A HOLD ON ME

A HOLD ON ME

A Dark Heart Novel

PAT ESDEN

KENSINGTON BOOKS

www.kensingtonbooks.com

KENSINGTON BOOKS are published by

Kensington Publishing Corp.
119 West 40th Street
New York, NY 10018   MAR 0 2 2016

Copyright © 2016 by Patricia A. R. Esden

All Kensington titles, imprints, and distributed lines are available at special quantity discounts for bulk purchases for sales promotion, premiums, fundraising, educational, or institutional use.

Special book excerpts or customized printings can also be created to fit specific needs. For details, write or phone the office of the Kensington Sales Manager: Kensington Publishing Corp., 119 West 40th Street, New York, NY 10018. Attn. Sales Department. Phone: 1-800-221-2647.

Kensington and the K logo Reg. U.S. Pat. & TM Off.

eISBN-13: 978-1-4967-0006-3
eISBN-10: 1-4967-0006-6
First Kensington Electronic Edition: March 2016

ISBN-13: 978-1-4967-0005-6
ISBN-10: 1-4967-0005-8
First Kensington Trade Paperback Printing: March 2016

10 9 8 7 6 5 4 3 2 1

Printed in the United States of America

For Dad:
You were right.
There wasn't anything under the bed,
at least nothing I couldn't face.

Acknowledgments

It takes a lot to get a story into the world. To thank everyone would take far too many pages, so I'll limit myself.

Much credit goes to my agent, Pooja Menon, and my editor, Selena James. I am forever grateful for your faith in me and the series, and for your beyond wise guidance. I don't want to forget Pooja's interns and my agency-mates—thank you so much for everything. Special thanks to all the Kensington Publishing staff who had a hand in bringing *A Hold on Me* to life and into the world. I'm thoroughly aware that at every step there were many of you working and reading behind the scenes—dare I say like shadows. You guys rock, each and every one of you.

To my writing friends who have been on this journey with me the longest and whose support means everything to me: Ginger Churchill, Laura Andersen, Suzanne Warr, Becca Fitzpatrick, and Karen Kobylarz.

To Jaye Robin Brown, who deserves her own paragraph. Huge northern hugs to you. No one could ask for a more honest, inspiring, and caring friend and critique partner.

Denise, Jessica, and Nicole, you all get gold stars for patience and support. And, most of all, to Russell for putting up with the insanity that comes with being married to a writer.

All right, here's where I'm sure I'll mess up, so I'm going to stop before I forget someone. But I am grateful to each and every one of my writing friends who critiqued the whole manuscript, chapters, or even just paragraphs, and to my beta readers as well. And to my sisters, Ruby Rice and Robin Rice Lichtig. You guys are the best.

Oh, yeah. Last but not least, I want to thank all the readers who picked this book up. Without you there would be no beginning, middle, or end.

A Note to the Reader

Like life, stories are never simple. This is particularly true of
A Hold on Me. Though the entire series takes place over a couple of months, it is the culmination of events that have built up
over eons. So I've chosen to add quotes at the beginning of
each chapter from journals written by Annie's ancestors, spells
etched in blood and carved into stone, advice found on ficti-
tious Internet sites, words screamed against the darkness and
whispered into lovers' ears. Think of these quotes as stars and
moons, tiny additional pieces brought together to reveal the
true expanse of this story's universe, through time and into
other worlds and dreamlands as well.

CHAPTER 1

There are things darker than night, darker than the souls
of wicked men or a woman of unchained passions.
Believe me, for I have known them well.

—Josette Savoy Abrams
Beach Rose House, Bar Harbor, Maine

Most people went to church to save their souls, but not Dad and I. We went there to see the priest about treasure.

It was a cold day in February and the church was an abandoned stone chapel on a back road near our home in Vermont. With its gloomy stained-glass windows and carvings of gargoyles under its sagging eaves, the chapel was exactly the kind of place where antique pickers like Dad and me could find the weird treasures and the gothic furniture our customers loved to buy. And, as luck would have it, the bishop had given the local priest permission to sell the entire contents as he saw fit.

The priest glanced once more at the grungy pews and the statue of St. Anthony with its chipped fingers and peeling paint. "Now that you've seen everything, are you still interested?"

Dad gave my shoulder a squeeze. "What do you think, Annie?"

"Ah—" I let my voice crack as if my jitteriness were nerves instead of excitement, then I met the priest's eyes. "One price for everything, right?"

"For all the contents. That doesn't include anything that's part of the structure. No windows, attached light fixtures, doors, none of those sorts of things." His tone left no room for debate.

Dad looked down, scratching his elbow while I took a scrap of paper and a pen from the turned-up sleeve of my bulky sweater. I jotted down the offer he and I had covertly agreed on when the priest had turned away for a moment, then handed it to the priest.

The priest's brow furrowed as he studied the paper. He ran a finger under his collar, cleared his throat, and finally glanced at Dad. "Perhaps you should look at this before we agree?"

Dad waved off his suggestion. "This was her idea. The offer is hers to make."

"All right, then," the priest said. "We have a deal."

I counted out a thin stack of hundreds and gave them to him. In turn, he passed Dad the church keys, all neatly labeled. The truth was, he wasn't the sort of person who would have ever believed a twenty-year-old girl with ripped jeans and a stud in her nose could know the first thing about valuing antiques—as Dad and I had hoped.

"Sorry I can't stay and help," he said, "but I have to get back to St. Mary's in time for Mass. When you're finished taking what you want, leave the keys in the box outside the door. I hope you find enough to make this worth your effort."

"I hope so too," Dad said, without cracking a smile. But, as soon as the priest went out the front door, he did a little victory dance and gave me a kiss on the cheek. "Perfectly played. If I'd given him an offer that low, he'd have thought I was up to something for sure."

Every inch of me tingled with anticipation. "So, where do you want to begin?" I asked.

Dad jangled the keys. "It appears the priest neglected to give us one very specific key. The one to the only room he didn't take us into or even mention. I don't know about you, but that makes me curious."

"The sacristy?" I said.

"That would be the one. Did you notice how he fidgeted with his collar, too?"

"I figured he thought everything was junk—that he was nervous I'd offered too much and that you'd back out."

"That's possible. But don't ever underestimate your opponent. There could be something else behind his uneasiness. Perhaps he hid something in the sacristy, something of value he hoped the diocese would forget. Priests are men, after all. They come in all shades of honesty, like the rest of us." He stroked his chin, a sure sign that he was about to launch into one of his home-brewed tales. "You remember the story about my wicked great-uncle Harmon and the Canary Island sirens? He always claimed to be a spiritual man, forthright and faithful to his wife. . . ."

I loved listening to Dad's crazy stories. But, as he began an abridged version of a tale that easily could have gone on for an hour, the word *faithful* sent my mind veering in a different direction—to me and Taj and a matinee of *Romeo and Juliet,* to his practiced fingers slipping under my skirt, up my inner thighs. The rush of desire. His words hot and moist against my neck: "*Oh, baby, c'mon. I want you so bad.*"

Men come in all shades of honesty for sure.

Shoving Taj from my mind, I smiled at Dad and cut him off. "I'm going to run out to the car and get the tool bag."

"Don't forget the thermos and flask," he called after me. Dad most always kept a thermos filled with coffee in our '68

Mercedes. He loved his cup of joe and it had become our tradition to toast successful deals by lacing a cup with a bit of brandy from his flask.

When I returned from the car, I found Dad crouched in front of the sacristy door, studying the keyhole. I set the flask and thermos on a pew, got the screwdriver and stiff wire he used for picking locks out of the tool bag, and gave them to him.

As I watched him work, sunlight crept in through the stained-glass window behind us, smearing the back of his old leather flight jacket with purple and blue. He glanced over his shoulder at me, the colored light now bruising his face. His eyes glistened with excitement. "What do you think we'll find inside—hidden treasure or a glorified broom closet?"

I hugged myself against a sudden chill. Either way the sacristy was bound to be windowless and dark, as black as a cellar or the space under a bed, black like death. I forced a smile. "Treasure," I said, because I really did hope we'd find something valuable.

"Well, we'll soon know for sure." Dad turned back to his work.

He pivoted the screwdriver and the lock clicked. Throwing me a triumphant grin, he reached for the latch, readying to open the door—

Suddenly, a thin, man-shaped shadow appeared on the wall next to the door, slithered toward Dad, and vanished.

I whirled around.

"What the heck?" I said, scouring the pews and aisles to make sure the priest hadn't returned. But there was no one in the church besides us. No one who could have caused the shadow. I turned back toward Dad. "I could have sworn—"

My voice died in my throat.

Dad was staring at me in a way I'd never seen him do before, his eyes dark and vacant.

I took a step back. "Dad?"

His tongue grazed his lips as if he was lost in thought.

"Are you all right?" I asked.

He didn't say a word. He just kept staring at me.

Trembling, I lowered my gaze to avoid his deadpan eyes. Dad's expression was exactly how he described the faces of the sleepwalkers in the creepiest of all the stories he'd ever made up. But this wasn't one of his tales. This was real. And I didn't have the faintest idea what I should do.

My stomach twitched from nerves as I made myself glance up. I couldn't just pretend nothing was wrong. I had to do something.

To my surprise, he appeared normal. The familiar sparkle had returned to his eyes, and he was grinning.

He chuckled. "What's wrong with you? You look like you've seen the Devil."

Totally baffled by his transformations, I could only gape.

He shrugged halfheartedly like he was done trying to figure out what was going on with me, then cocked his head at the sacristy door. "Be a good girl and lend me that flashlight of yours, so we can see what we've got in here."

"Uh—sure." My voice stuttered a little as I fished my flashlight out of my jeans hip pocket and handed it to him.

He gave me a quick wink, then opened the door and headed into the sacristy.

As I watched him disappear into the pitch-black room, I shook my head. What was I thinking? Slithering shadows. Sleepwalkers. That was ridiculous. There was nothing wrong with Dad. It was me. Me and my childish fear of the dark. Plus, I was overtired and had stupidly got myself worked up about Taj again. I hadn't eaten all day and had drunk way too many coffees; enough to keep me awake for a week. No wonder I was imagining things.

Giving myself a mental shake, I inched closer to the door. Dad's voice echoed out. "Broken cups and napkins." He laughed. "Not even enough for a bad garage sale."

I blew out a relieved breath.

There was definitely nothing wrong with Dad.

FIVE MONTHS LATER

CHAPTER 2

*Though some myths exaggerate, they all sprout
from a kernel of truth. Many—as an enlightened scholar
soon comes to realize—are remarkably correct.*

—Dr. Rupert Bancroft Walpole,
A Comparative Study of History and Folklore

I'd driven all afternoon, across Vermont, into New Hampshire, and up the seacoast of Maine. Fog as well as darkness was closing in. My eyes ached from staring at the road too long and my stomach grumbled, but at least Dad had finally settled down.

I glanced in the rearview mirror to where he huddled on the backseat, staring blankly out the window. I now knew for certain that at least part of what I'd seen in the abandoned church wasn't imaginary. The vacant expression on Dad's face had a name: dementia.

For months, I'd made excuses for his forgetfulness and lapses into confusion, for his ever increasingly bizarre behavior. But then his lawyer discovered the situation and to my horror a judge turned down my petition for custody and placed Dad in the care of his older sister, Kate. At the time, Dad's lawyer, the judge, the doctor who evaluated Dad . . . everyone involved in the custody thing had ignored my opinions like I was twelve instead of twenty. That had pissed me off, but I wasn't naïve enough to think my age alone had made the judge favor Kate. I suspected the real reason was money and power, the old boy network. I also suspected the major player behind me losing wasn't Kate. It was my grandfather.

The bitter tang of nausea climbed up my throat and settled on my tongue. As long as I could remember, Dad had hated his family, hated them so much he refused to talk about them. Well, except when he made them characters in his wild stories or talked about how he was certain they'd lied about some aspect of my mother's death.

I turned my attention back to the road. Ahead, streetlights and scattered houses appeared. The village of Port St. Claire, I assumed. A mini-mart materialized out of the fog, its lights haloed in misty gray. A woman in a yellow rain slicker dashed inside the store. A guy was pumping gas.

As I passed a snack bar, I rolled down my window. The rush of cool air brought with it the scent of fried food, pine trees, a hint of the ocean. In the distance a foghorn sounded.

I sighed under my breath.

It was true: I didn't like or trust Dad's family any more than he did. But I did wish I remembered something from the time I lived here in Maine with them. To be perfectly honest, I wished I remembered them, too. It wasn't surprising that I didn't. I'd been barely five years old when my mother died and Dad fled the family estate with me in tow. But I did know two things for certain. I trusted Dad's opinion of people—and every mile we traveled brought us closer to the one place he'd sworn to never return to.

Switching the headlights to low beam, I squinted through the mist, struggling to read the road signs as Port St. Claire's streetlights and stores, and even the faint glow of its harbor disappeared, replaced by the blurred outline of trees and guardrails. After a few more miles, the mist consumed even them, leaving nothing ahead except a narrow tunnel of haze and darkness.

Finally, I spotted the turn I was looking for and pulled the Mercedes into a private drive.

A gate loomed out of the fog, blocking the way. Spear-shaped finials glistened across its top. Wrought iron scrollwork spelled out the name: Moonhill.

Swallowing hard, I brought the car to a stop. My chest tightened and every ounce of confidence I'd built up drained away. Oh my God. We were here.

I squared my shoulders and sat up as tall as I could. I couldn't lose my nerve now. I had to stay strong. Everything was going to be all right. The doctor who evaluated Dad in Vermont suspected he had Korsakoff's dementia. Most often it was caused by alcoholism or malnutrition, which didn't make sense in Dad's case; the only condition Dad had was a slightly weakened heart. But having Korsakoff's did mean that with the help of the specialist Kate had hired, Dad was likely to improve. Once that happened, he could get out from under Kate's custody, we could get out of here, and I could go back to working toward my ultimate career.

I wanted to be a certified fine art appraiser. Dad always said a person could make a good living appraising and buying art and antiques for collectors. It was something I liked and I already had a lot more knowledge and experience in the field than most young dealers. Last fall, I'd started working toward my certification by taking online classes. I'd even applied to Sotheby's summer program, to take their Arts of Asia class in London. I'd gotten accepted, too. But then, Dad began acting strange, so I'd had to withdraw. Once things went back to normal, the first thing I was going to do was reapply for that program. A summer on my own in London would be amazing. And Dad needed to get used to the idea that I wouldn't be working full-time and living with him forever.

The rustling sound of Dad stirring to life came from the backseat.

"Well, now," he said, a little louder than necessary. "This looks like a place that'll be packed to the gills with antiques, and I'm talking about the good stuff."

My gaze flicked from the gate to the rearview mirror. "I'm sure it is. But we're not here to buy anything. We're guests."

He snorted. "Not buy anything? We'll see about that." His voice filled with disgust. "Who are you, anyway?"

My fingernails dug into the steering wheel's leather cover as frustration crashed through me. I closed my eyes and took a deep breath, holding it for a second before I released it.

"I'm Annie, your daughter," I reminded him for the zillionth time.

He flumped into his seat. "Like I believe that."

Gritting my teeth, I resisted the urge to argue with him and instead clicked the windshield wipers on and peered through the misted glass.

Just beyond the gate, the headlight beams trapped the outline of a stone cottage. The blue glow of a television throbbed in one window. Someone was obviously home, maybe a security guard or groundskeeper. They might not like coming out this late at night, but opening the gate was probably their job.

I honked the horn, then swiveled around to see why Dad was so quiet.

With his index finger, he was drawing jagged designs on the steamed-up window.

A loud creak made me turn back. Up ahead, a guy with the build and swagger of a Navy SEAL was shoving the gate open. As chilly as it was, I was surprised to see he had on a sleeveless T and no shoes. Maybe he'd been working out or something.

He waved for me to drive through and I eased on the gas.

As I approached him, he nodded. He didn't look much older than me, twenty-three or four at the most. His dark hair was cropped short, his face clean-shaven. My first impression was that he came from some kind of Mediterranean heritage, Greek or maybe Turkish. But it was impossible to guess in the dark and fog.

I tapped on the brakes and put on a smile. "Thanks," I said through my open window.

But the guy wasn't listening to me or even admiring our classic car. He was glaring at the window Dad had drawn on.

Dad shook his fist. "Vermin!" he shouted at the guy.

Heat flooded my face and I tromped on the gas, not waiting for the guy to reply. As the car lurched forward, the headlight beams slashed through the darkness, throwing shadows all around us.

Once the cottage was out of sight, I glanced back at Dad. I wanted to yell at him for being so rude, but instead I gritted my teeth and swallowed my anger. It wasn't right for me to lose my temper or be embarrassed by his behavior. He'd never lost his cool with me. Not even when I'd driven the Mercedes over a box of expensive porcelain at an auction—or when I'd thrown up during the private Vatican tour because I'd partied a bit too much the night before. It wasn't his fault he was sick. Besides, it didn't matter what people thought of him. We weren't here to make friends.

Turning my attention back to the road, I noticed the driveway ahead was climbing steeply upward. On either side, stone walls and black-limbed trees flickered through the fog. As we reached the top of the rise, the fog and trees gave way to a moonlit vista. The view was so spectacular that I slowed the car to take it in.

Below, Moonhill's main house shimmered in the silver-plated darkness. Its peaked roofs and shingled turrets blended into chains of glimmering windows and wide terraces. One wing jutted toward the west. A glowing solarium faced east. Behind it, the

ocean and sky stretched like an ebony-and-pearl backdrop.
The information about Moonhill that I'd found on the Internet didn't do it justice.

Then again, I hadn't uncovered any modern photos, only a
couple of faded etchings and articles on how the Freemonts,
my family, had lived on the property since the first settlers
came to Maine, and made their fortune in the salt mining business. Even the satellite views I'd found hadn't revealed anything unusual, just a sprawling house surrounded by solitude.

I rubbed the tingle of goose bumps from my arms. Actually, Moonhill looked exactly like how Dad described it in his
crazy tales.

Dad leaned forward and gave a low whistle. "A man could get
used to living in a place like this." He glanced toward where the
brass jar holding my mother's ashes sat on the front seat, nestled in
a blanket. "What the heck is that?" he asked.

"Ah—don't worry about it," I said. "It's nothing—just a
vase."

A lump clogged my throat. For as long as I could remember, Mother's jar had sat on our living room mantel, except
when we traveled and Dad brought it with us. Deep inside, I'd
always hoped someday he'd be ready to let the ashes go. But
for now, I'd make sure the jar was close by, easy for him to spot
when he started to recover.

I pulled up to the mansion's front steps. And, as Dad squinted
out the side window and muttered something about the carvings
over the door, I slid Mother's jar into my oversize bag. Later, I'd
take it to his room and make a special place for it. It wasn't like
the family would want it on their living room mantel, considering Mother's cremation played a big part in the rift between
them and us.

"Wait here," I said to him. Then I shouldered the bag, hurried up the front steps, and rang the bell.

The heavy door muted the bell's echoing tones. No footsteps followed.

I rang again.

An eerie sensation swept over my skin. Someone was watching us. I was certain of it.

Craning my neck, I looked upward, past the carved symbols of bees and triangles to a second-story window. Someone stared down at me through parted curtains. Then the curtains fell back in place and the small figure disappeared.

I hugged my bag against my chest and frowned as I quickly rang again. It seemed like they could hurry up and answer the door, instead of making me stand here while someone checked us out from a window. I doubted the watcher was either of my two cousins. The stare was too intense for a younger person or even a teenager, more like an art collector studying a painting to determine if it was real or a forgery.

Dad shuffled up beside me with his rumpled flight jacket draped over one arm. He reached for the enormous brass doorknob, but the door opened before he could touch it.

An aristocratic-looking woman in a white blouse and charcoal-gray slacks stood on the threshold.

My breath caught in my throat, and I squeezed my bag tighter. Her high cheekbones and waves of espresso-colored hair looked exactly like mine. Since I was little, Dad had told me I looked like my aunt Kate. I was expecting a resemblance, but holy freak show we were mirror images of each other, except she was about twenty-five years older.

"Welcome home, James," she said to Dad in a cool and controlled voice. She inclined her head at me. "I'm Kate. I assume you're Stephanie?"

"Yes. But everyone calls me, Annie—if you don't mind."

If she heard me or noticed the similarity between us, she gave no sign. She just waved us in. "We might as well get on with this," she said.

"If you insist," I answered, stepping inside.

My eyes widened in disbelief. I'd been in a ton of wealthy homes, heck, our home in Vermont had been packed with fine antiques, but stepping into Moonhill's foyer was like beaming into the Metropolitan Museum, complete with a full-size polar bear in one corner and floor-to-ceiling oil paintings all around. Spotlights illuminated a cabinet, which held Middle Eastern artifacts and terra-cotta oil lamps. Dad had taught me quite a bit about spotting reproductions and fakes. These looked real. I also suspected a number of them were no longer legal to buy, unless you were a museum.

Dad grinned at Kate. "Impressive collection."

"It is, isn't it," Kate said. She swiveled toward me and lowered her voice. "I'm a frank woman, Stephanie, and I intend to be frank now. I would appreciate a moment alone with your father. Perhaps you'd like to see your room and freshen up?"

My eyes went to Dad and back to her. No way was I leaving him alone without time to adjust. "It's probably better if I go with you," I said. "It's been a long trip. He can be—" I didn't want to say the word *difficult* out loud in front of him. It made him sound like a child.

Kate rested her hands on her hips. "I was not making a suggestion. Tibbs will be right in with your bags. He'll show you to your room." She turned from me and took Dad by the elbow. "Perhaps you'd like to come to my study for a nightcap?"

Dad's voice lifted. "Brandy? That would be lovely, especially if that girl doesn't follow us. She's always trying to make me drink coffee."

She patted his hand and they started across the foyer toward a hallway. "Don't worry about her."

My jaw clenched as I glared at the back of Kate's head. I hadn't expected a warm welcome, but she was downright demeaning and rude. No wonder she wasn't married. No man would want such a total bitch.

Something rock-solid and heavy thumped the back of my knee.

Pulse thundering, I wheeled around.

A short, dapper old man in a tweed jacket and a bowtie stood an inch behind me. He had one of my suitcases in each hand. "These yours?" he, undoubtedly Tibbs, asked.

I gulped a quick breath and nodded.

"Follow me," he said, muscling the bags toward a flight of marble stairs, which curved upward, just to one side of the front door.

I glanced back to where Kate and Dad were vanishing down the hallway and scowled. I didn't like this. Not one bit. What I should do is follow them, to hell with her commands. But that wouldn't help our situation. Besides, it would only take me a minute to get settled in my room, then I'd come back and find the study. For the life of me, I couldn't figure out why Kate had wanted custody of Dad to start with. What's more, I had the sneaking suspicion Kate wasn't in on this alone. I was willing to bet that Grandfather was waiting for them in the study, lurking behind the scenes while he got others to do his bidding, the way he used the old boy network during the custody battle. Well, I'd soon know for sure.

Tearing my gaze away from the now empty corridor, I followed after Tibbs, up the wide staircase to the second floor, then down a heavily carpeted hallway. Silence swallowed our footsteps as he ushered me past closed doors and draped windows.

"I imagine keeping this place clean is a hellish job," I said to him.

He mumbled something about someone being worth her weight in macaroons.

We went around a corner and up a couple more wide steps, then into another hallway. This one was longer and had a glistening white marble floor, like the churches Dad and I had visited in Rome. A moment later, we passed through an archway and entered a dimly lit gallery full of oil paintings and sculptures of ferocious angels. The statue of a three-faced goddess glared down at me from a shadowy alcove. A Siamese cat dashed past us and vanished into a dark corner. The room was so creepy it raised the hair on my arms. I hugged my bag and hurried my pace, rushing to keep up with Tibbs. We zigged and zagged through the expansive room and into another series of gloomy corridors.

After we'd walked for what felt like an eternity, Tibbs set the bags on the floor and rubbed his shoulder.

"Does anyone else live on this side of the house?" I asked. The place wasn't covered in spiderwebs and the carpet was fairly new, but I couldn't see or hear any signs of life.

His watery blue eyes sparkled with delight. "Why? Are you afraid to be alone?"

"No," I said sharply. It wasn't as much a matter of loneliness that bugged me as the idea of being surrounded by endless rooms filled with nothing except darkness. I hiked the strap of my bag up higher on my shoulder. "I was mostly wondering who stayed in this wing, in case I needed to ask someone how to get back to the main staircase."

"Something wrong with your sense of direction?"

"No, I just—" I snapped my mouth shut. Usually, when we visited places, I got along great with the employees. But this guy was strange—the Edgar Allan Poe of butlers, testing to see which torture chamber would work best on me: the hall of disorientation or perhaps the isolation tank.

He picked up my bags and grumbled. "Nowadays, most people have suitcases with wheels on them."

"I'd be happy to carry one," I offered. At least, this comment of his made sense. I loved my vintage Louis Vuittons, but lugging them was sometimes a pain in the ass.

He snatched them and strode off down a slightly brighter hallway with alcoves on each side, mumbling to himself.

Finally, he thumped the suitcases down and opened a door. "The Grecian Room," he said, motioning for me go through first.

With dread knotting in my chest, I stepped past him and into what was most likely a dark, musty guestroom where my chances of getting any sleep were zero.

My mood flip-flopped. Soft light swirled down from a chandelier, giving the room an airy and sunlit feel. The walls were papered in pale shades of sapphire and green with faint images of Grecian columns. A wonderful upholstered chair and a writing desk sat beside a window. The window's drapes matched the chair and were drawn tightly closed, blocking out any sign of the darkness beyond them.

But what took me back most about the room were the carvings of ribbons and cherubs that decorated the bed's massive headboard. Definitely high-end Victorian, pristine and incredibly valuable. The room reminded me of the supposedly haunted bed and breakfast Dad and I'd stayed at when we'd gone picking in New Orleans and met the Santeria priest.

I smiled slightly as memories from those weeks drifted back to me: sheer curtains fluttering in front of a whirring fan, dappled light and the scent of gardenias flooding in from the yard. Once, while Dad and I were there, we'd gone to an auction. At the end of the day, the auctioneer had sold a pile of boxes without letting anyone look at what was inside them. We'd bought the so-called *mystery* lot, hauled it back to the bed and breakfast, and into the parlor. Then, we'd sat there on the carpet for hours, talking and laughing, sipping sweet tea and going through everything—Dad, me, the owner of the bed and breakfast, and her little twin daughters. We found tintype photos of weddings, old marbles, games, lace hankies and costume jewelry, feathered masks, and arm-length kid gloves. After that, the owner had invited Dad to put Mother's jar on the parlor mantel instead of keeping it in his room. Perhaps it was because we let her have a diary we found in one of the boxes or because she was up for anything that might make her bed and breakfast come across as more haunted, maybe both. But it made us feel like a part of her family. I really wanted to go back there, someday.

Tibbs shuffled past me and thunked my suitcases down by the bedside stand. He nodded at a doorway on the other side of the room. "Bathroom's in there. Breakfast's at eight," he said. Then he left and shut the door behind him. So much for Maine's warm hospitality.

I set my bag and the suitcases on the bed and started for the bathroom. It would only take a second to wash up, then I'd find my way back to Dad. Maybe Kate and Grandfather thought they could manage him, but they didn't know him like I did. Besides, he would never have deserted me or left me alone with someone I hated.

As I stepped into the marble-floored bathroom, I spotted, just beyond the toilet and shell-shaped sink, a small grotto with walls painted to resemble a Grecian temple. In the middle of the grotto was the most gigantic claw-footed tub I'd ever seen. My pulse jumped with excitement at the thought of lounging in sultry chin-deep water. But I didn't have time to dream about relaxing and baths, not right now.

I turned on the sink's faucet and splashed cool water on my face. It tingled against my skin and stole the heat from my eyelids.

A sudden realization slammed me in the chest.

Tibbs had said, "*Breakfast's at eight,*" with finality, like I wasn't expected to go back downstairs until then. But, Dad—at the very least, I had to make sure he'd settled in okay.

I turned off the faucet, went into the bedroom, and headed for the door. Opening it, I stepped out into the hallway—

Utter darkness crushed in around me. Darkness as black as the stone in the poison ring I'd sold for Dad last month.

I retreated into the doorway, struggling to catch my breath. Damn it.

The dark had terrified me for as long as I could remember. No matter what I did or how hard I tried, I couldn't get over it, like most people did when they were still little. There was no justification for it either—except, perhaps, that I had an unusually hyperactive imagination or that Dad had let me watch too many horror movies when I was too young.

Taking a deep, shaky breath, I stepped forward and peered out. Except for where the light from my room brightened a narrow strip, I couldn't see anything else.

I slid my hand down the hallway wall as far as I dared, hoping to feel a light switch. Nothing. Not even a dimple in the wallpaper.

Inside my door, there was a single switch. I snapped it off and on. The overhead light responded, but the hallway remained completely black.

I scowled at the darkness. "You're not going to win that easily," I said.

Dashing to my bed, I opened my smallest suitcase and reached into the pocket where I kept my trusty flashlight. My fingers found my shampoo bottle, my cosmetic bag, and blow-dryer exactly where I'd put them, but no flashlight. I patted down my clothes. My mouth went dry as I checked my other suitcase. Still, no flashlight.

I'd never forgotten it before. Even at home, I slept with it my under my pillow, forever and always, like some kind of childish idiot.

A prickling sensation swept across my scalp. Tibbs had been alone when he retrieved my suitcases from the car. Though it didn't make sense for him to steal an old pink flashlight, he'd had enough time to rummage through my stuff. He was odd, and undoubtedly knew where the light switches were.

But why turn them off—because he was a nut or simply not thinking before he did it? Or did someone else know about my fear and put him up to these things?

I shook that thought from my mind. I was starting to think like a crazy person myself. Besides, it wasn't like I was trapped in my room.

Grabbing my bag, I slid my hand under Mother's jar and retrieved my phone. I turned it on, went back to the doorway, and stepped into the hall.

The phone's blurry light pushed against the darkness, transforming the first few yards of black into writhing gray shadows. But I could still see the darkness, daring me to step toward it, waiting to blind me, to smother me.

I shuddered and backed into my room, and shut the door. The light wasn't enough. I'd have a full-fledged panic attack before I got halfway down the hallway. I turned on the desk lamp, then the bedside light, then paced back to the desk. I didn't want to do it, but there was one painfully obvious solution to this.

With a sigh, I slumped into the chair and phoned Kate. Dad's lawyer had given me her number in case the car broke down on our way to Maine. I'd ask her where the light switches were and the easiest route to the foyer. It wasn't a big deal. My ego would live through it.

My call went to her voice mail.

"Kate, this is Annie," I said. "Could you please call me right away?"

I sagged even deeper into the chair, staring at the phone, heaviness settling over me.

After a minute, I went online and checked a couple of places to see if any of my friends were around. No one. If this had been last summer instead of now, I'd have been able to find at least one of them. I could have texted or chatted with someone if for no other reason than to break the silence. But most of them had gone away to college last fall, one friend had gotten married, another had gone into the service, most were deep into relationships. My friendship with Taj was totally screwed. I hadn't told any of them about Dad's condition. Six or seven months ago, I might have ignored the slight bittersweet tang of friendships moving on and called someone anyway, but now reaching out felt as impossible as crossing the gulf between stars.

With a sigh, I set my phone on the desk.

Kate wouldn't call me back. I knew it in my heart.

CHAPTER 3

When my bed is cold I embrace the dark,
When it's you, when it's you I want to hold.
Oh, embrace the dark for my love is gone.
Embrace the shadows of the night.

—Susan Woodford Freemont
Ballad favorited on www.NorthTunes.com

As I expected, Kate never returned my call and the next morning I woke up with a million nightmares crashing around in my brain. Some were about Dad getting lost in a maze of hallways, but most were a crazy quilt patched together from scraps of his made-up stories. One thread involved Great-grandmother Freemont using the leg bone of a cat to become invisible, another was his favorite story about a treasury in the cellar filled with jars of plotting genies.

But woven in with all the fabricated tales were flashes of Mother's death, narrated by my father's voice: "*They told me, she was walking in the graveyard when it happened. It was foggy, and the grass was wet. She slipped, and her head collided with a marble lamb. She died that instant: her skull cracking open, her dark-red blood staining the small white stone. By the time I got home, nothing of your mother remained, except for a jar of ashes.*"

I wiped my sweat-dampened hair back from my face. Why

couldn't Dad have provided me with more happy stories about my family, instead of just material for nightmares?

The plush carpet silenced my footsteps as I got out of bed and went into the bathroom. It didn't take me long to decide what to wear. I'd learned from watching Dad swagger into upper-end auctions in his worn-out chinos and slouchy fishing hat that when you were nervous about the crowd you were going to face, the best thing to do was dress like you had all the confidence in the world. In other words, like you were beyond having to dress for success. Be yourself, and then some.

I put on a comfy T-shirt, then shimmied into my favorite worn jeans. I topped off the outfit with a pair of bright-red spiked heels I'd found at a yard sale. Nothing says confidence like a touch of red, except perhaps the ability to strut while wearing spikes.

Grabbing my bag with Mother's jar still inside it, I headed into the daylight-brightened hallway. Judging by the way the sun's rays filtered in through the window at my end of the hall, I guessed that my room was in the east wing. If I'd taken the time to open my curtains, I'd probably have seen the ocean. Well, there'd be time to enjoy the view later, after I found Dad and had breakfast.

I strutted down the hallway. Here and there window-brightened alcoves broke up the relentless parade of closed doors. As I zigged and zagged, I watched for light switches. I didn't spot any, but there was plenty of time before dark. I'd just have to ask someone where the switches were.

The gallery was hot and airless when I entered it. The only traces of brightness trickled down through a dome-shaped skylight. My heels clicked a staccato rhythm as I started across the room and silenced when I stopped to admire a nineteenth-century painting of castle ruins. I turned my attention to the statues. Fury contorted the angels' cold marble faces. Their hands gripped swords. One had snakes writhing around its base. From the depths of her alcove, the three-faced goddess sneered at me. They were all truly fear-inspiring masterpieces, and it was amazing to think my family owned such priceless works of art.

In fact, the entire gallery was magnificent, except for an odd man-size stain marring the alcove wall closest to the goddess. It was black and oily and about six feet in height. The shadow in the abandoned church hurtled into my mind, and my chest tightened with fear.

I clenched my jaw and forced myself to not look away. This was ridiculous. I was going to drive myself nuts if I kept thinking imaginary things were real. This was simply a stain. Nothing more, nothing less. Certainly nothing alive.

My legs resisted, but I took a step toward it. The shape was oddly manlike, a head, neck, and wide shoulders. I was about to take another step, when the tap of fast-moving footsteps sounded behind me and I turned to see who it was instead.

A gangly, thirtysomething woman in a stretched-out gray cardigan and long black skirt scurried toward me.

"I went to your room to get you, but you'd already left. I was afraid you'd get lost." Her throaty accent sounded vaguely Russian or Eastern European.

She flashed me a toothy grin like she was thrilled to see me, but her gaze skimmed disapprovingly down to my spikes.

I narrowed my eyes. "I haven't gotten lost, yet," I said defensively. I thought about complimenting her worn-out slippers or asking for my room's GPS coordinates, but decided it was better not to rock the boat before I knew where I stood.

The woman draped a bony arm across my shoulder. "That's good to hear. You'll get used to the house soon enough. If you ever want company, our apartment is on the other end of the hallway. You come see us anytime."

As she drew me into a motherly half-hug, I resisted the

urge to push her away. I liked the idea of not being as alone as I'd suspected and her friendliness softened me a little. But I didn't need a mother hen clutching me to her nonexistent bosom and expecting me to visit her for Russian tea and potentially lethal gingerbread—at least her burn-scarred fingers and the magenta and orange stains that crescented her fingernails made me wonder what she'd been brewing up.

She gave me another squeeze. "I hope you like your room. My daughter, Selena, picked it out. She turned eighteen last month, not that much younger than you. You're going to be close friends. I know it."

I wriggled from her grip. Though I didn't remember her at all, I had a strong suspicion who she was. "Are you my aunt?" I asked.

Her hands fluttered to her mouth as if she was totally mortified. "Oh, my dear. I'm so sorry. How silly of me. Yes. Of course. I'm your aunt Olya. My husband is David, your father's little brother."

Like giant, freaky-colored moths, her stained fingers settled on my arm. I tried not to flinch as she went on about Selena and her eleven-year-old son, Zachary, and how my uncle David was away on business at the moment. Selena and Zachary. If Dad had ever mentioned them by name, I might have tried to connect with them on the Internet.

Still chattering, Olya steered me toward the far side of the gallery. I might not have known much about them, but it quickly became clear that she knew tons about me. She was totally aware that I'd been homeschooled and dealt antiques with Dad. She knew I'd gotten two speeding tickets, liked indie rock and cheesy popcorn. Unnerved, I began to wonder if she knew about my stupid fear of the dark as well. Dad's lawyer was the only person who might have known all these things, other than Dad. But, even before the dementia, Dad never talked to people about our personal stuff. Perhaps the old boy network was behind me losing custody. But now I was also wondering if Dad's lawyer had been spying on us and reporting to Grandfather for years.

Olya and I were almost all the way across the gallery when the dark stain I'd spotted near the three-faced goddess slid back into my mind. Maybe from this angle I could tell what it was.

I glanced back.

The stain was gone. Just like the shadow in the church.

My feet froze to the floor.

"What's wrong?" Olya asked.

A bead of sweat dribbled down my spine. "I thought I saw something—a big, man-size stain on the wall—by the goddess. But it's gone now."

Her eyes flicked to the wall, then back to me. She was smiling, but her face had paled. "Oh, yes. A shadow. The statues sometimes cast them. Very lifelike. I'm not surprised it startled you." She laughed nervously. "I should warn you, Zachary, he likes to play tricks. Ghost noises. Jumping out at people. Don't tell him what you saw or he'll paint shapes on every wall in Moonhill—just to terrify you."

Her anxious tone did nothing to ease my fear. If anything, it spiked my suspicion that I might have indeed seen something supernatural—a ghost or some kind of phantom stain imprinted on the wall.

I faked my own laugh, and said, "I'll remember that."

But my eyes went back to that place by the goddess, and an unsettling sense of recognition came over me. It was impossible as I had no memories of this place, but still the feeling lingered, joined by an unrelenting rush of fear as if darkness had suddenly boxed me in.

A chill sent goose bumps across my skin. I hugged myself against it and took a deep breath. I needed to stay strong for

Dad, so I could help him get well and get us out of this creepy place—and fast.

As we left the gallery and went down the main staircase to the foyer, I listened while Olya talked about how Zachary had tried to frighten Selena by hiding a motion-activated recording of ghostly voices in the family library. Great. Just what I needed. Real mysterious things and fake ones.

We had just passed the cabinet filled with artifacts when I heard a door squeak open behind us. I looked back and spotted a lanky guy with scruffy red hair shuffling out of a door under the staircase. With his brown work pants and matching shirt, I would have assumed he did maintenance around Moonhill, except that he was carrying a silver bowl filled with fresh fruit.

"Good morning, Tibbs," Olya greeted him. "I'm not sure if you met Stephanie last night."

Tibbs? I gaped. But Tibbs was an old man who wore tweed and a bowtie.

"Are you all right?" Olya said to me.

"Yeah. It's just—" I tore my gaze off Tibbs. "I thought the guy who showed me to my room last night's name was Tibbs."

"Not me," Tibbs said. "I had the night off. Probably Chase—guy my age, buzz cut, built like a boxer?"

That sounded like the military-type hottie Dad had yelled at. "No. He was up by the gate. The guy I'm talking about was old with a bow tie."

Olya's fingers once again fluttered to my arm. She gave me a couple of pats. "That would have been your grandfather. Ever since we found out about the situation he's talked about nothing except you and your dad. He's so glad—we're all so happy you're here with us."

I took a step back. "But he didn't even tell me who he was."

"Did you ask him?" Olya said. "He probably assumed you knew."

She was probably right about that, but it still seemed oddly presumptuous.

With Tibbs trailing behind, Olya escorted me across the foyer toward the hallway that Kate and Dad had vanished down last night. As we passed a thick, velvet braid, hanging beside a doorway, she flagged her hand at it. "If you need something pull any bell rope. Tibbs or his mother will come. You can phone or text them as well."

"I'll be in the kitchen for most of the morning," Tibbs said. "Stop by after breakfast and I'll give you the numbers." He had a gentle voice, a little shy but not girly.

I glanced over my shoulders. "Thanks, I'll do that."

His cheeks and ears flushed bright red. He was a bit too skinny for my taste and gingers didn't turn me on, but some girls would have really gone for him. In my book, he looked mostly like a potential ally.

"Tibbs is a godsend," Olya went on. "If he or his mother aren't available, there's always Chase. If something happens at night, stay in your room and use your phone."

"I'll do that," I said. It sounded a lot smarter than trying to call Kate again.

We left the hallway and stepped into an elegant dining room.

Kate sat on one side of a long mahogany table, her shoulders square and her spine as straight as if she had a broomstick taped to her back. A boy with spiked hair, most likely my cousin Zachary, slouched across from her, slurping cereal. At the head of the table, the old man from last night—my grandfather—sipped on a coffee. A little bit of it dripped off his chin and onto his bowtie. In the daylight, he appeared less dubious and more like a gentleman from an old BBC movie.

He looked over the rim of his cup and winked at me.

I gave him a warm smile, as if nothing from last night had struck me as odd. Then I glanced around the room and leaned in close to Olya. "Where's my dad?" I whispered.

Before Olya could reply, Aunt Kate's voice took command of the room. "Your father's in town at a doctor's appointment. I thought it was wise to get his treatments started, don't you agree?"

My jaw clenched and a few choice words gathered on the tip of my tongue. It was great Dad was getting help. But I hadn't expected it to happen so quickly and without me being notified.

A smile twitched at the corner of Kate's mouth and in that instant I knew what she was up to. She was baiting me, trying to get me to lose my temper and yell at her.

Well, two could play that game. I took a second to flick a strand of hair back from my face, then steadied my voice. "It's just, so early—and I would have liked to have gone with him."

She cut me off. "He'll be back around teatime. Now, fix yourself something. Breakfast hours are almost over." She jerked her chin toward a buffet covered with breakfast food and carafes.

Anger and worry stole my hunger, but I wasn't about to give her the satisfaction of knowing it. I nonchalantly strolled to the buffet, then snatched a blueberry muffin from a basket, stabbed it in half, and jabbed some butter onto it. Teatime. That was four o'clock. Seemed absurdly long for a doctor's appointment, even for a specialist. Dad wasn't going to deal with that very well. Not at all.

I sucked in a deep breath and set the knife gently next to the muffin. Then I strengthened my resolve. I had loads of reasons to be upset, but I'd never get anywhere if I let Kate and Grandfather unhinge me. Besides, Dad had raised me to keep my cool. And he'd taught me more than just how to dress like I was beyond dressing for success.

He'd taught me how to come out on top at auctions by

staying quiet and watching body language, doing the unexpected and anticipating the opposition's moves, not to mention a bit of faking and bluffing. Moonhill might be full of practiced liars and perhaps they'd see right through my pretense, but I wouldn't go down without trying. First, I needed to make them think I was gullible and inexperienced, like Dad and I had done with the priest back in Vermont.

I let Olya fix me an extra-sweet coffee with cream. Then I carried it and my muffin to the table and sat beside Zachary, and as far away from Kate and my grandfather as possible.

Grandfather leaned forward, his eyes zeroing in on me. "You've got that same uppity chin as your aunt Kate, but you have your father's sly eyes. Definitely a Freemont, through and through."

His words sent heat rushing across my face, and as much as I would have liked to meet his stare, I submissively dropped my gaze to my plate. So much for not letting my emotions show.

Olya settled into the empty chair on the other side of me. She glanced toward Zachary. "You need to hurry up. You don't want to keep the Professor waiting," she said.

Zachary groaned. "I just started eating."

I turned my attention to Zachary, much better than having the conversation go back to me. "A professor? So, you're going to summer school?"

"No. He's my private tutor." Zachary's voice grew shriller. "I know, it's crazy. This is supposed to be vacation time. But I have to do homework."

Olya shook a finger at him. "Mind your manners, young man." Her accent was a thousand times stronger than her son's.

A scowl darkened Zachary's face. "It's not fair. Chase and I have other stuff to do."

Kate cleared her throat. "We're very fortunate, Stephanie. The Professor is from Oxford. He's overseen a variety of archeology

projects the family's funded. But he had some time off this summer and agreed to work with Zachary." Kate's voice dropped off,
presenting me with a chance to say something.

"Sounds like a wonderful opportunity," I said, bringing my
coffee cup to my lips. I wasn't sure if she was baiting me again
or not.

"Well, as I was saying," Kate went on, "we're lucky to have
him. Sometimes, Selena even sits in on his lectures. She's taking
a gap year before going to Yale. In her case, a short break is a
good idea. On the other hand, someone avoiding college for two
years"—she wrinkled her nose at me as if she'd caught a whiff of
something rotten—"that tells us all we need to know about your
academic abilities and ambitions. You did manage to graduate
from high school, right?" She sat back in her chair, her eyes
challenging me.

My fingers tightened around my cup and a voice inside my
skull screamed for me to wing it at her head. But instead I
calmly matched her pose and told her what I suspected she'd
already learned from Dad's lawyer. "As a matter of fact, I grad-
uated with top honors—and it so happens I didn't take a gap
year. I'm simply not attending college full-time."

Grandfather laughed. "There you go, Kate. She's a perfect
likeness of you when you were her age."

Flustered, I glanced at Kate. Wrinkles fanned out from the
corners of her dark eyes and her lips pressed into a firm line, undoubtedly holding back a comment as tart as the ones I longed
to say.

As fast as I could, I sucked down my coffee and gobbled
my muffin. Then I excused myself and headed off to get the
numbers from Tibbs.

The kitchen was right behind the swinging door under the
front staircase. The one Tibbs had come out of with the bowl of
fruit. He and a gray-haired woman with a face as weathered as
an old barn were slouched over a bucket, peeling potatoes.

Tibbs introduced her as his mother, Laura. Once I'd introduced myself, I got the numbers and asked for directions to Dad's room. With him at the doctor's, it was the perfect time to sneak in and situate Mother's jar.

A few minutes later, I'd found my way through a maze of corridors and was on the second floor, sprinting down the bleak west wing hallway. Dad's room was the last one on the right. It couldn't have been any farther from where I was staying if they'd tried, which was exactly what I suspected someone had done. I didn't believe for a second that cousin Selena had chosen my bedroom.

As I stepped into Dad's room, a musky odor hit my nose, like someone had recently snuffed out a stinky candle or like the lingering smell of incense in a church.

I dashed past the massive four-poster bed to where a sitting area had been arranged in front of a white marble fireplace. Opening my bag, I pulled out Mother's jar and set it on the mantel. Perfect. Dad would probably think it had been there all along.

BANG! The door to the bedroom slammed shut.

I spun around, my heart in my throat.

Childish snickering came from the other side of door, followed by the patter of running footsteps. Zachary.

A chill went through me as I realized how dark the room had become. Only a streak of brightness wedged its way between the drawn curtains. I sprinted for the door. The brat had probably used a key to lock me in. I'd be stuck here until Dad or someone showed up or at the very least until I could find a way to pick the lock.

I yanked on the knob.

The door opened.

Drawing in a relieved breath, I turned to take one last look at Mother's jar. Rising toward the mantel on either side of it were oily black, man-size shadows, like the stain I'd seen in the gallery, only leaner, and definitely not attached to the wall.

"Holy crap," I said under my breath.

The shadows whirled to face me.

I froze with my hand on the doorknob. The room was blistering hot now, and sweat drizzled down my face. A caustic smell prickled my nose as I watched them swirl and coil like blue smoke. Suddenly they stopped swirling and swooped toward me.

I bolted into the hallway and yanked the door shut. As I took off at a dead run, I heard a thump as if one of them had collided with the closed door, then a second thump.

Full tilt, I sprinted back toward the main part of the house, my heels hammering with every step. Dad always said to believe in everything until you had solid proof it wasn't real. I didn't have firsthand experience with the supernatural. Still, I was certain ghosts existed. But these shadows didn't resemble any ghost I'd ever heard about or seen on television.

I turned a corner and went down another hall. Finally, I slowed a little and dared a glance over my shoulder. Nothing was following me. No shadows. No movement of any kind. I couldn't hear or smell anything either.

Folding my arms across my chest, I tucked my hands in my armpits to keep them from shaking and jogged toward the main staircase. My pulse banged in my ears. My legs felt wobbly. This was stupid. I had to calm down, stop acting like a girl in a horror movie and start using my brain.

When I reached the staircase, I paused to catch my breath. Below, the cabinet filled with artifacts sparkled under the chandeliers' glistening light. It seemed impossible that people who collected stuff from all kinds of cultures and religions didn't have some level of awareness and interest in the supernatural, the way I did. For sure Olya knew something, and I couldn't believe she was the only one. But why hadn't she told me about the shadows when I mentioned the stain?

I rested my hands on the staircase's sweeping banister and closed my eyes, questions whirring like crazy in my head. What I needed was to get someone to tell me the truth. But in order to avoid being misled by them or filled with lies, I'd have to ask my questions with finesse like the way Dad used his tools to coax a lock open.

CHAPTER 4

Drink cautiously from the sea of comprehension.
For once filled, the soul cannot unlearn.

—Carved above the entry to Moonhill's library

I was still deciding on my next course of action when the front door swished open and a willowy blond girl in red-framed sunglasses and designer jeans sashayed in.

Fast as I could, I backed away from the banister. I really didn't want to face anyone until I'd calmed down a bit more.

But she spotted me and waved. "Hey, Cousin. I've been looking for you."

This had to be Selena. "Hi," I said. It came out meeker than I'd preferred.

I heaved my bag's strap higher on my shoulder and strolled down the stairs, my heels clicking with every step. Despite her expensive clothing and confident air, Selena had an unmistakably naïve vibe about her. For sure, every sorority at Yale—and fraternity—would open their doors the second she stepped onto campus.

She shoved her sunglasses up on top of her head. "I thought you might like to hang out for a while, have a tour of the grounds and check out the beach."

I hesitated, my fingers tightening around the end of the banister. I wasn't sure about spending too much time with her.

I'd never been very good at the girlfriend thing. But her smile was infectious and I did want to see the ocean. It also seemed like she might be the perfect person to ask about the shadows.

Selena hooked her arm through mine and towed me out the front door. As we stepped into the sunlight, the sudden brightness reminded me of something I'd wanted to do.

"Before we go to the beach, I'd like to grab a couple things out of my dad's car. Do you know where it is?"

"Sure. It's in the garage. Come on."

We rushed along the front of the house, past a vine-covered gazebo to where the garage and a black sedan sat at the end of a small cul-de-sac. Selena gave me the code, so I could unlock the garage's side door, and showed me where the car keys were stored. Then, while I unlocked the Mercedes, she hovered over my shoulder. "Anytime you want to go somewhere, just call Tibbs. He'll bring your car around to the front door. He'll do anything if you flirt a little."

I snagged Dad's mini-flashlight out of the glove box and shoved it in my hip pocket, then laughed. "I can probably manage to get my own car."

"Aunt Kate wouldn't like that. She thinks it's uncivilized. Well, actually"—Selena pursed her lips and blew the hair off her forehead—"I think it's because she likes to know what everyone else is doing all the time." She lowered her voice. "Whatever you do, don't try to go anywhere after dark. The main gate's locked from sunset until morning. Only Grandpa, Kate, my parents—and Chase, of course, have the key."

I glanced at her. "You've got to be kidding."

She rested her hands on her hips. "Seriously, don't bother trying it. There's no way to get through."

"Kind of like a prison?" I said.

"Pretty much." She leaned in closer and whispered, "But there is an escape route." She touched a finger to her lip to silence me. "I'll tell you about it later."

I grinned and nodded. The idea that I'd found an ally in Selena lifted my mood. Still, anger simmered beneath my skin. Spooky shadow things. Locked gates. It was a wonder my father hadn't fled this place long before my mother's death.

I grabbed my spare sandals from under the passenger seat and tossed them into my bag, so it wouldn't look like the flashlight was the only thing I'd wanted. The sandals might come in handy if we went to the beach as well.

Once the Mercedes was locked back up, Selena's gaze went to my feet. "Your shoes are amazing, by the way," she said.

"Thanks. They're my favorites." In a way she reminded me of the girl I'd bought the shoes from, all red and white designer everything. The girl had told me the shoes had belonged to her older sister. How they used to swap clothes and even dates, when they were younger, before her sister went away to college and they drifted apart. That's one thing I loved about antique picking, everything came with a story, with a heritage, a soul. I smiled at Selena and this time it was totally real. "You can borrow them sometime, if you want."

"Mother would kill me." Her eyes glistened. "Can I try them on?"

Before I could say yes, she hauled me out of the garage and to the gazebo. We sat down on its steps and she slipped out of her glittery flip-flops. Wiggling her toes, she motioned for me to hand over my spikes. I shook my head, amused by her enthusiasm, and gave them to her. When she slid them on, they actually looked better on her, given her legs were skinnier and longer than mine, and because her sunglasses and red-tipped fingernails perfectly matched the shoes.

Selena stretched out her legs and admired the effect. "They're gorgeous. They'd be perfect for—" She paused abruptly and glanced around as if looking to see if someone was within earshot.

"Perfect for what?" I prodded, hoping it would get her to start spilling again.

She wriggled closer. "There's this guy, Newt. He and a bunch of his friends called the Beach Rats have parties. That's why I had to find an escape route. Your shoes would be perfect with my new outfit. But if Mom and Dad ever found out what I wanted them for—" She made a cutting motion across her throat with her finger.

"Yeah, and then some," I said. Then I realized she'd given me an opening that could solve not one but two problems at once. "How do you sneak out of the house, anyway? Last night, I wanted to go downstairs and meet everyone, but the hall was pitch-black, and I couldn't find a light switch. I was afraid I'd get lost."

"There're switches on both ends of the hallway, near the windows. But we won't want to turn them on when we go out." Selena hesitated dramatically. "The light attracts *things*."

I shuddered as images of oily black shadows materialized in my head. "Things? Like what?" Freaking shadow-ghost things, no doubt.

"Like Zachary and Aunt Kate. And you really have to watch out for Chase, he's on permanent stealth mode."

"Chase?" I couldn't believe I'd heard right. She was talking about people.

"He looks like he might be cool," she said, "but he's all security this and that. It's awful."

My shoulders slumped. I'd really thought she was going to start telling me about ax-wielding ghosts and blood spilling from the walls—not complain about how well the local eye candy was doing his job. "Sounds like it's lucky you get out at all," I said, grumbling a bit.

"I'm actually very lucky. Grandfather can't stand the idea of security cameras watching him, otherwise I might not. You can only cover a camera so many times before someone notices. Newt told me that—and he knows." She gave my arm a friendly squeeze. "But enough about me and Newt. Do you have a boyfriend?"

Caught off guard by the sudden change in topic, I could only blink at her. I generally didn't discuss my personal life with people I'd just met, especially someone I wasn't supposed to trust. But it was hard not to like Selena. Plus it would feel good to finally tell someone and I doubted she'd be judgmental.

Gathering my nerve, I took a deep breath. "There was one guy, Taj. He's an intern at the Metropolitan Museum. I met him a long time ago through my homeschooling program. We used to text and stuff all the time. We were best friends. I went out with some guys he knew. Then last winter, when Dad and I were in New York, he asked me out and we kind of hooked up." I lifted my head and looked her in the eyes. "A couple weeks later, I saw a photo of him and some girl online. They were all over each other. It said they were *in a relationship*."

She stuck out her bottom lip in a sympathy pout. "That's awful."

I shrugged. "I should have known better."

My throat choked up and I could feel a little wetness at the corners of my eyes.

I blinked it away. Taj didn't deserve my tears. He was a total shithead. Besides, it was time to get this conversation back on track. "I asked what kind of *things* you saw at night because I thought you meant ghosts."

"Oh, I can see how you might think that," she said.

When she didn't continue, I nudged again. "I was just wondering if there were any. When Dad and I went to New Orleans, we stayed in a haunted bed and breakfast. I never heard or saw anything, but the owner swore she'd seen shadows and heard a woman singing." The part about the shadows was made up, but the rest of it was true. If this didn't get her talking about the shadows, then maybe nothing would.

"Singing?" Selena's eyes widened with sudden understanding. "You're not wondering about ghosts in general, are you?"

"What do you mean?" I asked, puzzled.

She shifted her weight from one hip to the other, looking distinctly uncomfortable. "You mentioned the woman singing because you want to know if your mother"—her eyes rose to meet mine—"if she's a ghost. My dad says she had a beautiful voice. It was awful, the way she died."

My mouth fell open and a tremor of panic went through me. "Are you saying what I think you're saying?" It had never occurred to me that Mother might be haunting Moonhill. She couldn't possibly be one of the shadows. They'd felt malevolent.

Selena shook her head. "I don't think she is. At least no one's ever seen a ghost in the house, but if she was haunting the graveyard, no one might have noticed. That's where her accident happened, you know." She glanced at the hillside, just north of the driveway.

Through the scattered trees I could make out a domed mausoleum on top of a hill and white monuments climbing toward it. The graveyard. Somewhere up there was a white marble lamb—a lamb, perhaps still stained with my mother's blood.

"You want to walk up there later?" Selena asked.

I swallowed hard. "No," I managed to say, but my voice trembled more than I would have liked. The truth was, even when I'd looked at the satellite photos, I hadn't realized the graveyard was so close to the house. And I definitely didn't want anyone with me when I went up there.

I wrapped my arms around my knees and rocked forward. The other truth, the one I hadn't admitted to myself until now, was that even if Dad hadn't gotten sick, one day, at some point in time, I would have returned to Moonhill on my own.

Even if it was to do nothing more than walk where Mother had gone, and to see where she had died.

What few memories I had of her were from Dad: her love of the ocean, her thirst for adventure and fondness for skinny-dipping, her fiery temper and bright silk scarves, her musical voice and wild beauty—*like a selkie stolen from the sea,* Dad had always said. Her death, a fluke, a one in a million freak accident. Dad racing home from a business trip. His anger at his family. His blame. His guilt. His grief that he had never overcome. These memories felt real to me, but they were threads from stories that belonged to Dad.

I wanted my own memories, even if it was just a small one.

CHAPTER 5

The following day, we anchored in a small cove, rowed ashore,
and found our way to the top of the cliff. There we discovered
the hill we'd been told of, shaped like a crescent moon.

—Memoir of Henry Freemont
Volume IV, 1601–1609

Selena gave me an extensive tour of the front gardens. She showed me the beach from the cliff top, a glistening wet crescent of stone and sand reached only by a treacherously steep set of stairs.

I would have given anything to have gone down there and walked along the shore alone, the waves washing my feet, the sun heating my shoulders. I could barely focus on what she was saying, the history of our ancestors discovering and settling on Moonhill, way back when the first explorers came to Maine. About the family's salt mine here and the larger ones they later established in Canada. My mind was with Mother, seeing her blood on the lamb, wondering who found her body, and if I'd been with her that day.

As we started back toward the house, through another series of gardens punctuated by statuary and stone walls, I swapped to thinking about the absence of ghosts in the house. That meant there shouldn't be anything weird going on. No shadows. No stains. But I hadn't imagined everything. I was sure of that.

Selena stopped where a garden curved around a sundial. "This is Grandma Persistence's Shakespeare garden. Every plant in it is mentioned in at least one of his works. There's columbine, poppies—and monkshood, some people think it was the poison in *Romeo and Juliet*. Isn't it fascinating how so much of modern medicine is based on what they already knew back then?"

"I guess," I said. Actually, it sounded a little creepy. But who was I to judge? Dad and I had certainly bought enough bizarre antiques in our time.

She took me by the elbow, snuggling me close. "I'm so glad you're here. I want to have some fun this summer. I'm dreading next fall so bad. I was supposed to go away to Yale for pre-med, but Dad decided I was too young and is making me wait a year."

"That's shitty," I said. Then I backpedaled and clarified. "I don't mean the taking-a-year-off part. I did the same thing. Well, sort of. I took some classes online. But it's ridiculous that your dad didn't let you decide."

"Exactly. I knew you'd understand."

Ahead, the garden path transformed into terraces and wide stone steps, leading up to what appeared to be a flagstone terrace, surrounded by Grecian columns and roofed with vine-covered lattice. A low hedge made it impossible to see if anyone was on the terrace from our angle, but as we neared, Zachary's voice echoed out.

"The *Iliad*?" he said.

"Indeed. It's an absolutely brilliant work," a distinctly British guy's voice replied.

I leaned in close to Selena. "Is that the Professor? He sounds young. I thought he was old, like a retired professor."

She giggled and lowered her voice. "Not at all. He's twenty-six. People just call him the Professor because he's super smart, got his doctorate at like twenty-two. His real name's Rupert Wal—pole." She drew out his name, making it sound very posh. "Wait until you see him. He's hot, like cliché-movie-star-archeologist hot. Really uptight, though. I think he needs to get laid."

"Maybe he and Kate can help each other out," I said, totally deadpan.

She slapped her free hand over her mouth, sealing in a laugh. "Oh my God. That would be hysterical."

As we reached the top step, she let go of my arm and led me past a glass door that went into the house and around a potted cedar tree.

On the farther end of the terrace, wicker chairs circled a glass-topped table. Zachary was slouched in a chair. The Professor sat next to him, studying a laptop. He finished what he was doing and turned the laptop toward Zachary. "Let's start with this line. Once you're done translating it, we'll take a quick stroll to the garage and find that troublesome kitten you're worried about."

I bit my lip to keep from smirking. From his scholarly glasses and sandy brown hair all the way down to polished brown loafers, every inch of the Professor looked exactly as Selena had described. Except he was a bit more effeminate than I'd expected.

Zachary sliced a scowl at Selena and me. "What are you freaks doing here?"

The Professor swiveled toward us and peered over his glasses. "Well, this is a wonderful surprise." He flashed me a smile. "You must be the infamous Annie."

"I don't know about infamous," I said, my face heating. "I'm more of a totally normal sort of Annie."

He laughed. "That I doubt. I understand you have an interest in ancient history?"

"More like artifacts and antiques, than pure history," I said. Clearly someone had filled him in on my background, most likely Grandfather. "I've always wanted to go on a dig. It must be really interesting."

"Ever so much—" His gaze darted to something behind me. "Glad you could join us, Chase," he said.

"Sorry I'm late." A male voice, hard-edged and quick like a boxer's punch, came from beside me as the hot guy from the gate strode past and dropped into a chair across from Zachary and the Professor.

Zachary looked up and grinned.

Selena scoffed. "Late? More like almost in time for lunch."

"Had to wait for the mail." Chase shoved up his hoodie's frayed sleeves, then reached around to his back pocket and pulled out a graphic novel. He plunked it down on the coffee table. "I expected it yesterday."

The Professor gave the graphic novel a cursory look. "I'm really terribly sorry to tell you this, but that's not the sort of literature I had in mind."

Chase jabbed his finger at the title. "*Arabian Nights*—a classic and it covers the foreign language requirement as well."

I studied the cover. He wasn't lying. The title was in Arabic. Not that I could read Arabic, but the shapes of the letters looked familiar. About a month ago, it had been my duplication of an early Arabic inscription that had alerted Dad's lawyer about the dementia. To conceal Dad's forgetfulness, I'd corresponded with one of his clients about a poison ring she wanted to purchase. I sold it to her, but hadn't included a translation of the inscription like Dad would have done. I was hoping she'd overlook it as well as the ring's questionable authenticity. But she met Dad's lawyer at a cocktail party and bitched about the missing translation. The lawyer had come to see Dad about it. Next thing I knew, the lawyer called a doctor and the old boy network swung into action. It was the stupidest move I'd ever made. And, I wasn't in the clear yet. The woman could still complain to the police about the ring's authenticity. Then my chance of becoming a certified appraiser would be screwed.

The Professor sighed. "All right, Chase, you may begin with that version. But I want you to check in the library. I believe there's a copy of Galland's eighteenth-century translations of *Voyages of Sinbad*. I think it would be absolutely wise to put some effort into it as well."

"That's fine," Chase said. His head snapped toward me. I tried to glance away, but his gaze trapped mine.

And, for a heartbeat, the depth in his smoke-blue eyes took me back and stole my breath. What was going on behind that unflinching gaze? And who was he to the family, besides an employee? I had a hard time believing Grandfather or Kate would pay for his tutoring out of the kindness of their hearts. On top of that, he looked more like a guy who belonged in a fight club than studying classics.

My cheeks heated, and I lowered my eyes. I wasn't sure what he was thinking, but the thrum just below my belly button told me it was safer to stick to talking about graphic novels than plunging into that mystifying depth. I looked back up and put a lilt in my voice. "You're way ahead of me. I'd never be able to read that version."

"I doubt that," he said. His low tone lowered. "I suspect you catch on to things real fast."

"I—uh. Whatever." My words came out softer than I'd intended.

The Professor cleared his throat. "While you're all here, I want to extend an invitation. I finished cataloging a splendid group of new artifacts last night. I thought you might enjoy seeing them this evening."

"Cool," Zachary said.

I nodded. "I'd love to," I said. Then my shoulders slumped as reality nosedived into that daydream. "But I can't. I need to sit with my dad." I hadn't seen him in over twelve hours already. "Would you mind showing me the artifacts some other time—next week or later this month?"

"If we're lucky," Chase said, "you and your father will be long gone by then." His voice was hard this time, but those cool, ocean-deep eyes of his didn't hold any resentment. In fact, the way they studied me radiated keen interest . . . and something more. He cocked his head as if watching for my reaction, and I shivered under the intensity of his gaze. Oh, boy. I'd have to watch out for this one.

Selena swatted his shoulder. "Don't be an ass. I for one am glad to have her here." She grinned at me. "We're going to have a fantastic time."

I nodded to Selena, but I let my eyes flit back to Chase's. I actually hoped he was right. Archeology or not, the sooner Dad and I got out of this place, the better off I'd be—especially with the addition of this tall, dark, and dangerously tempting distraction. Man, I couldn't wait to get out of this place and get my freedom back.

Chase flashed me a grudging smile. "I didn't mean that the way it sounded," he said.

"I know." I waved a dismissive hand in the air, but I was still confused as to if he was interested in me or preferred we leave Moonhill. It was, however, abundantly clear which option my hormones preferred.

"By the by, Annie." The Professor brought my attention back to him. "I believe I know a friend of yours."

"You do?" I didn't have that many full-fledged friends.

"Indeed. Last winter, I was employed to do some work at the Metropolitan. One of the interns went on at great lengths about you. Taj, I believe his name was."

My stomach curled up into a ball and launched itself up my throat. "Wow, small world, isn't it?" I managed to choke out.

The Professor gave me a knowing smile. "Amazingly so."

The sick feeling in my throat hardened. I was going to puke. Taj had told the Professor I was a slut. I just knew it.

Selena tugged on my sleeve. "We need to get out of here or they're never going to get anything done."

"Yeah, right. See you later," I said.

She towed me to the other side of the terrace, but it wasn't until we were safely inside with the glass door between us and them that she let out a gasp. "Can you believe that? Taj, of all people."

"I thought I was going to die of embarrassment," I said.

I glanced back through the door to where the Professor was now studying the laptop and nodding as if Zachary had done a good job. Chase had moved into the shade and was standing with his hips resting against a low wall as he read the graphic novel. As I watched him, my fears about what the Professor might have heard faded, unimportant in comparison to the more tantalizing mystery that was Chase.

"What's the deal with Chase, anyhow?" I said to Selena. "He's not a relative, is he?"

"God, no. Chase is Grandpa's charity case. You'd know what I mean if you'd seen him when Kate and my father dragged him home. He was a mess, scuzzy, beat up. He had a long, skanky ponytail. Chase never talks about his past, but they were in South America visiting a dig when they found him. Dad told me Chase ended up on the wrong side of a cartel. Those guys don't mess around, you know."

"Sounds like it was lucky he escaped." I glanced back at Chase and he looked up, his eyes catching mine again. His lips crooked into an amused smile. My mouth went dry and I dropped my gaze. Mysterious and dangerously distracting.

A clanking sound, like a pan hitting the floor, reverberated out from a swinging door just down the hallway from us. As

Selena glanced toward the sound, her stomach growled loud enough for me to hear.

"Sorry about that," she said. "I skipped breakfast and I probably shouldn't have. You want to grab something to eat? Laura makes amazing cookies."

I squeezed my bag against my chest. "Actually, I should go finish unpacking." In truth, I was done with that. But I desperately wanted some alone time to sort through everything that had happened—before I got any more overwhelmed.

Selena pointed me in the direction of a servant's staircase that was only a few steps from the kitchen door. Then, as I headed for it, she took off to get a snack.

Unlike the elegant main staircase, the servant's stairs were steep and narrow. But when I reached the top, I was only a few doors away from my room.

I stopped in my tracks, every muscle in my body on high alert.

The door to my room was open. And I was certain I'd left it closed.

Quickly, I covered the distance to my doorway, stepped inside, and snapped on the overhead light. The bed remained half made as I had left it. No one had opened the curtains.

As I set my bag on the bed, something crunched under my heels.

A quarter-size dribble of what looked like white sand glinted on the otherwise pristine carpet. I dampened a finger and touched the grains, so I could collect a few and get a better look at them. Up close, they appeared more like salt than sand.

I touched my finger to my tongue and tasted them. It was salt, but definitely not salty beach sand, which anyone might have tracked in on their shoes. This was table salt. And not just a few grains that might have fallen off a handful of pretzels or chips, this was a small pile. What Olya had said about Zachary liking to play tricks came back to me.

Kicking off my shoes, I scoured the room again. Then, I checked the bathroom to see if there was a new bag of bath salts by the tub—one he might have spiked with something that would turn my skin purple or make me stink like a skunk.

But there was nothing new by the tub or sink, or anywhere.

I returned to the bedroom, struggling to think of a prank that might involve salt. It wasn't exactly a dangerous or scary substance. In fact, on television shows about the supernatural, salt was used as a protection against evil. When I'd gone to Salem, Massachusetts, the tour guide witch had talked about how sprinkling salt across a doorway could keep demonic spirits contained during an exorcism and generally ward off nasty things. But Zachary had no reason to assume I'd connect salt to witchcraft or the supernatural. Heck, twenty-four hours ago I wouldn't have either. In fact, the supernatural would have been the furthest thought from my mind. On top of that, I couldn't figure out when Zachary would have had the time to mess around in my room. There had to be more to this.

My pulse began to drum even harder as I noticed a different salt dribble that went under the bed's dust ruffle. The bed was high enough off the floor for someone to have climbed under it and done something. But what?

Kneeling down, I reached for the ruffle—

My hand stopped in midair, refusing to move another inch.

No matter what else was under my bed, there was one thing there for sure:

Darkness.

I couldn't remember how many nights I'd lain awake barely able to breathe while I waited for darkness to creep out from under my bed, like the evil escaping from Pandora's box. I'd fully expected it to slither up the mattress, clamp my ankles, weigh down my body, and smother my mouth and nose until I gasped for air. Darkness smothering me until I forgot everything.

With a fortifying breath, I pulled the mini-flashlight from my pocket, turned it on, and pointed it toward the ruffle. Still, my hands shook as I grasped the fabric. I could do this. I had to do this. There was probably nothing under the bed. It probably wouldn't even be that dark.

I lifted the fabric.

The flashlight's beam pushed the shadows aside and illuminated the outline of a five-pointed star made from salt. It was the size of a dinner plate. A pentagram. A freaking witch's star!

I dropped the ruffle and scooted backward.

Witchcraft. Real witchcraft. In my room. Under my bed.

I gulped a breath, and then another.

I rubbed my temples. What the hell was going on here? Were Kate and Grandfather part of a coven? No. That was ridiculous. There might be a couple of strange things going on, but a group of witches performing evil rituals in my room was not one of them.

Wiping my sweaty hands on my jeans, I lifted the ruffle again and trained the light on the pentagram. It wasn't haphazard. It was precisely made and at its center—I leaned closer—there was a gray-blue coinlike object.

My heart climbed into my throat, and I dropped the ruffle.

Even if he had found the time, Zachary couldn't possibly have made it. Maybe the kid was school smart. Perhaps he'd even beat me on an IQ test. But no antsy, cereal-slurping eleven-year-old was capable of creating a pentagram that exact—or, for that matter, meticulous enough to come up with a bizarre detail like the coin.

I pressed my fingers against my eyes. If I believed the television and the tour guide witch, then salt was a good thing. But I couldn't just assume the weird pentagram was as well.

Last year, when we'd sold a Victorian funeral portrait to the Santeria priest in New Orleans, just being around him gave me the creeps. The owner of the bed and breakfast had told us the priest could cause all kinds of things with his charms and spells: sickness, miscarriages, nightmares, bleeding, obsessive love—

Hope and worry coiled inside me. I raked my fingers through my hair.

My mother's death was written off as a one-in-a-million freak accident. But that didn't mean it was one. Perhaps Dad had good reason to suspect someone after all, like someone who was into witchcraft. Someone, perhaps, who could also call up evil shadowy figures and cause sickness.

I scrambled to my feet, hurried to the window, and shoved the drapes aside. Sunlight washed over me and flooded the room. I pushed the window up and took a deep breath of the ocean-scented air.

Closing my eyes, I focused on the seagulls' cry and the warmth of the sunlight against my skin. Selena's mother, Olya, definitely wasn't mainstream. The stains on her fingers looked like something that might have come from handling herbs and oils. Most likely, Olya was the resident witch. But with all her mother hen urges, I couldn't see her creating anything evil. Hopefully. Anyway, good or bad, it didn't seem smart to take a chance and remove the pentagram and have whoever made it know I was onto them. I'd just have to live with it for now. It wasn't like I could bring it up casually at dinner: *Hey, by the way, there's this witch thing under my bed and I was wondering if it was evil.*

I opened my eyes. Beyond the window stretched a sweeping view of the lawn and gardens, the cliff top and the ocean. It was beautiful. Peaceful.

Suddenly a flash of movement caught my eye. Someone was scurrying through the gardens, toward the cliff top.

I gasped.

Dad!

What was he doing here? He wasn't supposed to be home this soon. And why was he alone, and hurrying toward the cliffs?

Terrified, I grabbed the sandals out of my bag and crammed my feet into them, then tore down the hall to the back staircase. In a second, I was on the first floor. The door to the terrace was straight ahead of me. I flew out of it and found the terrace steps. Before I knew it, I was on the path, pumping my arms to run faster as I passed the Shakespeare garden and sprinted toward the cliff top. Where was Dad?

I got to the top of the stairs that led down the beach. Dad was striding toward the ocean.

The steps thundered as I hurtled down them.

"Dad!" I shouted above the crashing waves. "Wait for me!" I screamed, hoping to distract him from whatever he was about to do.

Slowly, he turned toward me.

I stopped, my hand seizing the railing as if it might shackle me there forever.

The man in front of me was indeed Dad, but the hard line of his mouth and the dark fury in his eyes didn't hold a trace of the lighthearted father I knew, or even the vacant stare of the sick man I'd become used to. Something must have happened at the doctor's appointment. Something bad.

"Come here, girl," he commanded.

I winced at the tone of his voice and blinked at his narrowed eyes and rigid posture.

He had something in his hands: Mother's jar.

I glanced at the ocean and back at the jar. I'd always hoped the moment would come when Dad was ready to let Mother go. But not like this. This frightened me more than his forget-ting, more than having to come to Moonhill, more than a pen-tagram of salt or shadows or even a dark hallway.

"Dad," I said, forcing myself to go down the rest of the stairs. "We should go back to the house."

He heaved a disgusted breath. "What about my order was too difficult for you to understand? Get over here. I've already had to stomach this for longer than I would have preferred." He set the jar on a flat outcrop of rock that reached into the ocean.

I walked toward him, the damp sand and pebbles giving slightly under my weight. "We'll have a cool drink on the ter-race. Lemonade with a little wine, your favorite."

Dad reached into the pocket of his chinos. "I would not ask for help if my hands were steady." He lied. I could see his hands were steadier than they'd been in months. "Confining a soul like this is despicable."

Then, before I could turn and run, Dad closed the distance between us. The old-time straight razor he used for shaving appeared in his fisted hand, the cutting edge flipped open, like a switchblade ready for a fight. What the hell?

He grabbed my hair in one hand, yanked my head back, and sliced the back side of my ear with the blade.

Pain zinged across my skin.

He sliced again and warmth trickled down my jawline.

I twisted against his grip. "Dad, stop!"

He wrenched my hair tighter, leaned in close, and whis-pered, "If you run, I will catch you and slit your throat. Now shut your mouth and do as I say."

My pulse banged louder than the waves against the rock. I clamped my mouth shut, but the voice inside my head screeched, *Dad, no!*

He yanked my hair again, then released me.

I staggered backward, my hand going to my ear. It came away

wet with blood. I couldn't think. I couldn't breathe. I glanced toward the stairs. He'd catch up with me before I could ever reach them.

"Over there." He nodded at the rock and Mother's jar.

As if trapped in a nightmare, I stumbled to it.

Dad edged closer and held out the razor. "Open the jar," he commanded. But when I went to take the razor, he locked his grip. "Do not get any foolish notions, daughter of these loins."

Daughter of these loins? He sounded ludicrous, like a bad actor in a cheap movie. But this wasn't a movie. It was reality, a terrifying reality where the dangerous stranger my father had become recognized me as his child—when my loving father did not. I swallowed hard and nodded that I understood.

He released the razor. I took it, sat down on the edge of the rock, and put the jar between my legs to hold it firm. Dad had told me a million times how he would have bought a rosewood box for Mother's ashes. But by the time he was told of her death and traveled back to Moonhill where Mother and I had lived, her ashes had been put in a brass jar and sealed in with beeswax.

The beeswax curled off in ribbons as I worked the blade around the jar's mouth. Under the wax I discovered a cork. Pausing for a second, I reached up and ran my fingers behind my ear. The trickle of blood had slowed to a sticky seep. Dad had cut me. He'd cut me, and he might do something worse if I didn't do as he said. I had to stay calm. Otherwise he would just get angrier, and he'd never snap out of this. Whatever this was.

"What are you waiting for?" he snarled.

With trembling hands, I pried the cork out. "I-I'm done," I stammered, holding the jar out to him.

His eyes sliced toward where the waves slapped the shore, then retreated. He took a step backward. "Pour them in the water."

My jaw tensed. No. I couldn't. Once he got better, he'd regret doing it like this. But I couldn't refuse him either. He was stronger than I was. I'd never make it to the stairs.

"Now, girl." He glared at me. "Do it while the tide is still going out."

Leaving the cork and razor on the rock, I yanked off my sandals and rolled my pants legs up. Then, with the jar in my hands, I waded into the shallow waves, the bone-cold water numbing my feet and ankles.

For a split second, I looked at Dad.

His face quivered. His hands clenched.

My fingers tightened on the jar. All right, I'd do this, but this moment belonged solely to honoring Mother and nothing else. Not to whatever was going on inside Dad's head or the tears burning in my eyes, or the pain throbbing behind my ear, or the fact that I really hadn't known my mother at all. Nothing was going to steal this moment from her, not even fear.

"Mama, I love you," I said under my breath, as I tilted the jar and let the ashes fall.

Then, I bowed my head in respect and watched them ride the waves, washing over a starfish, over stones and sand and shells, as the tide drew them into deeper water.

Something the size of a small earring shimmered amongst the last of the ashes.

Before Dad could shout another command, I reached into the water with my free hand and scooped it out.

I hesitated, expecting Dad to demand what I'd found. But only a whisper in the back of my mind had anything to say. *It's not yours. Leave it with the ashes.*

Opening my hand, I gave it a quick study. It was sapphire-colored and shaped like a raindrop with a small hole on the slender end. Not a gem. More likely sea glass. Why had it been in with Mother's ashes?

And why was Dad so quiet?

I shoved the sea glass in my pocket and raised my head.

He slouched on the flat rock, his knees tucked to his chest, his head bowed. The razor and cork sat untouched beside him.

"Dad?"

He looked up, his eyes wide with confusion. "I've met you before, haven't I?"

CHAPTER 6

Like the ocean you wash over me.
Like death you steal my heart.
Like a shell you whisper in my ear,
"What is it you desire?"

—"Song of the Stolen Heart"

While I rolled down my damp pants legs and slid into my sandals, I took one steadying breath after another and willed my pulse to slow. Normally I would have found Dad not recognizing me upsetting, but right now I didn't care as long as the violent version of him was gone.

Dad listened quietly as I wiped the blood off my jawline and explained who I was. He didn't react at all when I folded the razor closed and slid it into my pocket. I wanted desperately to ask why he wasn't at the doctor's. However, chances were, he wouldn't know what I was talking about any more than he'd remember attacking me. What I needed to do was keep him calm and get him to the house.

I took Dad by the hand. He allowed me to lead him up the stairs to the cliff top. But as we passed the Shakespeare garden, he slanted his eyes at the unsealed jar in my other hand. His knees locked and he yanked his hand from mine. "I know what that is. You're going to kill me and put my ashes inside it! Aren't you?"

"No. Dad." I set the jar on the ground far enough into the garden so leaves hid it from view. "See, I'll leave it right there. No one wants to hurt you."

His eyes became slits. "You can't lie to me. They told me about you."

The cool I'd managed to patch together evaporated. My voice became shrill. "They? Who? What in the hell are you talking about?"

"They came to my room and told me to warn you to stay out of their way." The terrifying glisten in his eyes told me he wasn't talking about the doctor or any member of the family. It was something more sinister.

My mind raced, searching for answers to a remark that I shouldn't have even been taking seriously. "Are you talking about the shadows?"

His lips pressed into a guarded smile, and his eyes went to something behind me. He leaned in and whispered, "He belongs to them, you know."

Instinctively, I glanced over my shoulder to see who he was talking about.

Chase was striding toward us. A trace of sweat darkened the front of his olive-green sleeveless T and a few leaves clung to his low-slung jeans. He must have shed his hoodie and traded in his graphic novel for yard work while I was in my room.

"Need a hand?" He didn't look me in the eyes, but he sounded sincere.

I opened my mouth to say no. Dad would never want a stranger involved, no more than he'd want anyone to ever know what had happened on the beach.

My hand went to my ear. It no longer seeped blood, but it was still painful. Oh God. I hated this. I didn't want help and I didn't want Dad going back to where I'd seen the shadows, but we couldn't just stand here forever. I forced my head to nod

yes. "I was taking Dad inside," I said, my voice edged with unwanted tears.

No sooner were the words out of my mouth than Dad took
off at a trot. "I can find my own room, thank you very much."

Wiping my eyes, I jogged after him with Chase close behind. "I don't know what happened at Dad's appointment this
morning, but he hasn't been himself since he got back from
town."

"Back?" Chase said. "What are you talking about? No one
went anywhere."

I stopped and swiveled toward him. If Kate had taken Dad
off his regular medicines and not taken him to a doctor, that
might explain everything. "Are you saying he didn't leave the
grounds?"

"I didn't see anyone." He rubbed his neck, his fingers pausing when they touched a jagged scar on the left side of his collarbone. "But I wouldn't have, I was working inside the sheep
barn."

My voice became harsh. "That's bullshit. You were watching for the mailman, so you could get your graphic novel."

A nerve twitched at the corner of his eye. "That was
later—and he was the only person I saw. Earlier, I was in the
barn."

"Oh, okay," I said, like I believed him. But I was certain he
wasn't telling me everything.

The terrace door slammed and Dad disappeared inside.

"I've got to catch up with him," I said.

Chase's voice gentled. "You look like you could use a break.
Let me take care of him."

I bit my lip. He was right. I did need a break to process
what had happened, and what I'd just learned. But how could
I trust Chase, when it was obvious he was hiding something?
And how could I forget the unwelcoming way he'd glared at

the Mercedes's window when we arrived? And what did Dad mean by: *He belongs to them?* My hormones definitely wanted to trust Chase, but look where that had gotten me before.

Still, I was good at reading body language and Chase's kind smile and relaxed stance said he was sincere. I really didn't want Dad to be alone, especially in his room. Besides, there was something else I had to do before I lost my nerve. Kate had legal guardianship over Dad, but that didn't mean I couldn't confront her about his care, or lack thereof.

"Do you mind staying with him? I'll be up as fast as I can," I said.

He smiled. "Don't worry. He'll be safe."

My stomach twitched at the word *safe,* but his smile softened me. To be honest, it wasn't Dad's safety I was worried about. It was mine. The mere thought of being alone with Dad terrified me, making me feel both guilty and sad, which in turn felt totally foreign and wrong. Even the idea of running into the shadows again didn't begin to compare to the memory of what had happened on the beach.

"Thanks," I said.

His eyes lingered on mine, communicating something else, something deeper that made the air between us simmer and left me more than a little breathless. Then, he turned and jogged toward the house.

As I watched him, I noticed a curtain fall shut in an upstairs window. Someone had been spying on us, and it had been from a window at the end of the hallway where my room was.

Heart hammering, I made a beeline into the house and dashed for the back stairs, then skidded to a stop. There was no point in trying to catch the person. He or she would be long gone by now. Plus, I had something more important to do. I turned to start in the opposite direction, but the kitchen door swung open, missing me by inches, and Olya flew out.

"Your Dad, have you seen him?" she asked, breathless. Her gaze darted to the terrace door, then toward the other end of the hallway.

My hands shot to my hips. "Why didn't anyone tell me he was back?"

She hesitated, toying with the hem of her sweater and averting her eyes from mine. "He returned a little while ago," she said. "He asked me if I could get him some lemonade. When I brought it back to his room, he was gone."

She was obviously lying. Still, I doubted she was the mastermind behind whatever was going on. And it was probably smarter to stay on her good-witch-mother-hen side than turn her against me. "I found Dad outside. Chase is going with him to his room right now."

Relief washed the worry lines from her face, and her craggy fingers fluttered to her breastbone. "Thank goodness."

"Do you know where Aunt Kate is?" I asked, trying to appear as cool and collected as possible.

She shook her head. "There's no need to tell her what happened."

"If you tell me where Kate is," I said, "I promise I won't mention Dad's escape. I'm really grateful you're helping take care of him."

Olya's gaze slid toward the staircase and then back to me, like she wanted desperately to get back upstairs to Dad. "Kate's in her study. On the first floor, last doorway on the west wing hall, right under your father's room." Her throat bobbed as she swallowed hard. "It's better if you talk with her at lunch. She has a visitor right now."

"I'll do that." I lied.

I waited just long enough for the sound of Olya's footsteps to vanish up the stairs, and then I rushed to the foyer, past the dining room, and into the west wing hallway. I could only hope that Olya wouldn't text or phone Kate and warn her of my impending visit. Then again, Kate probably never answered her phone.

Both sides of the hallway were lined with closed doors and mirror-backed display cases full of ticking clocks and bizarre whirling apparatuses that looked like Leonardo da Vinci might have invented them.

When I reached the door to the study, Kate's demanding voice and an unfamiliar man's deeper tone came from within. I paused, my confidence wavering. If I went in now, I wouldn't be able to confront her, not with a stranger in the room. That would make me look like an ignoramus, and I didn't want that any more than I wanted yet another person to know why Dad was here. Olya was right. I needed to wait.

As I turned to leave, I heard the door open.

"Stephanie?" Kate's voice said.

I whirled around and gave her a sheepish grin.

Kate looked down her nose at me.

"I—I wanted to talk to you, but if you're busy, I can come back later." My voice stammered and a dribble of sweat fell down my spine. I clenched my hands, and fortified my resolve. I had to stay strong.

Kate stepped into the hallway and a gray-haired man in a dark suit with a white clerical collar came out with her. A priest.

He dipped his head to greet me. "You're Stephanie Freemont, I presume?"

Unable to find my tongue, I nodded. I'd met loads of priests and ministers over the years, but coming face to face with one here was the last thing I'd expected. On top of that, the only way he'd know my name was if he and Kate had been talking about me.

"Well, nice to meet you, Stephanie." The priest smiled at

me, then turned back to Kate. "Like I said, I don't think we should delay." He gave me another quick nod and headed down the hallway, most likely toward the front door.

"You might as well come in." Kate's voice brought me back to attention. She waved me into the dimly lit study and closed the door. "I assume there is a reason for this impromptu visit?"

I straightened my spine and marched straight toward the chair beside her desk. If I sat there, then she'd have to sit at her desk rather than lording over me while we talked.

"Don't make yourself too comfortable. We'll be talking over there." Kate waved an imperious hand, indicating a high-backed settee that faced away from us and toward a fireplace. It was a beautiful piece of eighteenth-century furniture with brocade upholstery, and so tall it would have protected anyone sitting in it from cold drafts and hidden them from view as well. But I wasn't here to admire the antiques.

Head held high, I followed Kate across the room. As she went to stand by the fireplace, I started to sit on the settee, but leapt up when I realized Grandfather already sat in it.

"I'm sorry," I said, backing away. "I didn't realize you were there." My neck and face burned from embarrassment.

Chuckling, he scooted over. "You are a skittish little thing." He patted the cushion next to him. "Now, what is it that you want to talk to Kate about?"

Determined not to let him think I was that flustered, I lowered myself onto the settee and casually crossed my ocean-dampened legs at the ankle. I looked at Kate.

Behind her and above the fireplace hung a huge oil painting of frolicking cats. The absurdity of it hanging where I had expected to see a portrait of some grim ancestor gave me the will to smile as I steered the conversation in a very specific direction. "I wanted to know how Dad's appointment went."

"Given time and proper treatment, your father may recover." Kate glanced away from me and ran a finger down a

porcelain ginger jar that sat on the mantel, like she was checking for dust. Then her eyes rushed back to mine, narrowed and
hard. "The doctor said your father's recovery would have been
ensured if he had received help sooner. In the future, Stephanie,
you must refrain from keeping secrets."

I planted both feet on the floor. She had no right to lecture
me like that. Biting my tongue, I dropped my gaze. No. I wasn't
going to let her get to me. I wasn't going to lose my temper. No
matter how hard she pushed.

Grandfather cleared his throat. "Secrets breed trouble," he
said quietly.

But his words barely registered in my brain as I braced myself and then asked a seemingly innocent question. "The doctor, what did you say his name was?"

"Dr. Jerome," Kate said without hesitation. "He's a world-
renowned expert. The best in these sorts of cases. We're lucky
he's close by."

I knifed her with a glare. "It must be very close. I asked
Chase and he said he didn't see anyone leave the property or
return this morning."

Her lips pursed, like she'd sucked on a sour pickle. "My,
don't you think you're the clever one, seeing conspiracies
where there aren't any. Just like your father."

Every muscle in my body tightened, and I started to rise,
readying to lunge at her. Grandfather tugged me back into the
settee.

"That was uncalled for, Kate," he said. He squeezed my
arm. "I understand you're upset. You've been through a lot.
But Kate didn't mean anything by that. She's just on edge. We
all are."

"I'm sorry," I said. And I was. Not for what I'd said, but for
the attitude I'd walked into the room with. He was right. I
could feel it, worry permeating the air. And, as much as Kate

pissed me off and Grandfather had freaked me out before, now at least his closeness was oddly comforting.

Kate blew out a noisy breath. "Shall we try this again?" She rolled her shoulders as if relieving a cramp, then went on. "We expected your father's appointment to last longer, but the visit was cut short. I was about to come find you and let you know." Her tone darkened. "In reality, there's no reason for me to answer to you—"

"Maybe because he's my father?" I snapped.

"Well, be that as it may," she said. "You should know I would have been surprised if Chase had seen people coming and going. First thing in the morning he has barn chores, then he spends time at the house with the Professor."

I shrugged. "Okay, so I believe you," I said, though suspicion still bristled inside me, warning me that I wasn't getting the whole story, just like with Chase.

I licked my lips, considering whether I should come clean myself by telling them what had happened on the beach. But I decided against it. Better to keep something to myself for now, and in doing so I would be able to keep my promise to Olya. Besides, if Dad and I were lucky, his lapse into violence was an isolated incident, brought on by the stress of visiting an unfamiliar doctor.

Something warm brushed my ankle. I looked down in time to see a calico cat, then an orange one streak away from the settee, dash under a bookcase, and out of sight.

"Stephanie," Kate said, snapping her fingers at me. "We're discussing something important here. Your father is a very sick man."

Grandfather cleared his throat again and shot her a pointed look. "Don't mind her," he said to me, "your father's going to be fine. But we need you to tell us everything. When did he first start acting odd? The more we know, the easier it will be to help him."

The muscles along my spine tensed at the thought of telling

them any details. I mean, yes, they were family. But if Dad hadn't trusted them, then why should I? Still, despite my reservations, I was certain Kate wanted Dad to get better and for us to leave as much as I wanted to get away from Moonhill. Although, Grandfather did seem to genuinely care.

"All right," I said. I closed my eyes and let my mind drift back. I told them how it had begun last winter, shortly after Dad and I came back from doing the Met antique show. That the first time I'd noticed anything was when we were going through the contents of an abandoned church. How I'd seen a shadow and turned around to see what had caused it and, when I looked back, Dad had a strange blank expression on his face.

I hesitated, giving them time to react to my mention of the shadow. But neither of them even so much as flinched. Grandfather just softly nudged my shoulder and motioned for me to go on. "What happened next?"

Closing my eyes again, I pretended I was telling myself the story, trying to make sense of it, like I'd done a million times since that day in the church.

I told them how, after that day, Dad would often stare into space or act distracted. "At one point, I even thought, I don't know, perhaps he had a girlfriend and was afraid to tell me—or in love." I laughed bitterly and brushed my hair back from my face, feeling their eyes on me, and feeling sure they thought I was a childish imbecile. "But when I asked him about it, he told me I was imagining things. Later, I decided maybe his forgetfulness was from a lack of sleep. He was up all hours of the night, wandering around. I gave him chamomile tea and tried to get him to take sleeping pills, but nothing worked. He kept saying he felt fine, to quit pestering him. Then it got worse. It was like flipping a light switch: One day he was a little off, but wheeling and dealing like always. The next, he lost all interest in the business. He started talking to himself and refused to answer the door. Sometimes he even forgot who I was. I didn't want his clients to stop buying from him, so I started doing all his e-mailing and phone calls—you know, running the business. No one caught on that he wasn't working behind the scenes. Well, until I failed to include the translation with a ring and the customer complained to Dad's lawyer." I bit my tongue, resisting the urge to tell them that I was fully aware that the lawyer had been spying on us.

"This ring," Grandfather said. "It was a poison ring and the inscription was in Arabic?"

I nodded. "Gold with an onyx stone. I copied the inscription and tried looking the letters up. I think they were a form of ancient Arabic, maybe Sabaean—though they sort of resembled modern Arabic as well. Weird, actually." I frowned. "But what does this have to do with Dad's illness?"

"You told the woman the ring was from the eighteeneighties?" he continued, ignoring my question.

"I, uh—" I cleared my throat, guilt twisting in my stomach. "She was in a hurry and I didn't want to lose the sale. I kind of—I made up that part." I gulped. Hopefully, he was done asking questions about the ring and that stupid sale.

"You do realize—if the writing was a form of Sabaean—that could date the ring all the way back to the sixth century or even before, perhaps to the time of Solomon and Sheba. Which would make it substantially valuable."

For a blissful half second, a sense of relief swept the tension from my body. Great. It was the ring's value and nothing else that interested them.

My guilt returned with vengeance, and I hung my head as shame for what I'd done caught in my throat.

I peeked up at Grandfather. "To be perfectly honest, I was convinced the ring was an early piece. But then"—man, this wasn't going to be easy to admit—"I couldn't find any record of it in Dad's inventory and it had been stored in the safe near his personal, everyday jewelry. So I examined the ring again, really well, and I decided . . . I know it was wrong. But I was desperate. We'd gotten overdue notices for the power and car insurance. There wasn't any money in the bank." My voice cracked. "When Dad's lawyer called, I was terrified. I thought the woman had figured out what I'd done and called the police. I knew the ring wasn't Victorian. I decided it wasn't an early piece, either. It was a reproduction, a high-quality one Dad had picked up to wear, maybe at a museum shop—or it was a gift. Dad has a friend who makes really good"—I braced myself, then said it—"forgeries."

Grandfather slapped his knee and laughed. "I certainly wasn't expecting that." His face went serious. "There was no need for you to feel that desperate. You simply needed to tell the lawyer or us that something was wrong. No one would have ever let you go without or not reached out to help your father."

I met his eyes, my anger flaring. "Why would I have done that? You've never once tried to see me. You never e-mailed or phoned. You never so much as sent me a birthday card." I swallowed hard, my face going cold. That was how I felt, how I'd felt for years. But damn, I wished I hadn't let it slip. Not only did I sound like a spoiled kid, but I shouldn't have allowed them to see how much their lack of interest in my life had bothered me.

Grandfather shifted closer and rested his hand on my knee. My leg tensed and I longed to shove his hand away, but a part of me refused. Instead, it cherished the touch, a touch I'd hoped to feel for as long as I could remember.

His voice was soft. "Annie, believe me when I say that wasn't our doing. That was your father's choice. We never forgot you or didn't care about you. We simply were respecting your father's wishes. You are my eldest grandchild, you know?"

Kate groaned. "Oh, my God. Enough of this sentimental hogwash. Who's kidding who? If James wasn't such an idiot none of this would have happened."

Grandfather's hand left my knee. His voice toughened. "Don't speak about your brother like that."

Kate's words made my jaw clench, but it was hard not to smile at Grandfather's reprimand. I glanced from one to the other and back. They seemed to have forgotten about me as they glowered at each other.

Finally, Kate looked away and huffed. "It is infuriating."

"Yes, my dear, it is," Grandfather said. Then he turned back to me. "Whether you're a budding criminal or you sold an incredibly valuable ring for a pittance, doesn't matter at this point. Your uncle David will get it back. What's important right now is that the sale led us to knowing about your father's condition, and you're here with us as it should be."

I nibbled my lip as worry about how the sale could destroy my future resurfaced. Grandfather claimed he wanted to help. He had connections. It was silly to let my pride and one stupid move ruin everything. "Ah—about that sale. I was wondering if—you—"

"What is it?" Grandfather said.

"Um—Is there a way David could make sure the woman hasn't or won't complain to anyone else about the ring, like to the police? I kind of need a clean record when I apply for colleges and jobs."

"I'll have him look into it," he said. Then he sanded his hands together, as if wiping away the last remnants of the conversation. "Now, if we're all done, I'd like to get to the dining room, have a cup of chowder and maybe some of Laura's macaroons." He braced his hand on the arm of the settee and started to rise.

I jumped to my feet, took Grandfather by the elbow, and

helped him up. A musty incense smell clung to his tweed jacket, reminding me of Dad's room. My fingers recoiled from his arm.

"Thank you, child," he said, apparently oblivious to my abrupt withdrawal. "Politeness is always a good sign."

Kate harrumphed. "I wouldn't call bringing half the ocean into the house polite." She sliced a glance at my damp pants legs, then scrunched up her nose as she scanned the rest of me.

"No need to worry about me," I said tartly. "As long as Dad *is* getting the proper care, I won't be around long enough to offend you."

Grandfather chucked. "You see, Kate, manners and spine. Very much like you."

With a dismissive toss of her head, Kate marched toward the door. She opened it and another cat, this time a pure black one, skittered inside and streaked under the bookcase.

"They certainly are riled up," Grandfather said as he scuffled into the hallway.

"They aren't fond of strangers," she answered with a snap, but her voice betrayed more worry than her words, and I was left with the distinct feeling that there was a deeper meaning behind the seemingly innocent retort.

CHAPTER 7

The darkness borrows things: black satin slippers,
a hair from the old cat's tail. It gives things too:
dreams of soft touches, and kisses where
only a lover's mouth should go.

—Night Magic
By Anonymous

Instead of having tea with Grandfather and Kate, I excused myself and headed for Dad's room. Chase had probably left as soon as Olya showed up, but I still felt obliged to check in like I'd promised. It wasn't like I could avoid the room forever.

I touched my ear and flinched. Okay, those reasons were only part of it. In truth, I couldn't live with myself if I let fear keep me from helping Dad.

As I rounded the corner and started down Dad's hallway, I heard a squeak. When I glanced toward the sound, I spotted a shadow vanishing into a wall.

Adrenaline shot into my veins. I might never know if Dad had really gone to the doctor's, or if Olya had made the pentagram under my bed, or if someone was actually watching from the window. But clearly, the shadows were not just a figment of my imagination.

Determined to not make any noise, I slid out of my sandals

and crept toward where the shadow had vanished. When I got there, I discovered a paneled door with a brass push-plate instead of a knob.

The door squeaked as I eased it open. I slipped inside and found myself standing on a second-story balcony overlooking an enormous library, hazily lit by a stained-glass skylight.

On either side of me and below, dark stacks held thousands of books. Ornate desks and leather chairs lurked here and there in the dim light. Nothing moved, but the prickling hairs on the back of my neck warned me I was not alone.

I pulled my flashlight out of my pocket and searched from right to left, one inch at a time, looking for anything out of place—the same way I'd use a black light to scan a piece of porcelain for repairs or embellishments. When I reached the book stack closest to me, I saw the angled jut of an elbow.

Quick as I could, I pinpointed my flashlight's beam on the shape.

The darkness shattered into a stark image of Chase haloed by the library's muted blue light.

"What are you doing here?" I said. I had no idea what or who I'd expected to unmask, but it hadn't been him.

He raised his hands in surrender. "I'm not the one playing cops and robbers with the flashlight."

"Sorry." I clicked off the light, and his face dimmed to a less stark shade. "It's just. I thought I saw . . ." Words failed me as I weighed whether to tell him about the shadows or not. Clearly this time, I'd been deceived by something much more ordinary—perhaps the swiftness of the door swallowing his outline combined with the angle I'd seen him from.

He came away from the book stack and moved toward me. I could smell his outdoorsy scent, bonfires and fresh-cut wood. But, despite how enticing that was, the grim twist to his mouth told me he had something disturbingly serious on his mind.

I took a step back and found myself against the balcony wall.

"I saw what your father made you do on the beach," he said.

My heart beat so fast it made my head light. Exactly how much had he seen?

"What did you find in the water?"

With trembling fingers, I brushed the outside of my jeans pocket, feeling the lump of sea glass that I'd all but forgotten. I met his unflinching eyes. "Nothing much."

He cocked his head. "Did it belong to your mother?"

My breathing faltered. "What do you know about her?"

"Nothing. Except those ashes aren't her. She's alive."

I gasped. "What are you talking about?"

Hesitating, he frowned. "What happened to your ear?"

"It's nothing," I fired back. He definitely hadn't seen everything that had happened at the beach. Desperation filled my voice. "Don't try to change the subject. I want to know about my mother. She's alive?"

He rubbed his collarbone as he'd done earlier. It had to be an unconscious habit of his, a tell that most likely meant he was uncomfortable. "I didn't mean it like that. She's alive in your memories, like my mother is to me. That's all," he said with almost too much force.

I folded my arms across my chest. Idiot. How could he not have realized I'd misinterpret what he meant?

As a pained look flickered across his face and vanished, the full meaning of what he'd just said struck me at a deeper level and I unfolded my arms. With his strong features and severe military haircut, he looked so tough. I'd never stopped to think his question about what had happened on the beach might stem from personal heartache. I softened my voice. "How long ago did you lose her?"

He took another step toward me, his expression now un-yielding. My heart stumbled. One inch closer and the front of his shirt would press against mine. "Too long ago to waste time worrying about her. You should do the same." He started to turn away.

"Wait!" I grabbed his arm and the secret I'd kept safely locked inside bubbled out. "Something about my mother's death bothered Dad. I really don't know what. I think he believes she didn't die the way he was told."

I'd wanted for so long to share that with someone, but now that it was out in the open, I was afraid I'd said too much, without thinking, without really knowing Chase. Maybe it would have been okay to tell him if we'd met someplace nor-mal, like at a party or college, anyplace but here. Maybe.

I let go of him and pressed my fingers over my eyes. "I'm sorry. I'm just overwhelmed. I shouldn't have said anything."

His warm hands cupped mine and drew them away from my face. "You're right, you shouldn't have. Don't say it again, not to me or anyone, especially your father."

I pulled away from his grasp. It felt like he cared about me. Actually, it felt a lot hotter than that. Yet he said things that made me feel like he didn't want me to trust him or Dad. He was willing to watch over Dad and keep him safe, but he didn't like him. It was too confusing, too weird and wrong. "I don't get what's going on. But I'm not going to just ignore every-thing."

"If you don't, your life will never be the same. You'll regret it. If you live."

Intense cold swept my skin and seeped into my very core. I opened my mouth, but couldn't think of a sensible thing to say.

Chase clutched me by the shoulders, his smoldering eyes locking onto mine. For a heartbeat I thought he was going to kiss me, hard and fast like in a romance novel. But instead his lips tightened and his voice deepened to a husky whisper.

"Leave Moonhill and soon," he said. Then, he turned around and fled, his footsteps a hushed murmur as he disappeared into the shadows.

CHAPTER 8

We saw it in the time between the lightning and the thunder.
And we knew beyond a doubt it was not the flag or sail
of a friend or foe. It was death, her skirts spread out
on the horizon, horrifying and supreme.

—Journal of Stephanie Freemont:
14th May, 1801. Indian Ocean.

In a daze, I wandered down the hallway to Dad's door and knocked lightly. Chase telling me not to talk about Dad's suspicions concerning Mother's death made it pretty obvious someone was covering up something. But how could it be that dangerous—and, of anyone, why shouldn't I mention it to Dad?

I raked my hair back from my face. This whole thing wasn't fair. A person was supposed to be able to trust their family, especially parents and grandparents. On the other hand, not trusting Chase made sense. But deep inside I wanted so badly to trust him as well.

Dad's door opened partway and Olya stuck her head out. "It's good you're here. Your father's asleep. But"—she opened the door a bit wider—"I could use some company."

The room was silent and dark, except for a bleary glow and muffled voices filtering out from the television. Thankfully, a pleasant lemony aroma had replaced both the musty incense smell and the more acrid one.

I followed Olya to the sitting area in front of the fireplace. As I settled into one of the wingchairs, she gestured at a silver tea set and lifted an eyebrow to ask if I wanted some. I nodded. Then we sat without speaking. She watched the TV, her head bobbing as she dozed off. I shoved Chase's words to the back of my mind and sipped tea while I kept vigil over Dad and the fireplace, ready to pull my flashlight out at a moment's notice.

But no shadows materialized, human or otherwise. And Dad slept curled up under a puff of blankets, snoring gently like everything was right with the world.

Hours later, Tibbs came in and whispered that supper was ready. Olya and I got up to leave, but stopped when Dad rolled over and opened his eyes.

"Annie," Dad said in a hoarse voice. "I love you. Never forget that."

I smiled at him. "I love you too, Dad." I thought about the beach and what Chase had said in the library, and added, "No matter what."

Supper dragged on forever. When it finally ended, I decided to take the Professor up on his offer to look at the artifacts instead of going straight back to Dad's room.

While Zachary charged ahead, the Professor, Selena, and I walked slowly to the library. Once there, I couldn't help but glance up to where Chase and I had stood on the balcony only hours ago. My breath quickened as I thought about the husky tone of his voice and the smolder in his eyes when he'd warned me. The warmth of his body, so close to mine. What was he doing now, eating his supper with Laura and Tibbs or alone in the stone cottage by the gate?

"Hurry up," Zachary shouted from where he was vanishing into the stacks.

I followed the Professor and Selena through the alleys of

books, past where a circular staircase rose up to the balcony, and into the archeology workroom.

Stunned, I stopped and stared. Unlike the library or the rest of the house for that matter, this room was brightly lit and ultra-modern. It wasn't big, no larger than a two-car garage. Smaller than some I'd seen at museums. But it was spotless, all gleaming stainless steel, white paint, and glistening glass. Not one computer or piece of equipment looked out-of-date or worn. The only thing vaguely old-fashioned was the journals lying open on the massive desk.

"Wow, this is amazing," I said.

The Professor motioned for us to sit around a table, then he turned on one of the computers and a wall-size monitor came to life. The top third of the screen showed a distant satellite image of a dig site. I was sure of this because a series of close-ups spanned the bottom of the screen. One appeared to be infrared, and another was the image of a 3-D model.

Zachary bounced in his seat. "That's where the stuff came from," he said.

I studied the image. Amazing was an understatement. "Where is it?"

"Greece," Selena said. "Our family's been involved in this site for decades."

"Indeed," the Professor said. "I was about Zachary's age, the first time I went there." He handed out cotton gloves for us to wear, then started to pass around pottery shards and other trinkets. His eyes widened as he lectured about them. Everything was fascinating, an incredible experience.

"This one's sweet," Zachary said, passing me a gray-blue coin the size of a nickel.

I blinked, then blinked again and stared. I couldn't believe it. The coin looked almost exactly like the coin in the center of the salt pentagram.

I set it on my palm. The coin had the image of a centaur stamped into one side—I flipped it over—and a bee on the other.

Closing my fingers around it, I thought about the penta-gram. I was pretty sure Olya had made it. Selena might have had a passing interest in medicinal herbs from Shakespeare's day and age, but she didn't strike me as a kneeling-on-the-floor-chanting-spells kind of girl. It certainly wasn't Zachary. And, if the Professor had used the coin in witchcraft, it didn't seem like he would pass one around for everyone to see.

I opened my fist and studied the coin. If no one here had made the pentagram, then this was a good time to ask. "Pro-fessor, this coin, what is it?"

Ignoring me, the Professor zeroed in on Zachary. "The point of showing you these artifacts is that I don't expect you to merely dabble with the *Iliad* translations. I want you to gain an exceptional appreciation for the Greek culture and history. Their military commanders studied the *Iliad* to learn the art of combat. You will need to put effort in that area as well."

Zachary waggled his eyebrows. "No problem, Prof. Weapons are cool."

The Professor shook his head and continued his lecture, going on about the exact location where each artifact was found and how that significance worked into various theories. I wanted badly to interrupt and ask about the coin again, but maybe it was smarter to hold off. Tomorrow, I'd catch him alone and find a way to bring the subject up.

As he returned to discussing the *Iliad,* my mind wandered back to when Chase and I were on the balcony. The dig and Greek history were interesting, but they were mysteries that for the most part had been unearthed—but, Chase, now there was a tantalizing story that begged to be explored. How had he ended up fleeing for his life? Where had he come from before that?

Laughing at myself, I sat back in my chair. Why did I even care about any of that? I barely knew Chase. As a rule, I didn't obsess on random guys like some girls did. Not even freaking movie or sports stars.

I touched my shoulder where his hands had held me captive. His grip determined and forceful.

Closing my eyes, I imagined his face. His eyes, steel blue and deep. His inviting lips. His strong jawline and dark brows. His hair. If I ran my fingertips over it, what would it feel like, bristly like a rottweiler's scruff or softer like cut grass? Would touching it send shivers across my skin? For sure, and then some.

I breathed in through my nose, recalling his outdoorsy-bonfire scent. The warmth of his hands cupping mine. For a heartbeat it had felt like he might actually kiss me, hot and fast, impetuously. Chase didn't seem like the type to preplan those kinds of things.

I let my mind wander deeper, imagining what would have happened if I'd encouraged him with a tilt of my head, or if I'd kissed him first. I pictured closing the gap between us and reaching for his neck . . .

But before I can kiss him, his arms go around me, pulling me hard against him. His lips are on mine, eager and hungry, as if he can't hold back. They open, asking, offering, demanding more. Heat floods my body, and my legs weaken. I grip his back, my hands twisting into his shirt as I return the kiss with equal passion. His tongue finds mine. The kiss deepens, hardens. His hand strokes the outline of my cheek, slides down my neck. Pleasure ripples through me and I gasp as he kisses my throat, caresses my—

"He did, too." Zachary's voice brought me crashing back to reality.

I dropped my hand from my throat. What the hell? Chase. I was having full-blown, no-holds-barred fantasies about him now. Oh my God. Had I gone totally nuts?

Shifting in my seat, I crossed my legs and squeezed them together to ease the embarrassing thrum that pulsed between them.

Selena gave an exasperated sigh. "That's bullshit, Zach. Chase would never say that. You're such a pervert."

I shifted again and uncrossed my legs. Zachary was staring at me.

"It's the truth," he said. "Chase thinks you're hot and I think, instead of a book report, I should make a toga for you."

The Professor closed his eyes and pressed his fingers against the bridge of his nose, as if he'd suddenly acquired a headache. "That will not be happening. Togas would be Roman not Greek, and terribly inappropriate for other reasons."

Selena leaned toward me and whispered, "Don't pay any attention to Zach. It's not that Chase doesn't like girls or anything, but he never talks like that. He's always, 'blah, blah, blah, knives, blah, blah, sword fighting and weight lifting' and Aunt Kate's stupid sheep."

Hopefully, she was right. The last thing I needed right now was a romance—especially with a hot, baffling guy who said scary shit, told half-truths, and had already sizzled his way into my fantasy life. Though a small part of me couldn't help but feel incredibly, stupid happy. Chase thought I was hot.

Tucking this new information away for later, I focused on Zachary. Something else had clicked in my head. Zachary had given the Professor the perfect opportunity to slide in a snide comment about Taj and our relationship, but the Professor hadn't so much as given me a sly look. Taj had treated me like crap and didn't deserve my gratitude for anything. Still, I was thankful and relieved that he apparently hadn't spread rumors about me. The last thing I needed was for Kate to find out and start making even more judgmental comments about me and my upbringing.

By the time the Professor stopped talking and we left, it

was almost nine. Selena and I checked on Dad. Then, since he had already gone to sleep for the night, I suggested we go out on the terrace and watch the stars come out or something. It would give me a chance to discover what else she knew about Mother and, even if we ended up talking about nothing important, it would help me relax before bed.

Selena grimaced apologetically. "I'd love to hang out, but"— she lowered her voice—"Newt's expecting me to chat with him, like as soon as Mom thinks I'm in bed asleep."

"You really can't tell her you're seeing someone?" I didn't know what else to say. There were millions of reasons her parents might not approve of him: too poor, too wild, too conservative or liberal. The wrong religion or background.

"It wouldn't matter who he was. They think I'm too young to see any guy."

"That doesn't make any sense. You're eighteen."

She shrugged. "What can I say? My parents are weird."

As we walked toward the east wing and our rooms, Selena told me about how she'd met Newt last December in a Bar Harbor bookstore. Her dad had dropped her off to do some shopping while he visited with an old friend. She and Newt had started talking. He'd bought her a coffee and a white-chocolate muffin. After that, they'd kept in touch, texting and chatting online, and meeting in person when they could. He was going to be a senior at Harvard next fall, an Economics major. He was a little old for her, but he didn't sound at all creepy.

She showed me were the light switches were, and then we talked for a couple more minutes in the hallway outside my room. Finally, Selena took off for her family's apartment, and I went inside and closed the door behind me.

Though darkness hadn't stolen the entire view from my window, it hovered in the garden and seeped in around the edges of my room.

I turned on the overhead light and rushed to the window and drew shut the curtains.

Breathing a sigh of relief, I stashed Dad's straight razor in my suitcase. Then I went into the bathroom to examine my ear. The cut wasn't very deep and the scabbiness was confined to the back of the earlobe. Still, it stung and began to bleed again when I washed it.

I dabbed the cut with toilet paper to stop the flow, then changed and headed for the bed.

My heart leapt into my throat.

The pentagram. I couldn't go to bed.

Even if I dared lie down, I'd never fall asleep. And I definitely didn't want to remove it and chance that something worse might happen. Or move to a different bedroom and have whoever made it suspect I was onto them, especially if they were part of the danger Chase had warned me about.

I swallowed hard. I could sleep on the floor or in the chair. I grinned as the perfect solution came to me.

First I snagged the pillows and the quilt off my bed, then the mini-flashlight and a large blanket. I hauled them all to the bathroom and piled them into the claw-footed tub. It certainly wasn't as comfy as the bed, but it wasn't bad, and it was a witch-craft-free zone.

I'm not sure how long it took before I dozed off, but I woke with a start when my bedroom door rustled open.

"Annie. Where are you?" Selena's voice said.

Shit. I leapt out of the tub, sprang for the bathroom door—and came face to face with Selena.

She craned her neck around me. "You're sleeping in the bathtub. What's wrong with the bed?"

My mouth went dry and I couldn't begin to think of a lie or a reason not to tell her.

I led her to the bed and lifted the ruffle. "Look," I said, motioning at the pentagram.

She leaned forward and squinted. "Oh," she said, bolting upright.

"I don't know if it's good or bad, but it wasn't here when I first got to my room, then it was."

Selena stared at the floor, nibbling her lip.

I clasped her by both arms. "You know who made it, don't you?"

With a sharp exhale, Selena looked up. "It was me," she said hesitantly, then with more force. "I made it. It's—it's to give the room good vibes."

"You?" I shook my head. No way. She'd been far too surprised when I showed it to her.

"I know it's weird, believing in magic and stuff. I'm not that into it. I just toy around with love potions, good luck charms, and things like that." She stuck out her bottom lip and her chin trembled a little. "Don't hate me. I thought it would help you sleep."

I let go of her arms. She was lying. I knew it. But what could I do short of tying her to the bed and torturing it out of her? "I don't hate you. I—I'm just surprised. So it's not evil?"

"Cross my heart." She sounded truthful.

I moistened my lips with my tongue. "I've heard of using salt and pentagrams," I said, "but what the heck's the coin for? It looks like the one the Professor showed us."

With a smug smile, she flounced past me, gathered up the quilt from the tub, and paraded back to the bed. "It's not so much the coin as the bee. It's my totem, kind of. The Queen Bee's a powerful goddess. Honey's used in medicines. A bee's on the Freemont coat of arms, too." She turned toward me and rested her hands on her hips. "Now, let's get this bed made."

I took two corners of the blanket and helped her spread it across the bed. The witchy image didn't match the rest of Selena's look and personality, but the bee-is-my-totem thing fit with her love of medicine. It definitely sounded like she had some expertise and could have made the pentagram. But I doubted it.

"Where did you ever learn about this stuff?" I asked.

Her voice hesitated, like an amateur con artist trying to pawn off a fake. "The Internet," she finally said.

"Oh." It was better than calling her a liar.

"So"—Selena belly-flopped onto my bed and looked up at me—"aren't you going to ask why I woke you up?"

"I figured you were sneaking out or just getting home. What time is it anyway?"

"Three o'clock. But I wasn't out, at least not tonight." She giggled. "Newt and the Beach Rats are having a party tomorrow night. He asked me to go. You're invited too."

"That's nice." I lifted my voice in an attempt to sound excited, but failed miserably, if the disappointed look on Selena's face was any indication.

She scowled. "Don't even think about chickening out. It's going to be great." She sat up and curled her legs to one side. "If you're worried about leaving your father, I'll make you a deal. Tibbs is cool. I'll ask him to text me if we need to come home for any reason. Please, please, please."

I frowned and shuffled my feet. Dad was one reason I didn't want to go, but there was another. I hated big parties. It was a weird thing. I did fine out with a couple of friends, hanging around and doing whatever. I was totally at ease in auction houses packed wall-to-wall with yammering older people. But put me in a crowded party with people my own age and I instantly transformed into a quivering mass of brain-dead Jell-O.

"I—I'll think about it," I said.

She gave me another one of her patented pouts. "It's the witchcraft, isn't it? You think I'm a freak, and you're still mad about the pentagram."

"No. I'm not upset with you." I took a long breath. I didn't want to go to the damn party, but going was probably a smarter

move. Most likely there'd be drinking and, once Selena got a
buzz on, it would be easy to coax her into revealing who made
the pentagram. "I am a little scared of the witchcraft, and I'm
worried about leaving Dad, but if Tibbs will go along with it
then I'll go."

She let out an ecstatic squeal. "It's going be so much fun!"

I narrowed my eyes. "This isn't going to be high school–age
kids, right?"

"Of course not. They're mostly in college, like Newt. You're
going to have a great time, promise."

I sank down on the bed next to her and pasted on a smile.
One thing was certain, if the pentagram was harmful, Selena
wouldn't be lying on the bed.

At least, I hoped.

CHAPTER 9

Βεωαρε οφ φρεεδομ ωρουγητ φρομ φεαρ.
Beware of freedom wrought from fear.

—Etched in blood into the sands of the Red Desert

Only a couple of hours after Selena left, I was awoken by the nonstop shriek of gulls outside my window.

Trying to block out the noise, I clamped a pillow over my head and squirmed deeper into my nest of tangled blankets. I'd managed to sleep, despite the pentagram and all the crazy thoughts whirring in my head, which was a good thing. But I couldn't afford to stay in bed any longer. Somewhere, amongst all the tossing and turning, I'd come up with a plan—one that required me to get going fairly early.

I wrestled free from my blankets, swung my legs off the bed, and sat up. Then, out of habit, I grabbed my phone from the bedside stand. Checking it wasn't part of my plan, but if I didn't look to see if I'd gotten any messages it would drive me nuts until I did.

I smiled at a text from Selena.

You're the best! With the GIF of kittens doing the mamba.

There was an e-mail from Dad's lawyer. Bastard. I wanted to delete it unread, but I gave it a quick scan. He said I didn't have to worry about anything. Our house in Vermont was safely closed up. He was taking care of the bills as prearranged.

Yeah, right. I didn't have to ask where the money had suddenly come from. Grandfather. But it was a relief at the same time.

I bit down on my bottom lip, enjoying a tingle of anticipation before opening the next e-mail. It was from Nastja Domashevich. She had done my admission interview when I'd applied to Sotheby's summer program. With her gruff Russian accent and large stature, she'd come across as tough. But once we got talking, we'd totally clicked. She'd congratulated me when I got accepted and sounded sad when I'd decided to withdraw. In fact, she'd been so supportive that I'd opened up and told her about Dad's condition. But I hadn't expected to hear from her again.

My pulse jumped as I read the e-mail. Because my recommendations and test scores had been so strong and since I'd withdrawn because of an unforeseeable hardship, Sotheby's was extending an offer for me to attend any of their fall short courses without going through the readmission process. Hot damn!

And, the offer stood for next year's London summer programs as well.

Attached was a list of courses that still had openings, their deadlines—the first of which was next week—and their costs. The courses weren't anywhere near as expensive as going to college full-time, but I was broke. Then again, Grandfather wasn't.

Another thought wriggled into my head and my stomach sank. The poison ring. If Sotheby's found out that I'd sold a forgery, they'd drop the offer for sure. Grandfather had said he'd look into it, but that wasn't the same as guaranteeing he'd fix it. I needed to talk to him again, tell him how important this was. Maybe I could even ask if he'd loan me some money.

I set the phone down and scrubbed my hands over my face. Was I crazy? I couldn't trust the family. The last thing I needed was to get even more indebted to Grandfather. Stupid. Totally stupid.

Besides, there was a way for me to do this on my own. I didn't have much money, but I had enough for a bus ticket. I could go to New Orleans. The woman who owned the bed and breakfast where Dad and I stayed had said she'd hire me if I was ever looking. I could help take care of her twins, chamber-maid for her, and get a second job at an auction house. If I scrimped, I could easily make enough money to attend the London summer program next year. I could apply for a scholarship as well. The only problem was—I sighed—I couldn't do that or anything yet, not as long as Dad was sick. He wouldn't desert me and I wouldn't do it to him, either.

The sinking feeling in my stomach grew heavier as the horrible truth I'd kept locked away bubbled to the surface. Dad might never get better. And, in all honesty, he wouldn't have wanted me at Moonhill to start with. According to Chase, if I didn't leave, I could end up like my mother. Dead.

My mind went back to the plan I'd come up with in my sleep. If everything went as I hoped this morning, then I'd soon know if Dad was getting help or not. That would give me the ammunition I needed to confront Grandfather and Kate. Once that was done, I'd have a clearer idea of Dad's situation and could put some more serious thought into classes and when to leave Moonhill.

With that decision firmly in mind, I sent a reply to Nastja. Fantastic. I was thrilled. I'd get back to her before the deadline. I didn't specify which one. With my whole heart, I hoped it would be soon. No. I was going to do my best to make sure it was.

In record time, I bathed and did my morning bathroom rituals. I pulled my damp hair into a casual ponytail, then put on my good jeans, a loose white blouse, and my vintage charm bracelets. No bright red this morning. What I had planned called for a more subdued appearance.

After I tore off a finger-size strip of toilet paper, I headed for the hallway. Up until now, it had felt like I was trapped inside a game where I didn't know the rules or even how to win or drop out, nothing, except if I lost, my dad might get stuck here forever. That, however, was about to change. It was time to add a few of my rules to their game.

I dampened the end of my finger with my tongue and used the moisture to stick the toilet paper to the doorjamb. Then I shut the door. If anyone opened it while I was gone, the paper would be on the floor when I returned.

Satisfied that my silent alarm system would work, I loped to the back stairs and tiptoed down them. Once I got across the terrace, I strolled toward the garage. Hopefully, if someone saw me from a window, they'd think I was simply taking a walk before breakfast.

Yeah, the rule was: breakfast at eight. But no one ever said I had to be there.

That part of my plan went without a hitch. And a few minutes later, I was behind the wheel of Dad's Mercedes, its engine whispering elegantly as I drove away from the house. If I had things figured right, I'd be back in less than an hour.

Light fog shifted through the fields and threaded over the top of the crescent-shaped hill. The drive was a lot less spooky by daylight than it had been when we arrived at night.

As I reached the peak of the hill, I glanced north, through the shielding trees to the family graveyard. The early morning sun splattered the mausoleum's roof with red. Between the ornate gravestones and monuments, black sheep raised their heads to watch me pass.

My foot retreated from the gas pedal. What had happened up there so many years ago, the day my mother died? It had to have been something awful for the family to have hidden it from Dad.

I looked back at the driveway ahead, my hands trembling

as I eased on the gas. I took a deep breath to steady myself, and then another. I'd be at the gate in a second. If Chase came out to let me through, I needed to look relaxed.

His cottage came into view, then his parked truck, then the fence's spear-embellished top.

"Hell yeah," I muttered. The gate was open and no one was around!

Every inch of my body wanted to punch the gas and squeal through the gateway, but I resisted the urge and maintained a painfully slow speed.

However, when I reached the main road, I let out a whoop and drummed my hands on the steering wheel. I'd escaped and no one was the wiser. Selena had said the gate was unlocked at sunrise, but I didn't expect it to be this easy. Also, it appeared Kate and Chase hadn't lied about him not being around first thing in the morning. Clearly he wasn't.

I hadn't gone more than fifty yards down the road when the black sedan I'd seen parked near the garage yesterday approached me in the other lane. Its turn signal began to flash, indicating it was going to Moonhill. Damn it. If it was Kate or Grandfather, there was no way they wouldn't recognize Dad's car.

As the sedan zipped past, I stole a look at the driver. The priest. I narrowed my eyes. Why was he going to Moonhill again, and so early in the morning? Dad. It couldn't have anything to do with him, could it?

My shoulder muscles tightened and the urge to turn the car around raced through me. I clenched the steering wheel harder. I had to stay focused. Untangle one set of truths and lies before I moved on to the next. I couldn't fall into the trap of playing by their rules. I had to do the unexpected. That's what Dad would do.

Ten minutes later, I sped into Port St. Claire. I stopped at the mini-mart I'd noticed the other night, went inside, and came out with directions to Dr. Jerome's office and an iced latte.

I set the latte into Dad's makeshift cup holder, then double-checked the directions on my phone. It was hard to believe that my luck had continued to be so perfect. Not only was Dr. Jerome's office just a block away from the mini-mart, I could see it from where I sat—a modern two-story building overlooking the harbor.

With butterflies in my stomach, I got out of the car and hurried down the sidewalk toward the building. It would have been quicker to park in front of his office instead of walking. But if someone from Moonhill happened to drive by and spotted Dad's Mercedes, they'd have known I was up to something for sure. At least the mini-mart parking lot wasn't quite as obvious. Maybe.

When I got to the office and went inside, a middle-age woman sitting on the other side of the reception window looked up and smiled. "May I help you?"

I pulled my shoulders back. "I'm Stephanie Freemont. I'd like to speak with Dr. Jerome for a moment. I believe my father, James Freemont, saw him yesterday."

Her brow wrinkled. "Freemont?"

Unable to breathe, I nodded. Hopefully, I wouldn't run into some kind of doctor-patient confidentiality issue.

She punched some keys on her computer. "Are you sure it was yesterday?"

"Yes. It was an early appointment, before eight."

"Let me check with the doctor." She got up from her chair and vanished into another room.

I shifted from one foot to the other and wiped my sweaty palms on my jeans.

The woman reappeared. "I've spoken with the doctor. I'm afraid your father isn't one of his patients. You probably should double-check the doctor's name with your father."

"That's strange." I shrugged. "Well, thanks anyway."

I dashed out of the office, my head down as I fast-walked

back to the Mercedes and collapsed into the driver's seat. I didn't know whether to smile at my success or cry because this meant all my fears were founded. Dad wasn't getting professional help, and I was the only one who could do something about it. Kate and Grandfather had lied.

I picked up my iced latte and held it against the side of my face, letting its frostiness steal some of the heat from my skin. As tears began to burn in my eyes, I took a long breath and another. I couldn't fall apart. I had to stay strong.

Once the worst of the jitteriness subsided, I started the car and backed out of the parking space. At least, I'd made this trip without anyone spotting me.

That thought had barely left my mind when the steering wheel jerked hard to the left and a *flump-flump* noise came from the Mercedes's rear end. I pulled back into the parking space and got out. Damn, a flat tire. Just what I needed.

I weighed my options. I could phone a garage to come fix it, but that would take a while, and I didn't want to be here any longer than necessary. I could fix it myself. Or—I grinned— the mini-mart most likely sold cans of Fix-A-Flat. It was a temporary solution, but it would keep the tire inflated long enough to put some distance between me and Dr. Jerome's.

Feeling a million times better, I thumped the side of the car with my knuckles, a celebratory fist bump of sorts. Maybe it was my jubilation at having found a solution to my tire dilemma or for having discovered the truth behind my dad's treatment, but I was so lost in thoughts that when a pickup truck pulled up next to me, it took me a full minute to realize who was behind the wheel.

Shit.

Chase's head poked out the window. "Trouble?"

Before I could respond, he hopped out and strode over. "Got a spare?" he asked.

"Yeah," I said.

For a moment our eyes locked, his lips parted as if drawing in a sharp breath, and—despite my suspicion that he might have seen me leave Moonhill and not so much found as followed me—memories of my daydream rushed back and I flushed.

"Well?" He folded his arms across his chest. "I can't get the jack out if you don't open the trunk."

"Oh—sorry." I opened it and he went to work.

"I'm not surprised it went flat," he said, wriggling the tire off. "There's no tread left. Your father should replace them more often."

I gave the tire a closer look and a prickle of embarrassment went up my neck. He wasn't lying. The insides of the tire showed through the rubber. "It's my fault. Honestly, I never thought to check them."

Chase heaved the tire into the back of his truck. "I'll ask Tibbs to put on some new ones."

"Thanks," I said.

He hauled out the spare and put it on the hub, then went to work tightening the lug nuts, his arm muscles flexing, the defined cords of his neck and shoulders getting into the action as well. He really was the definition of mouthwatering hotness.

Then, as I glanced at the equally bald but not in the least bit soft front tire, a suspicion began whispering in the back of my mind. Just because a tire was crap didn't mean something sharp, like a knife, couldn't have helped it go flat. But why would Chase or Kate or anyone want to delay me? Unless delaying me wasn't their intention. Maybe they just wanted me to know that I'd been caught at Dr. Jerome's—hence Chase's convenient appearance.

As if he sensed my train of thought, Chase shot a look over his shoulder. "Just so we're clear, I owe your family a lot. But that doesn't mean everything I do is on their say-so."

"Ah—what are you talking about?"

He stabbed at the tire with his fingers, then turned away and went back to work.

Puzzled, I replayed the gesture in my mind. Was he saying what I thought he was saying?

I opened my mouth to ask, but the rigid set of his jaw told me he was done talking. Try as I might, I suspected the only thing quizzing him would accomplish was a slowdown of the tire-changing progress and that was something I didn't want. What I needed was to stay focused and get back to Moonhill as soon as possible and talk to Dad. There was a one-in-a-million chance that a good night's sleep could have left him more lucid than usual. If he was, then he might be able to re-call what had happened yesterday morning when he was sup-posedly at the doctor's.

It didn't take long for Chase to finish tightening the last lug nut and put the jack away. After the trunk lid was closed, I rested my hand on his arm and smiled. No matter what he had or hadn't done, I was grateful for his help.

"Seriously, thanks for doing this. I owe you one," I said.

His lips curved into a smile that touched his eyes. "There is something you could do for me."

"Yeah, like what?" The flutters inside me gave a hopeful kick, and a thought slipped into my mind. Maybe he was going to ask me out.

"What did you find in the water?"

"Huh?" I said, then I realized it was same question he'd asked yesterday.

"Was it a starfish? An earring?"

"Why do you care?" I asked, suspicion making my voice sharp.

He folded his arms across his chest, staring at me while he waited.

Finally, I threw my hands up in surrender. For the life of me, I couldn't see how a tiny bit of glass could have any importance. But perhaps I could learn something from his reaction. "A piece of sea glass with a hole in one end. That's it."

"Thanks," he said, then he swaggered to his truck.

Blinking, I watched him get in and put on his seatbelt. Okay, so that was the most unreadable reaction ever. I really shouldn't have said anything to him. Damn hormones.

CHAPTER 10

Don't ever underestimate your opponent.

—James William Freemont

Alll the way back to Moonhill, I tried to think why a piece of sea glass could be so important, but I didn't come up with anything sensible. To top it off, Chase and the sea glass and even how they might relate to my mother's death weren't things I needed to focus on right now. Dad wasn't getting the care he needed. And, for the life of me, I couldn't think of a reason why the family wouldn't want him to get help. One thing was for sure, by not taking Dad to the doctor, Kate had violated the custody agreement and given me a legal foothold.

I tapped the brakes, slowing to a snail's pace as we went around a curve, and then another. Chase didn't strike me as a guy who'd drive like a terrified grandma, but that was exactly what he was doing. And, the longer I followed him, the more I began to believe he was doing it on purpose rather than from a lack of skill.

Finally, we crept up the driveway and went through the gate. To my surprise, Chase didn't turn off at his cottage. He kept puttering along ahead of me all the way to the house, where he parked next to the priest's sedan.

I zinged the Mercedes into the garage and leapt out.

"Annie!" Zachary dashed from the depths of the garage

with a struggling tiger-striped kitten clutched against his chest. He let go of it and snatched my hand. "I was looking for you. Mom and Selena went to Bar Harbor shopping. They wanted to take you, but you weren't around."

I would have fought against his grip, but he was dragging me out of the garage and toward the house and I'd planned on going that way anyhow.

As we passed Chase's vacant truck, I glanced around. He'd already vanished and it didn't shock me. I'd figured he'd take off to warn Kate and Grandfather that I was back, if he hadn't already called and told them. Maybe he had the hots for me, but he hadn't minced words about his devotion to the family.

My gaze landed on the priest's car and an uneasy feeling wriggled inside me. The priest had been here yesterday when Dad was supposedly at the doctor's, and here he was again. I had a hard time believing he and Kate were simply socializing.

Zachary tugged me harder. "The Professor's waiting in the workroom. He got out some artifacts to show you."

"Ah—I really don't have time right now. How about if I stop by later?"

He stuck out his bottom lip in a very Selena-like pout. "Laura left a bunch of chocolate chip muffins in the library, but the Professor won't let me have any until you get there."

I had the sneaking suspicion the muffins and artifacts were another tactic designed to keep me busy and out of the way, like the flat tire and the invitation to go shopping. But I pretended like I was amenable and rushed along with Zachary, through the front door and into the foyer. Actually, the library wasn't out of my way. From there I could take the circular staircase up to the balcony and the use the secret door to get into the hallway by Dad's room. It seemed like the most obvious place for Dad to be—and, yesterday when the priest was here, it had smelled of incense.

We passed the dining room and couple of other rooms, all empty and silent.

"Where's your aunt Kate and Grandfather?" I asked.

"I haven't seen them. You'll love the muffins, they're the best. Laura made banana smoothies to go with them. They're the Professor's favorite."

When we got to the library, its lights were dimmed. The only bright spot was the distant outline of the workroom's open doorway, like a beacon designed to keep us from straying too far. Or a candle left lit on purpose, to attract unwary moths.

I let Zachary usher me toward it, playing along as we went deeper into the stacks. But when we neared the circular staircase, I halted. "Is there a bathroom somewhere around here?" I asked.

He nodded at a door next to the staircase. "It's small and kind of stinky, but it works."

"Great. Tell the Professor I'll be there in a minute."

I waited just long enough for him to vanish into the workroom. Then I sped up the staircase, careful not to make too much noise. Full tilt, I headed toward the secret door.

A hand seized my shoulder.

Yanking free, I whirled around. It was Chase.

A vein pulsed in his tightly corded neck. "Go back downstairs," he said.

I glanced over my shoulder at the hallway door, and then back at him. "What's going on?"

"Please, Annie. Just do it." His eyes begged me to obey.

"No," I said, not trying to hide my anger. "Tell me the truth."

"Annie, trust me. You don't want to know."

A yowling sound came from the far side of the door, like an animal being skinned alive.

"What the hell was that?" I screeched.

"Nothing." Chase had me by the shirtsleeve now. Sweat dribbled down his face. "Don't worry. He'll be fine. Just go back downstairs."

My jaw clenched. His fingers tensed, like he was readying for me to try to pull free.

Instead, I moved in close to him, inches from his face. My voice growled. "You think you can stop me?"

"Annie, I'll tell you everything. Just don't—"

I didn't hear the last of his words as I broke free, dove for the door, and hurtled into the west hallway.

I gasped.

The hallway was arctic cold, and frost coated the mirrors and windows. The acrid stench of church incense burned my nose. A cat ran past me and then another. Then they both ran back, circling and yowling like they had gone crazy or had rabies. What the hell!

"Annie." Chase was coming through the door. "Wait."

I covered my mouth and nose with my hand to keep out the smell and staggered toward Dad's room. Damn them. Damn them all. Whatever was going on, I'd get Dad out of here. Go somewhere. Anywhere.

"Don't," Chase shouted.

Salt crackled under my feet as I shoved Dad's bedroom door open and stepped inside.

I stopped. Unable to breathe or move, I could only stare.

Orange candlelight pulsed like a heartbeat through the darkened room. The priest and Kate stood beside Dad's four-poster bed, so focused they didn't even glance my way.

The priest raised his arm, his wide sleeve blocking my view of the bed. "I adjure you, Satan, deceiver of the human race, acknowledge the Spirit of truth and grace, who repels your snares, confounds your lies." His voice echoed. His breath was an icy vapor in the frigid room.

Fear, disbelief, and horror all roiled inside me. An exorcism. They were doing a fucking exorcism on my dad! I opened my mouth to scream.

But Chase grabbed me from behind, one hand clamping my mouth, the other pinning me against his chest. "Shush," he said.

The priest lowered his arm and I saw Dad, lying motionless, his eyelids wide open, his eyes rolled back so only the whites showed. Spittle foamed from the corners of his mouth. His arms and legs were tied to the bedposts.

The priest took a bottle from Kate and began sprinkling Dad with holy water. "Depart, unclean sprit!" he commanded.

Dad writhed against the ropes. His back arched. He howled in pain.

I thrashed against Chase's grip, struggling to break free. He seized me tighter.

Grandfather's voice came from beside me. "Be still. We're trying to save him."

I turned my head toward him and glared. Kill him was more like it.

"Begone, spawn of Satan!" the priest shouted.

A demonic voice hissed from Dad's mouth. "No false servant attended by witches can command me!"

I looked back at Dad, my heart fumbling. The shadow in the church. The stranger Dad had become on the beach. I didn't want to believe this. Exorcism. Demons. This couldn't be real.

A chill—colder than the room—sliced though my veins. Overwhelmed, I let my arms drop to my sides and quit fighting against Chase.

He released me and Grandfather propelled me toward the sitting area and into a chair. "Sit," he whispered. Then he and Chase folded their arms across their chests and stood in front of me like prison guards.

Kate was sprinkling more salt across the doorway.

The priest was making the sign of the cross over Dad. "In the name of the Father, Son, and the Holy Spirit."

Dad spat at the priest, hitting him in the face. He cackled. "We're not afraid of you."

Without wiping off the spittle, the priest continued, "In the name of God, depart!"

The mirrors, the paintings, everything that hung on the walls began to rise and fall in a deafening rhythm, pounding faster and louder like an oncoming train. The air pressure climbed until my ears rang from it. The cold deepened. Shivering, I hunched over, tucked my chin to my chest, and covered my ears against the howling noise. The floor began to vibrate. The smell of sulfur overwhelmed the incense.

"NEVER!" Dad's voice wailed. "No!" A demonic voice screeched.

Electricity crackled through the room. My head felt like it might explode. My stomach heaved and the taste of vomit coated my tongue. Please, let this be over.

"Begone!" the priest shouted.

I glanced up.

The priest crossed himself and then made the sign over Dad again.

Dad's entire body jerked, fast quick spasms. "No" hissed from his mouth as the air pressure plummeted.

My ears popped. Dad went limp. His eyes closed, and the entire room went deathly silent.

A second passed. Then another.

The priest glanced at Kate. "It's over," he said.

While the priest and Kate untied Dad's arms and legs, Grandfather poured a glass of water and helped Dad take a sip. Chase pulled the drapes open, sunlight streaming in.

I couldn't make myself move. It was like I was sitting in the audience watching an old black-and-white movie sputter in front of me.

Dad's eyes flittered open. He rubbed his wrists, ringed with rope burns.

"I'll have Olya bring you something for that," Kate said.

Sweat matted the priest's hair and darkened his robe. His shoulders slumped as he took the gold chain and crucifix off from around his neck, kissed the cross, and then touched it to Dad's forehead.

"Thank you," Dad mumbled weakly.

"Thank the mercy and power of the Holy Spirit," the priest replied. He put the crucifix back on and pulled a blanket up over Dad's legs and body. He turned to Grandfather. "He'll be fine, but he should rest now." He tilted his head at the door. "If you don't mind, I'd like to speak with you and Kate for a moment, outside in the hall."

Kate cleared her throat. "We should talk in the study. Chase can stay with James." She flicked her fingers at me. "She should come with us."

The priest nodded. "Yes, that would be a good idea."

Their sharp tones yanked me from my daze. Kate's face was tight with anger, her eyes flinty and cold. My stomach dropped. Once I got to the study, I was going to get one hell of a lecture about how my barging in could have caused the exorcism to fail. I was certain of that.

I sliced a couple of looks in her direction. It wasn't my fault. If they'd been honest with me in the first place, then none of us would have had to resort to subterfuge and secrecy. How was I supposed to trust them, if they were going to lie to me?

Mostly, I was glad and grateful that I'd witnessed everything—felt the demon's presence, heard it, smelled it, tasted it. If I hadn't, I probably would never have accepted Dad's lightning-fast recovery as real—or, later, believed Dad when he explained a demon, not dementia, had caused his illness. I would have thought he was making up another one of his stories.

I nodded to say I'd follow them, then went to the bed and slipped my hand into Dad's.

His fingers were hot and clammy. His face was pale. But he looked more at peace than he had in months, his eyes warm, his mouth curved into a gentle smile, the muscles in his shoulders visibly relaxed.

Grandfather opened the door and let the priest go into the hallway first.

"Come along, Stephanie," Kate said, waiting for me to follow.

I glanced at Dad. "Are you sure you don't want me to stay?"

"It's okay, Annie. I'm so tired." He stopped rubbing his rope-burnt wrist and scratched his elbow three times.

I drew a sharp breath. It couldn't be. The priest, Kate, Grandfather, Chase, everyone was acting like it was over. Heck, *I'd* thought it was over. But, was it possible we were all fooled?

I bit my tongue and fought to keep a sedate expression on my face. Dad's eyes and mouth, his shoulders, his arms, everything about the way he held himself indicated he was tranquil and as innocent as a newborn lamb.

But could he be faking it? The three elbow scratches had always been Dad's only tell. A tell that told me that under his relaxed exterior, he was ecstatic a plan was coming together.

Right now, however, there was no reason for him to hide his delight about the exorcism succeeding. Unless—

I pulled my hand from Dad's, so he wouldn't notice it trembling.

Unless the exorcism hadn't succeeded, and making everyone think it had was Dad or the demon's true goal.

CHAPTER 11

*Before full possession is reached, the symptoms can
mimic dementia interspersed with moments of clarity where
the host or the demonic presence breaks through.*

—Prevention, diagnosis and treatment
www.SerpentWrestler.com

I rushed ahead of everyone, down the hallway and stairs to
Kate's study.

As soon as the door closed behind us, I blurted out, "Dad.
The exorcism." My words faltered as I gulped a breath. "He's
still—"

The priest turned toward me. Despite the dark circles
under his eyes, his gaze was unwavering and intense. "I understand your father visited an abandoned church?"

"Yeah, we did," I said. "But that's not important. I have to
tell you something."

The priest thumped his fist on the back of the settee and
bellowed as if he were addressing a congregation. "Deserted
churches are a favorite playground for Satan's minions. Your
father was very fortunate. He easily could have fallen prey to a
higher-ranking demon. You could have become possessed as
well."

"I didn't. And that doesn't matter!" I huffed.

The priest jerked back, his eyes bulging as if I were the

spawn of Satan. "Doesn't matter? Are you out of your mind, child?"

"Listen!" My voice tore from my throat, raw and forceful. "Dad's not fine. He's still possessed. The demon isn't gone."

Grandfather lifted his hand to silence me. He narrowed his eyes at the priest. "Is she right? Is this why you suggested we meet where James couldn't hear?"

The priest shot Grandfather a hard look. "Certainly not. I only wished to let your son rest and clarify our arrangement in private." His eyes cut toward me. "What you're suggesting is impossible. A possessed man could not lie still with a religious relic under his mattress and a crucifix over his head."

I opened my mouth to protest, but Kate's talonlike fingers dug into my shoulder. "Stephanie, listen to him. He's experienced in these matters. You certainly are not."

I clenched my teeth. I had to make them understand.

The priest folded his arms across his chest, his dark sleeves billowing. "If your father were still possessed, he would not have been able endure the touch of a crucifix against his skin. Welts would have risen and the demon would have cried out in anguish." The priest held up his index finger. "But do not make light of the hold even a lesser unclean spirit can have. It's only God's strength and mercy that allowed your father, an un-baptized man, to be freed from the Devil's grip."

Grandfather nodded at the priest. "I have every reason to believe you're correct, and James is free. But"—he turned to me—"why do you believe he isn't?"

I shoved Kate's hand from my shoulder and faced them all. "When I was holding Dad's hand, he looked peaceful. But I'm—" I took a deep breath. There was a good chance they'd think I was being ridiculous, and they might have been right. But I had to trust my gut, and it was telling me something was still wrong. "I'm certain it was all an act." My chest tightened. Was I that certain? Dad and I had always been super close, but that had changed over the past six months. Was there a chance I could be wrong? I knew next to nothing about exorcisms or demons. Part of my brain was even laughing at how crazy it all sounded. Still, I had to tell them what I'd seen.

I pitched my voice lower. "When there's something at an auction Dad's really excited about bidding on, he acts super relaxed like he isn't interested in anything at all. That's his poker face. The only way to know he's faking is if he scratches his elbow three times."

Kate groaned as if exasperated. "What you've failed to consider is that most often scratching is no more than a man relieving an itch, and your father had been restrained for some time."

A sinking feeling gathered in my throat, then dropped into my stomach. As much as my pride wanted to argue with them, logic told me Kate and the priest were right. I'd seen the cross over Dad's bed. I'd seen the priest touch his forehead with the crucifix. I'd even noticed part of a small linen bag sticking out from under the mattress, which I now assumed held the relic of some dead pope or saint. And, truthfully, it was possible he'd scratched more than three times and I'd failed to notice it.

I hugged myself, shoulders slumping. "You're probably right," I said.

Grandfather's eyes gentled. "Your misinterpretation is understandable. And I'm very sorry we couldn't tell you what was going on, but we were certain you wouldn't believe us and would try to run off with him."

My fingers clenched as I resisted the urge to nod. That was exactly what I would have done.

"This isn't the first time we've faced this situation." Grandfather's voice softened even further. "If we're lucky, it will be the last."

I touched the back of my ear. At the beach, Dad had seemed like a stranger, but when I'd held his hand after the exorcism, all

I'd sensed was my loving Dad. He had called me by my name, too. Kate was right. Sometimes a scratch was just a scratch.

"You did what you thought best," I mumbled. Then I looked up and said with gratitude, "You saved Dad."

Grandfather smiled. "We wouldn't have dreamed of doing anything less." He turned away, stepped quickly to the door, and opened it. He looked back at the priest. "Father, we could go on about this all day. We certainly are thankful for all you've done. But we're rather exhausted." He inclined his head at the hallway.

The priest nodded. "Yes, of course, I must be going." His eyes went to me. "If you don't mind, I do have one more question before I go. Do you know what your father acquired from the church?"

Given a minute to think, I probably could remember everything: pews, the statue of St. Anthony, a couple of gothic chairs and a musty tapestry, the broken cups and napkins from the sacristy.

I glanced at Grandfather. Why wasn't he or Kate offering to e-mail the priest a copy of Dad's inventory? I'd seen Dad's lawyer send it to them after Kate had been granted custody.

Ever so slightly, Grandfather shook his head, indicating for me to say nothing.

I looked at the priest and shrugged. "Off the top of my head, I can't recall exactly."

Kate stopped fiddling with her signet ring, an amazing piece of jewelry with a carved purple stone. "Is it necessary to put her through this right now? Can't you see the girl's dead on her feet?"

"Yes, of course, I'm beyond tired as well," the priest said to her. Then to me, "If you recall what else he bought or just want to talk, feel free to stop by the church."

"I doubt she or her father will have time for that," Kate said. "Once James has rested, they'll be leaving."

Leaving? My pulse leapt and I couldn't hold back a smile. Of course, we could leave now. Wow. This was great. Our life would go back to the way it had been, with just me and Dad, and we could put this whole nightmare behind us. I could register for classes and not worry about having to back out this time.

Uneasiness quivered in my stomach. I was beyond thrilled Dad was better. Leaving was all I'd wished for—except, it meant I might never get the chance to find out more about Mother's death. And after what Chase had said in the library, I'd never be content until I did.

"Well, good night." The priest stepped into the hallway, but glanced back at Grandfather. "We're agreed about the relic, right?"

Grandfather nodded. "It'll be dropped off at your office next week, and I speak for the entire family when I say, we are glad that we are able to return it to the church."

The priest dipped his head. "I'll personally see to it that it's delivered to Rome."

Once the priest's footsteps faded, Grandfather smiled at me. "You did well," he said.

Kate pulled a tissue out of a box on her desk and dabbed the sheen off her face. "All I'm grateful for is that it's over, and that the possession had nothing to do with that so-called poison ring you sold for your father."

"That certainly would have complicated the situation, perhaps even made it impossible," Grandfather said. "As it is, all we're left with is a priest who's hoping he's made converts out of us, and who's annoyingly curious."

I laughed. I couldn't help it. This was all so bizarre. It felt like the right reaction, but the sound died in the room's stillness.

Kate stroked her throat and grimaced at me as if she'd caught the scent of armpit odor.

Grandfather's lips pressed into a grim line, but as he spoke his voice softened a little. "The church and our family have always been close allies, Annie, but caution must be taken. Some believe their power has weakened in this modern day and age. That, however, is far from the truth."

Dropping my gaze, I watched a semi-rabid-looking cat streak across the room and disappear under the bookcase. Kate and Grandfather talking candidly while I was in the room almost made me feel like they had accepted me as part of the family and, for a second, I wanted to be. But I knew neither feeling was real and that I couldn't afford to open up to them. All I'd have to do was ask about Mother, and they'd go as cold and silent as her grave. At least, I strongly suspected they would, considering how they'd hidden the truth from Dad.

Kate cleared her throat. "Annie, you do realize that you're not to talk to anyone about the possession or exorcism. Out of respect for your father's privacy. And there's no need to frighten Selena or get Zachary's curiosity up, either. Silence is golden. Understand?"

I nodded yes. It was crystal clear. They were temporarily letting me be a part of their secret dealings because they wanted me to lie for them. Just like they expected Chase to lie.

"That's a good girl," Grandfather said. "Now, why don't you go upstairs and sit with your Dad."

The knots of tension released from my neck and shoulders as I left the study behind and headed for Dad's room. It would be nice to spend some time with him without worrying about the stranger he'd become or him not recognizing me. It seemed likely the exorcism would have driven off the shadows in his room as well as the demon, especially since the cross and relic were still in there.

A heavy feeling rose up from deep inside me and gathered force, like an impending storm. It didn't seem like it would take long for Dad to be strong enough to leave, two days, maybe three at the most. Maybe David would return with the ring by then and I wouldn't have to worry about it ruining my future. Kate acted like she thought I might be wrong about it being a forgery. I could only hope I was that lucky. At any rate, maybe the whole family would treat me and Dad decently for the next few days, maybe not.

But one thing was certain, if I wanted to ever know what really happened the day my mother died, I needed to start digging—and now.

CHAPTER 12

The coat was made of bearskin with two dozen mink hides as fringe around its collar. Fastened to its breast with a pin from a Scotsman's kilt was a note, written on hairless hide. Try me on, it said. No words have ever been more enticing or treacherous.

—James William Freemont
The Tale of Samuel and the Snake Mound Furrier

When suppertime came, Dad was still very weak. But he managed to sit up long enough to down everything on his plate, except for half a pork chop.

"It's tough as shoe leather," he whispered. Then he winked at me. "Too bad we can't transform it into a rack of lamb with a smidge of mint jelly on the side."

That made me smile. My old Dad was back. My misinterpretation of his elbow scratching had scared the crap out of me, but, thankfully, I'd been wrong about what it meant.

The humor fled from Dad's voice and his face became somber. "I'm sorry you had to go through this, Annie. But, in a couple of days, we'll be able to leave this rattrap. Think about where you'd like to go—the Cape, the Adirondacks. It's your choice." He waggled his eyebrows. "How about New York? If I'm not mistaken there's an intern at the Met you might like to see."

A crawling feeling went over my skin and I shuddered.

Definitely not New York and the Met. If I didn't ever see Taj again it would be too soon. Maybe London, but that would have to wait. I wanted to go there by myself, to take a class and hang out.

"Don't worry about me. I'm just glad you're okay," I said. It seemed too soon to tell him our house was closed up and our bank accounts busted, except for whatever Grandfather had siphoned into them.

Not long after that, Dad fell asleep. When Laura came by and offered to watch over him, I beelined for my room.

More than anything, I needed time alone to think. A couple of days. That didn't give me very long to find out about Mother. And it wasn't like I could tell Dad what was on my mind. He'd tell me not to go prying into the past, to be civil while we were here, and then move on with our lives as soon as possible. Dad was sweet and funny. He was all the world to me. But he didn't believe in forgiveness. Even a million good deeds wouldn't change his mind once he'd made it up about someone, like his family.

I was almost to my bedroom door when I spotted the toilet paper I'd stuck in the jamb lying on the hallway floor. Son of a bitch. Someone had gone into my room again.

The door banged against the wall as I flung it open. My eyes scoured the room. No one. I dashed into the bathroom. No one was in there either.

I went back and closed the door.

As I turned around and braced myself to check under the bed, I noticed a small gift bag sitting on one of the pillows.

My heart leapt into my throat and I backed away. Not just a gift bag. It was black and the handles were tied with an equally black ribbon. There was nothing benign about that color choice. Black stood for death, for witchcraft, and darkness. And the bag was the perfect size to hold something nasty, like a blood-soaked voodoo doll or a decapitated sparrow.

I raised my chin and crept forward. I'd survived the penta-gram and a freaking exorcism. I could deal with this. Whatever it was.

With two fingers I tugged the bag off the pillow and dragged it across the bed toward me. There wasn't a card to indicate who'd left it.

Carefully, I untied the ribbon and looked inside.

Pink tissue paper. Lots of it. Happy and cheerful, a real gift, not something horrible like my overactive imagination had as-sumed.

I took out the bundle of tissue paper. Inside it was a pot of lip gloss, sparklers, and a nip of peppermint schnapps. Selena. Damn. The party. I'd totally forgotten all about it.

With a bit too much force, I slapped the sparklers on the bedside stand, then flopped down on the bed and twisted open the lip gloss. Its citrusy aroma mingled with the quilt's freshly washed scent. It was bizarre how Selena's brain could black out or skip over all the weird things going on around the house—and focus on partying and Newt. Had the oddness of Dad's ill-ness even vaguely occurred to her? It seemed like she might have noticed that, especially since she had an interest in medi-cine and supposedly knew about witchcraft.

As I started to slide my index finger across the surface of the lip gloss, I hesitated. The texture looked right, as did the shine. But there were unappetizing gray swirls and nubby green flecks scattered through it.

I set the pot down, picked up its cover, and studied the label:

Mind-Blowing Citrus Lip Gloss—try me

The printing looked like it had come from a home com-puter, not a factory. That didn't mean anything in itself. But there was no list of ingredients; even hippie cosmetics included them.

No way was I going to slather on this could-be-a-hallucinogenic-or-aphrodisiac homemade slime because the label said *try me*. I wasn't stupid like Alice in Wonderland, who ended up tall as a house after munching on a cake that said *eat me,* or Samuel in Dad's Moonhill story, who went feral after he'd dressed in a fur coat he'd found buried in an Ohio snake mound, simply because a note commanded him to *try me on.*

Perhaps the gloss was harmless. But I wasn't about to take a chance, any more than I was about to sneak out tonight like some high school kid and party with a crowd I didn't know.

Rubbing the cover between my fingers, I gave that decision a rethink.

Screw it. Dad would probably sleep until noon tomorrow. I'd built my life around him for months. I deserved a break. It wasn't like I'd never had a good time at a party, or like my sneaking-out days were that far behind me. I could relax, get a little buzz on. As long as I stayed more sober than Selena I'd be all set. I could even ask her about my mother's death as well as pressure her into telling me who'd actually made the pentagram.

I put the cover back on the lip gloss, then headed to the bathroom and stashed it in the medicine cabinet. If I went to the party, I could also take some photos, nothing too raunchy, just some candid party shots I could strategically share on the Internet, a little revenge for the pictures I'd discovered of Taj and that girl.

The room filled with steam as I fixed a bath. Once the tub was full, I took a couple of sips of schnapps, then slid in. Closing my eyes, I focused on the warmth of the water against my skin: the relaxing scent of gardenia bubble bath, the *slush-slop* sound of the water, and the smoothness of the porcelain against my shoulders. It would be fun to dance and meet some new guys. Hopefully, a lot nicer than Taj.

Taj had been such a good friend for so long. The day when everything changed, he'd taken me to The Cloisters, so I could finally see the Unicorn Tapestries. As we'd toured the exhibits we talked about what I'd been up to, about his internship at the Metropolitan, and the Near Eastern artifacts he was helping categorize. Later, we snuck a bottle of wine into a retro movie theater and drank it while we watched *Romeo and Juliet*. I could still see Taj, his dark hair flopping over his face as he leaned in to kiss me, his mouth sweet with wine. We left before the movie got over and had sex twice at his parents' loft. We did it three more times in my hotel room later. It was amazing, too. I'd never had sex like that before. Fun. Kinky. No holding back.

Really late, like after two in the morning, I'd heard Dad return to his room next door. He'd gone to the theater and for drinks with friends. I was surprised but relieved he didn't look in on me. Not that Dad had any reason to get angry or shocked that I had a guy in my room—after all, I wasn't a kid. It was just that I wasn't ready for him to see in my eyes what I had only just discovered for myself.

Until that moment, I'd never believed I would find love as fierce and enduring as my dad had for my mother. They'd only had a few short years together before she died. Still, she remained the only woman he desired. He lived in the memory of their time together. A love so powerful and profound that even death couldn't lessen it. I'd aspired to love like that, but I wasn't sure it was possible—until that moment, lying in the arms of a guy who'd been a best friend for years, every inch of my body humming from sex. Right then, I believed I'd found it.

Wiping tears from my eyes, I scrambled out of the bathtub. Not that I cared about Taj anymore. I definitely didn't. And this wasn't the time to go all girly and depressed—or, for that matter, for relaxing or meeting new guys. I'd go to the party, but the only reason would be to get information out of Selena.

Another guy muscled his way into my thoughts: his outdoorsy scent surrounding me in the library when I'd thought for a second he was going to kiss me, him holding me back in Dad's room, his hand stopping my screams, his arms pinning me hard against him, his arms folded across his chest as he glared at the Mercedes's window. His smoke-blue eyes, hiding so many things.

Yeah, I didn't have time for guys, with one exception: Chase.

He definitely knew something about my mother and I wouldn't mind spending some private time with him. Unfortunately, I doubted he'd be at the party. Keeping track of Selena may have been one of his jobs, but it sounded like she'd found a way to escape without him knowing.

I heaved a sigh. So much for asking him. Most likely it was for the best, considering the effect he had on my crazy-ass hormones.

A few minutes after eleven, my bedroom door opened and Selena slipped inside.

She grinned at my cami top and jeans. "You look great."

"I love the lip gloss," I lied before she could ask.

"I made it myself." She grinned. Without hinting that there was anything special about the gloss, she unzipped her hoodie and gave me a flash of her bright red and bare-shoulder top.

"Wow! You look hot." I didn't have to fake my reaction. She looked amazing, like a cover model from Victoria's Secret.

"Thanks, and don't worry about bringing the schnapps or sparklers. You can save them for some other time." She zipped her hoodie back up. "We better get going. Our ride's waiting in the garage."

Our ride? I swallowed hard. I'd been so focused on what I

could gain by going to the party that I hadn't stopped to consider anything else, like how dark it would be and that we couldn't simply drive out the front gate.

I slipped my hand into my jeans pocket, double-checking that the mini-flashlight was still there. "So, how are we getting to this party? I'm assuming it's at someone's house?"

"It's on the beach. About ten minutes away—if you know the trail and have an ATV, like we do." A gleam twinkled in her eyes. "All we have to do is roll the ATV out of the garage and down to the woods. From there it's a cinch." She sighed. "But I'll have to take a rain check on borrowing your red shoes. The wet sand would snap off their heels."

I barely heard what she said after *ATV*. Holy insanity! We were going riding through the pitch-black woods to a beach in the middle of the night.

My stomach flip-flopped and an acidy taste coated the back of my throat. "I—ah. I can't go," I said.

"You've got to be kidding. You're all dressed. A second ago you were excited." Her hands went to her hips. "Tell me the truth."

I looked down at my sandals. If I wanted to get the truth out of her, it would help to give her something first. Besides, given a minute to think, she'd probably guess why I was hesitating.

I took a deep breath. "I know it's stupid. But I'm—I'm scared of the dark." I held my breath, waiting for her to laugh. I'd never told anyone, except Dad, about my fear before.

Her voice gentled. "That's awful. But you know"—she picked up my cardigan off the bed and handed it to me—"the only way people get over fears is to face them. And this time you don't have to do it alone. I'll be with you. I promise I won't do anything stupid, like turn the ATV's lights off or leave you stranded. I'll stick with you the whole time."

My fingers trembled as I took the sweater. She was right

about facing my fear, and she sounded sincere. Besides, if I didn't go, I'd blow what might be my only chance to find out about my mother. I'd never be able to live with myself then.

Selena gave me a hug. "If you need me to, I'll turn around and come home. Promise."

"Okay," I said. This wasn't going to be easy. But I had to do it.

Fifteen minutes later, I was wearing a helmet and sitting on the back of an ATV, my fingers white-knuckling both sides of the seat. As the engine rumbled to life, I forced my fingers to let go and wrapped my arms around Selena's waist. Then we zinged into the woods.

I clamped my eyes shut. There was no denying it, I'd gone totally insane.

"Hey!" Selena shouted over the ATV's grumble. "See, it's not so bad."

I cracked my eyes open. Not bad? Yeah, right. If I didn't barf it would be a miracle.

Icy sweat drizzled down my back as she gunned the gas and the ATV leapt to light speed. Branches clawed out from the darkness and limbs hung down. Streaks of moonlight broke through, brightened the trail for a split second, then vanished as we rushed headlong though the overwhelming blackness.

I looked past Selena's shoulder and focused on the jouncing headlight beams. The whole idea of encouraging her to get a buzz on seemed worse than crazy now. If she got drunk, we'd get into an accident for sure. We'd end up stranded in the woods—or dead. Shit. What if she'd already taken or drunk something, or wiped something on her lips? I had no idea how to drive an ATV.

We careened out of the trees and plummeted down a sand dune. My stomach dropped as the ATV tilted to one side, then righted itself when we thumped onto a beach.

Long wedges of moonlit sand and glimmering tidal pools stretched toward the surging waves and horizon. The smell of wood smoke and the thud of music echoed in the air. A short ways up the beach, the orange glow of a bonfire and a pillar of sparks rose into the night.

As we sped closer, I could make out a crowd of at least forty or fifty people gathered around the massive fire, drinking and dancing. Kegs and coolers covered picnic tables. The glint of trucks and cars dotted the shoreline.

Selena skittered the ATV to a stop.

I stared longingly at the distant firelight. "Why are we parking so far away?"

She pulled off her helmet and hoodie and began finger-teasing her hair. "I don't know about you, but I don't want anyone calling me a helmet-head."

Keeping my eyes on the bonfire's brightness, I took off my own helmet and shakily finger-brushed my flattened hair until its waves returned.

"You ready for some fun?" Selena asked.

"I guess," I said, and we were off again, speeding helmetless toward the party, my stomach cartwheeling like one of those nasty up-and-down-and-all-around rides at a fair.

Selena parked on the edge of the firelight, then hooked her arm through mine and pulled me into the crowd. She snatched a Twisted Tea out of a kiddy pool filled with ice and waved for me to take one. I snagged a wine cooler instead, popped it open, and took a long swig.

The drink's coolness settled my stomach a little, but the beat of the music and the sheer number of strangers swarming all around me, everyone moving, dancing, laughing, all the voices, strobing firelight, the heavy scent of pot, made my head swim. I took another slug and a deep breath. At least a majority of the people were around my age, like Selena had promised.

I leaned in close to her. "Where's Newt?" I asked.

She went up on her tiptoes, looking over the crowd. "I don't know. But he's got to be around here somewhere."

"You sure he knew we were coming?"

Playfully, she punched me in the arm. "Of course. He's got a surprise for you, too. C'mon."

As she dragged me through the swarm of dancing couples, I worried about Newt's so-called *surprise*. I was pretty sure I didn't like the sound of that.

She shouted introductions to a couple of guys and girls. But we were moving too fast for me to connect faces with names. She veered out of the crowd for a second, pointing at a black Mustang and giggling something about Newt, condoms, and spilling something or doing something. Sweat glistened on her forehead. Her eyes were wide. Still, she didn't look stoned or drunk, at least not yet.

Finally she let out a squeal, ran ahead, and latched onto the arm of a tall blond guy in shorts and a rugby shirt.

She hauled him toward me. "This is my cousin, Annie," she said. "Annie, this is Newt. Isn't he amazing?"

He had floppy hair like Taj and a Boys of Summer tan. I gave him a smile and said, "Hey." I could see why Selena had the hots for him, but—

Keeping the smile plastered on my face, I gave him a second look. Something about him seemed . . . *incongruent* was the word that came to mind. I'd caught a glimpse of a tattoo on the inside of his left wrist: entwined snakes or maybe just one twisted up like a pretzel. Not anything unusual in and of itself, but it drew my eye to a charm on his gold bracelet. It wasn't any fraternal symbol I'd ever seen.

With a shake of my head, I shoved my uneasiness aside. What was wrong with me? He was a normal guy. Preppy, rich, and Harvard, just like Selena had told me.

"Glad you could come," he said, elbowing the guy behind him.

The guy turned toward us. He was wearing a U of Maine sculling team hoodie, but he was blubbery-chunky and his skin was as pasty-pale as a slug. He was maybe nineteen at the most.

"This is Selena's cousin. Remember I was telling you about her?" Newt said.

The guy gave me a body scan and an approving grin. "Annie, right? You want to dance?" He reeled off the questions like they were rehearsed—and I suspected they were.

I folded my arms across my chest. Something told me this guy was Newt's *surprise*. Why hadn't Selena warned me? Yeah, right. Because I would have said *no*.

"Go on." Selena nudged me toward him. "He's Newt's brother."

I turned to scowl at her, but she and Newt were already vanishing into the crowd. Man, I hated this.

The guy swaggered toward me. "Come on, I won't bite, unless you want me to," he said, wiping his hands on his shorts.

Reluctantly, I let him take my hand and lead me into the dancing crowd. But, as we danced, I searched the crowd, hoping to catch a glimpse of Selena and Newt or one of the girls she'd introduced me to earlier, anyone safe to hang with.

But no one looked familiar, their faces brightened, then shadowed by the pulsing orange light. The smoke stung my eyes. The pounding music dug its way into my brain. Newt's brother jerked his pelvis and flailed his arms, dancing like a slug on fire. My legs felt heavy as if they were made of lead. Worst of all, it was clear I wasn't going to get my chance to pump Selena for information. This was one of my worst ideas ever.

Without warning, the music went from throbbing to slow. Newt's brother snatched me like I was his favorite blow-up doll, one hand fastening me against him while his other weaseled its way up my body. He leaned in close, his crotch grinding. "Let's get out of here," he said.

Teeth clenched, I strategically twirled away from him. Where the hell was Selena?

He snagged my wrist and yanked me from the dancing crowd, and toward the picnic tables and coolers. "I'll make us some drinks," he said.

A thousand ways to kill Selena flashed through my mind. I couldn't deal with this, especially tonight. But I couldn't leave the party until she did and I was done hanging around with this jerk.

He unscrewed the top off a half-empty bottle of foamy orange liquid, poured a little into two plastic glasses, then pulled out a hip flask and added whatever it contained to the drinks.

Holding one out to me, he licked his lips. "I've got a blanket in my car. I'm real good at the horizontal two-step, if you know what I mean."

I started to reach out for the drink, then pulled my hand back. "Give me a minute." I winked to throw him off the track and added, "Nature calls."

I fled back into the dancing crowd, around the fire, past a table covered with pots full of steamers and corn on the cob, by someone throwing up and a couple humping on the sand, and finally slid to a stop.

Ahead, the ocean rolled toward me, black and undulating like a mass of writhing snakes, rushing over the tidal pools, waves crashing higher and closer than when we'd arrived. Flashes of firelight and moonlight sizzled across the water.

I looked to my left. A bunch of people were stripping off their clothes, readying to go skinny-dipping. I glanced the other way: to the very edge of the firelight and beyond, to the night-shrouded dunes—and Selena's ATV.

I shifted my weight from one leg to the other and considered my choices. Newt's slime-mold little brother. A bunch of naked strangers. Or the ATV and darkness, terrifying but as familiar as my own name.

Shivering, I tucked my hands under my arms and jogged toward the ATV. I could feel the dark watching me approach, as alive as the demon that had taken over Dad's body.

I slumped down with my back against the machine, the night air chilling my skin.

Digging my heels into the sand, I stared straight ahead, my body hidden by shadows, my eyes focused on the firelight. I forced my childish fear into the furthest reaches of my mind. Instead, I bristled at what Selena and Newt must have said about me to Newt's brother in order for him to think he was going to get lucky, and chastised myself again for ever thinking that coming to this party was a good idea.

Slowly, my anger drained. My muscles relaxed. My mind wandered.

I pulled my knees to my chest. Everything that had happened until now, coming to Moonhill, Grandfather pretending to be Tibbs, the shadows, Dad cutting my ear, even the way Chase made my body thrum. It all seemed so unreal, so distant and strange.

In a cold rush, an image of Dad thrashing on the bed and the demonic voice coming from his mouth flooded my brain.

Burying my face in my hands, I rocked forward. I was too tired, too on edge to think about this. I needed a break. Dad had told me so many stories about Moonhill and the supernatural. I'd seen artifacts and exhibits about cursed Egyptian tombs, African shamans, the Romans, the Mayans, all kinds of cultures and religions. I'd talked to the Salem witch and the Santeria priest. But there was a huge difference between suspecting magic and supernatural were real, and having them invade your life like they had mine.

And I couldn't afford to just not think about it either, even for a second. I knew this as surely as I knew the dark was daring me to turn around. A demon, a living, breathing spawn of the Devil, had possessed Dad. And I had gone into the church with him. The demon could have possessed me.

"Hungry?" A guy's voice came from right in front of me.

My pulse jumped. I dropped my hands from my face and jerked my head up.

Chase crouched in front of me. He was wearing a black hoodie and his trademark low-slung jeans. There was a bowl of steamers in his hands.

His eyes settled on mine, lingering, leaving me breathless for a second.

"Want some?" he asked.

"Not really," I stammered.

Chase set the bowl on the sand. "I went through a lot of trouble to fix you this picnic."

I snorted. "More like you filched it from a bunch of drunks."

"That too." He pulled a pair of beers from his hip pockets and set them on either side of the steamers, then took off his hoodie, spread it out on the sand, and indicated he'd put it there for me. "Come on. Humor me. Think of it as a peace offering to make up for earlier today."

As I scooched onto Chase's hoodie, I caught a hint of his outdoorsy scent. But it wasn't a bonfire smell like I'd thought. It was actually a purer, hotter smell with a metallic tang, like a welder's torch.

Chase sat down on the other side of the beers and bowl. "Isn't this more comfortable?"

"Yeah—" My brain staggered, searching for something chit-chatty to say. Finally, I blurted, "You're lucky I didn't kick you in the shins when you grabbed me in Dad's room. And how slow were you going on the way back from Port St. Claire? Like ten miles per hour?" I gulped a breath, then gave him one last reaming. "And you really scared me the other day in the library— with that *if you live* bit."

He gave me a pained look that sent a shot of guilt tumbling around inside me.

Pressing my fingers over my eyes, I grimaced. "Sorry. That was totally rude." Man, I needed to lighten up. He was trying to be nice and I was giving him the third degree. Totally the wrong way to get things sizzling. Not that I was intent on hooking up with him right now, but I didn't want him to run for the hills, either.

Chase twisted the top off a beer and handed the bottle to me. "The situation has changed anyway."

The bottle chilled my lips as I took a tiny sip. "Because of what happened today with Dad?"

He looked away from me and reached toward his boot. I took advantage of the moment and dumped some of my beer onto the sand. If I didn't catch a buzz and he did, I might be able to pump him for information like I'd planned on doing with Selena.

His hand came back up, clutching a glinting dagger.

What the hell! I sucked in a breath, my hands braced behind me, readying to push up and run. First Dad with a razor, now this.

Chase laughed. "Sit down. I'm not going to use it on you." He took a steamer from the bowl and, with a flourish, used the dagger to open the shell and spear the meat. "Here." He held it out to me.

Gingerly, I took the clam off the blade's tip. "Thanks," I said, trying to look as cool as possible while I struggled to get my pulse back under control. I popped the meat in my mouth. It was tender and left a delicious smoky aftertaste on my tongue. I smiled at him. "So does Selena know you're here?"

"That's something I generally try to avoid. It makes life happier for the both of us."

I swallowed what remained of the clam. "You're not going to tell Kate about the party, are you?"

"Not unless I have to." He pointed his knife at my beer. "Drink up. There's plenty more."

As I took a tiny sip, I eyed Chase's nearly full beer. "Kate asked me not to tell Selena about Dad, and I don't think she's figured it out on her own." Talking about Selena seemed like a good way to find out how much he knew and to get him to trust me more.

"What makes you think Selena isn't a better actor than you?"

It took a second for what he'd said to sink in. I glanced past him toward the bonfire, double-checking to make sure Selena wasn't within earshot. Then I lowered my voice. "What do you mean?"

"Think about it." He reached behind him and brought out another beer. He held it out to me. "Here, you deserve it. Seeing your father like that couldn't have been easy."

A flash of Dad tied to the bed slammed into my mind, him arching and thrashing, his eyes rolled back into his head so only the whites showed.

A sob built in my chest and I turned my head away from Chase, swallowing hard and digging my hands into the sand to keep from crying out in anguish. Why my dad? Why something so awful?

I felt the cool-damp brush of the second beer as Chase set it down next to my hand. Then, his hand covered my clenched fingers, squeezing them gently and sending a comforting wave of warmth across my skin.

His voice deepened. "What did you get by coming here, clams and some beer? What did Selena get by bringing you here?"

Blinking my eyes open, I struggled to regain my composure. "What are you talking about? She just wanted to see Newt and have some fun. She wants us to be friends."

"Are you sure that was all? I told you to be careful." Chase looked away from me and stared toward the incoming waves.

With him distracted, I dumped out the rest of my first beer, then gave his half-empty bottle a sideways glance. As slow as he drank, the chances of him getting tipsy were next to nothing. On the other hand, I felt as mixed up as if I'd drunk a twelve-pack already.

After a few minutes, he turned back toward me. "I'm sorry I scared you in the library."

"That's okay," I said, waving his apology away. "Did you tell me not to talk to Dad because"—I forced the words out— "because of the demon?"

"No. I told you not to talk to anyone about your mother. I still feel that way. Except, I need you to tell me how your father thinks she died."

My throat squeezed and my mind raced. "Why do you care about that?"

Chase set his beer down. His gaze went to my face, then abruptly dropped to the sand beside me. In horror, I realized his eyes were focused on the spot where I'd dumped the beer.

"Uh, so—" he said.

Bowing my head, I stared at the bottle beside him and tried to think of a witty comeback.

Next to his bottle was a shadowy spot. No. Not a shadow: a wet spot. He wasn't drinking his beer either.

My eyes went to his and we both began laughing. I laughed so hard that tears moistened the corners of my eyes. I wiped them away with my fingers, relief flooding through me.

He gave another laugh. "Great minds think alike, huh?"

"Maybe we should just be straight with each other," I suggested.

He smiled, his beautiful eyes lighting up like I'd given him the best gift in the world. And, once again, those sexy flutters began dancing inside me. Only this time I let them take control, reverberating, rocking me to my toes with a surge of desire. I wanted to feel the sand against my back and his body pressed against mine. I wanted to forget everything else, except the sensation of his hands and lips against my skin. I wanted to make the daydream I'd had about him come true. Why not? Dad and I were leaving Moonhill soon. I could see in his eyes that he wanted me as much as I wanted him. This wasn't like Taj. I had no misconceptions about it leading anywhere.

Without letting my gaze stray from his, I shifted in close to him, my pulse beating a frenzied rhythm as I tipped my chin up, parted my lips and waited, hoping.

"Annie," he murmured. He lowered his head toward mine, one hand sliding down my back, bringing me in even closer until our lips were a breath apart.

My heart stumbled. I closed my eyes. I could smell his white-hot scent, feel the warmth radiating off his body. For a long moment, I feared he was going to retreat. Then his thumb grazed my bottom lip, leaving me breathless and trembling.

Finally, his lips touched mine, warm and tender, a gentle caress, growing harder, more demanding. Desire exploded through me. I opened my mouth, surrendering. I didn't care if someone saw us. I didn't care—

His mouth was gone from mine, cold air once more separating us.

Stunned, I blinked my eyes open.

He was scrambling to his feet. Turning away, he raked his hands over his head and groaned. "Annie, this is a bad idea. If you knew me, you wouldn't want to—" He stopped midsentence and cocked his head.

My breath came in short pants. "I—I'm not expecting anything—"

"Shhh." He turned back and raised his hand to silence me. Every sign of passion had drained from his face.

"What's wrong?" I whispered.

After a few tense seconds, he grabbed my arm, pulling me up. "You and Selena have to leave. Now."

"Why?"

"Wait here. I'll go get her," he said, his jaw muscles clenching.

But before he could move, someone shouted, "Cops!"

Three cruisers, maybe more, squealed into the parking area. Searchlights flooded the beach. Screams filled the air. The music died. People scattered everywhere. I snatched Chase's hoodie from the ground and thrust it at him. Selena was running toward us. "Get on the ATV!" she shouted.

I glanced at Chase. There was no room on the ATV for three.

"Don't worry about me. Get out of here."

Selena started up the engine and we flew across the wet beach, through the incoming tide. Sand sprayed out behind us as the ATV took the dune and sped into the shelter of the trees. Once we were out of sight, she slowed to a stop and we both looked back.

In the early morning light, I could make out the dying bonfire. A dozen or so partiers slouched beside the cruisers. A cop hauled someone across the sand, and a naked couple hid behind a dune.

"I don't see Newt, do you?" Selena asked.

"No," I said, though from this distance it was impossible to tell.

She blew out a breath. "That was close." She gave me a friendly cuff. "Hey, what happened to Newt's brother? And what were you and Chase doing, all by yourselves?"

I shrugged. "Nothing. Having a beer, talking." I touched my lips, remembering the warmth of his kiss.

"Yeah, right. About knives and skinning sheep." She laughed. "I can see why he turns you on. The secretive outcast image, the muscles and all that stuff. But be careful."

Sighing, I looked back to where Chase and I had sat. Any sign that we'd been there was gone, washed away by the surging waves. "*If you knew me, you wouldn't want to—*" he'd said.

For a second, my mind went back to a moment not long after Dad had made me pour Mother's ashes in the waves. What was it that he'd said about Chase? *"He belongs to them, you know."* I shivered as a chill swept up my arms. But it didn't make sense to be disturbed by those words or even think about them again. Most likely, it had been the demon talking, making up things to mess with my head.

I hugged myself. Still, I needed to figure out what was going on, who I could confide in. I wanted it to be Chase, but I actually had loads of reasons not to trust him. And Chase had told me I couldn't trust Selena. It was all so confusing.

Selena wrapped her arm around my shoulder and pulled me into a quick hug. "We should get going. We're not home free yet."

The ride back through the woods wasn't wonderful, but a whisper of daylight filtered through the trees and that made me feel less anxious about the darkness.

When we got to where the trail ended and Moonhill's yard began, she cut the engine and we pushed the ATV toward the garage.

There were no lights on in the house. The yard was hushed. But as Selena opened the garage door, I spotted, up on the shadowy hillside near the graveyard, the beam of a flashlight swaggering our way.

"Selena," I whispered sharply. I jerked my head to indicate the light.

She rushed back to the ATV and we pushed it as hard as we could.

It thumped as it went over the threshold and into the garage, but we managed to close the door noiselessly behind it.

"Maybe it's Chase," I said.

Selena pulled off her helmet. "Couldn't be. He didn't have enough time to get ahead of us."

The rustling sound of someone's quick footsteps came from outside the garage. We dashed away from the ATV and hid behind a car. After a second, Selena snuck to one of the side windows.

"Who is it?" I whispered.

"I'm not sure. The Professor, maybe."

I hurried over and looked out.

A slightly plump man with his hat yanked down low and his flight jacket collar pulled up strode away from the garage and toward the house. Selena might not have recognized him, but I knew him in an instant.

It was Dad. And my missing pink flashlight was in his hand.

CHAPTER 13

Τηιρτεεν ισ ωιχκεδ ιν αλλ ιτσ δισγυισεσ
Thirteen is wicked in all its disguises.

—Whispered into Solomon's ear

Only a few hours later, Selena and I were slouched on the terrace drinking coffees and nibbling raspberry croissants. It was muggy-hot, but neither Selena nor I felt like hanging around the air-conditioned dining room talking with Grandfather and Kate.

Selena lowered her voice. "Sorry about the early wake-up, but I didn't dare stay in bed. I think Mom's suspicious. She was vacuuming—back and forth, back and forth—outside my bedroom door."

I laughed. "Maybe it's the universe getting even with you for fixing me up with Newt's brother."

"Myles isn't that bad."

I nearly choked on my coffee. "What do you mean? He's the definition of *jerk*."

The dull headache that I'd woken up with began throbbing in earnest, and I pressed my temples to ease the pain. Selena hadn't actually woken me up. Despite the headache, I was about to leave when she'd knocked on my door. I'd planned on slipping out of the house before she got up to see if I could figure out where Dad had been coming from. My guess was that he'd been in the graveyard, visiting the spot where Mother's accident had happened. It didn't make sense why he'd gone at night, especially when he was supposedly bedridden. It was time for me to do some serious digging. And, I needed to do it alone and before the impending thunderstorms arrived and made retracing his footsteps impossible.

Selena touched my arm. "You okay?"

I dropped my hands from my temples. "My head aches a little, that's all."

"Man, can I relate to that. I've got the worst hangover. Newt told me not to mix beer and liquor. But did I listen? Oh, no."

"Well," I said, balling up my napkin and tossing it into my empty coffee cup. "I think I'm going to go lie down again."

Selena hopped up. "No need for that. I've got the perfect cure."

I tried to argue with her, but it was impossible and a second later we were on the other side of the terrace, headed through the solarium's side entrance.

Damp warmth and the smothering scent of jasmine surrounded me as Selena led the way down a gravel path, between beds of towering trees and plants of every description. Overhead, dense leaves and shadowy green light replaced the sky. Astonished, I scanned a row of pots teeming with orange fungus and mushrooms. Long, contorted pods hung from a tree with grotesque growths on every branch.

"Wow, this is quite the collection," I said.

Selena slid her fingers across a silvery plant. "It took Kate years to gather it all—and a ton of messing around with genetics and cross-pollinating as well." She rolled her eyes. "Kate calls this place—her *little* hobby."

I laughed. "Whatever happened to knitting?"

"That would be Chase's hobby," Selena said, without missing a beat.

I gaped at her. "You're kidding, right?"

"Not at all. He made me a gorgeous scarf for my birthday."
She shrugged it off. "Must come from being around the sheep
too much, shearing them and stuff. He makes knives, too, that
kind of seems more fitting."

My breath faltered as an image of Chase opening the clam
with a flourish of his knife came back to me: his strong hands,
the gorgeous planes of his cheekbones shadowed in the low
light, the comforting warmth of just having him near, the
moist heat of his lips against mine, then the cold air coming
between us. He really was a man of mystery and mixed messages. But since last night, I'd had time to think about the way
he'd ended our kiss. His holding back made sense—and not
the kind of sense that involved demons and shadows. He'd had
a crappy childhood: lost his mother and ended up nearly
beaten to death by a cartel. Those kinds of wounds might make
it hard for anyone to open up or realize they were desirable.
Well, it was about time someone helped him break down those
walls and showed him some fun, at least for a few days. Someone
like me.

"Hey!" Zachary's voice came from a ways up the path. He
sat on a wall that surrounded a small fishpond, tossing pieces of
bread to a school of surfacing koi. When we got up to him, he
added, "You haven't seen the Professor? He was supposed to
meet me here."

"He probably overslept," Selena said, shooting me a knowing look. She held out her hand to Zachary. "Can I borrow
your knife for a minute?"

He produced a jackknife and she used it to peel a toothpick-
wide strip of bark off a miniature willow that sat nearby.

"Chew this," she said, giving me a smidge of it.

I grimaced. "Thanks, but no thanks."

"Go on. I know what I'm doing," she said.

Zachary snorted. "Just don't spit any of it into the fishpond. It'll kill them for sure."

"No it won't, Zach." Selena flicked her hair back. "Aunt Kate developed this plant from the common weeping willow. It's called *Salix brainus*. It should cure things like headaches."

"Yeah, right," Zachary said. "*Should cure* isn't the same as safe." He turned to me. "She put leeches on Tibbs's face and one of them migrated into his ear."

Selena shot him a dark look. "That wasn't my fault." She turned to me and widened her eyes. "Please try it. Promise, I'm not a total moron." She popped some of the bark into her own mouth. "See. Delicious."

Thoughts of Alice in Wonderland's mushrooms went through my head, but I shoved them aside. It was a tiny piece and a lot better than having her slap leeches on my face, maybe. Besides, I wanted to get this done with so I could escape and head for the graveyard.

I stuck the bark in my mouth and then tucked it into my cheek. I could always spit it out later.

Selena tsked. "You have to chew."

I chewed a couple of times. A bitter taste filled my mouth and a slippery coating anesthetized my tongue. Oh, God. Something was happening.

Zachary leaned forward, studying me intently. "Aunt Kate said it could make people pass out."

I stared from him to Selena. This wasn't good.

"That's not true either," Selena said. "Kate said it could *possibly* make someone dizzy for a few minutes." She smiled at me. "I'm going to go take a bath and relax. In a half hour we should both feel on top of the world."

The slam of the solarium's side door echoed through the plants, followed by Olya's voice. "Zachary!" She came hurrying down the path toward us. Something pea-green streaked one of her cheeks and splotched her apron. Her bony fingers were as orange as carrots. "Zachary, no classes today. The Professor is not feeling well."

"Booyah!" Arms flailing, he did a victory dance.

Olya frowned. "That's not nice. The poor Professor has the stomach bug."

Selena elbowed me. "Told you it was him," she whispered.

I nodded, trying to keep my face expressionless. Until I got to the bottom of this, that was probably the best thing for her to believe.

Less than ten minutes later, Selena had headed off to take her bath and I was sticking toilet paper in my doorjamb. She was right about the willow. Though my ears were ringing a little, the headache had subsided and I didn't feel faint at all. Maybe I wouldn't throw the lip gloss out after all.

After giving the door one last tug, I hurried down the hallway. But when I got to the gallery, my feet froze at the entrance. It was even hotter and darker than it had been earlier in the day, when Selena and I had passed through to get our coffees from the dining room.

I thought about going back and taking the other stairs, but pushed the idea away.

"Get a grip," I told myself. Last night, I'd ridden through the dark woods on an ATV. I'd walked across the sand in the dead of night and sat down by myself. I'd been through this stupid room just over an hour ago and hadn't seen anything.

Taking a deep breath, I strode into the gallery, my sandals squeaking on the floor. I passed the first angel, his marble face as stark as bleached bone, his sword thrust skyward with fierce determination. As I neared the angel with the snakes coiled around its base, the clouds must have broken over the skylight because dazzling light flooded all around me.

A movement in the alcove near the three-faced goddess caught the corner of my eye and the same disturbing sense of recognition I'd felt in the gallery before came over me once more.

Fear electrified every cell in my body, telling me not to look, to run and get out as fast as I could. But I couldn't do that. I had to prove to myself once and for all that this was nothing, like Olya had said, even if the otherworldly shadows in Dad's room had been real.

I forced myself to remain still, to pretend I was admiring the angel with the snakes, while on the periphery of my vision, a dark cloud coiled and rose, widening into a—it couldn't be—human-shaped shadow.

My heartbeat banged in my ears as I slowly slid my hand into my pocket and gripped the flashlight. It's a juxtaposition of a statue and the light, I told myself—like Olya had said or like the shadow puppets I used to make with my hands and the flashlight's beam.

I listened intently and sniffed the air, struggling to figure out if I'd missed any of the warning signs. But there was nothing. No strange smells. No creepy noises. No change in air pressure. Nothing to be scared of.

In one swift motion, I flicked on the flashlight, swiveled, and pointed it in the direction of the coiling cloud.

A pure-black shadow, five times broader than a large man, whipped toward me. Its cavernous mouth stretched open and an earsplitting yowl vibrated across the gallery. I stumbled backward into the angel. Then I ran, screaming in utter terror, out of the gallery and down the halls.

I didn't stop until I got to the main staircase. Gasping for breath, I bent over with my hands on my knees, so dizzy I thought I might pass out. Holy shit. What the hell was that? This shadow was bigger than the ones in Dad's room. Much bigger.

As I struggled against surging lightheadedness and to push the ghastly yowling from my mind, the answer came to me: Selena's stinking willow. The damn stuff had made me see things. Sure the shadow had been there, just like Olya said it might be. A trick of light, most likely. The yowl could have come from any of a zillion cats I'd seen, probably a Siamese.

Selena had said, "*In a half hour we should both feel on top of the world*." She was right about the timing, but it was more like a hallucination straight from hell rather than an on-top-of-the-world high.

Sucking in one more deep breath, I willed my pulse to slow. The room had stopped spinning, so I grabbed ahold of the banister and made my way carefully down the stairs and into the hazy sunshine. Never ever, ever again would I take or use anything Selena concocted. And, just to be on the safe side, once I returned from retracing Dad's steps, I'd tell Grandfather all about the shadows.

By the time I got to the place where Dad had walked past the garage, I wasn't feeling shaky anymore. In fact, I felt better than I had in months. I looked up toward the hillside. When Selena and I had first spotted the flashlight beam coming toward us from the graveyard, only a few minutes had passed before Dad had appeared, so the path he took must have gone directly down the hill and across the field.

With my eye on the hillside, I started across the driveway.

But the sound of a shrill squeak made me jump and whirl toward the garage.

Tibbs stood on a camo-colored ladder, washing the garage's side window. He set his squeegee down and smiled at me, his blue eyes brightening. "Did you have fun last night?" he asked in a hushed tone.

Strolling over to him, I nodded. "I guess. But not as much as Selena did with Newt."

"Newt?" His Adam's apple bobbed and his mouth drooped. "Oh, I should have guessed," he said, like I'd just given him the most depressing news in the world.

Then it dawned on me. He had a crush on Selena. "I—um—

I meant, Newt and the Beach Rats. That's what her friends are called, right?"

"Yeah," he said. But I had no doubt he'd seen through my cover-up. Watching his forlorn face, I wondered how long he'd had the hots for her. He was about the same age as Newt, but other than that he wasn't even close to Selena's type. I couldn't help feeling sorry for him. Selena would never take him seriously, and there had to be other girls in town who would. I wished I could tell him that.

Shifting uncomfortably, I glanced at the sky. "I better get going, if I want to sneak in a walk before it rains."

He gave me a listless nod and then resumed his cleaning.

I glanced at him one last time and turned around. As long as I acted nonchalant and pretended like I knew where I was going, he probably wouldn't even think about reporting my whereabouts to Kate.

Squaring my shoulders, I hiked straight across the rest of the driveway without stopping and came to the field.

Sure enough, a well-worn path went across it to the hillside. Here and there, the dirt was scuffed as if someone had come this way recently. In one place, I could make out well-defined shoeprints, but there were both larger and smaller ones. Clearly, a number of people had taken this path over the last few days.

As the path wound its way between dense thickets and sprawling trees and up the hill, I noticed the ground wasn't sandy, nor did it have any rock outcrops, like I'd expected this close to the ocean—not that I was any kind of nature expert. Then again, a graveyard would require dirt and a lot of it, and I was certain that's where the path was taking me.

A shoulder-high stone wall surrounded the graveyard and a narrow, filigreed iron gate blocked its entry.

Flakes of rust sloughed off it as I rested my hand against

the gate's spiraled bars and peered at what lay within: close-clipped grass and ancient hydrangea trees, lines of white grave-stones, obelisks and statues and, near the top of the hill, the domed mausoleum fronted by pillars. Somewhere amongst all those things, a marble lamb marked a child's resting spot, and the place where my mother died.

A sheep's blat brought me back from my thoughts of Mother. A dozen of them, all as black as onyx, grazed their way past the mausoleum and into view. Not that black sheep were weird, but I'd never seen a flock that didn't contain at least a single white or speckled one.

Black as night, black as witchcraft, black like death—

Stop that! I told myself.

The gate creaked as I opened it and latched it behind me. Beyond it the worn path dissolved into grass and any trace of footprints vanished.

The sheep raised their heads and watched as I brushed my hair back from my sweat-dampened face, then walked toward the closest obelisk.

FREEMONT was chiseled in bold letters, and in smaller script names and dates going back to before the early 1800s. *Phillip:* died in the War of 1812. *Martha:* mother of twelve, devoted wife of Samuel, struck down in the winter of 1832. *Stephanie:* daughter of Zachary and Prudence, born 1770, drowned at sea 1811.

A knot tightened in my chest. I traced the words *drowned at sea* with my finger and felt a stab of sadness. Dad loved history. He loved antiques. He loved telling stories about Moonhill, about pirate treasure and ransacked Egyptian tombs, oil lamps hauled up from the ocean's depth, escaped yetis and ship-wrecks on the way home from digging Aztec gold, and about Samuel going feral and his glass heart breaking. But before, when I'd listened to Dad tell these stories, these people, my people, the people my name had come from, hadn't felt real. And now . . .

The wind picked up and, as it pushed through the graveyard, the hydrangea trees swayed.

In the distance, thunder grumbled.

I checked the clouds. They'd crowded the sky, their underbellies now as dark as the flock of sheep.

My eyes went back to my name on the stone, then past it to the windblown hydrangeas and lines of monuments and graves. Though I wasn't sure if I'd ever really be ready to see the spot, I had to find the marble lamb and make sure that was where Dad had gone.

I walked deeper into the lines of crowded graves, moving toward the mausoleum at the top of the hill, scanning on both sides for the small stone. Despite the cooling wind, sweat gathered on my upper lip. I wiped it off, but the taste of salt lingered. Maybe the graveyard wasn't public now, but early on it must have served the entire settlement of Port St. Claire. It was much too large for just one family.

A line of newer gravestones caught my eye. And even as I stepped toward them, I knew what I'd find. This wasn't what I'd come for, but my heart could not resist going near.

Susan Woodford Freemont

My mother's name, birthday, and the day of her death were chiseled into a glistening white stone. Above her name was an etching of seagulls circling between swirling clouds. Below, it was the likeness of a family of seals resting on a cliff top surrounded by wild roses.

But her name was not alone on the stone.

I swallowed hard.

James William Freemont

Dad's name was carved next to hers. It only lacked his death date.

And then mine: *Stephanie Persistence Freemont*

I stiffened and stood motionless, the wind chilling my hot face, the smell of the impending storm all around me—and the numbing reality of how short life was and how many lives had gone before mine settled in my bones. No matter what happened or where I went, in the end, I'd come back to the beginning.

To Moonhill.

To the family Dad had tried to leave behind.

It could not be denied: I was a Freemont. I was one of them. And more than that, I wanted to be a part of them, of their heritage, their story, my story. My family.

Shoving my hands into my jeans pockets, I looked away from the stone. As easy as it would be to stand here and get lost in thoughts about my past and a future that might never happen, I needed to keep in mind why I'd come, and how little time I had.

I turned my back on the stone and continued up the hill toward the mausoleum.

When I reached it, I flopped down on its hard steps and stared back the way I'd come. The graveyard wasn't small, but it wasn't that huge, either. The lamb should have been easy to find.

I bit my lip.

Unless there wasn't one.

Maybe that was what Dad had come to double-check.

Thunder rattled again, closer this time.

The sheep stopped grazing and scuttled off toward the back side of the hill, past a bowed hydrangea tree.

As the tree's branches scraped the ground and rose again, my eyes caught a hint of something white and low to the ground.

My pulse jumped.

I blinked to make sure I'd seen right.

Under the overhanging branches was a small, solitary monument.

A lamb!

My fingers gripped the edge of a rough step. For a long moment, all I could do was stare at the monument. My mother had slipped on the wet grass and died there. Her blood had stained that stone and soaked into the ground around it. I couldn't help but wonder who had found her body, and if I had been with her when she died.

I gazed beyond the lamb to the spiderweb of trembling dark trees and the roiling black clouds. Probably I would never know why, but she must have had a good reason for coming here that day.

Struggling to my feet, I made my way across the distance.

I ducked under the hydrangea's branches and knelt.

The dirt's dampness soaked through my jeans and chilled my legs. I touched the lamb, its body rough from age and cool beneath my trembling fingers as I traced what remained of an inscription. *Sacrifice* and *innocence* were the only two words I could make out.

All around me the hydrangea's leaves clattered. I licked my lips, my pulse drumming in my temples, and waited for something to happen—for a leaf to rustle, for a soft voice to reach my ears, for the sensation of a hand on my shoulder. Something of Mother.

But the wind died and nothing happened.

I squeezed my eyes shut.

Nothing. Not even tears.

It seemed like I'd feel a trace of something.

Suddenly, a thought pricked at the back of my mind. I pressed my hand against the hard-packed earth, bare dirt, flat as it could be, and so thickly canopied by the hydrangea that not a single blade of grass grew, and hadn't for years and years. For a lot more years than the fifteen my mother had been dead.

I shimmied out from under the branches and scrambled to my feet.

Wheeling around, I scanned the graveyard, searching for a different lamb.

There were no others.

No one could possibly have slipped on the wet grass and hit their head on this lamb, like Mother supposedly had done. It was impossible. There was no grass. The tree's overhanging branches would have broken the person's fall.

Someone had lied about Mother's accident.

And Dad knew it.

A gust of wind whipped my hair across my face. The hydrangea's leaves murmured, whispering like cousins sharing secrets in the dark.

I cocked my head as a fainter sound reached my ear. People talking, just beyond the hilltop.

Taking the same route the sheep had, I crept toward the voices.

As I crested the hilltop, I saw two familiar figures standing just below me. Zachary and Chase. It had probably been Zachary's smaller footprints I'd seen on the way to the graveyard.

Quickly, I ducked behind a tall gravestone and peeked out at them, my mind still reeling with thoughts of my mother and dad.

"You've got to be kidding. You expect me to hit a pea?" Zachary whined.

"Not hit. Slice. Now, watch carefully this time." Chase shook his arms out, like a gymnast loosening his muscles. "Now, when the wind calms, throw the peas as fast and high as you can."

A second later, the wind let up and Zachary started heaving things into the air. As fast as he threw, Chase flicked his wrist and, one after another, knives sliced the air.

Zachary gathered up the knives and brought them back to Chase. "That was awesome. You hit them all. I'll never be that good."

"With practice, you might." Chase reached into the pocket of his hoodie and pulled out an apple. "We'll try something larger. Wait until you can't feel the wind on your face. Watch your stance and focus. Don't think about the apple. Think: your eye, your wrist, the—"

Chase raised his hand, like he'd done to shush me at the party.

"What's wrong?" Zachary asked.

As if he had sensed my presence, Chase swiveled toward me.

I stepped into clear view and waved at them. "Hey, I thought I heard you guys."

Dad had always said: The best way to not get accused of eavesdropping—like at auctions—is to pretend you just arrived.

Chase took the knives from Zachary and began tucking them into his beltline. In a few quick strides he closed the space between us, with Zachary following on his heels.

Before he could put the question to me, I asked, "What are you guys doing up here?"

"Chase is teaching me how to throw knives—and hatchets." Zachary beamed.

"Nice," I said. I let my eyes find Chase's. I wanted him to know everything was cool between us.

He smiled, like he'd gotten my message. But his gaze quickly left mine and went to Zachary. "You two better get back to the house. It's going to rain any minute."

As if on command, a drop of rain hit my arm, then another. A deafening clap of thunder came from directly overhead. Rain pelted down. Lightning crackled.

"The mausoleum!" Chase yelled, and we all ran toward it.

But the mausoleum's portico offered little protection from the torrential downpour and streaks of lightning.

"C'mon!" Zachary yanked the mausoleum's door open and dashed inside.

I followed him, grateful to be out of the rain and within the thick walls that muffled the thunder's noise.

Chase bent over and picked up a chain and padlock from the floor. "It's convenient for us. But this place is supposed to be locked."

"Someone cut it?" Zachary asked.

"No. The lock's open, like it was picked. More likely grave robbers than just kids messing around."

I stepped back farther into the mausoleum, uneasiness twisting in my stomach. Dad. He'd picked it. This is where I'd seen him coming from. I was sure of it.

Goose bumps raced up my arms as I glanced around, trying to figure out what he possibly could have been looking for.

In the dim light, interment vaults, some empty, a strip of them sealed, rose from floor to ceiling like honeycomb in a hive. In the middle of the floor two caskets, one steel with gold filigree and the other pure white, rested on marble slabs. In every corner and out-of-the-way place, spiderwebs and darkness huddled.

Zachary wiped his hand along the white casket. "When I die, I want to be put in here. But I want to be stuffed like the polar bear." He raised his arms and growled.

I pulled my flashlight out and flicked it on.

Chase eyed me. "Prepared, aren't you?"

"S—sometimes." I stuck to one word, but my voice still gave away my fear.

He tilted his head to one side, first studying me, then my light.

Unnerved by his stare, I forced a laugh. "Tell me you don't think this place is creepy."

"It's not creepy." Zachary's voice came from the rear of the mausoleum.

Chase stepped closer to me, his voice low. "You're afraid."

I backed up. My heart pounded like crazy. "No. I don't like dark places. That's all."

"Fears all have a root. Why the dark?"

Outside, the thunder rumbled even louder and rain pummeled the mausoleum's roof.

I glanced out the open door. Every muscle in my body wanted to push past him and escape. "I don't know," I said. "I've always felt this way."

"Always?"

"Yes," I said, but my quivering voice made it sound like a lie, even to my own ears.

Chase's eyes locked on mine, ocean-deep and unflinching. "Are you sure?"

I looked away from him, to the flashlight's beam. Then, I forced myself to step toward the middle of the mausoleum. "See, doesn't bother me at all," I said.

Resting my free hand on the white casket, I stared into the darkness to further prove my point. If this didn't work, I'd switch things up and ask him about his childhood fears.

In the shadowy light, I could just make out the faint outline of candelabras and sword-wielding angels standing guard on either side of a stone altar.

My breath stalled in my throat. There was a time I could remember—a time so faint I could only recall it in the moment between sleep and waking: my mother's warm arms wrapped around me, her singing, beautiful, soft, the smell of sandalwood. There had been a time when I didn't fear the dark.

There was no sound to warn me, but the hairs on the back of my neck prickled and my chest tightened as Chase moved in closer behind me. His hands clasped my upper arms, a determined grip. "What happened?" he asked.

"I don't know," I said. "I can't remember." Then, as I squeezed my eyes shut to hold back a surge of unwanted tears, I felt a trickle of warmth run from my nose and I tasted blood. I wiped my hand across my upper lip to check if my nose had suddenly started bleeding, but my fingers came away dry and a surreal feeling closed in around me.

"Tell me." His voice buzzed in my ear, distant and dream-like.

An image flashed in the back of my mind, a split-second memory fighting to get free, like a bird trapped in a black box, struggling for daylight. I did know something. Something about my mother's death.

I opened my mouth to tell Chase. He'd lost his mother, he'd understand. But I didn't dare say a word; one sound from me or anyone else might stop the flickering image from taking form.

I glanced at the altar with its candelabras and angels standing guard, angels with their arms thrust skyward like the one in the gallery.

Zachary's voice echoed out. "Look at this!"

Chase's hands fell from my arms. "Don't touch that vault," he said, nearly bringing me back to the here and now.

"The Professor would want me to. There's writing on it. It's in ancient Greek: *In service of Hecate, the Three-faced Goddess, Protector of the Gateways.*"

The darkness in my head wavered for an instant and I gasped as the image clarified instead of vanishing. The feeling of recognition in the gallery. The human-shaped shadow. It wasn't a trick of light. Or a hallucination brought on by the willow. It was a living, breathing, horrifying being!

The shadow's darkness, it was the root of my fear.

My mother died in the gallery.

The shadow had been there.

"Mother." The word tumbled from my lips and every trace of the memory slipped back into the darkness, but there was no question I'd witnessed my mother's death.

Chase wrapped his arm around my shoulder. His voice softened even more. "Are you all right?"

Trembling, I leaned against him. I had to tell him. I couldn't keep this to myself. "I need to talk to you, alone," I whispered.

He took his arm off my shoulder and looked me in the eyes. "I have to get the sheep into the lower pasture. After that, I'll find you."

"All right," I said, barely able to breathe.

His eyes narrowed to bands of unflinching steel. "Promise, you'll tell me everything."

"I will. Cross my heart and hope to die."

He pressed a finger against my lips. A warm rush shot though me. Nerves, excitement, fear, desire, so many emotions balling into one.

"Don't say that," Chase said.

Zachary's voice came again. "I bet we could pry the vault open."

"Get over here." Chase's tone was tough, almost too hard.

Zachary stomped back to us. "I wasn't doing anything."

"Your grandfather's going to be unhappy enough about the break-in without you damaging something by mistake."

My eyes widened. Grandfather? Even though I wanted desperately to tell Chase what I'd discovered about Mother's death, I didn't want anyone to know I suspected Dad had broken in. First I needed to be sure why he'd done it, and how it connected to everything else.

Quickly, I swept the flashlight's beam across the dust-coated floor.

"What are you looking for?" Zachary said.

I flicked the flashlight off. "I was checking to see if the burglar left any footprints." If Dad had left any, the three of us walking around had wiped them out. I couldn't be sure, but I hadn't seen any signs that Dad had touched or taken anything either.

CHAPTER 14

We who now must work in the shadows shall
one day be the lights of the world.

—Jeffrey White, President
Sons of Ophiuchus

A s fast as the storm had arrived, it blew over, leaving everything
soaked but the sky blue and the air cool.

Chase called Kate and told her about the break-in. I wasn't
surprised he mentioned I was with him, and it didn't matter
since Zachary would have told everyone anyway.

After that, I hurried back to the house and straight to the
west wing. It was time for Dad and me to have a heart-to-
heart about Mother's death and what he'd been doing in the
graveyard. While I was at it, I'd ask about my flashlight—
though I suspected Dad had stolen it while he was possessed
and probably had no memory of doing it.

When I reached Dad's door, I raised my hand to knock,
but froze when an unfamiliar hushed voice crept out from the
other side. "Easy as skinning a cat," it said.

"Yes, indeed." A deeper voice snickered.

A memory careened into my head. A month ago, I'd gone
shopping and come home unexpectedly early. When I'd stepped
into the house, I was certain I'd heard voices. But no one was

there besides Dad and it had felt like he'd turned the heat up, really high.

Slowly, I lowered my hand to the doorknob. The sound of my pulse thudded in my ears and fear, cold and sharp, shuddered up my spine. Part of me wanted to run, but I gritted my teeth and stood firm. If Dad was in there, maybe there was a reason he wasn't saying anything—or couldn't.

The deeper voice cleared his throat. "I believe we're not alone."

I threw the door open and catapulted inside.

A blast of sweltering air hit me. An eye-burning stench stole my breath.

Faintness rushed over me. I staggered back against the doorframe, clutching it as my head whirled and the floor tilted up to meet the ceiling.

I gulped a breath, and then another. Holding onto the doorframe, I clawed my way back onto my feet. Five more breaths and the room stopped spinning. The air temperature plummeted back to normal and the overwhelming bleachlike odor faded.

Dad had me by the arm. He walked me over to a chair. "Sit," he said.

Shivering from the sudden drop in temperature, I pushed my sweat-slicked hair away from my face. The heat and the smell had been like a super-charged version of the last time I'd seen the shadows in Dad's room, and not at all like the dizzy and surreal feeling I had experienced in the mausoleum.

Wide-eyed, Dad stared at me. "Fascinating," he said. "You are as white as a clam."

I glanced around the room. "I heard voices. It was so hot. Was someone in here?"

A smug little smile lifted his lips. "I was."

My jaw clenched. The Dad I knew would have run to get

a cool compress for my head, held my hand, threatened to phone 911. Instead, he looked amused.

My eyes went to the bed. The cross hung over the headboard and the bag with the relic in it was still tucked partway under the mattress. The priest had said no demon could stand being around such things.

I blew out a couple of short breaths, trying to gain control. Maybe Dad had really gone insane. Or maybe these *things* were something other than demons, things a priest and his tools couldn't drive off. Maybe I was right about the exorcism failing.

Trying to mask my fear, I looked him in the eyes. "Dad?"

His eyes bore into mine. "Yes, child."

I flinched. He didn't even sound like himself. But, no matter what was going on, I couldn't believe the Dad I knew wasn't still in there somewhere. "I think I should go back to my room and lie down. Promise, I'll come back later."

He dipped his head. "A promise is best when skillfully worded."

"Yeah, right," I said as I wobbled to my feet and made for the door. Whatever was going on, I had to get Dad help. And now.

My wooziness faded with every step, and by the time I was halfway to Kate's study, hardly a trace remained. Kate was not my favorite person, but I was certain that she wanted Dad well, if for no other reason than so we'd leave Moonhill.

I dashed down the stairs and just as the first-floor hallway came into view, I saw Kate rushing into her study.

"Wait!" I shouted, but the door slammed before she could hear me.

Hurrying my steps, I knocked once and let myself in.

I shut the door behind me and turned to face Kate.

She wasn't there.

Man, I was getting sick of this vanishing-people thing.

On the wall opposite the fireplace were three doors. Kate had to have gone through one of them.

"Kate, are you here?" I called out, just in case one of the doors led somewhere private, like to a bathroom, which could definitely explain her rushed disappearance.

I gave her a minute to answer, then knocked and opened the first door.

It was a closet: rubber boots, jackets, sneakers, and a smock Kate probably wore when she worked in the solarium.

Behind the next door was a small storage room, its shelves loaded with trays of seedpods, pressed leaves and bark, notebooks and neatly labeled boxes.

With a frustrated huff, I tried the last door.

It was a bathroom with a sink, a toilet, and a small table with a basket of toiletries and makeup on it. A dressing mirror hung on the wall and a stall shower took up one corner. I glanced into the stall just to be sure it wasn't a James Bond–style elevator.

Leaving the bathroom, I rubbed my neck. Shadows could vanish, weird voices could disappear, people could get in and out of my room without me seeing them, but Kate hadn't just dematerialized.

A scratch-scratching noise caught my ear. A fat, gray cat was sharpening its claws on the high-backed settee.

"Pstttt," I said to get its attention. It didn't make any sense to let a cat destroy a two-hundred-year-old piece of furniture.

The cat hissed, then streaked across the room and vanished under the bookcase like the small herd of cats had done the other day.

I smiled. Maybe the shower stall wasn't a super-spy elevator, but I'd toured enough historic homes and castles to know that bookcases sometimes hid passageways.

I shoved my hand in my jeans pocket, fingering my flashlight as I looked for a decorative carving or brass plate, a book whose cover showed more wear than the others, something that might trigger a mechanism and open a secret panel—if there was one.

A statue of a three-faced goddess stared out from one shelf: *Hecate, the Three-faced Goddess, Protector of the Gateways*, that's what Zachary had said when he translated the inscription on the vault.

A sense of danger flickered inside me as I moved toward the statue. If it opened a secret panel here, then perhaps Zachary had discovered a mechanism that opened a similar panel in the mausoleum. Maybe that was what Dad was looking for. And maybe there was also a connection to the three-faced goddess in the gallery where my mother had died.

The statue was secured to the shelf. I tried twisting it clockwise.

It turned. But nothing else happened.

I tried counterclockwise.

Nothing again.

Nibbling my lip, I studied the writing around the statue's base. It wasn't in English, but that probably didn't matter. It wasn't like it would be instructions on how to open the panel.

I tried touching the letters and words, one by one in hopes of finding some kind of switch. Then I gave up and just ran both hands down the length of the statue starting at the head. As my little finger skimmed the statue's base, something clicked, and one section of the bookcase slid behind the others, revealing a narrow door-size opening.

Holy cow, I'd done it!

Adrenaline shot through me as I took my flashlight out. If I found Kate, I'd tell her about Dad, of course. But I also needed an explanation for how I'd found the hidden passageway. I could say I saw it closing behind her.

I flicked on the flashlight. The passageway was probably lit with flaming torches or something, but better safe than sorry.

Calling up all my bravery, I stepped out of the study and

into a room no larger than a port-a-potty with dead smelly air. My mouth dropped open. Disappointment and shock surged through me. Whatever else I'd been expecting, this wasn't it. In one corner, there was a trashcan and a jumbo bag of cat litter. Between there and where I stood, every inch of the floor was covered with plastic litter boxes.

I wrinkled my nose to block out the cat-urine smell. Even if there was a second secret panel within the room, no way could anyone get to it without tripping.

Backing out of the secret room, I put my flashlight away. Then, I felt around the statue's base. Relief coursed through me when I heard a click and the missing section of the bookcase glided back into position. Okay, so that was a huge dead end.

Dejected, I glanced over the fireplace at the frolicking-cat painting. It seemed even more absurd now than the last time I saw it.

Just as I was about to turn away, my eyes zeroed in on a detail in the painting.

Holy shit! All six of the cats had raindrop-shaped bobbles hanging from their collars.

I slid my hand into my pocket and fingered the piece of sea glass I'd almost forgotten was in there. The bobbles were identical to it. But it didn't make sense why a bobble off a cat's collar would be in with Mother's ashes.

Barely able to breathe, I lowered my gaze from the painting to the fireplace's cluttered mantel. Five containers sat on it; two were porcelain ginger jars, and three were brass and looked exactly like the jar that had held Mother's ashes. All of them were sealed with wax, just like Mother's jar.

I studied the painting. Undoubtedly, the jars on the mantel held the cremains of the cats in the painting, someone's beloved pets. But there were six cats and only five sealed containers on the mantel. Where was the sixth container?

Numbness swept through me. Dad had told me a million times how he would have bought a rosewood box for Mother's ashes. But by the time he was told of her death and had traveled back to Moonhill, her ashes had been put in a brass jar that was then sealed with beeswax.

I squeezed my eyes shut as realization dawned on me. I knew where the sixth container was. It was sitting in the Shakespeare garden. Where I'd left it after Dad had made me pour what I'd believed was Mother's ashes into the ocean. But they hadn't been Mother's. The cremains had belonged to a cat.

"You are a clever one." Grandfather's voice came from behind me.

I swung around, my hands fisting. Not only had they betrayed and lied to Dad in the worst way possible, they had also let him believe he had his wife's ashes with him all these years.

Grandfather winked at me. "I'm sure the cats gave away the location, but how did you find the lever?"

With a hard, fortifying breath, I swallowed my anger. Grandfather had seen me close the secret panel, but he hadn't noticed me looking at the painting. And as much as I wanted to scream at him and demand answers about Mother, it was smarter to think things through before I revealed what I knew. Besides, Dad needed help, and that couldn't wait.

"I was looking for Kate. Something's wrong with Dad," I said.

Grandfather's forehead wrinkled with concern. "What happened?"

I studied him for a second, then began telling him what had gone on in Dad's room, including the shadows I'd seen in there before the exorcism and the more recent voices.

Fear flashed in Grandfather's eyes, sending a fresh wave of panic through me. He pulled out his phone. "This isn't good, not good at all," he said. "I'm going to make a call, then go up to your father's room. I need you to find Selena and Zachary. Stay with them, but don't tell them anything. Understand?"

My anger about Mother and how they'd kept secrets from Dad flooded back. I wasn't going to be left in the dark. Not this time.

I folded my arms across my chest. "What the hell is going on?"

Grandfather raised a stern finger, silencing me. "Annie, your father's situation is more complicated than it appeared. But if you hadn't told me what you found out, then it most likely would have become impossible. As it is we may have a chance. But you must do as I say. Immediately—and without question."

I could tell by his resolute stance and the firm look in his eyes that there was no way I was going to get anything from him right now. I also believed he was right—there was no time to waste on fighting. On top of that, he'd just given me a huge clue without realizing it.

After the exorcism was over and the priest had left, Kate had said, *"All I'm grateful for is that it's over, and that it had nothing to do with the ring."*

"That certainly would have complicated the situation, perhaps even made it impossible," Grandfather had replied.

The words Grandfather had used then and now were too similar for it to be a coincidence. He was certain the poison ring and whatever was going on with Dad were connected. All I had to do was figure out what was so worrisome about the ring myself, then I'd know the real truth.

I stepped toward the door but looked back. "You'll tell me as soon as you know what's going on, right?"

"Yes, of course. Now, get going." Grandfather waved me off with a flicker of a smile that didn't match the worry lines fanning out from his eyes.

In return, I forged my own smile, then opened the study

door and sprinted down the hallway. Hopefully, Grandfather wouldn't check to make sure I was with Selena and Zachary because I had no intention of trying to find them. I was going to my room.

I had an old e-mail I needed to find and a new one I had to send.

CHAPTER 15

*Darkness has a hold on me, but it shall not take me
to the grave or wrench the fight from my rebel heart.
I will have freedom. And, I will have revenge as well.*

—A Hold on Me. By Anonymous

To avoid going through the gallery, I took the back stairs up to
my room. I was surprised and relieved to find the toilet paper
still in the doorjamb. But, to ensure that my privacy continued, I
braced a chair against the door. The last thing I needed was
someone barging in and asking what I was up to.

I sat down at the desk and dug my phone out of my bag.

It only took a second to get into my sent e-mail folder and
find the information I'd given to the woman who'd bought
the poison ring, complete with a sketch of the ring's inscription.

I studied the inscription's jagged letters. If only I'd tried to
translate them. But at the time, selling the ring fast so I could
get money and pay the overdue bills was the only thing on my
mind. I'd never dreamed it was anything other than a forgery
or at best a newer reproduction—certainly not ancient, or for
that matter cursed or whatever.

Resting my elbows on the desktop, I blew out a breath.
Telling Grandfather and Kate that I'd thought the ring was a
forgery had been the right thing to do. But man, they had to

think I was a piece of work, after hearing how I lied and cheated a customer without compunction. Though, now, it appeared the only person I'd cheated was myself. The good thing was—no customer in their right mind would complain to the police about buying a ring for far less than its real value.

My gaze went back to the phone. I'd told Grandfather I thought the inscription was a weird form of Sabaean, an ancient form of Arabic. Unfortunately, I had no more ability to translate that now than I had back then.

I grinned. However, I knew someone who could: Taj.

And, considering how shitty he'd been to me, it seemed like he owed me one. It was a good thing I'd totally forgotten about taking or posting revenge photos on the Internet. That would have ruined any chance of playing on his guilt—that was, if he had any.

After attaching the sketch of the ring's inscription, I composed a short note about needing the translation as soon as possible because I had a buyer and that I'd phone him in a couple of hours. Okay, that wasn't much time, but the message wasn't very long, and the sooner I heard back from Taj, the better. If I'd had a choice, I'd have avoided having anything to do with him, like I had back when I'd sold the ring to the woman. Who'd have ever believed, after all the things Dad had taught me about spotting fakes, about bluffing and reading body language, that I'd get taken in by a guy-friend with floppy hair and a wallet full of rubbers.

My fingers tightened on the phone. There was a chance Taj might think I'd made up the inscription and was pretending I needed help as an excuse to get in touch with him. He might even laugh at me.

I rubbed my neck, thinking. I could include photos of the ring, too. But the inscription was on the inside of the ring, barely visible at all. No. I didn't need to complicate things. I just needed the damn translation.

I lifted my chin and hit send. Once I had my information, it didn't matter what Taj thought. I'd simply hang up on him and that would be the end of that.

I'd barely had time enough to go into the bathroom and wash up when my phone rang.

Queasiness twisted in my stomach as I answered it. "Hello?"

"Is the inscription on a ring?" Taj asked.

I pressed my lips together. I didn't want to chitchat with him, but he could have at least said hello before firing a question. "Yeah, an old ring," I answered.

"Tell me it doesn't look like a poison ring."

"Why does that matter?"

Taj lowered his voice to a hushed tone. "Annie, you need to get rid of it. Forget you ever saw it."

My legs wobbled and I slumped into the desk chair, holding the phone tighter. "What does the inscription say?"

"Don't worry about that—Shit, my supervisor's coming. He saw me working on the translation. I didn't tell him about your e-mail."

"What does it say? Please."

"No. Don't ask me about it again. Never. Get rid of it. Before you wind up in jail. It was stolen from the Met, Annie." He hung up.

For a long moment, I stared at the phone, fear blanketing me like a shroud on a stiffening corpse. Dad was slick, but he wasn't a thief. It was just as likely Taj's nosy supervisor or one of his horny friends stole it. But he was one hundred percent wrong if he thought it was Dad or me.

Oh, God. I hadn't stolen it—but I had sold it.

Sold stolen property . . . Shit. The police. My future. Dad.

Overwhelmed, I dropped my phone back into my bag and rubbed my neck, struggling to figure out what my next move should be. One thing was for sure, even if I wanted to, I couldn't waste time thinking about my future—or lack thereof. David was hunting down the ring. When he got back, Grandfather could use his pull with the old boy network to get me off. Maybe, hopefully. Right now, I needed to focus on Dad.

Taking a deep breath, I got up and paced across the room. I really didn't want to wait until Grandfather or Kate told me what they thought was wrong with him, and hope like hell I could tell if they were lying or not.

An idea hit me. I grabbed my bag and flew out the door. There was someone else who knew some Arabic and could help me, someone who I'd already planned on talking to: Chase.

Granted, the letter had looked like a weird cross between ancient Sabaean and the modern Arabic in his graphic version of the *Arabian Nights*. But maybe there was enough similarity for him to be able to translate it, or at least get the general idea of what the inscription was about.

I moved fast down the stairs, shortcutted through the solarium. In less than a minute, I was backing the Mercedes out of the garage.

When I reached the front gate, I parked, sprinted to Chase's cottage, and knocked on the front door.

The cottage probably had one bedroom upstairs. The small windows and the thick lintel over the door told me it was old, maybe even eighteenth century. A boot scraper and a pair of muddy sneakers sat beside the door, but the cottage lacked any girly touches like window boxes or lace curtains. Definitely, a single guy's place.

The bleat of a lamb echoed out from the hillside. I glanced toward the sound and spotted a line of black sheep tripping over each other to get into a shedlike barn. Maybe it was feeding time and Chase was up there passing out supper.

Holding my bag against my chest, I jogged between the puddles and up a path to the shed. As I approached, I could hear Chase's voice coming from inside.

I paused, waiting to hear if he was talking to the sheep or a person, or something else. But all I could hear now was the trickle of water and the jostling movement of the animals.

I eased the shed door open and softly closed it behind me. If I could sneak up and watch Chase undetected for a moment, maybe I could learn more about him. After all, I was putting a lot of trust in him.

One step at a time, I moved away from the door and toward the sound of the sheep. Over the smell of wet wool and hay, I whiffed another scent—the thick, rich odor of fresh blood.

My stomach heaved, bile crawling up my throat. I wanted to leave, to turn and run. But I moved forward, past an old cupboard and grain bins to where a pile of hay bales blocked my view of the rest of the barn. A fly settled in my hair. I waved it off, then leaned forward and peered out.

Right in front of my face, a gutted sheep hung from a beam. Blood trickled out of it and into a basin filled with glistening intestines.

I covered my mouth and nose with my hand and swallowed the urge to vomit. The sheep didn't just look gutted. Its hide was mangled. Snapped ribs protruded at odd angles, bloody and raw.

A yard away, Chase stood with his back to me. His neck shone with sweat. Blood coated his hands and speckled his arms. He grabbed a rag and wiped it slowly across his knife's blade, meticulously, lovingly.

With my heart in my throat, I took a step back, then another. Maybe this was the normal way to butcher sheep—but I doubted it.

Chase slid the knife into a holster that jutted from the back of his jeans, then wheeled to face me. "You enjoy spying on people."

My eyes went deer-in-the-headlights wide. "No. I—ah."

I dropped my gaze and found myself staring at his low-slung beltline. Quickly, I looked up, past his blood-streaked T-shirt and his scarred collarbone to his steely eyes. This definitely hadn't been one of my brighter ideas.

I squared my shoulders. "I couldn't put off talking to you. Something happened. Can—can we go someplace—less bloody?"

For a long second, his eyes burned into mine, an unfamiliar and unnerving stare that I couldn't begin to read. I clutched my bag tighter. He could be so sweet and just being near him made me want to jump his bones. But that chilling look and hard-edged body didn't come from working out at a gym or by spending his summers sailing. I had the feeling whatever he'd been through before he got here had toughened him more than I'd realized, inside and out.

Chase jerked his head at the far side of the barn to where the rest of the sheep had clustered around an old bathtub overflowing with water. "Let me shut off the hose. Then we'll go to the cottage."

With his back to me, Chase stripped off his T-shirt, then rinsed the blood from his arms and neck with the hose. He grabbed a flannel shirt that lay near the bathtub and flung it on. Without taking time to button it, he turned and marched toward me.

When he got close, his pace slowed. He lowered his eyes and his voice softened. "Sorry I got angry. I can't stand people sneaking up on me." He glanced at the gutted sheep. "When she was born, I had to bottle-feed her for weeks. After I left you and Zach, I found her like this. Mutilated. It isn't right."

I opened my mouth to ask what happened.

But he cut me off. "Let's get out of here."

Chase followed close behind me as we left the shed and went down the path to his cottage. He opened the door and, as he stopped to let me go in first, his hand pressed the small of my back. "I'm glad you trust me," he said.

My knees locked. I wanted to overlook his toughness, his

secrecy, his fondness for knives and everything I'd seen in the shed just now. I wanted to trust the fluttery feeling deep inside of me and think only about the caring things he'd done for me. But I didn't want to be stupid, either. For heaven sakes, he'd even warned me about himself.

Folding my arms across my chest, I turned and faced him. "I promised to tell you the truth, and I need your help. Just don't make me regret this."

Chase pushed past me. "Take a seat. I'll be right back." He strode through an open doorway and into a room at the back of the cottage.

I eyed the couch, covered with an unzipped sleeping bag and flat pillows. I made my way past a coffee table to a saggy recliner. From there, I'd have a clear path to the door, if I needed to run.

"Want something to drink?" he called.

"Yeah," I said, hoping it would buy me a minute to compose myself and check out the rest of the room.

There were free weights and other exercise equipment in one corner. A whetstone, greasy rags, a few hunting magazines on the coffee table. There were no books or pictures or knick-knacks of any kind. There weren't any guns or electronics, or a television, either.

I scanned the room again. The night Dad and I'd arrived at Moonhill, there'd been the blue glow of a television coming from the cottage. Maybe he'd sent it out for repairs.

Chase came back with a bottle of orange soda in each hand and gave me one.

He sat down on the edge of the coffee table, his knees nearly touching mine. "So, what's this about?"

It was now or never. I took my phone out of my bag. "I was hoping you could translate something for me. It's an inscription on a ring that Dad had. It's important, seriously."

He laughed. "You're asking the wrong person. Try Zachary.

The kid knows a dozen languages. Or the Professor, he's a whiz too."

"It's Arabic, kind of."

"Oh." He set his soda on the floor and held out his hand. "Let me see it."

I pulled the image of the inscription up. But as I started to hand Chase the phone, my eyes lit on his collarbone scar. I could only see part of it sticking out from under his unbuttoned shirt. But it had the exact same jagged shape as the letters on the ring. And it wasn't a scar. It was wider than a mark a knife might make and uneven, like it was burned into his skin above his collarbone.

I yanked the phone away. *"He belongs to them,"* Dad had said about Chase.

It wasn't a scar.

It was a brand.

Chase's eyes were hot on mine. He snatched the phone and looked at it.

Unable to think, I watched, waiting for him to make the first move.

His face went rigid. He touched the brand. "Yes. I know what the inscription says. And yes, its first word and my mark are the same. But you already guessed that."

"No, at least, not until now." My hand trembled as I opened the soda and decided what to ask first. "What language is it?"

His lips tensed. "It's an ancient form of Arabic. A distant cousin to Sabaean."

Silence hung between us, tense and thick, as he once more stared at the phone. His cheek twitched.

"Chase?" I said. "I don't get it. You're trying to learn modern Arabic, but you can translate a weird sixth-century form with ease."

I set my soda on the table next to him. Despite the fact that

I was certain he could snap my neck in a second, despite him working for the family, and a bunch of other things, I was certain he'd been honest with me. So I decided to trust the flutter—and him.

"I'm scared, Chase. There are strange things going on around here. But more than anything, I'm terrified for my dad. I saw how you looked at him the night we arrived. I know you don't like him for some reason. I need you to tell me the truth. I'll tell you all I know about my mother's death, and I know more than I did at the mausoleum. But I have to know what the inscription says and how you can be so sure."

For a long moment, he didn't say anything. Just when I was beginning to think he wouldn't answer my questions, he ran his hand over his head and sighed. "You won't like what I have to say." His voice was low and for the first time since I met him, nervous.

I rested an encouraging hand on his arm. "Tell me."

"English is my first language, or it was when I was little and lived not far from here. But then I was taken from my mother." He paled and glanced at the phone. "This is my first language now, at least when it comes to writing."

"That doesn't make sense. It's a dead language, right?"

"Not exactly." Chase got to his feet. "I'm assuming your father got sick after he bought the ring?"

"Yeah."

"Earlier, you asked me to promise that you wouldn't regret telling me the truth. That's a promise I can't make. I have my own regrets and debts." He tucked my phone in his pocket. "We have to show this to your family."

For a moment, utter frustration stole my ability to say anything. On one level, I knew he was right. Then, anger boiled out of me. "Chase, they lied to Dad about how my mother died!"

He turned away and headed for the door. "We'll take your car."

Grabbing my bag, I rushed after him and snagged his arm. "All right. Fine. I'll go with you. We'll show it to them. But first, tell me what it says."

All emotion drained from his voice. Though his body stood in front of me, it was as unreadable as if his soul had gone into hiding. "The slave is the master and the master is the slave."

The words jumbled in my head, nonsensical and at the same time horrifying. The slave is the master. "What does it mean?"

"Your father is possessed, Annie. But no Christian priest can free him. Let your grandfather explain the rest. It won't be easy to accept." He rested his fingers against my cheek. "I really am sorry."

I closed my eyes, feeling the heat of his touch as fear and worry chilled me to the bone.

"I don't hate your father," Chase said quietly. "That night when you arrived, he drew something on the car window."

My mind went back to that moment, Dad drawing jagged lines on the misted glass. My eyes flashed open. "Your mark."

He nodded. "Your father recognized me that night. But I'd never met him before."

"Chase?" I let my eyes find his. "I won't ask anything else. But your mark, it's a brand, right?"

"It marks me as their slave, Annie. A slave to things like what's inside your Dad."

CHAPTER 16

*Hecate, Queen of the Sky, Protector of the Gateways,
of earth, heaven and sea.*

—Invocation to the Goddess

Once we got to the Mercedes, Chase used my phone to call Kate. He explained about the inscription and asked her to find Grandfather and meet us in the study. Then, as I steered the Mercedes away from the cottage and started up the hill, he slouched back in the passenger seat.

I wanted him to start talking again, to reassure me he was no longer a slave. More than that, I wanted to know who or what he was talking about. A creature that a Christian priest couldn't exorcise. An ancient form of Arabic. The thoughts twisted in the back of my mind, but I couldn't make heads or tails of them.

I cleared my throat. "I'm sorry about the sheep," I said, hoping a temporary shift in subject might draw Chase from his silence.

He shook his head. "I told your grandfather and Kate about your father's drawing. They thought I was imagining things. You know, they thought I was being paranoid."

"I can see how you might be. It must have been horrible.

A slave, it's hard to believe. But you escaped, right?" My fingernails dug into the steering wheel as I gathered my nerve. "Chase, you have to tell me, what kind of things or creatures are you talking about?"

"I can't. I owe Kate and your grandfather that much, and a lot more. If it wasn't for them, I wouldn't be free, Annie."

Silence settled around us again, but this time I let it win.

When I pulled the Mercedes up to the front door, Chase leapt out and barely waited for me to follow him before he strode toward the study.

Kate was waiting in front of the fireplace. While Chase handed her my phone, I settled down on the settee next to Grandfather. I wasn't about to stand up through this discussion.

After a moment, Kate let out a long breath. She gave the phone to Grandfather, and I helped him enlarge the inscription so he could get a better look.

"Who else has seen this?" she asked me.

I shrugged. "Dad, of course. A guy I know who's an intern at the Metropolitan Museum, his supervisor—who claims the ring was stolen from the Met—and the woman I sold the poison ring to. Dad's lawyer knows about the inscription, but I don't think he has a copy of it." I hesitated, then added, "Wouldn't he have given it to you if he did? He is your spy, right?"

Kate snorted. "Spy? That's a bit melodramatic. Yes, he works for us. But it's not like your father wasn't fully aware of it."

"You're lying," I said. "Dad would never have allowed that. He never wanted anything to do with the family."

"Not us, perhaps. But he didn't lose his fondness for our money."

Grandfather glared at Kate. "All right, that's enough." He turned toward me, his gaze still unyielding. "Kate's not lying about the lawyer. He deals with legal and financial matters for us and your father. Your father may not have wanted to have anything to do with the family directly, but the lifestyle and advantages you grew up with wouldn't have been possible without the supplemental income from his legacy, an income source you apparently were unaware of." He raised a finger to emphasize his next point. "That, however, is not the issue at hand."

Chase came away from the fireplace, like he'd been waiting for the chance to jump in. "Now do you believe me about the drawing on the window?" he said to Grandfather. His voice was solid, but he lowered his eyes like a humbled servant.

"We didn't totally disbelieve you before," Grandfather said to him. Then to me, "We honestly believed the problem stemmed from the church purchases—until you mentioned the shadows in his room and your father's worsening condition. We haven't had an issue like this for over a decade. Whereas we quite often run into Christian demons and their ilk."

Frustration got the better of me. I jumped to my feet. "Fine, I can accept all that stuff you just said about the lawyer and the legacy. But stop with the vague statements. Tell me what's going on. Christian demons, their ilk, inscriptions, supposedly stolen poison rings that aren't really poison rings. The shadows. A thing inside my dad."

Grandfather raised an eyebrow at Kate.

"It's up to you," she said. "I was against this from the start, but now that James is here and other things are out in the open." She pinched the bridge of her nose like she was staving off a headache. "Stephanie is one of us."

Grandfather smiled at me. "Indeed, she very much is." He motioned to the seat next to him. "Sit." He frowned at Kate and then at Chase. "For that matter, why don't all of you sit? Let an old man stand up and pace around like he's the king of his own castle for a change."

Once everyone was seated, Grandfather handed the phone back to me, then positioned himself with his back to the fireplace. "The poison ring, Annie, is actually a seal of sorts, a per-version as it were of the Ring of Solomon. Are you familiar with it?"

"I've heard of it. Solomon was in the Bible, right? But the inscription is in Arabic."

He stroked his chin. "I know nothing about the sort of spir-itual education your father gave you. But I assume he taught you to keep an open mind. Respecting all religions has been the backbone of our family, for each spiritual path has its own ele-ments of truth."

I nodded. Actually, I could now see how all our trips to museums and historic sites, churches and temples, reenact-ments, and all of Dad's lectures about culture and civilizations had centered on that very point.

"That being so," Grandfather continued, "it's easy to under-stand that there are places besides Heaven and Hell, that Adam and Eve and the snake were not the only beings present in the Garden of Eden. Other powerful creatures were cast out that day as well, and another place most Christians do not speak of was created: the realm of the djinn. Beings made of smokeless fire, powerful, conniving, and with free will just like God gave to human souls. Beings, some of whom can only appear in the form of shadows."

The air crushed out of my lungs as I gasped. "You're talk-ing about genies?" If Grandfather hadn't sounded so deadly serious and if anyone else had cracked a smile, I might have laughed. But instead, terror—as real as my fear of the dark—closed in around me. Some of Dad's most horrifying stories had involved Moonhill's cellar and the jars full of genies that were kept there, like an army of deadly preserved tomatoes or pickles.

Kate pursed her lips. "We're not talking Disneyland genies. The Devil doesn't even cross the border between his realm and theirs. But the djinn dream of one thing: claiming our world."

The whole idea was so overpowering that I could barely begin to comprehend what they were saying:

The djinn were real.

One of them had possessed Dad.

Chase was marked as their slave, but had somehow escaped.

As if he sensed me thinking about him, Chase added, "If your family hadn't helped me escape and given me a safe place to live, I'd still be imprisoned in their realm, or dead."

I pressed my palms against my cheeks. This was all so unbelievable—and it explained a lot, but there was so much more. I turned to Grandfather and steadied my voice. "So—so you're saying the ring somehow allowed my father to be possessed, by a genie?"

"To a degree," Grandfather said. "My best guess would be that the poison ring, like the lamp in the *Tales of the Arabian Nights*, held a genie. I suspect the genie fully intended to end up in your father's hands and to trick your father into allowing himself to be possessed."

I scowled. "That's ridiculous. The last thing Dad would have ever wanted was to become ill and be forced to move back here." I clamped my mouth shut. That was pretty rude.

Kate glowered at me.

Grandfather continued like I hadn't spoken at all. "The djinn are devious, and they've spent eternity spying on mankind, studying our weaknesses. We won't know for certain what happened or how to rectify this situation until we look into it further and do a bit of research. It's likely the ring and its inscription can be used to control the genie, but not while he's inside your father. If your father allowed the possession, then it won't matter what religious prayers or tokens we try. The exorcism will not succeed." He cocked his head at Chase. "Kate said you found a mutilated sheep."

"Near the graveyard." He rubbed his collarbone. "It was

ripped open and the heart was missing. It looked like their handiwork to me."

A sick feeling churned in my stomach and I hugged myself as an image of Chase wiping off his knife flashed through my mind. I didn't think Chase was lying about who mutilated the sheep. Still, it didn't make sense. "Dad wouldn't have done that. He loves animals."

Chase grimaced. "I'm sorry, Annie. It was him. Genies enjoy a lot of things humans find disgusting."

Kate got up from her chair. "More unpleasantness, that's just what we need." She squinted at me. "You do know not to say anything about this to anyone?"

"Of course," I said, a touch sarcastically.

"In particular," Grandfather raised his voice above Kate's. "We must all act as normal as possible around James, even if we notice the genie's personality coming through. Understood?"

I understood that perfectly well, but I also understood something else, which was as noticeable as the polar bear in the foyer. They still weren't telling me everything. For example, they hadn't mentioned the shadow in the gallery—and I was certain Olya hadn't kept that tidbit to herself.

And until I had a better idea what was going on, wise or not, I was going to keep the few secrets I had to myself—like what I'd discovered about the gallery and Mother.

Besides, could I even believe they were telling me the truth about genies?

CHAPTER 17

He who does not ask will not find answer.

—Fortune Cookie. China Wok
Port St. Claire, Maine

The first thing I did when I left the study was head for the solarium. It was quiet and peaceful, the perfect spot for undisturbed thinking, and I suspected Selena would pop in if I went back to my room.

I made it through the foyer and out onto the terrace without running into anyone, but as I opened the solarium door, Laura raced up behind me.

"Great. I found you. We're not having a formal dinner tonight, so your aunt Olya's invited you to have supper in their apartment. I'm taking everything up right now. I could use an extra pair of hands since Tibbs is with your father."

I forced a smile and said, "Great." Crap. Family night with Selena, Zachary, and their witchy mother was the last thing I had time for. But I couldn't refuse to go. I'd look like a total ass, and Selena would never talk to me again.

"Hurry," Laura said. "There are homemade French fries and onion rings. They won't be any good if we let them go cold."

I shouldered my bag. "Sounds wonderful."

Once we got to the kitchen, Laura handed me a tray of

condiments. "You take this. I'll get the cart," she said. Then she walked straight toward a wall.

For the life of me, I couldn't figure out what she was doing until she pressed a small red button and the wall slid open to reveal an elevator and a waiting cart, loaded with covered dishes and drinks; then it seemed obvious. An elevator made sense for such an enormous house. And if there were other elevators, it might explain how people vanished and appeared with such ease, though I hadn't come across one when I'd searched Kate's study.

I took a deep breath as Laura bustled into the elevator and waited for me to join her. A couple of years ago, Dad and I'd gone into an old warehouse to bid on a storage unit. We'd gotten into a rickety freight elevator and the only lightbulb had been burned out. I'd totally freaked. If this elevator was as dark as that one had been, there was no way I could hold the tray and reach for my flashlight. And this time Dad wasn't here to talk me down.

I craned my neck to get a good view of the interior.

Light glistened off steel and mirrored walls. Nice and bright. Not at all like the nasty freight elevator.

Making sure I didn't sideswipe anything with my bag, I squeezed in next to the cart. As the doors closed, the mouth-watering burger-joint smell coming from the covered dishes made my stomach rumble, as loud as Selena's had done the other day.

"Sounds like dinner isn't coming any time too soon for you," Laura said.

"It does smell wonderful," I admitted.

She beamed at me and began fussing with the linen napkins. I stared up at the ceiling and waited for the elevator to stop. Although the elevator didn't make any noise, my stomach felt like it was being yanked toward my toes, so I knew we were moving upward.

A suspicion nipped at the back of my mind and I let my gaze drift downward, along the shiny walls to the carpeted floor. I couldn't figure out what it was, but something about the elevator's design felt off.

I glanced up at the ceiling again to check if it was abnormally low. It didn't appear to be.

I scanned the buttons to check if the number of floors I assumed Moonhill had matched the number of stops. Basement. Kitchen. Second floor. Third floor. No hidden lower levels or secret stops between floors.

Laura tapped one of the covered dishes. "There's a special treat in here. Blueberry cobbler. It's your uncle David's favorite. He just got home, but I'm sure he'll be joining you for dinner."

Fear rushed through me and my mouth dried. David was supposed to be off tracking down the ring. If he'd already acquired it, then it seemed like Grandfather or Kate would have said something instead of spending so much time looking at the inscription on my phone. Damn it. Something was wrong.

I put on a cheerful voice. "It'll be nice to meet him," I said. To hell with secrecy, I'd obey Grandfather and not say anything to Selena or Zachary, but I'd straight-out ask David what had happened. This wasn't good. Not at all.

A moment later, my stomach stopped rising and went back to where it belonged. The elevator clunked and the doors whooshed open, revealing the alcove near my room.

As Laura pushed the cart into the hallway, a thought struck me. It wasn't connected to the ring and didn't seem connected to my suspicion about the elevator but, with all the mysteries going on, perhaps it was. "Do you mind if I ask you a question?" I said.

"Go right ahead, dear. I'd be happy to help, if I can." Laura sounded willing, but she blinked like someone who was preparing to lie if need be.

"Zachary said the jars on the mantel in Kate's study are filled with cat ashes. I wasn't sure if he was making up a story or not, and I don't want him to think I'm totally gullible."

Laura laughed. "Zachary is all boy. But this time he's not pulling your leg. In fact, until a few months ago, the brass vase containing your grandmother Persistence's ashes was up there as well. But personally, I'm more comfortable knowing she's resting in the graveyard now."

My fingers gripped the condiment tray so tight, my knuckles went white. The fact that Grandmother's cremains had been put in a similar jar and placed on the mantel next to the cats' made it even easier to believe that Dad wouldn't have questioned if the ashes were Mother's or not, even if he didn't believe the story about how she'd died. Poor Dad. Poor Mama. What had happened to her body? An overwhelming surge of emotions crashed over me: love, fear, sadness, anger. How different all our lives would be if none of the lies had been told, and especially if Mother hadn't died.

I paused for a second to settle my nerves and free myself from thoughts of what could never be, then I hurried a couple of steps to catch up with Laura.

The apartment was at the end of the hallway, like Olya had told me. It was huge, the size of a New York City penthouse, with pillars dividing a formal living and dining room. A gorgeous crystal chandelier hung down from an ornate tin ceiling and the tall windows revealed a view of the crescent-shaped hill and the ocean to the south.

The furnishings were as amazing as in the rest of the house, but here they reflected a love of the Empire period, and someone's obsession with silver tea sets and eggs: marble eggs and jeweled eggs and amazing eggs painted with intricate designs, displayed in primitive carved boxes and under glass domes.

Olya raced out from an open doorway. "I'm so glad you're here," she said to me. "Come, David's dying to meet you."

Making sure nothing toppled over on my tray, I followed her and Laura through the open doorway and into a basically normal den with cushy chairs and a big couch, a jumbo-size television and a computer desk. And a fish tank full of what appeared to be leeches. I bet Tibbs avoided them like the plague.

A man I assumed was David and Zachary sat on cushions around a low table. It looked like it belonged in a Japanese restaurant, except on top of it was an antique checkers-like board game.

Zachary pointed at the game. "See what my dad brought back from his trip. Sweet, huh?"

His dad gave me crisp nod. "Glad you could join us." With his polo shirt and white shorts, it appeared as if he'd just come back from playing tennis. But the sling on his arm, the fresh cuts and bruises on his face told another story.

"Um—I'm glad you got home fine," I said. No one else was mentioning his injuries, so I didn't either. I set the tray down and casually went on, "I'm guessing you didn't find what you were looking for?"

He ran his hand down the sling and studied me as if deciding whether to answer or not. Finally, he relented. "Actually, I did. I haven't seen it yet, but it'll be arriving here later this evening."

Relief flooded through me. "That's fantastic. Thank you. Thank you, so much." I stopped for a heartbeat, tempered my joy, then continued more discreetly, "You didn't happen to find out where my father got it?"

Before he could answer, Zachary interrupted. "The game's called Petteia. I can show you how to play, if you want." He waved one of the game's pebble-like pieces for me to see.

Frustrated, I gritted my teeth. "Not right now. Maybe later."

"Achilles and Ajax played it during the Trojan War." He waggled his eyebrows. "I think it'll get me extra credit from the Professor. It's so cool."

Olya began helping Laura unload the covered dishes. "Cool or not, you have to put the game aside for supper." She patted my arm. "Selena's bedroom is around the corner. Do you mind telling her dinner's ready?"

"Sure," I said. I looked back at David and jumped in with both feet. "A friend of mine told me it was . . . Ah-umm. Was it stolen from the Met?"

Zachary's eyes bulged. "What? My game?"

David's lips locked together as tight as if he'd sealed them with superglue. Just when I was a hundred percent sure he wasn't going to answer, he said, "Don't worry, your reputation is golden. It wasn't taken from there—or from anywhere else, at least in the last hundred years or so. It most definitely isn't a forgery, either."

"That's wonderful," I said.

His brows lowered and he gave me a disapproving glare. The message was clear. Sure, part of him was glad to meet me. But the other part wasn't going to let me off the hook that easily. I'd screwed up, big time. And, for that matter, Dad had too.

I dipped my gaze to show him I was sorry. When he didn't say anything to indicate forgiveness, I looked back up. He'd turned away and was taking a sip of his cocktail. Yup, I was on his shit list for sure.

Leaving him behind, I went to tell Selena dinner was ready. I found her lying on her four-poster bed, listening to something on her iPod. When she saw me, she took her ear buds out. "Hey, I was looking for you a little while ago. Where were you?"

I shrugged. "I went for a walk."

"Is that all? Zachary told me you were at the mausoleum, and not just about the break-in." She rolled her eyes. "You and Chase, again?"

"Zachary's lying, unless the other thing he told you was about the dead sheep Chase found."

She wrinkled her nose. "Didn't hear about the sheep." She swung her legs off the bed and lowered her voice. "We need to find you a crush-worthy honey, and fast, like tonight." She wiggled her fingers so I could see her freshly painted nails, the same shade of red as my vintage spikes she'd wanted to borrow. "The movie theater is having an after-midnight showing of *Zombie Bride Reanimated*. Everyone's going to that, then to a beach house. It's going to be epic."

"Sounds like fun, but I'd fall asleep before the movie even started." I wasn't sure what Selena was up to, but I didn't have time for it.

Olya's voice came from the other room. "Supper's getting cold, girls."

I stepped toward the door, but Selena leapt from the bed and snagged my sleeve. "Not so fast," she said in a hard whisper. "Me and you need to have a little talk first."

Startled by her change in tone, I pulled free and stepped back. "What's wrong?"

"What's wrong? You didn't see my father? He just got back from a family business trip. He almost died this time—and it's your father's fault. If your father hadn't deserted the family, my dad wouldn't end up doing everything on his own. It isn't fair."

I blinked at her, trying to make sense of what she'd said. Maybe my dad was responsible for her dad getting hurt this time, but that didn't seem to be what Selena was talking about. I suspected she meant family business trips in general, and I also suspected it wasn't my dad or me that she was really pissed at.

I lowered my voice. "I'm sorry about your dad. But what's really going on?"

She sank back down on the bed, her face in her hands. "My parents don't give a crap about what I want to do with my life.

All they want is for me and Zachary to take over their precious business, like little clones. Now they're talking about not letting me go away to college at all."

The strength of her dad's disapproving glare came back to me and my heart went out to her. "You need to stand up to them. What they're doing isn't right. It doesn't even make sense. Most parents would be thrilled if their daughter wanted to go to college, especially for medicine."

Selena lowered her hands, and a sly grin replaced her look of anguish. "If your father got better and stayed—or if you didn't desert the family like your father did. If you stayed, then you could join the business—and I could go to college."

I folded my arms across my chest. No amount of moodiness or bullying or guilt was going to make that happen. Once Dad was better and I knew the truth about Mother, I was out of here—even the hots I had for Chase wasn't going to stop me.

In a dizzying rush, the bond I'd felt when I looked at my ancestors' gravestones crashed over me, how all those people from Dad's tales—the treasure hunters, the pirates, the agents for the Vatican, the advisors to kings—centuries of Freemonts had felt real, and I'd felt a part of them. What harm could a little fib do? At a minimum it would make Selena feel good. At best, I might learn something more about the family.

I drummed up my own sly smile. "Who knows, I might stay. It's kind of hard to say. I mean, I'm not even sure if the family is still into salt mining or if funding the archeology digs is just for charity or if there's profit involved."

Selena's smile widened into a wholehearted grin. "We buy and sell stuff, pretty much the same as you and your father do. Some of it has to do with archeology, some of it doesn't, I guess. I really don't know much about it, except sometimes Dad goes to some dangerous places. They mostly treat me like a mushroom. You know how the rest of that goes."

"Yeah, they keep you in the dark and feed you shit."

Selena nodded. "Exactly."

"Girls!" Olya shouted. "You have one second."

She rolled her eyes again. "We better get going." She slung her arm over my shoulder and pulled me into a half hug. "Sorry about the bitch attack. It's just"—she hesitated for a second—"when Dad got home, he didn't say a word about what happened to him. He just started ragging on me about acting responsible and crap. Sometimes I wish he wouldn't come home."

I hugged her back. I could tell she didn't really mean that.

All through dinner my mind kept wandering from Selena's dad to my dad and genies, to what exactly a *normal* family's business trips might entail: probably not dangerous trips to exotic places, archeology, and supernatural mysteries. It actually sounded more intriguing than being an appraiser.

Luckily, no one noticed I was only half paying attention. Not that they ignored me, but they were busy talking about family things: whose turn it was to clean the leech tank, the new curtains Selena and Olya had bought in Bar Harbor, Zachary's chipped tooth. As Olya served up the blueberry cobbler, I sat back in my chair and watched. It was freaky how they simply didn't talk about the weird stuff and how much they looked like a normal family—or at least what I thought a normal family should look like.

Olya made a joke and I laughed along with them wholeheartedly. Then I sank back into my chair again. More than anything, watching them made me want to see Dad, but not like he was now. I wanted my old Dad. I wanted to eat chocolate doughnuts in the Mercedes and drink coffee laced with brandy. I wanted to talk with him about my career plans, about the legacy, and if I could afford to take a Sotheby's course this fall.

The trouble was, if I didn't personally do something, I might never have my old Dad back. Sure, I believed Grandfather, Kate and even David would try to help him. However, I was also certain they wouldn't risk their own security to do it. But if I could crack open their Pandora's box of secrets, find out what had happened to Mother, then I'd have a bartering chip and could make sure they did their utmost to help Dad. Then, I'd have hope.

And just maybe, if I was really lucky, I could even discover how to help Dad on my own.

CHAPTER 18

Caterpillar to butterfly, grapes to wine, dusk to dawn,
all things transform. All things end and return to their beginning.

—Inscription on Amulet of Transmutation

Once dinner was over, I excused myself and went back to my room. If I was going to crack open their box of secrets and find my bartering chip, I needed to get going.

Since a hot bath always helped me think, I filled the tub and climbed in.

Within minutes, my shoulders relaxed. The steaming bathwater cleared my head, and I let my mind wander through what I already knew. Grandfather had told me quite a bit about genies and the djinn. And I'd discovered a lot about my mother's death.

As I rested back against the tub, it occurred to me that I'd neglected to tell Grandfather and Kate an important detail. Namely, that when I'd spotted the shadows in Dad's room, they'd been moving toward the jar filled with Mother's ashes. Well, actually, a cat's ashes—but it was entirely possible the shadows hadn't known that, either. Grandfather and Kate also had no idea that I'd connected the shadow in the gallery to Mother's death.

Despite the heat of the water, I shivered. I scrambled to my feet and got out of the tub. I had nothing solid to base my suspicion on and no idea what it meant, but it was uncanny how

I'd seen the shadows in two places connected to my mother. And it was interesting that the one in the gallery had looked distinctly larger.

I threw on my sweats and hurried into the other room. It was probably a good thing I hadn't told them everything. The less they thought I knew about Mother's death, the better. At least for the moment.

Beyond the window, the last of the daylight glistened on the distant ocean.

Any minute now the darkness would fall. After that, even with the lights on, it would make no sense for me to go to the gallery and try to remember what I'd witnessed. Between the darkness and the possibility of seeing a shadow, I'd never relax enough to move past those fears and recall Mother's death, which most likely was equally terrifying.

I snagged my phone and settled into the chair beside the window. In the morning, I would go to the gallery. With the daylight on my side and a flashlight in my hand, there would be less chance that a genie or shadow or whatever they were would manage to sneak up on me, and I would be able to focus better. Tonight, I'd devote my time to learning what I could on the Internet.

Setting the phone on my lap, I closed my eyes. Where should I start? The djinn, the Ring of Solomon, maybe even the *Tales of the Arabian Nights* or non-Christian exorcisms.

I yawned. There was so much I wanted to do, but dinner and the bath had made me sleepy. A power nap, that's what I needed. Ten minutes and I'd be good to go all night.

Taking a long, slow breath, and then another, I drifted off, the shadows, the ring, Selena, Uncle David . . .

The room is bright, but foggy. Uncle David glares at me from across the supper table. He's saying something about the ring, but I can't quite understand him. His voice is too distant, more like the echo of a flute or a whistle, way far off. Now, he's gone and I'm in Selena's bedroom, except she isn't there. Chase is lying back on her four-poster bed with his arms folded behind his head, smiling invitingly at me. But the bed isn't in her room. It's in the gallery. The place is draped in silk and carpets, like a Middle Eastern harem. Throw pillows are everywhere. Blue smoke curls around us. It smells like sandalwood. And there are kittens, Siamese and tiger-striped ones, rubbing against my legs, disappearing under the bed.

And I'm on the bed with Chase now, straddling him, my hands moving up and under his sleeveless T, covering him with warm oil. Under my fingertips, his abdomen is even hotter than the oil, his skin smooth and silky, his muscles taut. My breath catches in my throat at the feel of him beneath me, and my stomach tightens. And an aching need begins to throb and build a bit down lower. My fingertips slide up his chest, defined and amazing. They touch the rough skin of his brand, and his hands clamp both my arms and his voice says something I can't quite make out. I glance up at his face. His beautiful eyes are on mine, blue-gray as the ocean. He licks his lips and in one swift motion, I'm on the bottom and he's on top of me. His mouth on mine, the full length of his naked body against mine. Hot skin against hot skin—

My eyes flashed open. Darkness stared back at me from beyond the window, pressing close against the glass. Holy cow. That was one hell of a power nap. I'd totally gone to sleep and had—Wow. Okay. Maybe Chase was just a tiny bit on my mind.

"Annie?" Selena's voice said. It rose an octave. "You're not dressed!"

I jolted fully awake.

Selena stood next to my chair, frowning down at me. Her hands went to her hips. "Don't try and give me some crap about being too tired."

Thinking fast, I teetered to my feet and held on to the chair for effect. "I—ah—I don't feel good. I think I caught what the Professor has."

"Bullshit. You were fine at dinner."

"Really, I feel awful."

"Newt's going to be pissed. To make up for his brother, he fixed it so you'd ride to the party with one of his lacrosse team friends."

"Please, just stop it. I told you I didn't want to go. Besides, I can find my own guys. And I'm not hung up on Chase." I swallowed hard.

"Yeah, right." Selena bent down and snagged my red spikes. "Stay here if you want to. I'm going to have fun." She stomped out of my room, leaving the door open behind her.

I dashed after her, but stopped in my doorway and watched as she disappeared down the hallway. I understood why Selena was mad at me for not going with her. I understood her swiping my shoes. Still, she really had turned bitchy since her father got home. Maybe it was more than her father harping on her, like mega-PMS or—a thought struck me—maybe Selena had a crush on Chase. She kept trying to fix me up with other guys and had tried pretty hard to make me lose interest in him.

Shoving the door shut, I retreated into my room and yanked the curtains closed. Newt was okay, but he wasn't that great. Selena knew if she went partying, Chase would most likely follow her. Man, would Tibbs be pissed if she and Chase started hooking up. And he wouldn't be the only one.

Squashing that ridiculous idea, I snagged my phone off the chair and flumped down on the bed. Whatever Selena knew or was up to or whoever she had the hots for, wasn't my problem. Not at all.

The glow of the alarm clock on the bedside stand caught my eye. Almost midnight. Selena's parents were asleep and no one else had bedrooms on this side of the house. Chase was busy tailing Selena, so he wouldn't be cruising the hallways.

Cramming my feet into my moccasins, I grabbed my flashlight and crept into the hallway. I didn't dare go to the gallery, but there was somewhere else I wanted to check out. Going there did mean I'd have to face the darkness again, but it didn't involve recalling horrible events from the past.

It took me less than a minute to find the elevator in the alcove near my room. I pushed the down button. Instantly the door slid open and bright light streamed out. A lot of Dad's tales involved Moonhill's cellar. He'd claimed it was a maze of tunnels and rooms that rivaled the catacombs we'd seen under Rome. At its center, supposedly, was a treasury that housed a host of mythical objects.

I pushed the basement button. My stomach rose, then dropped as the elevator descended.

From the mirrored wall, my reflection studied me. A sneaking suspicion about the elevator's design nipped at the back of my mind once more, trying to make connections—just like before when I was in it with Laura.

Dad had always taught me to trust my instincts. Right now, they told me this elevator had something to do with people appearing and disappearing so easily, which was logical. Except, they were also saying the vanishing acts weren't as straightforward as getting in and riding up or down.

My stomach settled and a second later, the elevator clunked and its door whooshed open.

Ahead was a maintenance room with a low ceiling, concrete floor, and storage cages.

The elevator door started to slide shut. I pressed my hand against it, holding the door open so I could use its light to study the room. What met my eyes was rather ordinary. A tool bench with a light fixture over it and a pegboard behind it. A table saw and some other power equipment. Shelves covered with boxes and, on every wall, mismatched doors, all tightly closed.

Still holding the elevator open, I fanned my flashlight's beam across the doors. A couple of them were crude and wooden. Some were made of iron and looked like they belonged in a prison. Over the top of an arched door, I could make out symbols of bees and triangles, just like the ones over Moonhill's main entryway.

The elevator door pulsed against my palm, trying to slide closed. If I let go of it and stepped into the room, total darkness would crash in around me.

Yeah, I could use the hold button, and I had my flashlight. Still, I could feel the chill of the darkness waiting for me to misstep. What if I dropped my flashlight and the shadows were somewhere down here?

I clenched my jaw. This wasn't a time to let my fear win. I could do this.

I took my hand away from the door and dashed for the workbench, switching on the light above it.

Slowly, I turned around.

The puddle of brightness I stood in filtered into the dark room, like a weak streetlight on a pitch-black night.

With my flashlight beam cutting a quivering path, I made my way past the red glow of the elevator buttons to the doorway with the symbols over it. I hadn't really studied the carvings over Moonhill's entry, but in the center of each of these triangles was a pentagram. Definitely not your average door.

Taking a deep breath, I tried the latch.

Locked tight.

I trained the flashlight beam on the old-fashioned keyhole and smiled.

"Thank you, Dad," I said under my breath as I ran back to the workbench. Maybe I wasn't an expert, but this was the same kind of lock I watched Dad pick at the abandoned church and many times before that. And, for the life of me, I couldn't see any sign of an alarm system.

I grabbed a thin screwdriver from a tool caddy, then rifled through the drawers until I found a piece of stiff wire.

Once I got back to the door, I grasped the flashlight between my teeth and went to work on the lock. A second later, I heard the mechanism click open.

Behind me, the elevator made a whooshing sound.

Light flooded the room.

Pocketing the screwdriver and wire, I pulled the flashlight from my mouth and swung around.

Grandfather's silhouette stood in front of the open elevator door. "A creature of many talents, aren't we?"

My pulse drummed in my ears. Damn! No way could I lie my way out of this one.

As Grandfather stepped away from the elevator, its doors remained open and I could see him more clearly. Like the symbols over the door, his backlit outline reminded me of the night Dad and I had arrived at Moonhill—or, more precisely, of the person watching us from the upstairs window.

I straightened up to my full height and toughened my voice as much as I dared. "You've been watching me all along—from the window when we first arrived and after that as well. When you carried my bags to my room, why didn't you tell me who you were?"

Grandfather nodded at my pocket. "You'll want to put those back exactly where you found them. Tibbs is fussy about his tools." His eyebrows lifted. "I suggest you do it now."

I scurried to the workbench and put everything away. He probably expected me to make for the elevator and run back to my room, or to apologize for picking the lock and forget that I'd caught him spying on me. But I'd come here for answers, and I intended on getting them. After all, I was as much of a Freemont as any of them.

I marched back to where he stood. "You told me a few things, but I know there's a lot more going on around here." I pointed at the symbols. "That isn't normal."

"You want to see what's behind the door?"

"Very much," I said. Hopefully this was a good idea and not the stupidest thing I'd ever done.

Grandfather dipped his head. "Go on. Ladies first. Open it."

A warning bell went off in my skull. Grandfather was far too unconcerned about having caught me lock-picking and way too eager to show me around. Still, this might be my only chance.

I reached for the latch. I wasn't going to chicken out. Not with Dad lying upstairs with a creature inside of him. Not until I knew everything.

The latch chilled my finger as I pulled the door open.

Beyond it a dimly lit tunnel arched. Gaudy-colored frescoes and ceiling-to-floor mirrors shimmered on its tiled walls. Only a few yards ahead, an Egyptian sarcophagus guarded one side of the tunnel and a suit of armor stood opposite it. Farther along, I could make out doorways and a wide alcove just before the tunnel curved out of sight.

Grandfather rested his hand on my back and nudged me through the doorway and into the tunnel.

"What is all this?" I asked, my voice quivering a little.

"Our collection," he said. "It dates back to when the first shaman drew on cave walls, to Eden, to ancient China and India, to the Great Father Snake and the Aztecs, and Mayans— to when dreams first entered man's sleep and anointed his mind with myths and magic." His voice rushed and tumbled, then blended into the tunnel's stillness. It sounded like he'd transformed from Grandfather into some kind of otherworldly tour guide. With another touch, he propelled me past the sarcophagus. "Enough of this esoteric mumbo jumbo," he said. "Let me show you our research room."

Sweat trickled down my spine. I hoped I could trust him. But if I was wrong, if he trapped me down here, no one would ever hear my screams. "It's late. I know I was snooping. I'm sorry. I don't want to keep you up."

"Hush, child." Grandfather stopped in front of a fresco that depicted people being burned at the stake and dancing demons. He breathed into his palm, then pressed it against a wall.

The wall slid open.

Beyond it was nothing except blackness.

My hand slithered into my pocket and clutched the flashlight. No. Flashlight or not, I was not going in there—if there actually was somewhere to go in there and not just an eternal pit of darkness. They'd probably already thrown Dad in. Now Grandfather was trying to lure me in as well.

Grandfather stepped forward.

Instantly overhead lights snapped on, throwing daylight-brightness down on everything inside. Surprised, I glanced at Grandfather. He was standing in a small, white-tiled vestibule. Next to him was a display cabinet filled with late-eighteenth-century English china and elaborately decorated eggs. Over it hung an amazing collection of swords. The vestibule itself overlooked an enormous room, which looked like a cross between the engineering deck on a starship and Dr. Frankenstein's laboratory.

"Wow." I stepped out of the tunnel and into the vestibule.

"You wondered what your family did." Grandfather smiled proudly. "I consider myself a sorcerer, though most of my magic is more science than witchcraft. The occult would be Kate and Olya's specialties. Not exactly professions we discuss with anyone, at least until we're sure they can be trusted."

I scanned the equipment, computers and electronic stuff, bubbling vats and giant prisms and copper pyramids. Dad had grown up in the middle of all this. He'd known all along what his family had and was into.

A realization struck me and I turned to Grandfather. "It wasn't just an accident that the genie possessed Dad. The genie wants something you have. Or you have something that belongs to it, like a bunch of jars with its family inside. It's using Dad as a Trojan horse, right?"

"That would be our assumption." Grandfather's shoulders rose in a slow shrug. "For as long as people and other beings have used magic to create tools, our family has sought out those objects, taken them for study, and safeguarded them from being misused."

I resisted the urge to roll my eyes. "Wouldn't it be easier to destroy them? So things like genies couldn't come and take them back."

"There is a fine balance between good and evil. Are we wise enough to judge what should be destroyed and what might be a savior in the future?"

I clamped my mouth shut. Now was not the time to debate about good and evil or if genies in jars were magical tools or living beings. Or why my family had deemed themselves the best guardians for all this stuff. Or why Dad hadn't told me anything. I needed answers I could hold on to, something normal. "I'm assuming Selena and Zachary, everyone knows about this?"

"Each to their own degree. After all, they are family—or in Tibbs and Laura's case, close to it." His lips pressed into a thin line. "Enough questions. It's my turn. Tell me, Annie, can you read Russian?"

I shook my head. "No. Why?"

He frowned. "Chinese?"

"No. I'm not good with languages. I know some French."

He nodded at the display of decorated eggs, every shade of yellow, green, and orange overlaid with black and gold symbols. Almost as many eggs as I'd seen in Selena's family apartment. "Art?" he asked.

"I can paint a little, but nothing like that."

"How about sports?"

Before I could stop myself, my voice turned sarcastic. "I can do the tango in spiked heels. Is that athletic enough for you?"

His frown deepened.

I pointed to the wall. "The second sword down from the top, right below the scimitar with the red symbol on its handle, is a Japanese katana. It could date back as far as the fifteenth century. If you remove the handle, there should be a maker's mark. That would help date it." I nodded at the display of china. "The teacup on the end would be English pearlware, probably 1810. The luster tells me it's unlikely to be a reproduction. It could have been professionally repaired or altered. I'd need a black light to check for that. As for the eggs, they appear to be Russian, but the patterns are unfamiliar, perhaps modern."

"Your aunt Kate's looks and your father's eye. You'd make an excellent fine art appraiser." Grandfather opened his mouth to say something else.

But I'd had enough beating around the bush. I knew where all this was leading. "If you think I'm going to stay here and join the family business, you're wrong. Even if Dad doesn't get well, I'll leave by myself if I have to. I have plans. I'm not going to be a part of this—" I waved my hand at the laboratory. "Madness."

Grandfather tilted his head. "Did I say anything about you being a part of anything?"

"Why else would you show me everything?"

He raised a warning finger. "Kate could wipe your memory clean with one sweep of her hand and give you nightmares at the same time. But Kate's and all of our abilities pale in comparison to the power of the creature inside your father." He took a deep breath. "I'm showing you this because I want you to understand how serious the situation is. You need to do as you are told. Treat your father as if you suspect nothing. Let the rest of us deal with the genie. Don't cause any trouble. No more snooping."

Taken aback by his answer, I fought against the urge to glare. Instead, I lowered my eyes and nodded as if I were agreeing. I understood what he was getting at, but I definitely wasn't going to promise anything. There was too much at stake.

"Now, come along." Grandfather shuffled toward the door.

We walked back down the glimmering tunnel, past the sarcophagus to the maintenance room. Grandfather locked the door, and then we got into the elevator.

With everything whirring around in my mind, I could barely think. But, as the elevator clunked and began to rise, I remembered something.

When Grandfather had caught me picking the lock, I'd heard the whoosh of the elevator doors opening, but I hadn't heard the clunk of the elevator stopping. Clearly, Grandfather hadn't ridden the elevator down from the house above. Which, as impossible as it sounded, left one other choice: Grandfather had walked into and out of the elevator from somewhere else on the basement level.

I studied the steel walls, then the mirrored one. There was nothing that hinted at the presence of a hidden doorway or a latch. Still, especially after what I'd seen in the research room, anything seemed possible.

My instincts drew my eyes back to the mirrored wall.

There were mirrors between the frescoes in the tunnel. In Kate's study, there was a tall one hanging in the bathroom. They were in the library and the gallery as well, all over Moonhill, now that I thought about it. Dad hadn't told me any stories involving mirrors. Still, I couldn't shake the feeling that they were connected to Kate and Grandfather's stealthy movements.

I looked down at my feet and struggled to keep my face expressionless. It would be easier and safer to do as Grandfather had asked and let myself be manipulated by all the half-truths. To play the part of a mushroom and let them keep me in the dark.

But there was no way in hell I was going to do that, not until I uncovered the truth.

The whole truth.

CHAPTER 19

Along with truth there is intentional deception
harbored within myths. For instance: genies and the
three-wish legend. This falsehood is propaganda created
by the djinn, a way to discover a human's greatest
weakness and subjugate a would-be master.

—Persistence Freemont
Notes and Warnings: Otherworldly Encounters

By the time I got back to my room, it was two in the morning. Even the idea of falling asleep was ridiculous. Besides, it made more sense to make up for the Internet time I'd missed earlier in the night.

I climbed onto the bed and sat cross-legged with my phone on my lap.

As I started to search the word *djinn,* the pentagram wormed its way into my mind. I laughed to myself. Only a couple of days ago, I'd freaked when I discovered it. Now the pentagram wasn't even on my list of worries—though I still wanted to know who made it.

It took me only a few minutes to locate a Web site with all kinds of myths about genies and the djinn. Well, not exactly myths. In one of the forums I found countless personal stories of people who'd encountered them. Terrifying stuff, and they sounded pretty real to me, too.

I pulled my knees up to my chest and continued to read. Holy crap. Kate and Grandfather hadn't lied or even expanded the truth about these creatures. They were dead right.

Like Grandfather had said, most types of genies could only appear in the form of shadows, at least in the human world. Some could briefly shape-shift from shadows or mist into animal or human form. But something about them always looked weird—like their eyes or movements—and they could only maintain the solid form for a short time. Cats didn't like genies and could detect them no matter what form they took on. Unfortunately, other supernatural presences made cats freak out as well.

Genies were basically gluttons. They loved human food, liquor, and any kind of sensual experience. They could influence and enter people's dreams, whisper to their souls, and hurt people physically. They could withstand injuries that would kill a human. They could supposedly die if hit hard enough with the stone from a fruit. Like I was going to face down a genie with a cherry pit. Not likely.

Another way to get rid of a genie was to bind it to an object or send it back to its own realm. The Web site, however, failed to mention how to do those things. In general, the djinn were strongest at night and in the dark. Sleeping with the lights on, as it turned out, kept them away. In their own realm, different kinds and tribes of genies fought with each other over territory and supremacy—and slaves. Apparently, there were also significantly fewer female genies than males, which naturally caused some major issues.

Blowing out a long breath, I went on to another Web page. It was hard to know how much of this information I could believe and what was made up. Unfortunately, I suspected the most terrifying stuff was the truest.

I tried another Web page. And, BINGO. Possession and exorcism. Exactly what I was looking for.

According to this article, it normally took months for a genie to gain full control over a human host. Until that point, the symptoms of the possession mimicked dementia interspersed with moments of clarity where the person or genie's presence could break through. Horrifying, but it sure sounded like the way Dad had been acting.

I stared at a medieval drawing of a priest holding a cross over a levitating man's bed. Clearly, the genie inside of Dad wasn't the first to pretend to be a Christian demon in order to fake his own exorcism. If anything, genies weren't stupid, though they were egotistical.

Middle Eastern scholars basically claimed: If the genie didn't want to leave the human's body, it couldn't be forced out, especially if the host had willingly allowed itself to be possessed.

Grandfather had suggested this was what had happened in Dad's case, but it didn't make sense for Dad to allow such a thing.

My legs started to fall asleep, so I lay down on my stomach and moved onto yet another Web site. There I found something particularly interesting. Genies couldn't untie or unlock anything. They couldn't even glide through a room's walls if all the entries to the room were secured with a lock or tie. This was good reason for the genie to need Dad as his personal Trojan horse. Dad had not only grown up exploring every nook and cranny of Moonhill, he could also pick locks and get into places where a lot of people as well as the genie couldn't.

But that still didn't explain why Dad would have allied himself with the genie, if in fact he had.

When I got to the point that all the information I discovered repeated something I'd already learned, I shut off the phone. It was almost four o'clock.

I slid off the bed, went to the window, and opened the curtains a crack.

Darkness owned the garden beneath my window, but ribbons of red and gray streaked the horizon and brightened the tops of the waves. Even thinking about what I should do next made my stomach queasy. However, it was the perfect time. Everyone was still in bed, but nighttime was fading.

Before I could stop myself, I grabbed my flashlight and Dad's razor. Even if it was a flimsy arsenal, it was all I had.

The hallway was silent, except for the pad of my moccasins. Faint light ghosted across the floor and washed the walls. I zigged and zagged. When I came to the threshold of the gallery, I took a breath and kept walking, through a puddle of misty gray cast down from a skylight, past the scowling angels.

I shone my flashlight's beam toward the dark alcove. The goddess, Hecate, Protector of the Gateways, glared back at me. My hands grew slick, and the terrifying feeling of recognition pulsed beneath my skin like a living creature. But I didn't see any trace of shadows. The air felt naturally cool and smelled of nothing besides morning dampness. I could only hope this would remain the case.

Sweat dribbled down my back as I crept toward Hecate and stepped into the small space between her and the alcove's back wall. With my heart pounding in my throat, I followed my instincts and turned around to face the center of the room.

At first, nothing happened. But just as I started to wonder if I was wrong, images began to flash through my mind— faded and slow at first, then faster and faster until they were too horrible to recall—like ripped pages falling from a brittle scrapbook:

My mother. Her hands over her eyes. "Ninety-eight, ninety-nine, one hundred."

Her hands part. "Ready or not, here I come."

The room is hot now. My mother's tanned face is white, pale as the wide scarf wrapped around the man's waist. Pale as the moonstone in his dagger.

He walks toward her. Broad-shouldered. Shaved head. Bare chest.

I've seen him before. Kissing Mama in a moonlit bedroom. They thought I was asleep. Dad wasn't home.

My heart is racing now. Racing and I cannot breathe. This isn't the game we were playing.

He holds out his hand. "No," she says, backing away. There are broad-shouldered men all around her. Dark men, like black paper cutouts. Black like shadows. "Stay away!" she screams.

"Mama!" I shout, running toward them. The glint of moonstone and a knife's blade flashes in my face as he wraps himself around her. A heartbeat later, he vanishes, turning into smoke, a whirling tornado of shadows. I can't see Mama anymore. Just darkness, as thick and real as congealing blood. So real, it burns my nose and eyes. "Mama!" I scream.

The images stopped flashing.

I crashed back to the here and now. Why had it taken so long for me to remember this?

As if in response to my question, the throb of an overwhelming headache came out of nowhere and dropped me to my knees. I buried my face in my hands.

And the flashes began once more:

I lie at the statue's feet. Sobbing. "Mama. I want Mama."

Cool hands touch my hot forehead. Fingers splay, cover my eyes. My eyelids feel oily. Warmth trickles from my nose. I taste blood. I smell violets. Aunt Kate's voice buzzes in my ear. "Hecate, Queen of the Sky, take these memories, Protector of the Gateways, of earth, heaven and sea."

I squeeze my hands into fists. "Mama. Don't leave," I cry.

All I see is darkness.

The memories stopped flashing.

But this time they didn't fade. Everything that had happened that day when I was five years old remained as solid and real in my mind as the djinn. "Mama," I whimpered as real grief hit me, fierce and overwhelming, rocking me to the core.

Suddenly the clip of fast-moving footsteps entered the gallery and headed toward the main staircase.

Drying my eyes with trembling fingers, I shifted farther into Hecate's shadow and raised my head, so I could see who was going through the gallery this early in the morning.

A broad-shouldered man dressed in black stopped beside one of the angels. In the low light, I could only make out his outline. His head swiveled toward me, like an animal sensing a hunter's presence.

I held my breath and stayed perfectly still. But his eyes homed in on me. I recognized him instantly. "Chase," I said with relief.

"What are you doing?" He hurried over. "You all right?"

I sniffed back what remained of my tears and nodded. Even if I'd tried, I couldn't have held back the flood of words. "I remember everything now. About my mother, how she died. They lied to Dad. She didn't fall or hit her head. A genie killed her, and I witnessed it. That's why I'm abnormally scared of the dark."

He crouched in front of me, his face level with mine. "Tell me everything."

"My mother and I were in here playing," I began, then I told him about the shadows and the genie with the dagger, the darkness, and how Kate had wiped out my memory. I told him every detail, even about my fear that Mother might have had an affair with the monster. When I got to the end, I sat back on my heels and squeezed my eyes shut. "I don't know if Kate took away my memories out of kindness, or if she had another reason for doing so." My voice faltered and I opened my eyes.

Chase ran his hands over his head. "Annie, your mother's not dead."

"No." My hands fisted. "You don't understand. There wasn't a body, but I saw the knife. She was fighting him. He was angry.

The ashes Kate gave Dad weren't hers. The sea glass was a bobble off a cat's collar."

"I'm telling you the truth," he insisted.

Heat blazed into my cheeks. "Don't give me the line about her being alive in my memories, like you did in the library. This isn't funny."

His voice was as solid as stone. "No, listen, Annie. I'm serious." He leaned forward and looked me square in the eyes. "When I was a slave to a genie called Malphic, your mother was in his harem. Five years ago, David and Kate tried to rescue her, but she let me escape instead. Until now, I could only guess how she'd ended up with Malphic. That's why I was curious about what you found in the water. I couldn't understand why you thought she was dead. I didn't know that's what they'd told you, or about Kate taking away your memories." His tone toughened. "I should never have let your mother stay behind. I'm going back for her, once I figure out how to do it."

For a second, the world spun around me as if I were riding on some kind of bizarre and otherworldly carousel. My mother, alive and trapped in a djinn harem? Sacrificing herself to let Chase escape. Kate and David's failed rescue attempt. It all sounded insane. So insane, it made perfect sense. My surroundings stopped spinning and slowly came into focus. Drained, I stared at Chase. He sounded so horribly ashamed about leaving Mother. I wanted to reach out and touch his hand, to comfort him. But I was terrified to do anything that might give him pause and make him wonder if he'd already said too much. And I had to know more.

"This Malphic, he was the one who kidnapped her?" I asked.

"You said he wore a white sash and had a dagger with a moonstone in it, right?"

"Yeah." I nodded.

Chase reached into his beltline and drew out a large knife. A moonstone glistened in its handle.

My breath caught in my throat. "That's it. How did you get it?"

He pressed a lever on the knife's handle and the moonstone retreated, replaced by a metal ring with a design at its center.

I glanced from the design to what I could see of Chase's mark. My stomach clenched and the taste of bile crawled up my throat. "That's Malphic's. It's for—"

"The handle's a branding iron," Chase said. He pressed the lever again. This time, the iron retreated and the stone reappeared. He tucked the knife back into his beltline. "Over the years, I watched Malphic use it to mark hundreds of us. Smelled the burning flesh. Heard the screams. But that day—the day I took this from him and your mother helped me escape—he was about to use it on a boy. He was five, maybe six. The same age I was when Malphic took me from my parents."

"You killed Malphic?"

He shook his head. "No." He shrugged. "But I did beat the snot out of him."

"He didn't come after you?"

"His men would have killed me that day, if they'd caught me. But no, Malphic hasn't, and I don't expect him to either. At least not the way you're thinking. Malphic"—Chase rubbed his forearm for a second, then looked up at me and grinned—"he respects strength. To him, triumph is honorable above all else. He sees me as a victor, a champion."

"A champion." Wow. That was amazing. I frowned skeptically. "For beating him up?"

Chase's mouth twisted into a grim line. "Annie, I wasn't kidnapped to be just any kind of slave. I was trained to become a Death Warrior, a gladiator for their pleasure. Malphic would have faced opposition at some point or the other. I just don't think he thought he would lose, and that it would be to me. I was a good fighter, but not the best. To be honest, if it weren't for your mother, I'd most likely be dead by now."

I braced my hand against the floor, a million different emotions and thoughts jumbling inside of me as I struggled to comprehend everything he was saying. The djinn realm sounded so barbarous, so much worse than anything I'd read or heard about before, I couldn't help but wonder how he had survived this long. And how he was able to function in this world at all.

I raised my eyes to his, tears once more threatening. "But why you? Why my mother? Why not someone else?"

With his thumb, he brushed the dampness from the corner of my eyes and a warm feeling washed my skin. "In the case of your mother, my guess is that your family had something Malphic wanted." He pressed his lips together like he didn't want to say the rest. Finally, he went on: "Seduction is one of Malphic's trademarks. He probably kidnapped her out of spite, after she refused to steal for him. He wouldn't tolerate that, especially from a lover."

A shiver went through me, and I felt a bit nauseous. But I was beginning to understand. "You're thinking Malphic didn't get what he wanted by using my mother, so he's trying again, only this time he's possessed my father?"

Chase laughed. "No way. The idea of entering a man's body would disgust Malphic. He's all about virility. His big dream is to be both Father and Master to a new order in the human world. If he seduced your mother, it wasn't simply to steal something. He had to have thought she would produce superior children as well." His lips tipped up into a smile. "She is beautiful, too—like you are."

Caught off guard, I blinked at him as a slow burn swept up my neck and across my cheeks. Then my fingers flew to my mouth, covering a gasp. "My mother. Malphic. Oh my God. He couldn't be—" I hesitated. "I'd know if I was half genie, wouldn't I?"

This time his laugh was more of a deep chuckle. "Annie, you look far too much like a Freemont to be anyone other than your father's child."

I blew out a breath. "This is totally crazy, sitting here with you in this gallery, talking about genies. I can't even believe I just suggested Dad wasn't my father. My mother's alive. It's overwhelming."

His voice once again went serious. "I promise. I'll find a way to get your mother back."

An exhilarating possibility hurtled into my mind and I grabbed one of his arms with both of my hands. "My mother, did she ever talk about me? She didn't give you a message for me, did she?" My excitement plummeted and I let go of his arm. "Sorry. Of course, she didn't. She was imprisoned in a harem and you were a fighter. You didn't really know each other."

"That's not exactly true." Chase's eyes took on a distant look as if he were seeing all the way back to the djinn realm. "She's an amazing woman, your mother. She used to slip away from Malphic's quarters to teach us reading, history, and philosophy. I don't know, maybe Malphic turned a blind eye and let her do it. She did talk about you, sometimes, and when she did, it was obvious she missed and loved you deeply. But, no, she didn't give me a message. There wasn't time for that. Neither of us knew about your family's rescue plan." He bowed his head. "Sorry."

I cupped his chin with my hand, his beard stubble sanding my palm as I lifted his face. Maybe I should have been angry because he was free instead of my mother. Maybe. But his regret was real. And I had no doubt he was telling me the truth. But more than anything, I wanted him to know he could trust me.

"You're right. We do need to free her. And we'll do it together," I said.

His eyes, deep and gray as the ocean, lingered on mine.

Warmth blossomed in my chest, spreading out. I released his chin and shifted in closer, my fingertips grazing his cheek. I wet my lips.

Flinching away, he pulled my hand from his face and held it captive. "I can't let you do that."

My heart squeezed. "Don't shut me out, Chase. I like you."

He rubbed my hand, his voice gentle. "I'm not talking about that. You can't have anything to do with rescuing your mother. It's too dangerous. I'll bring her back. But I couldn't live with myself . . . I couldn't face her if I let something happen to you."

Relief that I'd misinterpreted his words tangled with increasing fear for my mother. "Okay, maybe you're right about the rescue," I conceded. "But no matter what, you're not alone in this. We're together. Right?"

He nodded. Then his brow furrowed and his grip on my hand tightened. "I meant what I said at the party. You don't know me. I'm not normal and I never will be. And that's not something that you, or hoping, or even a magic wand can change."

The sadness in his eyes made my chest ache. "Being a Death Warrior, whatever you went through, it wasn't your fault. You were kidnapped. They did it to you. But you're not a slave anymore and I'm not going to let you just push me away. I'm not afraid of you."

"You should be," he said, his voice pitched so low it sent a chill slicing down my spine.

I sat back, breathing deep. My hands shook and brain staggered, as if I'd eaten a huge chunk of Selena's willow. I needed to focus. *One problem at a time.* That's what Dad would say.

Dad.

I swallowed hard. "I don't know if you're right or wrong, but I can't think about any of this right now. Not while that thing is inside my dad."

"That, I agree with," he said.

A shaft of early morning light slanted through the skylight, casting a stripe of brightness across the floor between us, and bringing with it another reality. It had to be around five o'clock.

"What are you doing here, anyway?" I asked. "Don't you ever sleep?"

Chase grimaced. "I needed to talk to your uncle. Selena's been arrested."

CHAPTER 20

⊕〰️♋♦♌♦□■♦〰️♦●♦□♌♦Ж●♌♦.

What tears also opens. What burns also builds.

—Engraving on the blade of Malphic's knife

Two hours later, I still couldn't get my head around everything I'd learned about the djinn, my family, and my past, not to mention the startling news of Selena's arrest. It shouldn't have come as a surprise after the raid at the beach party, but it had. Chase wasn't sure what she'd been charged with: disturbing the peace, underage drinking, trespassing. Hopefully, it was nothing worse than that. Like drugs, for instance. Her parents had to be pissed.

I padded across the foyer toward the dining room. I'd decided to wear jeans and a simple summer top. Probably there wouldn't be many people at breakfast. Still, it was a day to blend into the background, feel things out, and then decide what to do. It was sheer luck that I hadn't been with Selena when she got arrested.

To my surprise, everyone—including Selena—was already at the breakfast table when I entered the room. The only people missing were Laura and Tibbs, and Dad.

I lowered my head and made straight for coffee at the end of the buffet.

The Professor was there, measuring teaspoons of sugar into his cup.

"Feeling better?" I asked him as I poured my own coffee.

He nodded. "Very much, thank you."

Kate cleared her throat. "It would be nice if you two would finish up and join us at the table."

The Professor took off with his steaming cup and settled into an empty chair. I grabbed my coffee and a muffin and slid into the seat next to Chase.

I tossed him a smile. "Nice to see you're eating with us."

"Yeah," he said, staring at his coffee.

I glanced at Selena. Her head was bowed, and her napkin lay unfolded beside her plate.

Quickly, I scanned the rest of the table. Unlike Zachary, who was devouring his bowl of cereal, none of the adults were eating, and they weren't talking, either. This wasn't just breakfast. This was like a family meeting—or a firing squad for Selena.

Kate tapped her fork on her juice glass. "Now that we're all seated, there are some things that are best discussed as a group."

Out of the corner of my eye, I glimpsed Chase's jaw tense. That was odd. He didn't have a reason to be nervous.

"Our concern is not so much about the trouble Selena got herself into, it's that several of you covered for her," Kate said.

Selena's gaze stayed glued on her plate as her father rubbed her back sympathetically. His head swiveled toward me and he glared. "Selena would never have gotten into this situation if she hadn't been egged on."

I stared back at him. What the hell was he talking about? Sure he didn't like me, but I'd only been here a couple of days and just last night he'd ragged on her about responsibility. I gritted my teeth. This was stupid. What kind of story had Selena told them?

"Chase," Kate said. "You were asked on numerous occasions if there were any situations we should be aware of. You chose to lie by saying nothing."

He admitted his guilt with a nod.

My fingers tightened around my coffee cup. I wanted to jab him in the ribs. Tell him to say something, to defend himself. At a minimum, to say he hadn't forced Selena to sneak out.

My pulse slammed so hard, I felt it in my throat. Maybe I wasn't a part of their family, not really. Maybe everyone would be happy when Dad and I were gone. But I wasn't going to be falsely accused of things or watch Chase get browbeaten for something Selena did. It wasn't like any of them were lily white!

I thumped my coffee cup on the table and snarled at Kate. "You're calling Chase a liar! That's rich coming from you. You lied to Dad. You said my mother was dead and she isn't. You stole my memories! And you lied to me, saying Dad was seeing a doctor who didn't even know his name. What can be worse than that?"

Kate's mouth gaped for a second. Then she snapped it shut and turned to Grandfather. "Like I said before, no manners whatsoever. And frankly, if her father were placed in a mental institution, I suspect his issue might resolve itself in time."

My chair crashed over as I jumped to my feet. "If you think threatening Dad is going to make me become some kind of subservient bobblehead, then you don't know anything!"

Chase shot me a warning glance. Zachary shook his head and emphatically mouthed, *no*.

"No manners?" Grandfather rubbed his chin.

A hush settled over the room.

Selena's head was still bowed. But everyone else stared at me, undoubtedly waiting for me to stomp out of the room or do something drastic. But doing that would feed right into Kate's hands. I had to do the unexpected. I couldn't let them win by playing by their rules.

Biting my tongue to keep from saying something I'd regret, I picked the chair up and set it on its feet. "I'm sorry I got so angry. But if it wasn't for the lies, my dad—"

Suddenly Chase grabbed my wrist and gave it a quick squeeze. "Shush," he said, glancing at the doorway.

I turned to see what he was looking at, but no one was there.

When I looked back at the table, they were still watching me. It was time to switch the topic in a different direction, before my anger returned. "Selena," I said softly. "I'm glad you're okay."

She peeked up. "Thanks," she mumbled. Before I could say anything more, a voice cut through the dining room.

"Hi-de-ho!" Dad's voice came from the doorway. He swaggered into the dining room wearing nothing except a silk bathrobe and more gold necklaces than I realized he owned. Tibbs was two steps behind him. "The lad here was bent on me eating in my ivory tower." He jerked his thumb at Tibbs. "But I said it's time to join the masses. No more sickroom for me."

Fear and anger pulsed through me and I dropped my gaze to his feet. He reminded me of a murderous clown I'd seen in a horror movie, luring kids into a funhouse filled with warped mirrors. This was so not Dad. This was the damn genie.

Looking up, I turned on my best fake smile. "Dad, you look—well."

"I'm marvelous," he said. "Like a new man. It's amazing what a good night's sleep can do." He strode directly up to Kate.

Wide-eyed, she scuffed her chair back. "I'm glad you're feeling well?" It was more of a question than a statement.

"Thanks to your"—he shot Grandfather a wide grin—"both your quick thinking. I don't recall most of it or the last few months for that matter, or even the exorcism, but Tibbs—

kind lad that he is—filled me in." He winked at me. "Looking pretty as ever," he said. Then he rubbed his hands together and headed for the buffet.

As I watched Dad mound food on his plate, I hid my trembling hands on my lap. It seemed like the genie would realize how unlike Dad he was acting. After all, everything he'd done up until now had been above-average clever.

Then again, perhaps some of that cleverness had been Dad's doing and now the genie was the one in full control. There was another possibility as well, something I'd seen happen at auctions. Sometimes a person would start to think they knew everything and were smarter than everyone else. Then their super-charged ego would get the better of them and they'd start making silly mistakes. Just like the genie was doing. Trouble was, those people weren't any less clever. They were just more unpredictable and dangerous than anyone else.

Dad wolfed everything on his plate while talking nonstop about his new philosophy on how personal difficulties can help a man see the foolishness of past resentments.

When Laura wandered in with a fresh pot of coffee, Dad raised his voice. "Bring me a brandy, wench," he said to her. "And there better be mutton on the lunch buffet, or heads will roll."

Laura turned a deep shade of red, but produced a decanter and glass from the sideboard and hurried over to Dad.

"When you're done," Kate said to Dad, her voice a bit more subdued than usual, "perhaps you'd like to take the decanter back to your room. Maybe watch some television?"

Dad closed his eyes, sniffing the brandy fumes rising from his glass. "As enticing as that idea isn't, I think I'll take a tour about this place, reacquaint myself with the collections, and the nooks and crannies."

"I'd be glad to show you our latest acquisitions," Grandfather offered.

"No. I don't think so." Dad took a long sip of his brandy, swooshing it around in his mouth before swallowing loudly.

I raked my fingernails down my pants legs. Dad couldn't just wander around, not with the genie in control of his body.

For a second, my fear let up and a possibility came to me. With the genie in full control, it seemed like whatever came out of Dad's mouth would have to come from the genie's mind. I needed to learn all I could about genies, and who would know more than an actual genie?

"Dad?" My voice quivered more than I'd have preferred. It would be a miracle if I could pull this off.

"Yes, dear." He set down his empty glass.

"Would you like to take a walk in the garden? The sun might feel good after being cooped up in your room for so long." I bit my lip. Maybe that was a bad suggestion, considering the shadows fled from light and genies were stronger at night. But it would get him out of the house and away from the cellar and the treasury where the army of bottled-up genies were undoubtedly kept. And it would give me a chance to quiz him.

Dad shot up from his chair, his necklaces jangling. "What a fabulous idea. These old bones could use a bit of warmth. A nap on a sandy beach would be pure heaven. Then I'll take my tour."

My hand automatically went to my ear and touched where he had sliced me. The beach?

No. I couldn't think about what had happened the last time he and I were there. I had to do this. For Dad's sake. For me and everyone. At least this time the razor was in my pocket.

"Annie," Grandfather said, raising an eyebrow. "Perhaps Chase would like to go with you."

I gave Chase a pleading look. "Would you?"

"You couldn't stop me," he said, already halfway out of his chair.

As we followed Dad out of the dining room, Chase's fingers entwined with mine. I cast him a sideways glance. One corner of his mouth twitched into a smile and he squeezed my hand, which I hoped meant he knew what I was up to. Better yet, that he had an idea of what information we should try to get out of Dad. I sure didn't.

However, I realized we had another problem. Whoever was inside Dad knew Chase was an escaped slave. Maybe he'd attack Chase, for revenge or something. No. More likely he'd pretend to know nothing, at least for the time being.

When we reached the terrace, Dad stopped. Shading his eyes with his hand, he stared out across the gardens toward the ocean. "Beautiful, isn't it?"

He was right about that. Only a few white clouds and soaring gulls dotted the sky. Otherwise it was perfectly clear and blue. The chime of crickets and the scent of roses filled the air. It was balmy, but not sweltering hot.

Still, a chill swept my skin, like cold night air slipping in through a cracked window.

Dad thrust an arm into the air ahead of him as if he were a general leading a charge. "To the beach!" he shouted.

He took off at a trot, down the steps and through the gardens, his bathrobe flaring out as he hurried. Chase and I dashed after him, past the Shakespeare garden, where the vase that had supposedly held Mother's ashes still sat, down the metal steps to the rocky shore and a narrow crescent of sun-heated sand and pebbles, left untouched by the high tide.

With a sigh, he dropped onto a sandy spot and lay back with his arms folded behind his head. "Perfect," he said. "Absolutely perfect. It reminds me of Egypt." He raised his head and looked at me. "What are you waiting for, girl? Sit."

After I scanned the outside of Dad's bathrobe for any suspicious shapes—like a concealed weapon, for instance—I took a deep breath and settled down cross-legged, a few yards away from him. My fingers again went to my ear. He sounded good-natured, but that could change in an instant.

Chase crouched on the other side of Dad.

I raised my eyes to Chase's. He nodded, like he was waiting for me to ask something brilliant. But the only thing that came to mind was how terrified I'd been when Dad had pulled the razor on me.

A fresh jolt of adrenaline shot through me as I realized why Dad had made me open the vase. The genie inside him couldn't open locked things, like a sealed vase. Sure, Dad could, but perhaps not when the genie was in full control of his body like he was right now.

I untangled my legs and drew my knees up close to my chest. Probably the genie hadn't known for sure what was inside the vase. Maybe he thought it held an imprisoned genie that had died. That would explain why the shadow-genies had been so curious about the vase. Or maybe the genie dumped the ashes to show Dad he was in control, as a warning intended to make Dad behave. Whatever the genie's motive was, I didn't have time to try to puzzle it out right now.

I took a steadying breath and pasted on a confident expression, like I was about to talk a customer into buying a chipped piece of porcelain. "I'm so glad you're feeling better," I said to Dad. "You know what I've really missed?"

"What, child?" He pulled himself up on one elbow and gave me a crazy clown grin.

"Your stories. I've been bragging to Chase about them. It's such a beautiful day. Why don't you treat us? Tell us the one about the genies."

His grin narrowed into a sly smile. "I've got a better idea.

Why don't you tell *me* a story for a change? I'd like to hear the one about the Lamp of the Everlasting Flame."

I frowned. "I don't remember that story." It wasn't a lie, Dad never talked about that.

"I think he's referring to the Lamp of Methuselah?" Chase said.

Dad's gaze swung toward Chase, then he turned back and nodded forcefully at me. "Yes. That's it. That's the story I want."

I caught Chase's eyes and gave a slight shrug. I couldn't very well tell a story about something I'd never heard of. Besides, I had the strange feeling the genie was turning the tables on me—like Chase had tried to do with the beer at the party.

Chase cleared his throat. "The lamp was created long before the great flood. It was marked with sacred symbols, and filled with everlasting oil. It's said to burn with a flame as hot and smokeless as the genies who served Methuselah and Solomon. If broken, it will re-form itself and the oil will flow back inside."

Dad fanned his hand over his mouth and yawned. "Boy, your storytelling is as dull as listening to a camel snore. I want to hear the exciting version about how the family found it, the adventure, how it was brought back here—and hidden. I want my daughter to tell it the way she's heard it told to her." He sat up and scowled at Chase. "I've been denied time with my precious child, and I'd like you to leave us alone."

Chase shoved the sleeves of his hoodie up and squared his shoulders. "I don't think that's a good idea."

Dad sat up and folded his arms across his chest. "A bit insolent, aren't you, boy?"

Shit. This wasn't going the way I wanted. Not at all. But if I insisted Chase tell the story, the genie would get angry, and that definitely wasn't good, either.

I held my hands up in surrender. "It's fine, Chase. You have lots to do, and Dad's right, we haven't had any time together since he got well." I looked down, so neither of them would see the fear in my eyes. I could do this. I had to do this. I just had to make up a story. The genie would never know it wasn't real. I had to humor him and in return learn what I could.

Chase frowned at me and got to his feet, looking more and more displeased. "I'd like to hear the story too," he said.

Dad bristled and waved him off. "Don't you have sheep to tend, or boots to lick?"

A muscle in Chase's cheek twitched, and his hand swooped toward his beltline, like he was going to draw Malphic's dagger. Finally, he dropped his arms to his sides and gave me a worried look, then turned and stomped away.

Once the thud of Chase's boots against the stairs faded, Dad settled back down on the sand and closed his eyes. "You may begin now," he said.

Taking a deep breath, I did some fast thinking. Then I began to tell Dad's story about Stephanie Freemont traveling to the Middle East by ship in 1793. But instead of her excavating a cursed tomb and unearthing jars filled with Solomon's wisest and most obedient genies, I substituted it with the Lamp of Methuselah.

As I reached the part where the ship made it through a tempest of demons and anchored off Moonhill's beach, Dad sat up and leaned toward me.

He snagged my wrist. "Tell me the rest quickly, girl. Where did they hide the lamp?"

My gaze flicked to the cliff top, hoping to see Chase's outline. But I couldn't spot even the hint of a human shape.

I pulled against Dad's grip.

He squeezed my wrist harder. "Don't take all day, girl. Did they hide the lamp in the hill of salt?"

I gulped a breath. "They took it to the family mausoleum

and hid it in there. Under the floor. Where it would be safe from those who might misuse it." There, that was a safe ending. But what did he mean by *the hill of salt?* Moonhill? A salt mine, I presumed.

Fury burned in Dad's eyes. His fingernails dug into my wrist. "You're wrong!"

His outburst sent fear ricocheting through me. But I forced myself to look relaxed, blinked a couple of times, and then gave him a doe-in-the-headlights look. "Well, that's the way you always told it. Did you want me to make up a new ending?"

He let go of my arm and leapt to his feet. "Stupid bitch. Can't even remember a story right." He grumbled something about the old fool not having checked carefully enough, then stormed off the beach and up the stairs.

Letting out a relieved breath, I stretched out my legs and rubbed my wrist. Small bruises were blossoming where his fingers had gripped me. I certainly hadn't learned much about genies, but he hadn't learned anything useful about the lamp, either. In fact, it sounded like I'd made him wonder if Dad hadn't checked the mausoleum thoroughly enough. And that wasn't something Dad would have failed to do.

My chest tightened as I recalled Grandfather's warning. *"I want you to understand how serious the situation is. Let the rest of us deal with the genie."*

But Grandfather had let me go with him anyway. And I had kind of won this round, at least I now had an idea what the genie was interested in. Still, I couldn't, not even for a second, let my guard down. He was a genie and I had to fear him with all my heart.

With a sudden shiver, goose bumps rushed across my skin and I trembled. All during breakfast and here at the beach, every second, it had felt like I was with a stranger—and it had been terrifying. The thought of being afraid of my dad forever was something I couldn't live with.

I pulled my knees back up to my chest and hugged my arms around them. I had to keep fighting. I had to.

But if I found a way to get the genie out of Dad, what would be left?

Was my dad even still alive?

CHAPTER 21

*The assumption that magic and science are
not unified is a falsehood that must be overcome
before forward progress can be achieved.*

—General notes on alchemy
Hector Freemont

I stood on the beach, watching a sandpiper scurry along the
waterline, moving in and out with the crashing waves. I needed
to get going, make sure Dad hadn't wandered off somewhere—
like headed for the mausoleum, though I suspected he'd more
likely gone back to his room to talk things over with his shadow-
henchmen. But first I had to unwind for a minute, calm down and
try to make sense of everything I knew so far.

Grandfather had said our family sought out and safeguarded magic objects so they couldn't be misused. Assuming
the Lamp of Methuselah was here, it didn't sound like it could
be that dangerous. In fact, it sounded innocent and handy, like
a self-charging flashlight—though I imagined its real purpose
was much more important than simply casting light.

"Annie!" Selena's voice ricocheted from the cliff top.

I frowned. I didn't have time to deal with her and her bullshit problems. What did she think? That she could use me for
a scapegoat and I'd forgive her a second later?

She dashed down the stairs and across the beach to me. "I feel so awful," she said. "Seriously, I'm sorry I got you in trouble."

I scowled into her sunglass-shielded eyes. "What did you tell your parents, that I forced you to go partying?"

She stuck out her lip in a forgive-me-please pout. "Dad permanently grounded me."

"Well, isn't that too bad?" I said, totally sarcastic.

She shoved her glasses up on her head, revealing tear-rimmed eyes. "The cops handcuffed me, Annie. I was so scared. It was stupid to blame you, but I figured if Mom and Dad—if everyone thought I'd only snuck out a couple of times, like since you got here, then they wouldn't find out about Newt. But they did. Dad took my phone and my laptop. I can't even text him." She wiped her eyes on her sleeve. "Living with them is worse than a jail. You have to forgive me, you have to. I brought your shoes back."

The hitch in her voice and the sincerity in her eyes drained my anger. Although there was no reason for me to forgive her—after all, it wasn't like we'd been friends for years or even spoken before the last few days—I couldn't help but feel that if Selena's parents and all the adults around here had given her more freedom and respect, this wouldn't have happened.

The memory of that day and night with Taj drifted into my mind. He'd turned out to be a total loser and I'd been stupid to have sex with him. But I was glad Dad allowed me to make my own choices, even if they were wrong. Selena had never gotten that chance.

I held my hand out to her. "All right. Friends. But no more blaming stuff on me."

She threw her arms around me, pulled me into a fierce hug, and whispered, "Once this blows over, we'll have to figure out a new way to escape. We'll make sure Chase doesn't see us—or we could ask him to come with us. He's probably mad at me, too."

Wiggling free, I folded my arms across my chest. "I'm sure he is."

She looked down. "I really did make his job harder."

I bit my lip. It wasn't my secret to tell, but maybe she'd be nicer to him if she knew the truth about what he'd lived through. Besides, I needed to get all the information I could out of her and there was no better way to do that than by making her think I already knew as much if not more than she did. "I know where Chase came from—and it has nothing to do with drug cartels," I said. "He was a slave to the djinn."

Instead of laughing like most people would have, she gaped. "Oh my God, that explains a lot."

I didn't stop there. "I know about the research room, too. Grandfather showed it to me." Maybe she didn't know much about the family business, but I couldn't believe that wasn't a secret she'd kept from me.

Her eyes widened even more. "He did?"

"Yeah." I looked away from her, toward the crashing waves and sandpiper scurrying along the waterline. Then I lifted my chin and turned back. "Selena, I'm tired of all the secrets and lies. How about if we don't hide things from each other anymore?"

She smiled. "I'd really like that—like super lots." She linked her arm with mine and snuggled me close. "I need to get back to the house before Mom comes looking for me. But we can talk in my room."

I shook my head. "Maybe later. Right now, I've got to do some research."

"Can I help? You know, make up for being a jerk, and lies and stuff."

"Thanks, but—" I started to say no, that I could do it on my own, but that wasn't the way to keep the door between us open. Maybe it was a good thing for the both of us to work together. Besides, I was getting used to this cousin idea, sort of like built-in friends forever. "The other day the Professor said something about there being an old translation of *Voyages of Sinbad* in the library. Are there other books about myths or artifacts from the Middle East as well?"

"Sure. Some are in the vault, some on the shelves. I could find them for you, no problem."

"Great." I smiled at her. "I wish we'd gotten to know each other sooner."

"Me too."

All the way up the stairs and into the garden, Selena spilled family secrets, about the occult stuff her mom and Kate were into, and how they let her do some basic things. What they were capable of sounded way more powerful than anything that Santeria priest could have done. Of course, that shouldn't have surprised me considering Kate had the ability to wipe out memories.

Selena also mentioned that her mother was the last known practitioner of an ancient magic that involved etching symbols onto eggs, then dyeing them. That pretty much explained the gross colors on Olya's fingers and why Grandfather had asked me about art in the research room, not to mention having decorated eggs all over the house. Finally, Selena confessed that her mother had made the pentagram under my bed, but she stressed that it was for my protection. And this time, I was certain she was telling the truth.

Up ahead I spotted Kate, crouched in front of the Shakespeare garden with a pair of shears in her hand, cutting off spent flower heads or pruning or something.

I leaned closer to Selena. "I need to find out more about the djinn," I said softly.

She snickered. "So you can talk to Chase about his slave days?"

"No." I cuffed her arm and lowered my voice even more. "That's what's wrong with Dad. He's possessed by one of them."

"No shit—I mean, I'm sorry. I thought it was dementia." She glanced toward where Kate had stopped working and turned to look at us. Then she whispered, "If you want to know more about the djinn, you'll definitely need my help. It's not like any of them are going to tell you." She stopped talking and plastered a smile on her face as we neared Kate.

Kate put her shears and a sandwich bag into her gardening basket, and got up to greet us.

"Have you seen Dad?" I asked. I really didn't want her getting suspicious that Selena and I were up to anything.

"Slipped away from you, did he?" She sniffed smugly.

I lifted my chin and took a guess. "Chase was watching him."

"Indeed. He and Tibbs escorted your father back to his room." She narrowed her eyes on me and Selena. "Hope you two are staying out of trouble."

"Definitely," Selena said, pulling me toward the house.

Once the door closed behind us and we were outside the kitchen, I slipped my arm free. "One thing I am worried about is the Professor," I said. "If he's in the library or even the workroom . . . I like him, but we don't need him overhearing what we're talking about."

Selena nibbled her lip for a moment. "He and Zachary were headed that way after breakfast. But I've got an idea." She waved me off. "Go, tell the Professor that we're bored and want to listen in on Zach's lessons—make something up, ogle him a little. I'll be there in a minute. I'm going to make some iced tea for us to sip while we work."

Before I could offer to help, she turned on her heel and whisked into the kitchen. I started for the library. Actually something cool to drink while we researched sounded like a good idea. But ogling the Professor? Not so much.

When the Professor spotted me coming in through the library's door, he set the stack of books he was carrying on the edge of a desk and eyed me.

"Is there something I can do for you, Annie?" he asked.

"Selena and I thought we'd listen in on Zach's lessons today, if you don't mind."

"Unfortunately"—he patted the books—"today is reserved for translating. I suspect you two would find it exceedingly dull unless you happen to have an interest in ancient Greek or Arabic."

"We found it!" Zachary's voice came from deep within the stacks. A moment later, he appeared with a huge brass and leather-bound book in his hands. Chase followed close behind.

I smiled at Chase. "I thought you were with Dad?"

"I was, but he decided to take a nap. Anyway, Tibbs is with him." His gaze flashed to the book Zachary was carrying and back to me, indicating that it was why he'd come.

"Ah, you found it," the Professor said. "Be careful, Zachary. Why don't you let Chase handle it from here?"

"Don't worry. I won't tear it or nothing." Zachary gently set the book down on the desk.

As Chase settled into the desk chair, I squeezed in between the Professor and Zachary.

Chase undid the book's brass clasps and opened it to the first page.

Leaning forward, I studied the lettering. It reminded me uncomfortably of the inscription I'd copied off the ring. "How old is it?"

The Professor slid a finger down the edge of the book. "I would say, very seriously old. But it is not Galland's *Voyages of Sinbad* that I suggested Chase read."

"Whatever," Chase murmured as he turned the page, revealing a detailed woodcut of a man in a flowing robe, cupping a small clay oil lamp in his hand. The lamp's smoke coiled skyward, transforming into the shape of a bare-chested and particularly muscular man with a long black ponytail: a genie. A genie and a lamp.

I glanced at Chase, hoping to catch his eye again. But his head remained bowed over the page.

Zachary wriggled out from between the Professor and me, and went and hung over Chase's shoulder. "C'mon, Chase, read it aloud—in Arabic and English."

Chase frowned at him. "Sorry, buddy. I don't do out loud." He cocked his head at the Professor. "Galland's didn't have any references to Methuselah and that's what I'm doing my report on."

"That"—the Professor's voice ballooned like he was in a lecture hall—"would be because Methuselah is absolutely not in any of the *Arabian Nights Tales*."

Zachary tsked. "Yes, he is. Chase said so."

"What I said, Zachary, was that he should be in them." Chase flipped to another page.

I rubbed my neck. Probably a quick Internet search could prove whether the Professor or Chase was right about Methuselah, but my bag and phone were in my room. I also had faith that Chase knew what he was doing.

Another thought hit me and I glanced around the library. Damn. Why hadn't I thought of that right away? With all the dark corners and book stacks, we'd never know if a shadow was in here, listening to us and gathering information to take back to Dad.

The sound of ice clinking against glass came from the doorway and Selena sauntered in carrying a tray of drinks and pretzels. "Salty and sweet. The perfect brain food." She set the tray down on a stand by the door, picked up one glass, and came over to us. "This is for you, Professor. Extra sweet, just the way you like it. With mint to help settle your stomach."

"How perfectly thoughtful." The Professor took the glass from her and scanned us all. "Remember to be careful. One spilt drink can cause monumental damage in a library."

We all nodded and went to get our own drinks.

As much as I wanted to return to where Chase and Zachary were poring over the old text, I left them to their work and wandered into the stacks with my tea to look for any sign of shadows. All the research in the world wouldn't do us any good if the genie's henchmen figured out what we were up to.

As I reached the back section, the light grew dim. I set my tea on a small stand and skimmed my fingers down the outside of my pocket, feeling the shape of my flashlight.

I sniffed the air, checking for the scent of bleach, like I'd smelled when I almost fainted in Dad's room. Nothing, just the scent of beeswax polish and old books. Not even a trace of must.

I peered through the stacks, looking for dark shapes or movements.

Nothing, again.

The air temperature was normal, and I couldn't hear any strange whispers.

Now I just had to find a way to lock all the doors and windows without the Professor asking what I was up to, then the library would remain a genie-free zone.

"Are you sick?" Zachary's voice filled the library.

The Professor groaned. "No—yes."

I rushed out of the stacks just in time to see the Professor bolt for the door, hunched over, holding his middle like his guts were about to burst. "Must have been breakfast. Oh, my. I have to go. Oh, my." He vanished into the hallway.

Snickering, Selena shut the door. "*Have to go* is a good word for it. Go and go for the rest of the day will be more like it."

I couldn't believe my ears. "You gave the Professor the runs? I thought you liked him?"

Selena shrugged. "He's easy on the eyes. But we've got things to do. Friends forever, right?"

"I don't know what to say." I shook my head in amazement. "It is so wrong, but so perfect."

Zachary flopped down into the leather couch. "It's awesome, that's what it is."

"I'll go along with that." Chase's voice rose a little. "Unfortunately, I'm not finding anything new here."

Selena walked over to the desk and peered at the book. "You're researching?"

Chase glared at her. "I am capable of more than babysitting you."

"I didn't mean you're stupid. I just—I never took you for a library geek." Selena smiled. "Hey, and thanks, I didn't realize you never told them about the beach parties."

I cleared my throat. Chase was willing to help, and so was Selena. It was time for someone to speak up and make this officially a team effort. "I don't know about you guys, but I'm sick of being kept in the dark and lied to by Grandfather, Kate, and everybody else. We deserve the truth, all of us. And we are more than capable of helping." I looked at each of them in turn. "I assume you all feel the same?"

They all nodded.

Zachary pulled up his baggy T-shirt, revealing a Chase-like knife holstered on his belt. "Ready for anything," he said.

"Okay, then, how about for our first assignment we lock all the doors and windows?" I said.

Chase shook his head. "I wouldn't do that. It's too obvious. Leave them the way they are. Trust me. I'll know if we're not alone."

At the party, Chase had heard the cops coming before anyone else. He'd figured out I was in the sheep shed without turning around. Like his stealth mode, his time as a slave and Death Warrior training had probably left him super aware of his surroundings or something. "Fair enough," I said.

After that, I took a few minutes to tell Zachary and Selena all I knew about Dad's possession and my mother's kidnapping, and about the sea glass and the cat's ashes. "Grandfather's supposedly researching ways to help Dad. But I don't think we have that much time. The genie inside him is getting impatient—and bolder. Above everything else, we have to make sure the genie doesn't figure out we're onto him."

Chase confessed to Selena and Zachary that he'd also been kidnapped by Malphic and enslaved for years, and how he'd escaped.

"Way cool," Zachary said.

Selena listened intently and gasped at the right moments like she hadn't known anything. Once he'd finished, she tapped her lip in thought. "If it's not Malphic inside Annie's father, then who is it?"

"Malphic has a son, Culus," Chase said. "Most genies aren't powerful enough to possess a person, but he is. I'm sure he'd do it too. In fact, there probably isn't anything Culus hasn't or wouldn't try—as long as it brought him pleasure." He looked at me. "He also hates your mother because she has influence over his father. If Culus returned home, bragging about how he'd outwitted the Freemont family and stolen from them, he'd gain respect in the eyes of a lot of genies—and upset your mother at the same time."

"So Culus's motive is political?" I asked, unsure I'd followed Chase's logic.

"Partly. I'm also certain it's him for more obvious reasons. Culus likes gold jewelry, wears a ton of it the way your dad was doing earlier. Plus, he has a fetish for ripping open sheep and eating their hearts raw."

I grimaced. "That's really creepy and gross. But it fits."

Chase nodded. "If your father didn't find what Culus wanted

in the mausoleum, it would be like him to take out his anger on Kate's sheep. Using your father's body to do it would have been an added bonus to him."

Zachary pulled his knife from its holster. "If I saw a genie doing that, I'd—"

"You would do nothing," Selena said sharply.

"From what I've read, knifing won't do much good." I paused for a second, gathering my nerve. Hopefully, my Internet research wouldn't make me sound like a total sucker. "Is it true that you can kill a genie with a fruit pit?" I asked Chase.

Selena covered a snicker with her hand. "Sorry, couldn't help it."

"It can work," Chase said, dead serious. "But it's a nearly impossible throw, and the genie has to be in its solid form, not shadow or smoke. Actually, Zachary's right. Stabbing won't kill them, but it'll slow them down." He glanced at me. "A flashlight beam can hold off a weak one, for a while. But the best solution is to trap them or force them into something."

"And salt," Selena added. "There's not a single supernatural being that isn't repelled by salt." She turned to me. "That's why Moonhill was built here. But you knew that, right?"

"Uh—no. I mean, I knew about the mines. But I never stopped to think the family wanted the salt for any reason other than making money."

"Well, they did," she said. "And the underground tunnels and caves that were left behind are pretty amazing too."

I ran my fingers through my hair, thinking. Culus didn't just need Dad for his knowledge about Moonhill and to unlock doors. He also needed Dad's body to protect him from the salt.

Looking back down, Chase flipped to the book's next page and huffed.

I walked over and studied the book. A woodcut of a dragon spreading his wings covered both pages. "What are you looking for?"

Chase flipped back to the previous page. "I read this section a while ago. I remembered there were only two pages about genies. But I was hoping I'd missed something." Hesitating, he rubbed his brand.

"What is it?" I asked.

His voice softened. "If the host willingly allowed the possession, Annie, there's only one way to make the genie leave. The host's death."

My heart leapt into my throat and I grabbed the back of his chair to steady myself. "There has to be another way."

"I'm sorry," Chase said. "As long as your father allowed the possession, I don't think anything else will work."

I stared at the book, strange letters blurring as tears stung my eyes. Death? No. I couldn't believe that. "Why would Dad allow such a thing? He couldn't have."

Selena got up and came over. The warmth of her arm surrounded me as she pulled me close. "We'll figure something out."

"Yeah," Zachary said. "One time, I saw this television show where they killed someone to get the demon out of him, and then they tried to bring him back to life."

"Oh my God!" I shrieked. "That's what Grandfather must be researching, I'm sure of it. They're going to kill my dad. What if they screw up? What if they can't revive him? Dad has a weak heart!"

"The guy in the movie died," Zachary said, his voice quivering.

Selena swatted the back of his head. "Shut up, Zach."

She led me to the couch and cleared away the pillows for me to sit. Trembling, I sank down into it. I wanted to run and find Dad, warn him. But telling him wouldn't free him. It would only put the entire family in danger.

"Don't listen to Zachary," Selena said, sitting down next to me. "He doesn't know what he's talking about."

I rocked forward and buried my face in my hands. "There has to be another way. They can't kill him."

Zachary crouched in front of me. "I'm sorry," he said, then he lowered his voice. "I bet you could trick the genie into coming out."

I sat up and blinked at him. "You're absolutely right," I said, stunned by how much sense his idea made. Why hadn't I thought of that?

"That may sound good, Annie," Chase said. "But if the trick fails, you'll end up with a pissed-off genie. Remember what Culus did to the sheep?"

I gritted my teeth in defiance, my body tingling with renewed energy. What did that matter as long as I could free Dad?

Selena got up and began to pace the room. "If Culus likes human girls as much as his father does, I could try to lure him out."

"No." The last thing we needed was Selena ending up kidnapped like my mother.

She shrugged. "You have a better idea?"

I stared past her to the stacks upon stacks of books. "Grandfather and the rest of them think Culus is here to rescue the imprisoned genies. But when Chase and I were on the beach with Dad, he wanted to hear about something called the Lamp of Methuselah. I made up a story, and when I told him the lamp was hidden in the mausoleum, he stormed off. I think he's after the lamp, not the genies. That's why you were looking for Methuselah as well, right, Chase?"

"Yeah," Chase said. "Not all genies like each other. There

are different kinds and clans. They feud all the time, and steal each other's women and slaves. It's more likely Culus is happy Solomon's genies are imprisoned."

Zachary waved his hand in the air, like a kid in school. "Why don't we just find Solomon's genies and let them go? They'd probably know how to help Annie's dad."

"I said it's *likely* Culus is happy they're captives. It's also possible the imprisoned genies could be a worse threat than Culus or Malphic."

I flopped back against the couch cushions and let out a long, dejected breath. "So this lamp, is it good for anything other than brightening dark places?"

Chase held his hands up in surrender. "Beats me."

"Maybe it can be used to see into the future?" Selena suggested.

I let my mind wander again, this time thinking about the Middle Eastern exhibit I'd seen at the Met last winter. The dark pottery, the jewelry, and the small terra-cotta lamps that a man could hold in the palm of his hand, like the man in the book's woodcut was doing. What did that lamp and the one in the museum have in common? What made the Lamp of Methuselah—the so-called Lamp of the Everlasting flame—different from other lamps?

"The oil!" I said, excitedly. "That has to be it."

"What?" Chase's brow wrinkled.

"The everlasting oil. It's not the Lamp of Methuselah itself that's special, other than that it can reassemble itself. It's the oil that burns forever without running dry."

Chase closed the book and got to his feet. "That makes more sense than you know."

"You've lost me," Selena said.

"I don't remember everything about when Kate and your father came to rescue Annie's mother. But I knew right away there was something off about them." Chase half-sat on the edge of the desk. "In the djinn realm, most humans appear as smoky shadows, the way most genies do in the human world. But, like some genies, some humans can maintain solid bodies for maybe an hour at the most."

Zachary sighed. "So what does this have to do with my dad and Aunt Kate?"

"When I saw them in the djinn's realm, they didn't look like shadows. They had solid bodies and looked exactly like genies. They wore the right clothes. Their hair was right. No one would have guessed they weren't genies, except they smelled bad—like wet sheep, cloves, and cabbage. Genies do nasty things, but they never have body odor like that. I'm certain it was their smell that gave them away to Malphic."

"What does body odor have to do with lamp oil?" As soon as the words were out of my mouth, the answer came to me. And everything I'd learned at the Met's exhibit snapped together, suddenly making sense. "Oh! A sheep smell as in lanolin, as in sometimes used as a lamp fuel back in Methuselah's time. You think Kate and David covered themselves in the oil to give themselves solid bodies in the djinn realm, but it also made them stink?"

"Exactly." Chase grinned. "Plus, I'm betting if the oil gives humans solid bodies in the djinn realm, then it will have the opposite effect on genies here. In other words, the oil will give them solid bodies in the human world. Since the oil is self-renewing, Culus would have an endless supply, enough to create an army of solid-bodied genies. People might overlook a few shadows, but they'd bow in terror if faced with an army like that." His eyes went ice-cold. "Like I said before, Culus has always wanted to prove himself. Taking over even part of the human world would do that and more."

With fear settling in the pit of my stomach, I got up from

the couch. I didn't trust Kate or David. I only half-trusted Grandfather, maybe less now that I'd figured out what he might have had planned for Dad. Still, I couldn't afford to make a mistake.

"I have an idea," I said. "But we have to find out from Grandfather if we're right about the oil. And now, before they decide to do something drastic. Before they . . ." I couldn't bear to say the rest out loud. Before they tried to kill Dad.

CHAPTER 22

Burn her body to a pile of ash, lest she
return and her spell be cast.

—Disturbing Nursery Rhymes
www.DarkCradleTime.com

Chase got out his phone. "I'll call your grandfather and find out where he is. It'll be faster than hunting him down." He held the phone to his ear for a second, then frowned. "It went to his voice mail. That's not normal."

I opened my mouth intending to suggest he try Kate next, but something occurred to me. I glanced at Selena. "When we saw Kate in the garden did you notice what she had in the sandwich bag?"

"Yeah." Selena nodded. "Nightshade berries. But that's not weird. She's always messing around with something." The color drained from her face. "Whoa, nightshade's poisonous. You don't think—"

"Oh my God! Zachary was right. They're going to kill Dad now!" I sprinted across the library and up the circular staircase. I had to get to Dad's room. I had to tell them my plan, before it was too late.

Behind me I could hear Selena's panting breaths and the squeak of Zachary's sneakers. If Dad's door was locked, I'd kick it in. I couldn't lose him.

"I hope you know what you're doing," Chase called out.

"I'm a hundred percent sure." I dashed past the book stacks, flung the secret door to Dad's hallway open, skidded out—and slammed into a food cart, and Laura.

The cart and dishes skittered to one side. Laura grabbed for the teapot.

"Sorry," I said as Chase, Zachary, and Selena piled up behind me.

Angry red blotches rushed up Laura's neck as she let go of the pot and straightened the jostled dishes. She scowled at us. "You need to watch where you're going." Her eyes darted to the dishes, and then back to us. "If you're hungry, I just put out sandwiches and lemonade in the dining room. This, however, is spoken for."

I eyed the cart. Food: the perfect disguise for poison. Tea. Macaroons. They were grandfather's favorites. The sandwiches, it had to be them.

Snagging a sandwich, I peeled back the rye bread: lettuce, tomato, what looked and smelled like roast lamb—with black-speckled mayonnaise. Laura might be delivering it, but Kate had probably made it.

Laura's hands clenched. "Put that back," she snarled.

"Dad won't miss just one." I reassembled the sandwich and opened my mouth.

Laura launched herself at me, slapping the sandwich out of my hand.

I snagged her by the wrist, twisting her arm. "Why don't you want me to eat it, Laura?"

Livid, she yanked away from me. "Leave it alone. Go away!"

Selena picked up the sandwich pieces and thumped them down on the cart. "We can't leave. Annie doesn't want her father poisoned, and we're going to make sure it doesn't happen."

Sweat beaded on Laura's upper lip. "Poisoned? That's— that's a preposterous idea."

"No. It's not," Zachary said.

Chase stepped toward Laura. "Who's in the room with Annie's father?"

"Their grandfather and Kate." Laura's gaze darted down the hallway to Dad's room and back. She lowered her voice. "If this is some kind of joke, you're going to be in big trouble."

"Zachary," I said. "Go tell Grandfather that Laura needs to talk to him. But don't say anything else, understand?"

"Yes, boss." He took off down the hallway.

I turned back to Laura. "I'm sorry you got caught in the middle of this."

She gripped the edge of the cart, her jaw so taut I expected to hear her teeth crack. "You're going to be sorrier once your grandfather gets here," she said.

A moment later, Zachary reappeared. Grandfather was a few steps behind. He had one finger crooked over his collar, loosening his bow tie. His face was totally unreadable. "What's the meaning of this?" he said as they came up to us.

I raised my chin.

His lips pressed into a thin line. *Just like Kate,* that's what he was thinking.

Laura pointed a shaking finger at the mutilated sandwich. "They think it's poisoned."

Grandfather cut her off. "Don't worry about that. While I'm straightening this out, why don't you go make sure Tibbs knows lunch is ready?"

With a toss of her head, Laura took off down the hallway.

Grandfather herded the rest of us back into the library where we could talk without being overheard.

"So, what is this all about?" he asked.

I squared my shoulders and stood up as tall as I could. "We know you are planning on poisoning Dad so the genie will leave. But you can't do it. There's another way."

Selena clutched Grandfather's arm. "Listen to her." She cut me a sideways glance and whispered, "I thought you were just going to ask him about the oil. But you have another plan, right?"

I nodded. Then I let my eyes meet Grandfather's. "Did Kate and David use the oil from the Lamp of Methuselah to make their bodies solid in the djinn's realm?"

The hard line of Grandfather's mouth tightened further. He rubbed his knuckles, studying me.

My stomach tossed and turned like I'd drunk some of Selena's special iced tea, but I kept my chin high and didn't break eye contact.

I drew a steadying breath. "When I was on the beach with Dad, he said something that made Chase and me believe the genie's after the lamp."

His expression remained firm, but the corner of one eye twitched ever so slightly. "Go on."

"I don't think Dad's ever seen the lamp, and neither has the genie."

"Culus," Chase added.

"So that's his name." Grandfather gave me a curt nod. "You're right. The lamp was acquired after your father left us. There's no chance he's ever seen it."

Sweat trickled down my spine. I gathered my nerve again and went on. "I think we could make a fake lamp and trick Culus into stealing it. All we have to do is make sure the lamp is from the correct time period and that the oil smells like the real stuff. Once Culus thinks he has the real lamp, he won't have a reason to stay inside Dad."

Grandfather turned to Selena. "You think this is a good idea as well?"

She blinked, like she was surprised he'd even thought to ask her opinion, then flipped her hair back. "Better than poisoning him." She tsked. "Annie's dad has a weak heart, you know."

"Oh. We weren't aware of that," Grandfather said. He folded his arms across his chest. "It sounds like a good plan. But what happens when Culus tries the oil and discovers it doesn't work? He'll know we tricked him—and genies are a vengeful lot."

I rubbed my neck, thinking. There had to be a solution. "Maybe we could use Kate's memory formula as part of the fake oil. Then when Culus tries it, he won't remember why he wanted the oil or where it came from?"

"That's a great idea!" Zachary said. "Then we could stuff him in the lamp, like in the stories." He scrunched up his face. "How do they make the genies do that anyway?"

Grandfather slid his hand into his jacket pocket and came out with something in his fist. "Fortunately, a courier delivered that answer late last evening," he said to Zachary.

Zachary craned his neck, waiting for Grandfather to open his fist. "What is it?"

Taking a relieved breath, I stepped back and let everyone else crowd closer. I had a good idea what he was hiding.

Slowly, Grandfather's fingers straightened, revealing an ornate gold ring with an onyx stone. The poison ring I'd sold for Dad.

Grandfather looked at me. "Culus purposely had himself imprisoned in this, so he could insinuate himself into your father's life. We're certain of that now."

"But how?" I said.

"The ring may not have been stolen from the Met. However, we discovered the man your father acquired it from works at the Met. He also happens to be married to the woman who purchased it from you. Interesting?"

"Very much," I said. It sure sounded like the man who sold Dad the ring could possibly have even been Taj's supervisor. "So they were in league with Culus?"

"Most likely he offered them something irresistible—a so-called wish. What that was, isn't clear. However, Culus's intentions are. By having the woman buy the ring back, he hoped to ensure that its inscription couldn't later be used to command him back inside. Culus knew your father would become irrational as the possession deepened. All the woman had to do was mention this abnormal behavior to our lawyer and . . . you know the rest. A brilliant plan, except"—a smile cracked Grandfather's stern expression—"we now have the ring and can use the inscription."

Selena rolled her eyes. "I hate to be a party pooper. But why are we even talking about poisoning and fake lamps? Why not just command Culus to get into the ring right now?"

"No one can command Culus as long as he's protected by a human body," Chase said. His voice lowered and took on a venomous tone. "But I can guarantee—once Culus has the lamp—if I challenge him to a man-to-man fight, he'll come out of Annie's father and try to use the fake oil to make his body rock solid."

My chest tightened. I wasn't sure why Chase was so confident that Culus would want to fight him, but I suspected the reason was more horrible than anything I could imagine.

I pushed that worry aside. I couldn't afford any distractions, not right now.

"On the beach," I said, "I told Culus a made-up story about our family finding the lamp and hiding it in the mausoleum. Even though he acted like he didn't believe me, I'm betting he'll go there to double-check as soon as he can sneak away."

"Actually," Grandfather said, "you chose a very appropriate spot. There's access to an old tunnel up there. It leads to what was once an underground treasury. It could be the perfect place to situate the fake lamp. However, I suggest you scout it out ahead of time to make sure there's a spot where it will look natural. Chase will also need to reset the tunnel's lock or even your father won't be able get inside."

Excitement filled my voice. "I take that to mean you're going to help us with our plan?"

He nodded. "Genies are strongest at night, that's why we planned on administering the poison and trapping Culus this afternoon. More than anything, I'd prefer not to have to endanger James's life." He looked at each of us in turn. "You have until an hour before sunset. After that, we'll have to go back to the original plan. I can't risk all our lives—not even to save my son."

"I understand," I said. "But we'll need Kate to help make the oil."

"Don't worry about her. She'll say yes. Just don't try to bully her into it."

An involuntary smile tugged at the corner of my mouth. She was just like me. Or, perhaps, it was more correct to say, I was like her.

Everyone began discussing what needed to be done: Selena and I would go with Grandfather to talk to Kate and Olya about making the fake oil. Zachary would help scour the showcases for the best lamp to use. While the oil was being made, Chase and I would take time to scout inside the mausoleum's secret tunnel and decide where to put the lamp. When everything was all set, whoever was sitting with Dad would have to let him slip away.

Their voices buzzed in the distance as reality chilled me to the bone. If anything happened to Dad, I'd be crushed. But was it fair to ask everyone else to risk their lives when poisoning Dad seemed to be a safer choice?

I closed my eyes and took a deep breath.

No. This would work. Everything would be fine.

It had to be.

One step at a time.

First, we had to talk to Kate—and that was going to be tougher than buying the contents of the Sistine Chapel from the Pope.

CHAPTER 23

Dark crystals, light crystals,
salt, rosemary, and virtuous pimpernel.
Protect this gateway. Seal the veil tight.
Protect us all, both day and night.

—Olya Freemont: Warding Spell

As soon as Kate joined us in the study, Grandfather explained everything to her, including how he'd given us until sunset to trick Culus into leaving Dad. Then he shuffled into the bathroom, leaving Selena and me to fill her in on the rest of the details.

Kate glanced at her wristwatch. "That gives you five hours and fifteen minutes." A slight smirk crossed her lips. "Then your father will be getting a special something in his evening meal."

Cold, furious anger crackled through my veins and my teeth clenched. I was certain Grandfather had left to see how we'd deal with Kate, but tact was the furthest thing from my mind. I wanted to rip her throat out.

Selena grabbed a peppermint out of a bowl on Kate's desk and began to unwrap it slowly. "There's something Grandfather forgot to mention. My mom can make the basic oil, but Annie thinks—" She stopped midsentence, popped the mint into her mouth, and nodded for me to finish what she'd been saying.

I met Kate's glare without flinching, then thought better of it. Kate was tough, but there was more to her than her haughty side. If I wanted her help, I had to put aside my ego and appeal to that part of her.

I lowered my gaze. I had to make this work. For Dad and all of us.

"Kate," I said, in the calmest voice I could muster, "we don't just want oil that looks and smells like the real thing, we'd like it to steal Culus's memories as well."

She raised an eyebrow. "I suppose you want my help for that?"

I shrugged. "I'm sure Olya could do it. But when it comes to spells and herbs, it's obvious your knowledge is far superior. I saw your hybrid plants in the solarium, they're amazing. Grandfather, the Professor, everyone says you're the best. That's what we need, a genius."

Kate laughed. "Laying it on a little thick, aren't you?" she said, but pride raised her shoulders a notch.

My compliment—or my begging—had won her over. But just in case I'd read her wrong, I added, "There's another thing we need to keep in mind. The djinn can go after the family anywhere or anytime, any of us—on business, at home. We need to show them our power. Make them respect and fear us. Your skills can do that."

"That," Kate said, nodding sharply, "is something I totally agree with."

She sashayed to her desk, sat down, and picked up a pen. She glanced at Selena. "I'll need quite a few things, and both yours and your mother's help." She grabbed a notepad and began jotting down a list. "The three *H*s: hemlock, hemp, and henbane. Walnut bark and rhubarb seed and wild violet root. These must all be fresh." She pointed the pen at Selena. "Don't forget to say the proper prayers as you gather them. And I'll need a head of cabbage and clove oil for the smell. When you have everything, bring them to the research room."

Grandfather sauntered out of the bathroom and grinned. "This is what I like to see, all my girls working in harmony."

Before I could stop myself, I shot him a hard look. When I realized Kate had done the same thing, my face heated. She raised her chin and I resisted doing the same. For a split second, a smile twitched at the corner of her mouth, then she went back to writing the list.

As Kate and Grandfather suggested places where Selena could dig the violet roots, I walked to the fireplace and took the sea glass bobble from my pocket.

It's not yours. Leave it with the ashes, the whisper in the back of my mind had said when I took it from the water. But now I was glad I hadn't left it there.

Certain Kate was watching, I set the bobble on the mantel next to the cats' cremation vases. That's where it belonged: with the other mementoes of the past. Why Kate and Grandfather had lied to Dad didn't matter anymore. What mattered was what they were willing to do for him right now.

"I'm—I'm sorry," Kate said.

I glanced back. Her chin was held high, but sincere regret shone in her eyes. I nodded, then walked out the door and closed it quietly behind me.

A few minutes later, I caught up with Chase and Zachary in the foyer.

Chase was moving artifacts aside on the top shelf of the display cabinet. On his knees, Zachary was going through the drawer beneath it.

I glanced around, then hurried over to them and whispered, "I'm assuming you're keeping a watch out for shadows?"

Turning toward me, Chase shook his head. "Culus is probably keeping them close to him. How many shadows did you see in his room, anyway?"

"Two." I hesitated for a second. "But the ones in Dad's room looked skinnier than the one I saw in the gallery. It was broader and darker. So that makes at least three."

Chase rubbed his brand for a second. "Two skinny ones. They'd be Culus's henchmen. But the other shadow, I doubt it's one of Culus's men. That sounds more like either Malphic or one of his spies."

Zachary's eyes bulged. "Malphic—himself?"

I swallowed hard as the memory of Malphic taking my mother flashed through my mind.

"More likely a spy"—Chase's voice brought me from my thoughts—"watching the family and reporting back. The kidnapping probably left a weak point between the djinn realm and ours. That would give a spy easy access."

I glanced over my shoulder to the top of the staircase and at the hallway that led to the gallery. "When I first saw that shadow, I told Olya right away. But I saw it again yesterday. You don't suppose she didn't tell Grandfather or Kate?"

"No. That isn't something she'd keep to herself. They probably strengthened the gallery's wards last night. I didn't sense anything when we were in there this morning."

"Wards? What the heck are they?" I asked.

"It's like sprinkling salt across a doorway. Charms, spells, sometimes symbols, things designed to act as barriers against intruders, like to keep genies from crossing at weak points in the veil. They aren't infallible. They get weaker over time and can be broken."

I stopped him with a wave of my hand. "I get the idea." Taking a breath, I forced my mind to stop trying to make sense out of everything and get back to the job at hand. "Did you guys find anything?"

Zachary plucked a broken lamp from the drawer. "The ones in here are cracked. They'd never hold oil."

Chase shrugged. "I've gone through most of the display case. Either the inscriptions and decorations are wrong, or they're not old enough."

"How about this one?" Zachary held out a small, simple terra-cotta lamp with a few lines and dots etched into it, so boring I'd never have bid on it at an auction.

I took the lamp. It was smooth to the touch, neither finely made nor coarse. It was a dark coppery-brown color. No way did it look priceless and one-of-a-kind, like something out of an *Arabian Nights'* treasure trove. But it was in perfect condition and the dots and lines easily could be taken as primitive sacred symbols.

"What do you think?" I said, handing it to Chase.

His fingers brushed mine as he took the lamp, and our eyes met and lingered. Oh, man. He could try to warn me off all he wanted, but I was sure he felt the electricity as strongly as I did.

Red-faced, I looked back at the lamp in his hand.

He flipped it over, examining all sides. "I doubt this is what Culus is expecting it to look like," he said.

I grinned. "Good. Then he'll be less likely to think it's a fake." I turned to Zachary. "Do you mind taking it to Grandfather? He'll want to get it down to the research room as soon as possible."

As Zachary took off with the lamp, Chase rested his hand on my arm. My pulse started thrumming again, but his serious tone made it easier to regain my composure. "I guess this means it's time for us to head for the mausoleum," he said.

My mouth dried. The plan was coming together perfectly.

Too perfectly. Something had to be wrong. "Maybe we should check on Dad first, make sure he's in his room."

Chase grinned. "One step ahead of you. I checked with Tibbs a couple of minutes ago. They're playing cards, and your father mentioned wanting to take a bath."

I let out my breath. That was perfect too. Now, if only I could be certain things would stay this way.

Neither one of us talked as we dashed through the hot sunshine, past the garage, and up the path. Chase went first, and I had to jog every now and then to keep up with his long strides as we wound our way toward the graveyard.

"What time is it?" I called to Chase.

He looked over his shoulder. "Around one thirty, I'd guess."

I hurried my pace. In the distance, sheep blatted. As we came up to the gate, they hurtled through the graveyard toward us, then followed like a shifting tide as we made our way up the rest of the hill to the mausoleum.

While Chase unlocked the padlock, I glanced back. The sheep watched us, their dark eyes gleaming. Behind them, the bright greens and stark whites of the graveyard had a surreal, motionlessness silence to them. A heat mirage, like a pool of water on a desert, wavered over what I could see of Moonhill's rooftops. It was odd and chilling how familiar this place felt, after only a few days. Like I'd been here all my life. Or like Moonhill had been waiting for me.

Chase said something.

Turning around, I blinked. "What?"

"I'm sorry." His shoulders sagged. "I should have thought to bring a lantern."

"That's okay." I took out my mini-flashlight and showed it to him.

"Great. I probably could reset the lock without a light. But this will make it easier." He stood aside and let me go into the mausoleum first. "Once we get inside the tunnel, there'll be torches I can light."

I fanned the flashlight's beam across the vaults until I found one with an etching of Hecate and an inscription on it. "I'm assuming that's the door to the tunnel. Does it go back to the house, like to the cellar or something?"

"When your father lived here it did. Back then, if someone knew how the doors and latches were disguised and had the keys, they could go anywhere." Chase pulled a jackknife out of his pocket and flipped open the screwdriver blade. "Almost everything's been closed off or remodeled in the last few years. In this case, the lock was simply disabled."

While I stood close behind him and trained the flashlight's beam on the vault, Chase tapped the screwdriver on what looked like a nickel stuck into the engraving about Hecate. Under the flashlight's white light, I could see that the nickel was a coin with a bee on it, like the one in the pentagram under my bed.

Chase pried it off, then twisted a screw that was beneath it. As he worked, I thought about the razor in my pocket. It was reassuring that—despite all the sorcery and mystical stuff going on—simple things like flashlights, knives, and razors still had their place.

"That should do it." Chase put the coin back where it had come from. "Now when your father tries to pick the lock, he'll succeed."

He turned toward me, his body so close to mine I could feel its heat.

My eyes found his, steel gray, mellowed to misty blue.

I lowered the flashlight and, for a breathless second, Chase's fingers skimmed the outline of my face. I took a shallow breath and leaned into his touch. Only a slice of air hovered between us. Closing my eyes, I tilted my face up, not expecting anything, but wanting it so badly.

His shirt pressed against mine. "This is wrong," he whispered, so close I could almost taste the words. His lips brushed mine, tantalizing and quick. They came back forceful, hot and moist as I'd dreamed. I slid my fingers along his temples, across his hair, bristly and soft. I shuddered as he crushed me against him. Openmouthed, I kissed him back. He groaned and I let him take control, lips, tongues, and hands frantically exploring curves and skin, necks and throats, eyelids and mouths again. Everything melted away, all my fears, the horrors, all the months and months of worrying about—

Dad.

I pulled away from Chase's embrace, gulping for air. My thoughts staggered as if I were drunk. "We—I want. Oh God, I want. But this isn't. Dad. The lamp. The timing is—"

Chase glanced down and scrubbed a hand over his head. "Worse than bad?"

"Yeah." I had to find a way to bring everything back under control, back to why we were here. I swallowed hard and settled on a question that my heart ached to ask. "Dad," I said. "I just don't understand why he did it. Why would he ever allow Culus to possess him?"

Chase's fingers swept up my arm, lingering when they reached the hollow of my throat, a spot he'd kissed just moments ago. Even in the low light, I could see the glisten in his eyes. "You really don't?"

"No." For a heartbeat, I hesitated, gathering my thoughts. "Dad never wanted to come back here. He hates his family. He probably thinks they killed Mother." Part of me wanted to know what Chase thought. Part of me wished I'd never said a thing. Just like the kiss and his hand against my skin, this wasn't the time or place—and what I was feeling for him was so much stronger than the onetime hookup I'd wanted to have with him on the beach.

Chase's eyes found mine again, holding me captive. "I don't think it was any of those things," he said.

"Then what?" I could barely breathe, let alone speak.

"I think Culus proved to your father that your mother's alive. Your father traded the use of his body for her safe return."

Surprised by his words, my fingers went to my parted lips. "You think so?"

His voice became a husky whisper. "I'd do it for you."

My heart leapt into my throat. Every inch of my body ached with the desire to rush back to his arms, press my lips against his, and get lost in the rush of warm skin and kisses. This was insane. This was wrong. And the timing couldn't be worse.

I punched Chase playfully in the chest. I had to do something to break the spell. "Very funny. Then I could turn my life story into a romance novel and make a million bucks." I frowned. "Are you going to just stand there or show me how this door opens?"

With an exaggerated sigh, Chase turned away from me. He pulled a key ring from his jeans pocket and slid a brass key into a slot. The slot was so cleverly integrated into the vault's designs, I could barely make it out.

The lock clicked and, with the grinding sound of stone against stone, a door-size grouping of vaults swung inward.

Chase chuckled. "Romance novel, really?" He glanced back at me. "Wait here a minute."

I took a deep breath and watched him vanish down the pitch-black tunnel. Chase's idea about Dad's motive actually made sense. Once Culus had the lamp, then Dad would get Mother. But what Chase had said about doing the same thing for me? Wow. Okay. That sounded as if he really liked me, like a lot. Maybe he'd been pushing me away—not for my sake—but because he was afraid of having his heart broken. I sighed. But who was going to protect mine from him?

Gathering my nerve, I shone the flashlight beam into darkness. Chase had told me to stay, but I should have gone with him. I had the only light.

A chill brushed my face as I stepped through the doorway.

The flashlight's thin light illuminated a few dozen yards, glistening off spiderwebs, and the stone ceiling and walls.

My breath caught in my throat. Where was Chase? It hadn't surprised me that he'd forgotten to bring a lantern. Heck, I—Miss-Never-Without-Her-Flashlight—hadn't thought of it either. But how could he see where he was going without it? It would be awful if something happened to him.

The scratch of a wooden match striking against stone came from a little ways down the tunnel, followed by a *whuff* and the bright flash of something igniting.

Chase appeared, holding a torch aloft.

Around his entire outline was an eerie blue glow. An aura.

My free hand went to my mouth, silencing a gasp. I'd have dismissed the glow as a trick of light and shadow, except I'd seen it before: the night Dad and I arrived, coming from the window of Chase's cottage, the cottage with no television. And I'd seen it one other time as well, in the library when I'd shone the flashlight beam on him. I couldn't even begin to guess what it was, but it wasn't a product of my imagination.

I lowered my trembling hand from my mouth that still tingled from his kisses. "*He belongs to them,*" Dad had said.

Chase had admitted he'd been a slave to the djinn and was being trained to become a Death Warrior. Maybe the aura was some sort of mark, like his brand—or a beacon. Chase acted like he hated the genies. He'd pretty much said Malphic wouldn't come after him for revenge, but maybe the aura was so Malphic could find him for some other reason.

Whatever it was—it wasn't normal. And I couldn't say he hadn't warned me.

Chase moved away from me, farther down the tunnel. Using his torch, he lit another one that sat in a bracket on the wall, then another. He turned back.

"Come on," he called. "There's nothing to be afraid of."

Oh God. What kind of guy had I fallen for this time?

CHAPTER 24

The creatures know the fruits and spice
that inspire a human woman to be with child:
cinnamon and apples under the new moon
for a boy, raisins and cardamom create a girl.

—www.MagicOfDjinn.com

As I hesitantly followed Chase, the blue aura vanished. But I knew I'd seen it. And I wished I hadn't. If only I were sitting in the Mercedes with Dad, driving to an auction on Cape Cod, or heading for a college interview, any college. If I could turn back time, I'd make sure Dad never got his hands on the poison ring. Then I wouldn't be here with my pulse going crazy and this war inside of me—was I wrong to trust Chase, could I trust myself, did I have something to fear or not?

Everywhere, spiderwebs swayed in the wavering torchlight. Silence pressed in, making the drum of my heartbeat as loud as thunder.

In one place a wall had collapsed, and stones and dirt littered the floor. A bat dove through my flashlight's beam. Trembling, I shuffled on, following Chase deeper into the darkness. I kept telling myself to forget about the aura for now. But I couldn't. Not with so much at stake. Not when he was someone I was trusting. I had to ask, even if I didn't want to.

When we came to where water trickled down the walls, I took a fresh grip on my sweat-slicked flashlight and glanced back toward the mausoleum, now gone from sight.

"How much farther do we need to go?" I asked.

Chase turned to me, his face masked with dancing shadows. "I don't know. I've never been in this far."

"Sure it's safe?"

"I'm certain it's not. But the old treasury should be just ahead."

An image of him wiping the sheep blood off his knife wormed its way into my mind. "Chase?"

"What?"

My throat contracted and I had to force the words out. "There was—you had. I saw a blue aura around you. Is that—did Malphic do that to you—like part of the brand? Some kind of magic?"

He lowered his torch and stood stock-still, staring at me. "Ah—something like that," he stammered.

Regret clenched my stomach. I wanted to kick myself for letting my doubts get the better of me. I was such an idiot for not trusting him, and a double idiot for wasting time we didn't have to ask him about it.

He opened his mouth to say something else.

But I spoke first. "Another scene for that romance novel, huh?" I said it with a laugh in hopes of relieving the tension.

He smiled. "It would be one weird book." His voice deepened. "I'll tell you more about it later. We really don't have time right now."

"I know—we need to get this done."

I jogged to him and we hurried on together, his torch and my flashlight casting circles of brightness into the dark tunnel ahead.

After a few minutes, the floor sloped downward and the

tunnel appeared to drop off into nothing. As we edged closer to the void, Chase's torch's light rippled across the top of a crumbling staircase and streaked the darkened outline of a chamber below.

"This looks like the perfect place to set a trap," he said.

I swept the flashlight's beam across the chamber. Huge black and gold statues that looked like Egyptian cats glistened under its fingering light. There were ceiling-high columns and a figurehead. And camelback trunks bound in copper, and carved boxes mounded with what looked like gazing balls and gleaming coins. "Holy shit! It looks like a pirate's treasure." My voice echoed off a distant wall.

"The lamp will fit right in," Chase said.

"Sure will." I fanned the flashlight across the chamber again. "I'm just surprised. Wow—this isn't the real treasury?"

Chase laughed. "No."

I glanced back at the tunnel. "We should get going. Kate's probably finished the oil by now."

"You do realize"—Chase's voice had a serious edge to it—"when we come back, we can't light the torches. The place has to look deserted."

Fear clogged my throat, but I swallowed it back. "I'll be okay."

"You don't have to come. Your grandfather and I can do it alone."

"No. I can deal with it." What was I saying? Hiding in the dark with a hotter-than-hell glowing genie-slave, waiting for a monster to emerge from inside my dad, this was beyond insane.

Sweat stuck my shirt against my back. My pulse slammed in my ears. I didn't want to do this, but I had no choice. If something happened to Chase or Grandfather, they would need my help.

This was my plan. I had to follow through with it.

I raised my voice. "When we come back, we should take a car and park it by your cottage. We can walk here from the back side. If Dad or the shadows spotted us a little while ago when we walked up here, it might not have raised a red flag. But if they see us returning, it's bound to make them suspicious."

"Good idea," Chase said. "Driving would be easier on your grandfather, too."

As we made our way back down the tunnel toward the mausoleum, Chase followed behind me, extinguishing the torches he'd lit.

After a couple of minutes, I looked back to make sure he wasn't watching, then shut off my flashlight and let the gloom close in around me. My fear of the darkness had come from seeing my mother kidnapped and having my memories stolen. Real darkness had never done anything to me.

In fact, when we returned, the darkness could hide and protect me.

I needed to remember that.

The trip back down through the graveyard went quickly. Chase seemed preoccupied, and I was too focused on keeping up with his long strides to talk.

When we came to where the path left the woods and emptied into the field, Chase's head whipped toward the garage. "Was that Tibbs?" he asked.

I shrugged. "I didn't see anyone."

"I could have sworn . . ."

Chase jogged toward the garage. "Tibbs should still be with your father."

"Maybe it was Zachary or David," I said, running after him.

Our feet crunched as we crossed the gravel to the garage door.

Chase punched the code into the lock. As he opened the door, a tiger-striped kitten tore past him and sped outside.

"Tibbs?" Chase shouted. He cocked his head, listening.

I held my breath. But there wasn't a sound.

Finally, Chase shrugged and shut the garage door. "I must have been mistaken."

"Well, at least you let the kitten out," I said lightheartedly, but my fake cheerfulness did nothing to relieve my building sense of apprehension. Hadn't I read on the Internet that cats freaked out when supernatural things were around—like shadows in the garage?

We were almost to the front door when Zachary bolted out. "There you guys are!" He lowered his voice to a whisper. "It's ready."

Two minutes later, we were in the kitchen elevator, heading down to the basement and the research room. I studied our reflections in the mirrored wall and thought about asking Chase and Zachary if I was right about the mirrors being doorways, and if either of them had seen what was on the other side—most likely a maze of remodeled tunnels and, somewhere, a treasury filled with objects—like the vases that held Solomon's genies and the Lamp of Methuselah.

The elevator stopped and the doors clunked open. Chase pulled the key ring from his pocket and unlocked the door Grandfather and I'd gone through last night.

We all hurried inside the tunnel. As we dashed past the suit of armor, Zachary tugged the back of Chase's T-shirt. "When I'm taller, I'm going to put on armor like that and challenge you to a duel," he said.

Chase swiped his hand across his sweaty forehead. "How about we live through today first?"

My legs felt like someone had strapped hundred-pound weights onto each of them. *Live through today*. Holy crap. This was a harebrained idea.

Before that thought could paralyze me, I pushed it aside. No time for second-guessing, not now.

Zachary rushed ahead and waited by the fresco of dancing demons. When Chase and I got there, he held up his hand, palm out. "Let me do it," he said to Chase.

"All right." Chase breathed on Zachary's palm, then Zachary pressed it against the tiles and the door to the research room swooshed open.

Zachary grinned at me. "Cool, huh? It works on DNA." He scowled. "Grandpa and Aunt Kate are lucky. They can get in here or visit the cursed skulls or the armory anytime they want. Me? They don't let me have access to nothing!"

"Shush," Chase said. "Once this is over, I'll talk to Kate. See if she'll give me access to the armory. Then we'll go there anytime you want."

"That'd be great." Zachary dashed inside.

I trailed behind them, blinking against the vestibule's brightness. A burnt-clove-and-cabbage smell irritated my nostrils. I pinched my nose to keep from sneezing.

"We're down here!" Selena waved from the laboratory below us. A black rubber apron draped her from chest to ankles. A bathing cap covered her hair. Beside her, Kate held a small copper funnel while Olya poured a liquid into the fake Lamp of Methuselah.

"How did it come out?" I asked.

Olya smiled as she finished pouring. "Good, I think."

"Adequate, is more correct." Kate set the funnel down on the workbench and took the lamp from Olya. "The memory formula needs time to mellow. But it should work."

The zing of metal against metal rang out behind me. I spun around, muscles tensed.

Chase had pulled the scimitar free from the wall display. He glanced my way. "Nice, isn't it?"

"You can't intend on waltzing through the house with that," Kate said, walking up the ramp from the lab and into the vestibule. "What if James sees you?"

Selena laughed. "You're talking about Chase. Knives and swords equal normal. Unarmed, that would be weird."

"Don't worry. No one will see a thing." Chase handed the scimitar to Zachary. "Hold this—and no fooling around." He pulled off his hoodie, revealing Malphic's knife and another one holstered at his waist. He took the scimitar from Zachary, and by the time he got it strapped to his back and his hoodie back on, not a single weapon was visible. "Does that pass inspection?" he asked Kate.

"It'll do." Kate held a small messenger bag out to me. "The lamp's in here. I've corked the spout and wrapped it in a cloth. But be careful with it."

I slung the bag over my shoulder. "Thanks for doing this."

"Just don't make me regret it."

"Don't worry, I won't." I glanced at Kate's watch. "It's almost three. We need to find Grandfather and get back to the mausoleum."

"Tell him I'll be up in a minute," Kate said. "I'll give you a half hour to get in place, then I'll make sure your father gets his chance to slip away." Her mouth worked like she wanted to say something more, but couldn't quite get it out. Then she added, "Be careful."

Selena galloped up from the lab and gave me a hug. "Good luck and be careful."

As Chase and I turned toward the door, Zachary stamped his foot. "It isn't fair that I get stuck here with the women. I really, really want to go."

Olya took him by the arm. "Young man, they're not going on a picnic. What they're doing is very dangerous."

"I know." He frowned. "I just want to help."

I gave him a serious look. "Staying here and watching over the research room is important." I smiled. "Besides, you've already been a huge help. You were the one who found the lamp, right?"

He puffed out his chest and grinned. "It was even better than the ones Chase found."

As I smiled back at him, a bittersweet feeling settled in my chest, and I couldn't help but wonder if he'd been as rambunctious as a toddler and I wished I'd gotten to watch him grow up, to know them all before now.

A minute later, Chase and I were in the elevator heading up to the first floor, and the bizarreness of the situation closed in around me. It was like I was playing a part in one of Dad's stories and had discovered a Trojan horse on Moonhill's terrace, jam-packed with genies.

I shook my head. No. This was very real. I couldn't allow myself to think it was a story or a game, even for a second. I had to stay sharp. I couldn't be afraid.

We found Grandfather in the study. His tweed jacket was draped across the desk, and he was putting on a shoulder holster, like a television detective getting ready to hit the streets.

Chase shut the door behind us. "Everything's all set," he said.

"Good." Grandfather picked up a handgun from the desk and secured it in the holster.

The hairs on the back of my neck prickled. Grandfather's gun. Chase's knives. I couldn't help but wonder if they realized how useless I'd be in a fight. I sure did.

BAM! The door to the hallway slammed open, almost making me jump out of my skin.

Tibbs staggered in. Blood gushed from a gash in his forehead and smeared his bruised face.

I caught his arm and half-carried him to the closest armchair. "What happened?"

"Your father—he wanted to see the tires I put on the Mercedes. He hit me—something hit me. I thought he was going to kill me," he babbled, his eyes slightly unfocused and wide with fear.

Grandfather crouched in front of Tibbs. "Did you see which way he went?"

"No. I don't know. He hit me with a tire iron. I was unconscious."

My breath hitched. He must have been lying there when Chase and I checked the garage.

Chase handed Tibbs a wet cloth from the bathroom. "Was he alone?"

Holding the cloth against the gash, Tibbs bobbed his head. "There were shadows."

"How many?" I asked. My fingers gripped the messenger bag so tight they began to shake. Hopefully, there weren't more than we suspected.

"Two," Tibbs said.

Chase let out a relieved breath. "Just Culus and his henchmen."

Grandfather took his phone out. "I'll get Olya to come up and take a look at you. We have to figure out where James went. If he's already at the mausoleum, then—" His phone buzzed and he answered it. "Zachary? Slow down, boy. Your mother? You need to calm down. Tell your sister to put pressure on the wound. Kate? He took Kate! What do you mean? All right. Hang in there. I'll phone your father. He'll be right down."

For a second, panic seized me. "What happened?" I finally managed to choke out.

"We found your father. He and the two shadows have taken Kate." Grandfather closed his eyes. "We underestimated him—or Culus. How did you get up here after you left the research room?"

"Kate said she was coming upstairs, right behind us," I said. "We took the elevator. We didn't see anyone in the kitchen." I bit my tongue to keep from rambling.

Chase's voice was steady as bedrock. "They must have taken the servants' stairs down to the basement or been hiding in the maintenance room when Annie and I went through. He could have picked the lock. They probably surprised Kate in the hallway or coming out of the research room. She has full access, right?"

"To everything." Grandfather held his phone back up to his ear. "David. We have a situation."

While Grandfather told David what had happened and asked him to call the Professor, I ran to the bathroom to get another wet cloth for Tibbs.

Tibbs would be okay. But Kate. It was my fault she was in danger. And I was certain there wasn't anything Culus wouldn't do to make her cooperate. Worse yet, I suspected the more agonizing it was for her, the more he'd enjoy it.

I trembled. Dad never would have hurt Tibbs's or Olya. He hated Kate, but he'd never hurt or murder her. But Dad's body wasn't his own anymore. Culus was in control.

"You're going to have to shoot him"—Tibbs's words made my chest clench—"and his shadow buddies, too."

Grabbing the cloth, I dashed from the bathroom. Grandfather was shoving the phone in his jacket pocket. "We should have used the poison," he said dryly.

Guilt knotted inside of me. But, as the weight of the messenger bag tugged at my shoulder, an idea formed. Clearly, Culus had figured out that Dad wouldn't be able to find the treasury because the tunnels had been remodeled, but Kate knew where everything was and had access.

"Dad and Kate must be somewhere in the passageway near the research room," I said. "But the real treasury and lamp are in the area beyond the mirrors, right?"

Grandfather's head snapped up and he blinked in surprise. "That's right. But how did you—" He shook his head. "You know what, it doesn't matter." His eyebrows furrowed. "What are you thinking?"

"Is there a shortcut to get from here to the treasury?" I patted the messenger bag. "We could still swap the lamps. Kate knows what we were planning. And I'm willing to bet she won't take Culus by the fastest route. She knows what the fake lamp and the real one look like, but Dad and Culus don't. They won't kill her until after they get into the treasury. As long as we have you, Grandfather, we'll have full access as well."

"It's a good plan," Chase said. "While they're in the treasury, the warding spells and salt will weaken Culus and the shadows. Culus won't risk leaving James's body, not until they have the lamp and are out of there."

Tibbs took the cloth away from his nose and glanced at Chase. "If it'll weaken them, then won't it—"

"Don't worry about that," Chase snapped.

"There is a shortcut," Grandfather said. "But I'm not as fast as I used to be and it isn't a lot shorter." His gaze went to Tibbs. "I hate leaving you like this."

Tibbs rested his head against the back of the chair. "I'm all right. Just kill the bastards."

"Let's go, then." Grandfather motioned for us to follow him and beelined for the bathroom. I would have thought it was a weird move, but I had a good idea what he was up to.

Once we'd gathered in front of the bathroom's full-length mirror, he turned to me. "Before we do this, there is a problem you should be aware of. Without your DNA in the system, if something happens to me, you won't be able to get out by chopping off my fingers and using them. The system is calibrated against the use of blood or body parts—as a safety precaution. And Chase doesn't have access where we're going."

I bit my lip. That wasn't very comforting, but there were other sources of DNA.

I scanned the bathroom. There might be a dirty tissue in the wastebasket. It would be gross, but not blood. I spotted the basket of toiletries on the stand. Rifling through it, I snagged Kate's lipstick. "How about this? It should be covered with Kate's DNA."

"That's a wonderful idea," Grandfather said as he faced the mirror. "Now, Chase, since you know the drill, you go first. Annie, you wait. Only one person can make it through at a time, another of my damn safety precautions."

Grandfather breathed on the mirror, fogging a patch of the glass with his breath. "Go," he said to Chase.

Without hesitating, Chase stepped toward the mirror. For a heartbeat it looked like he was going to smash into the glass. Then the mirror shimmered and liquefied, re-forming as he passed through.

Grandfather nodded at me. "Your turn." He took a deep breath, readying to fog the mirror again.

"Wait a minute." I put a hand on his shoulder to stop him. "I want to see if my idea works." Taking off the lipstick's cover, I made a Zorro zigzag on the glass, then stepped sideways into it. Better to hit my shoulder than break my nose on the glass. Oh, God. Here goes nothing.

It was like walking through a wall of super-cooled, burbling Jell-O.

Next thing I knew, I was on the other side, standing in what looked like the torch-lit hallway of a medieval castle, except a massive Easter Island–type stone statue glared at me from the farther wall and the torches were some kind of glowing crystal.

Chase took hold of my arm and yanked me aside as Grandfather came through what on this side appeared to be a gold-framed looking glass.

"That was—this is amazing," I said. I knew we were short on time, but I couldn't help being awestruck.

Grandfather smiled. "It is. So is your lipstick trick. Though I imagine you only have enough of Kate's DNA for a couple of uses. Don't squander it. But if something happens to me, take the real lamp, use the lipstick, and get it out of here as fast as you can." He waved his hand down the hall. "This way."

As Chase strode ahead, I hung back with Grandfather. He scuttled along amazingly fast for an old man, but sweat dribbled down his face as we hurried.

"This isn't exactly what I expected," I said, looking down at the unpolished stone floor. "I guess I thought the remodeled tunnels would look new."

"My dear, this is the oldest section. Much of it dates back to a long time before the Pilgrims." His voice lifted with pride. "It was deserted for centuries and looked much worse, until I gave it a facelift."

I stared at a mirror-bright suit of gold armor. "It's like a fairy-tale castle."

He chuckled. "More than you know, my dear."

The hallway narrowed. We dashed past an enormous stone panel with symbols carved into it and a frightening face at its center. My mouth dropped open. I glanced at Grandfather.

"An Aztec calendar stone." He confirmed my suspicion, before I could ask. "Your father is responsible for it being safeguarded. He was your age when he rescued it." As we neared a small niche with a glass front, he called out to Chase. "Wait. I need to show Annie something. You should see it too."

Chase turned around and jogged back. "Do we have time for this?"

"It's important." Grandfather puffed a couple of times to

catch his wind, then pointed to a bee carved into the wall over the niche. "If something happens to me, follow the bees. They will lead you to the correct treasury. There are four entries into it. Two are mirrors. The third is a hallway like this one. I'm quite certain they'll come through a mirror."

"There's more than one treasury?" I asked, though I probably should have realized it.

"No time for questions. Listen carefully. There's something else I need to tell you."

While Grandfather took another quick breath, I gazed past him to the contents of the niche: a large, hand-forged nail, brightened by a single blue spotlight. I couldn't even begin to imagine what was so important about it or why we'd stopped to look at it.

He pulled out a hanky and dabbed the sweat off his face. "Chase, you'll wait outside the treasury. Annie, you and I will go inside. I'm depending on you to switch the lamps while I keep watch. Once you've got the lamp in place, you and I will get out of the treasury and hide. When Culus arrives, Chase will call him into the hallway with a challenge. When Culus emerges from your father's body, I'll leave hiding and trap him in the ring."

"Sounds good," I said.

Chase frowned. "It's safer if I go with you into the treasury. Just in case."

"No." Grandfather's voice was firm. "You're not to go beyond the marks at the entry, understood?"

Chase dipped his head. "I don't agree, but I'll do it."

"Now that we have that settled." Grandfather pressed his hand flat against a dime-shaped indentation in the wall and the niche's glass cover rose. He turned his hand over, revealing to me that his gold wedding band was actually a signet ring with a purple stone, which he wore with the decorative side concealed. He wriggled the ring off his finger and held it out to me. "You'll need this to open the case the lamp is in. And you may keep it afterward."

Taking the ring, I studied it. A bee within a circle of pyramids and *F*s was etched into the stone. I'd seen a ring like this before. "It's like Kate's."

"By all rights I would have given one to your father by now, if he hadn't chosen to leave us." Grandfather nodded at the wall. "Try closing it."

The ring was too large for my fingers, so I held it and pressed it against the indentation in the wall. The glass slid back down.

Grandfather restlessly drummed his fingers on his leg. "The lamp's case will open the same way. But now we have to get going, or we'll be too late."

He scurried off like a man who'd definitely caught his breath, while I took a second to slide the ring into the messenger bag.

"Let's go," Chase said, touching the small of my back.

As we jogged to catch up with Grandfather, I held the messenger bag against my chest. I had no problem going into the treasury and swapping the lamps. But I still didn't know how to fight. I didn't even have a weapon, other than Dad's razor.

"I think you should come in with us, too," I said to Chase.

"No. Your grandfather's right." His tone told me he'd rather do the opposite.

I stole a sideways glance at him. In Kate's study, Chase had said Culus and the shadows would be weaker in the treasury. And Tibbs had replied, "*If it'll weaken them, then won't it—*" He hadn't finished because Chase cut him off. But had Tibbs meant that Chase would be weaker in the treasury too—like Culus and the shadows?

Chase's jaw tensed and his eyes stared straight ahead.

The blue aura. Him being able to see in the dark. His sharp sense of hearing. His stealth-mode movements. I was sure my heart didn't want to hear the answer to the question my head needed to ask.

"Why?" I said softly, wishing we had privacy, knowing I couldn't wait until later to ask. "Why shouldn't you go into the treasury? Is it the same reason I shouldn't get involved with you?"

Chase's pace didn't slacken. His eyes remained focused on what lay beyond Grandfather. When he spoke, his voice lacked all emotion. "In the gallery, you asked if Malphic was your father. He isn't. But he is mine."

I swallowed hard. "Culus is your brother?"

He looked back at me. "Half-brother. His mother is a genie. Mine was human. Still, the salt weakens me as it does him."

"That's why Culus hates you?"

"One of the reasons."

"And the aura?" I had to ask.

"Smokeless fire, that's what genies are," he said.

We were beside Grandfather now, the three of us hurrying down a grim hallway, the fake torchlight scarring our faces with flashes of orange and yellow. Chase was part genie. It made no sense. It made perfect sense. The salt. The scimitar. In a way, it was what I'd feared all along, that Chase was more than just a slave. And now, he was about to face a man who hated him. A man inside my dad.

I didn't want to lose Dad. Or Chase.

Or even Grandfather. Or Kate.

I glanced at Chase, every inch of him looked tense and battle ready, except—

I frowned and moved closer. Were those tears glistening in his eyes?

I reached out and laced my fingers with his.

His fingers tightened around mine, and he gave them a quick squeeze.

One of us was going to die. I was certain of it.

CHAPTER 25

Listen to the old tales, for in them
tomorrow's truths shall be revealed.

—Epitaph on Harmon Freemont's gravestone

A few yards ahead, Grandfather veered to the left and down a narrow passage, his pace slowing.

Packing crates and rolled-up carpets littered the passage's floor. Hundreds of skulls with symbols painted on them leered at us from niches in the walls. These had to be the skulls Zachary wanted to visit. A shudder slipped down my spine. It was beyond me why anyone would long to see them. They were beyond creepy.

After only a short distance, the passage tapered and became even more cluttered. We shimmied past a black sarcophagus and the skeleton of a man with a doglike skull.

An old fear replaced my bone-chilling certainty that some-one was going to die.

I slid my hand into my jeans pocket and felt the shape of my flashlight. Although I couldn't sense anything that made me think Culus's henchmen were close by, there was still plenty of darkness in the corners and rippling through the flickering torchlight, waiting to cripple me. I gritted my teeth. I couldn't let the dark get to me. It was supposed to be on my side this time. "Are you sure this is the way?" I called out to Grandfather, so I could hear a voice.

Grandfather raised his hand to hush me, then took a couple more steps and stopped next to a wardrobe with a cross carved into its door. He whispered, "Chase, you wait here. The treasury's just ahead."

Chase pulled off his hoodie, the scimitar glinting in the shadowy light. "There's not much room for fighting," he grumbled.

"But there are places for me and Annie to hide. And if Culus sees only you, it's less likely he'll retreat before I have time to use the ring and trap him."

The knots began twisting in my stomach again. "Let's get this over with," I said.

Grandfather rested his hand on my arm. "We'll be in and out before you know it."

"Run if you hear or smell anything out of the ordinary," Chase added.

My leg muscles resisted as Grandfather and I slipped out from the shelter of the wardrobe. For a couple dozen yards, the passage was eerily desolate. Then it ended at a wide-open doorway. Pentagrams, triangles, and bees decorated the stone floor and arched around the opening; those symbols had to be the marks Grandfather had mentioned—which explained why so many of the doors at Moonhill had them. Still, they didn't seem to keep much out.

As we passed under the marks, the air took on a salty taste and a prickly sensation raced up my spine and across my scalp. The prickles became full-fledged jitters when we stepped into the treasury, a small circular room with a high arched ceiling.

On the far side of the room another entryway gaped. Twin mirrors hung on either side of it. Brightly lit display cases with black stone bases dotted the entire space. One case contained a beagle-size scorpion with glistening eyes. Another held a glowing orange crystal. In the middle of the room a small terracotta oil lamp occupied a globe-like case.

I glanced at Grandfather. He held his hand up for a second, gave the room one more scan, then nodded for me to go on.

Quietly, I hurried to the lamp's case. Opening the messenger bag, I took out the signet ring Grandfather had given me and pressed its stone against a dime-size indentation on the case's base. The glass case unfurled, like a time-lapsed video of an opening tulip.

The real Lamp of Methuselah was deep brown and embossed with a woman's face and three symbols, such a simple vessel to hold a substance that would allow one race to invade another's world. Genies into our realm, or us into theirs.

I put Grandfather's ring on my thumb, then took out the fake lamp and set it in the display case next to the real one. Luckily, they were almost identical in size. The case would close perfectly around it. This was great.

I turned toward Grandfather to ask if I should take the real lamp with me or stash it somewhere in the treasury, but he wasn't looking at me. His entire focus was on one of the mirrors, like he'd heard something.

My hands trembled as I bunched the cloth around the real lamp and shoved it into the messenger bag. It was most likely nothing. Chase would have picked up on any sounds and warned us if there was something to worry about. Nevertheless, the heavy feeling in the pit of my stomach made me deeply uneasy.

I rushed to Grandfather and tugged on his sleeve. "Let's go," I whispered.

He nodded. But as we turned to leave, a low burbling sound made me look over my shoulder. An oily-black human shape seeped out from one of the mirrors, another one followed close behind. Shit!

"Hurry." Grandfather started toward the passageway.

A loud hissing sound came from behind us. I glanced back.

Holes riddled one of the shadows. It writhed and dropped to the floor.

"Look," I said to Grandfather. "The salty air's burning it."

The next thing I knew, the shadow rose up and transformed into blue smoke. It streaked across the floor toward us, like a snake on fire. Damn it. I'd spoken too soon.

"Run!" I shouted. Too late.

The thick smoke lassoed Grandfather's legs, yanking him to his knees. Invisible claws shredded his jacket. I kicked at the smoke, but a second coil snagged my legs, trying to drag me down.

Grandfather drew his handgun. The shadow lashed like a whip, sending the gun flying. I pulled out my flashlight and trained its beam on one coil of smoke, then the other.

The smoke hissed, retreated, and circled around us like wolves planning their next attack.

To protect the lamp, I shoved the messenger bag around so it hung against the small of my back. "I thought salt weakened them," I said, helping Grandfather to his feet.

"This is weak." He nodded to where Chase hopefully waited. "Get your light ready. We need to get out of here before—"

A low laugh echoed in the room. "Daughter of these loins, and this body's dear sweet father. What a pleasant surprise."

I whirled around to face the sneering voice, which sounded years younger than Dad and totally pissed off.

Dad stood near the mirror the shadows had come out of, freshly shaven and dressed in chinos, his flight jacket, and a ton of gold jewelry. He had one arm hooked around Kate's neck and the other fisted on his hip. An involuntary gasp escaped my mouth. The Kate before me was not the imposing woman I was used to seeing. Blood drizzled from a slash in her throat and down the front of her blouse. Her bruised eyes were swollen shut. Her arms dangled at her side, ragdoll-limp. Only her wheezing breath told me she wasn't dead.

I folded my arms across my chest and glared at him. "I'm no child of yours," I said.

Grandfather stepped between me and Dad. His voice rumbled. "Take the damn lamp. And take me to help you get out of here. Just let Kate go."

The circling smoke hissed, like rain on a hot tin roof.

Dad gave a one-shouldered shrug. "As you wish."

He let go of Kate and she crumpled to the ground, moaning.

Then Dad strode toward the lamp's display case. "Sorry I interrupted your little plan," he said.

I swallowed hard. I'd forgotten to close the lamp's case. But Dad thought I hadn't had time to remove the real lamp, so he couldn't steal it. Hopefully, Chase would shout his challenge before Dad had time to realize his mistake.

"It is quite lovely"—he picked up the fake lamp and sniffed it—"and smells exactly how I remember it." He smiled coldly at Grandfather. "My own father devotes his time to spawning an army of half-blood slaves to conquer this pitiful world. But with this, I can create an army overnight. Real genies, like myself. A continuously renewing legion of solid, full-bodied djinn that do not need to writhe like smoke or possess frail human bodies. We will kill, conquer, and rule mankind with fists, sword, and magic."

Dad stared off into the distance, like he was imagining himself ruling the world.

My grip tightened on the flashlight. When was Chase going to call Culus out?

A flicker of worry nudged the back of my mind. Something had happened to Chase, I was sure of it. Otherwise he would have been here by now. Or maybe, I bit my lip. No. There was no way he could have deserted us. Not in a million years.

"My own father"—Dad came back from his imagined king-ship—"will learn to respect his real son. He will grovel before me, as you will now do before your own son. You see, I keep my promises. Your son—this body I inhabit—wished to see you kneel and beg his forgiveness. He wished for another thing as well, the return of his bride, the human slut who taints my fa-ther's mind and harem with idiotic human beliefs of sanctity and peace."

Kate groaned. "Take the damn lamp," she said to Dad.

Dad tucked the lamp into his belt line. "A little late with that suggestion, my dear."

"Culus!" Chase's voice suddenly filled the treasury.

Dad's gaze whipped around, and he cackled with delight. "Half-breed slave, come out where I can see you, or are you too much of a girl to face me." He pointed his fingers like a gun. "Ah, there you are."

Like Grandfather, I glanced back.

Chase stood outside the treasury's doorway. With a casual flair, he sliced the air with his scimitar. "Father's right, you're as weak as a gelding, a pale-skinned maggot hiding in a human skin. The only thing you can make cower is an old man and women."

Dad sniffed with disdain. "Says the boy who let a woman take the punishment for his escape."

"I would have thought you'd approve of that."

For a moment neither of them moved, their eyes locked in a ferocious battle of wills. Then Dad's eyes sliced toward the circling smoke. "Get him!" he shouted.

The smoke streaked toward the doorway.

I shoved the flashlight in my pocket and grabbed Grand-father's arm. "Now! We have to get out."

He pulled against me. "We can't leave Kate."

"We can't save her if we're dead!" I shouted.

As we took off running, Grandfather's hand went into his

pants pocket and came out clenched. The poison ring. He was readying for Culus to emerge.

Ahead of us the smoke passed under the marks. Once on the other side, it rose up and transformed into shadows, black cutouts of lanky, muscular men.

We bolted between them. A wave of hot air and the stench of bleach choked the breath from my lungs. Grandfather coughed. Behind us I could hear Dad's laughter.

Chase waited, the scimitar drawn back and ready. His focus didn't waver as we passed.

When we reached the wardrobe, Grandfather waved me on. "Keep going. Get out of here. Keep *it* safe."

I flew past the sarcophagus and the skeleton with the dog head. I knew what he meant: Use the lipstick and get the real lamp to safety.

But when I reached the stacks of rugs, I stopped. No matter what Grandfather wanted—or even if I had the lamp, I couldn't desert them.

I whirled back around.

Under the arch of symbols, Dad stood with snarling shadows on each side of him.

"Come on," Chase said. "Shed that human skin. Face me, sword to sword. Or are you afraid a half-blood will kick your full-blood ass?"

Dad laughed. "This body is no mere skin. It is my finest weapon, my shield. Would you kill the girl's father to get at me?" He licked his lips. "Filleting you will be fun."

My stomach lurched. Shit. Culus wasn't going to leave Dad. This was bad, very bad. Even partly hidden by the wardrobe, I could see Grandfather take a step back. He was afraid too.

A sword appeared in one of the shadows' hands. He tossed it to Dad, a sword as black as the onyx in the poison ring.

"I'm betting your heart will taste as good as your sheep's did." Dad cut the air with the sword.

I crept forward, keeping out of sight. Grandfather had lost his gun in the treasury. I had my flashlight and the razor. If only I could get my hands on one of Chase's real knives. It couldn't kill the shadows, but it could slow them down.

Chase raised his scimitar in a mock salute. He stepped toward Dad, every muscle flexed, every movement measured.

"To the death!" Dad launched himself at Chase. "Get the old man!" he shouted to the shadows.

The shadows dove at Grandfather. The clang of scimitar meeting sword rang out. Grandfather punched a shadow in the face. It howled and grabbed him by the throat. The other shadow punched Grandfather in the stomach. He groaned.

Running, I pulled my flashlight from my pocket and trained it on one of the shadows' eyes. It hissed and shot toward me.

Chase shouted, "Son of a bitch!"

Dad pulled his sword back and swung again.

The shadow's darkness engulfed me in a wave. It clamped my wrist, forcing the flashlight from my shaking hand. Its other hand seized my throat. The air wheezed from my lungs. I gagged. My flailing arms slammed into the dog-headed skeleton. Its bones clattered to the ground.

I closed my eyes against the darkness, the shadow's darkness, the shadow's heat, the lung-searing stench smothering me. Cold sweat kissed my spine. In the distance, Grandfather moaned. I heard the sharp ping of a small piece of metal hitting the floor. The poison ring. Grandfather had dropped it.

"Leave the old man," Dad bellowed above the clank and slide of the swords.

The hand around my throat tightened. I could smell the shadow's breath, rancid as spoiled meat. My ears rang. Stars swirled behind my eyelids. Grandfather. Chase. Kate. The family. They'd risked their lives for Dad, for me.

"Two against one?" Chase laughed. "You don't have the guts to finish this by yourself?"

"Guts, yes." Dad said. "And a desire to see your guts on the floor before me."

A thump sounded. Chase grunted in pain.

My free hand found my pocket. Dad's straight razor, impossible to open in such a tight space. But I had to do it. My thumbnail bent backward as I struggled, pain running up my arm. I had to do this. Had to, before I blacked out.

The blade released.

Opening my eyes, I yanked the razor from my pocket and slashed its blade across the shadow's throat.

The hand released me. The shadow screeched and recoiled. I ripped the blade along its side. Hot fluid drizzled over my fingers. The shadow swung at me. I ducked, scooping up the flashlight. The shadow tripped over Grandfather's hunched body.

BANG! A gunshot rang out. The shadow slumped to the floor, its dark form writhing into smoke and vanishing.

In the doorway to the treasury, Kate belly-crawled with the gun in her hand.

In one stride Dad stood over Kate. "You bitch." He kicked her in the ribs, and then kicked the gun across the floor. "First the slave dies, then you." He sneered.

Dad whirled back around and marched to where Chase knelt, his arms pinned behind his back by the other shadow. The scimitar was on the floor, so was Malphic's knife along with another one.

Dad raised his sword over Chase's neck.

"NO!" I screamed. "I have the real lamp. I'll give it to you. Don't kill him!"

Turning toward me, Dad let the sword fall to his side. "Interesting, I could have sworn I had it."

As I stepped closer, Grandfather's hand brushed my leg. "Don't do it."

"I have to or he'll kill all of you." I took a deep breath, trying to slow my raging pulse. There was a way out of this. It wasn't what we'd planned to do—but if I was lucky, it might just work.

Chase glared at me. "He'll kill us anyway."

Folding the razor closed, I tucked it into my sleeve and shoved the flashlight into my pocket. I pulled the messenger bag around and took out the lamp. "He can't kill both Kate and Grandfather or he'll never get out of here. Genies can't undo locks." I took another couple of steps toward Dad. "He won't hurt the rest of us or I'll destroy the lamp. You do promise we'll be unharmed, right?" I asked Dad.

I knew it sounded stupid. I knew he wouldn't keep that promise. I knew even if being inside Dad somehow prevented him from killing me, his shadow would kill me for him. They'd kill Chase in an instant too.

But I had to get close to Dad, real close. The oil of Methuselah turned genies solid in our world. And I was betting the oil would do the opposite to a human, namely turn a person into a shadow in this world.

Dad smiled. A sickly grin that made my stomach lurch. "Of course, daughter of these loins. All I want is the lamp. I will even forgive you for trying to trick me." He held his hands out, palms up, like he intended only peace. "Give it to me, so I can compare the two of them."

The shadow holding Chase raised its head to look at the lamp. I could see its grip loosen ever so slightly. Chase had one more knife. I was sure of it. The one in his boot that he'd used at the party to open the clamshells. More than that, he'd had a chance to regain his strength.

I took another step and another until I was right in front of Dad. I held the lamp out to him.

Smiling, he took it and cradled it against his chest.

I whipped out my flashlight. Holding it with the wrong

end forward, I pulled my arm back like I was going to throw it at him.

Dad laughed. "What are you doing, child?"

Before he could move, I brought my arm down. A crack sounded as the flashlight smashed the lamp in his hands. Another crack rang out as I hit it again. The shattered lamp fell to the floor, chunks of my flashlight falling with it. The smell of cabbage, cloves, and lanolin filled the air.

Dad shoved me away. "Stupid girl."

"Your knife," I screamed at Chase. "Kill him. Now!"

Chase yanked free from the shadow that held him. He rolled to his feet, a knife in his hand. "No, Annie, I can't. Your father."

"Do it!" I shrieked.

The lamp's oil glistened on Dad's hands. It drizzled down his clothes.

And as the glint of steel flew from Chase's hand, Dad's body shimmered into a shadowy shape. The knife passed through the shadow and into the shoulder of a deeply tanned man with wild black hair and eyes as dark as night—solid and real as only the Methuselah lamp's oil could make a genie: Culus.

Culus clutched his hands around the knife, yanking it out.

In an instant, Chase threw another knife. I saw the glint of moonstone. A *thwack* resounded as it penetrated Culus's gut.

Culus staggered backward and dropped onto all fours. Curling up, he groaned. "I'll cut out your heart for this, bastard slave."

"Yeah, right." Chase yanked Culus's arms behind his back and secured them with plastic handcuffs.

My pulse leapt. One of the shadow-henchmen had vanished, but the other hadn't. Pulling the razor out from my sleeve, I wheeled around.

Grandfather was back on his feet with the gun in his hand. The shadow streaked up from the floor and zinged toward him. Grandfather pulled the trigger. *BANG!*

With an ear-piercing shriek, the shadow exploded into a million pieces. Then it re-formed, spinning wildly like a cyclone of black sand. Grandfather fired again. The cyclone disintegrated into an oily black mass and splattered to the floor.

Grandfather waved his gun at the wardrobe. "In there," he growled at the oily mass. It did as he commanded. Then Grandfather flipped the latch to lock it in.

"What happened?" Dad's voice came from behind me.

I turned to see what he was talking about.

His shadowy form knelt next to where Kate lay with her eyes closed, her face and clothes muddied with blood. All around them black droplets of Methuselah oil snaked toward each other, pooling and humping into a clinging mercury-like puddle, then flowing into the lamp that had reassembled.

Kate wheezed. "Secrets—secrets happened," she mumbled.

"James." Grandfather glanced at Dad. "Apply some pressure to the wound and see if you can get the bleeding to slow down. We'll get her upstairs in a minute."

As Dad reached out to press his palms against Kate's sliced throat, his shoulders stiffened. For a second, he sat back. "My hands. My body. I'm—I'm—a shadow."

"Dad," I said. "Don't worry. You won't be like that forever." I looked at Grandfather. "He won't, right?"

Grandfather nodded. "The oil will wear off at sunrise. After that, he'll be as solid as you and I." He glanced to where Chase was dragging Culus to his feet. "On the other hand, I don't think it would be wise to wait until our genie friend returns to his natural state before we test the ring's inscription."

Culus sneered. "You've got the brains of a dung beetle, old man."

"Is that so?" Grandfather smiled wickedly. "I suspect you don't believe I can force you into the ring as long as you're solid. But, at the molecular level, a solid body and smokeless fire are more similar than one might imagine." He sanded his hands. "Enough talk. We need to get this done."

"Wait a minute." Chase's voice rose. "We need to use the memory oil first. Annie, I saw Culus tuck the fake lamp into his sash. Can you get it?"

Culus fought against Chase's grip as I wriggled the lamp from his sash and unsealed it. Chase was right. Even if Culus was trapped in the ring, it was smarter if he couldn't remember what had happened or who had imprisoned him.

Chase grabbed Culus's head, holding it still. "Go on. Do it," he said to me.

Standing on my tiptoes, I poured the oil over Culus's forehead and massaged it down onto his eyelids. The smell of violets and the oil's slick chill brought back memories of Kate's fingers on my face. Blood trickled from Culus's nose as I chanted, "Hecate, Queen of the Sky, take these memories, Protector of the Gateways, of earth, heaven and sea."

As I settled back down onto my heels, a sinking feeling gathered inside me. I knew nothing about witchcraft. I wasn't a follower of Hecate. This wasn't going to work. "Please, Hecate, please," I said under my breath. I should have asked Grandfather to do this.

"Don't worry," Kate mumbled from behind me, "she knows who you are."

Warmth flushed my face and I stepped back.

Instead of fighting against Chase's grip, Culus's head was now bowed, rocking back and forth like a child on the edge of sleep.

Grandfather nodded at me. "Yes, very well done," he said.

Then, he held the poison ring up and his voice boomed as he recited the ring's incantation.

But what I heard, what I experienced was far beyond anything I could have imagined. The words of the incantation were living things. They brushed my skin with an electric prickle. Their breath filled the air with the scent of sandalwood and left the flavor of salt on my tongue.

Culus dropped to his knees and began to tremble, harder and faster until his body shimmered like a heat mirage. Then, with a loud hiss, he transformed into a greasy mass, spinning into a fine blue thread, tendriling toward Grandfather, and into the poison ring—which had started this whole mess.

CHAPTER 26

May the shadows never die away nor
the dark of night cease, without them
there would be no glory of sunrise.

—In Praise of Darkness

Once we got upstairs, we discovered Selena's family had set up a makeshift infirmary in their apartment. And Selena had taken charge.

She stood with her hands on her hips, barking orders to anyone who dared come near her. "Laura, get a fresh ice pack for Tibbs and make sure Mother's bandage hasn't bled through."

When she saw me, Selena rushed over and gave me a huge hug.

"I'm so glad you're all right," she said. "You'll have to tell me everything thing later." With one last hug, she breezed past me toward Chase, who had just lumbered into the apartment with Kate in his arms.

He glanced at her. "The bleeding's under control. But she needs attention right away."

Selena rubbed her hands with enthusiasm. "Put her on my bed." She turned to the Professor. "I'll need *Calvatica* spores for the smaller wounds. And a tranquilizer—well, you know, there's going to be pain when I start stitching."

I winced. Even Kate didn't deserve that. "Maybe she needs a real doctor," I said.

Selena harrumphed. "Our family has never trusted hospitals. Besides, how else am I going to learn?" She turned away from me and shouted, "Zachary, get me the suturing kit and more gauze."

David and Chase headed back to the treasury to find a more permanent home for the imprisoned shadow and hunt down the one that had vanished. It wasn't like either of the shadows could escape since the mirrors were the same as locks. Still, it would be nice to know they were sealed in jars or something, instead of slithering around in the basement. Also, we'd put the Lamp of Methuselah back in its display case before we came upstairs, but they wanted to move it to an even more secure location for safety's sake.

I fixed a cold compress for where the shadow had bruised my neck, then scuffled to the den and settled down on the couch next to Grandfather.

Dad's shadowy form stood in front of the window, staring out at the darkness beyond the glass. He scratched his elbow three times. He was thinking about something important, maybe about Mother or what he and I were going to do next. Clearly, he didn't remember a lot that had happened over the last few months. But I was sure what he did recall troubled him.

"I've been thinking," I said.

Grandfather picked up one of the pebble-like game pieces from the Petteia board and rolled it between his fingers. "About what?"

"Now that Culus is inside the ring," I said, "couldn't we take it to the gallery and tell Malphic's spy that we'll trade him the ring and Culus for my mother?" I glanced at Dad to see if he was listening.

He turned slightly toward us and cocked his head.

Grandfather sighed. "Malphic wouldn't go for it. To him,

Culus allowing himself to get trapped by humans is a disgrace. Genies aren't like us, Annie. They don't believe in forgiveness." His gaze went to Dad for a second. Then he set the game piece back on the board.

Hours went by and Dad continued to stand by the window. Silent and unmoving, like he might fade at any second. During that time, Selena finished treating everyone and David returned from the basement. It seemed impossible, but I fell asleep on the couch, and when I woke up, the apartment was hushed, except for the slow tick-tick of an egg-shaped clock.

Four-thirty. Almost sunrise. Soon the oil's effects would wear off and Dad's body would return to normal.

Grandfather patted my arm and whispered, "If you feel like stretching your legs, I'd love a cup of tea and one of Laura's macaroons."

The floor creaked as I hurried down the hallway to the elevator. When I got to the kitchen, I stopped at the sink to wash my hands before I fixed Grandfather's snack.

Through the window above the sink, I spotted a movement on the lawn.

In the silver-plated darkness, a shadow drifted through the gardens, toward the stairs and the beach, like ashes drawn seaward by changing tide.

Dad.

I slipped out onto the terrace. Here and there, slivers of light slanted down from the second floor. I crept down the stairs to the lawn, an ache building deep inside me. Soon the sun would rise, Dad's body would become solid, and we'd be free to leave Moonhill.

A hand touched my shoulder.

Pulse racing, I spun around.

"Sorry," Chase said. "I didn't mean to startle you."

"You're lucky I didn't—"

He pressed a finger against my lips. "Let me talk first. I'm sorry I scared you in the mausoleum tunnel. I usually have better control over"—he took a long breath—"over the aura thing."

"It's okay." I shrugged. "It was just a little unnerving." More like totally terrifying, but I wasn't about to tell him that.

"Adrenaline causes it, like when I'm working out or"—he gave me a crooked smile—"excited. It's been getting a lot harder to control lately."

I slapped his arm playfully. Then I remembered why I'd come outside and glanced toward the cliff top.

"Go on." Chase's voice was gentle. "Your father needs you." His fingers skimmed the line of my jaw and a flutter went through me. "We'll talk later," he said.

I went up on my tiptoes and kissed his mouth, letting my lips part just enough to lead him on. Then I pushed away. "We could talk or maybe find something more interesting to do."

"Hmm. I like the sound of that." He drew in a long breath, and then his voice became more serious. "Annie, I meant what I said, I will find a way to get your mother back."

I met his gaze. "She was like a mother to you, wasn't she?"

He nodded, but something flickered through his eyes, like I'd hit a deeper nerve.

"Oh," I said, as a realization came to me. "Malphic. Your real mom. When he kidnapped you, did something happen to her? Your parents are alive, right?"

He nodded. "Your grandfather tracked them down for me."

"They must have been thrilled to see you."

He laughed, but there was no joy in it. "My father used to call me *the little bastard*. Even as a kid, I knew it wasn't just a nickname. He could see I wasn't his." Chase turned away, his voice sad and distant, as he stared toward the gardens. "I remember sitting on a footstool, rolling up balls of yarn while Mother knitted mittens. It was our ritual, every Sunday after supper. She must have made hundreds of pairs, and gave them all away at Christmas. Mine were always blue and green. I was wearing them the night Malphic came." He punched his fist against his thigh. "I remember her begging him not to take me. The sound of her screaming. Screaming like he'd ripped her heart out."

"That's awful," I said. I hesitated, torn between my need to get to Dad and my desire to be there for Chase. Before I could make up my mind, Chase continued.

"Your grandfather and Kate think it's better to let her think I'm dead."

I rested my hand on his forearm and softened my voice. "They're wrong."

Chase squeezed his eyes shut. Light from the upper story of Moonhill glistened on his eyelashes and streaked his cheeks. "I'll only remind her of the horrible things that happened, between her and my father, of Malphic. My training, what I am, they aren't things a mother would be proud of."

"Chase, your mother loves you. She'd want to see you."

His eyes flickered open. "You really think so?"

"My mother cared about you. She didn't think you were just a bastard or a killer. She wouldn't have risked teaching you, if she did. I don't think that's what you are either. Your mother would see the child that was torn from her arms. You should go to her."

He pulled me into a hug, his arms wrapping me tight and warm. "Thank you," he whispered into my hair. Then he released me and glanced skyward. "It's getting lighter. Your father."

"You're right," I said. I drew a finger down his chest and smiled. Inside my body thrummed from thoughts of what could happen now that his secret no longer stood between us. "I'll be back. Promise."

I breezed through the gardens to the stairs, the darkness sliding off me like black oil from a lamp.

Dad sat on the stone outcrop: a hunched shadow staring across the ocean to where a thin line of dawn was replacing darkness. He didn't move when I sat down beside him.

Finally, he sighed. "If I knew how to get to her, I would go to her right now. Before the sun rises, while my body is still like theirs. If I knew how to get into their realm, I could bring your mother back to us." His voice was low, an echo of the water washing against the sand.

I covered his hand with mine. It felt strange to touch his shadowy form and have it feel warm and real.

"It's too late for tonight," I said, "but we will find a way to free her, you and me and Chase, even Kate and Grandfather will help. All of us. We'll do it together."

"No, Annie," he said. "Sometimes hate runs too deep."

"Dad, you can't go on hating them. Kate lied to you, but I don't think she was really trying to hurt you—or me."

The sound of morning birdsong filtered down from the garden, and a slice of sun appeared above the waves. Beneath my fingers, I not only felt the warmth of Dad's shadowy hand, but also, now, the softness of his skin.

"That's not what I meant," Dad said. "I risked everyone's lives. Culus promised not to hurt you." He looked at the sky as if he might find the words he needed written in the fading stars. "I don't remember much of the last few months, but I remember coming to myself and seeing the hurt in your eyes. I thought I'd be able to control him. But I was too weak. You—everyone has a million reasons to hate me."

I swallowed back the swell of tears. "No one hates you. Anyone might have done the same thing." For a heartbeat, I thought of reaching into my pocket and taking out the signet ring with the purple stone that Grandfather had given me. I could tell Dad that Grandfather forgave him, that he wanted Dad to have the ring, that he wanted Dad and me to stay at Moonhill forever, to be a part of the family.

I could give Dad the ring and lie.

But that would be no different than Kate giving him the vase of cat's ashes and saying it was Mother's. I would not do that to him. Instead, I'd tell him the truth, before I lost my nerve.

"Dad?" I looked down at our cupped hands.

"Yes, Annie."

"Dad, you know how much I love you. How much I love picking antiques, traveling, doing shows." I hesitated. I could stop now and everything would go back to the way it was before he met Culus—us doing shows, while I took classes online. I could even take one of Sotheby's fall classes, go to London next summer, become a certified fine art appraiser, have my freedom and own life, but sometimes work with him too.

The trouble was, things were different now. There was Chase and my family, not just my living family but my ancestors as well, and what they'd done and stood for all these centuries. They were a part of me. And I was a part of them.

"Go on," he said, still staring out across the waves. Here and there, the sunrays passed through his body like tiny spears. In other places, they brightened his solidifying skin and clothes.

I lifted my voice, trying hard to sound cheerful. "Grandfather showed me the Aztec calendar stone. He bragged about how you rescued it when you were my age. The family business is interesting."

Before I could continue, the morning light struck Dad's face and body, full force. He hunched over and groaned in pain. A hissing noise sizzled out from every inch of him and the stench of cabbage, cloves, and lanolin filled the air.

An instant later, it was over. Dad was once again solid and real, and the smell was gone.

I moved in close to him and wrapped my arm around his shoulder. "You okay?" I asked.

"I feel. Empty," he said.

"Don't worry. You're going to be fine. Everything's going to be fine. We'll get Mother back too. I promise."

He nodded. "I know we will." He squeezed my hand. "I never did tell you the story about the Aztec calendar stone and how I first met your mother, did I?"

I rested my head on his shoulder. "No, Dad, you didn't."

There was sadness and fear and uncertainty in his voice as he began, but I could hear his confidence returning. "Your grandfather and I were deep in a cave that was beneath an Aztec temple. It was a dark, creepy place with huge tarantulas and scorpions. The only sound was the scrape of our feet against the stone floor. Then, out of the darkness, came the soft lilt of a girl singing. It was your mother, Annie, and her voice was so pure and beautiful, so carefree. It was like I was spellbound." He laughed. Then his tone became serious. "Annie, I'd like to leave here, but maybe staying wouldn't be so bad, at least for a little while, until I'm rested and we find a way to free your mother."

I looked out at the waves and the sun and smiled.

Staying for a little while was the perfect way to begin.

Don't miss the next book in the Dark Heart series,

Beyond Your Touch

Available in September 2016
wherever books and ebooks are sold

CHAPTER 1

Bury the truth in robes of marble and ivy,
In halls of learned books and tomes ripe with
false beliefs, But it still breathes, still whispers and waits.

—Excerpt from *Devils and Djinn*
By Samuel Freemont

His neck tasted like strawberry jelly. Well, actually like jelly and powdered sugar—which was no surprise since we'd spent the last hour wreaking havoc on his freshly washed sheets, first by having a jelly doughnut fight, and then by making love in said newly created mess. Chase was no slouch when it came to lovemaking, far from it. But the doughnut fight had made me laugh until I cried. In all honesty, I'm not sure which I enjoyed more, the fight or the sex—or seeing him laugh, his mind and body off duty for a change, just there in the moment with me.

Chase rolled me onto my back and straddled me, his forehead resting against mine, his soft blue aura soaking my skin with warmth. We kissed again, gently this time, then I wiggled a bit lower and licked a lingering dab of jelly off his collarbone. He flinched when the tip of my tongue brushed the scarred skin just below his left shoulder, the fist-size mark created so many years ago by Malphic's branding iron.

It was hard to even begin to think about how different

Chase's childhood and mine had been: me traveling and dealing antiques with my dad, blissfully unaware that the stories Dad was telling about magic and his family were real—and Chase kidnapped from his human mother, taken to the djinn realm, branded and enslaved by his genie father, raised to be a Death Warrior until my family rescued him five years ago. It was crazy. Almost unbelievably so, but it was the truth.

The phone on the floor beside his bed jangled, and our private world evaporated as Chase climbed over me and sat on the edge of the bed to read the text.

"Damn. I was supposed to go see your grandfather this morning." He was up, grabbing his briefs and jeans, his aura fading with each step.

In less than a dozen strides, he was across his attic bedroom and inside the tiny half-bath. It wasn't like my growing relationship with Chase was a secret, something banned because I was a Freemont and he worked for my family. But finding any semblance of privacy had proven impossible with both of us living on my family's estate of Moonhill. In fact, since I'd come to Moonhill a month ago with my dad and Chase and I had met and things started to sizzle, we'd only managed to get together a dozen times—counting this morning.

I retrieved my jeans and shirt from the floor, then glanced out the window. It had been foggy and barely dawn when I'd driven the ATV up from the main house to *have doughnuts and coffee* at the cottage with Chase. Now the fog had lifted and sunshine brightened everything. It had to be close to eight or nine o'clock.

My eye caught the movement of a dozen black sheep drifting under Chase's clothesline and heading around the corner of the cottage toward the estate's front gate.

"Chase?" I turned toward the bathroom. "I'm guessing the sheep aren't supposed to be wandering around in your yard?"

"Crap!" He flew out of the bathroom and dashed down

the stairs. His footsteps stopped and he called back up to me. "Don't worry about the mess. I'm doing laundry later. And, Annie, I'm sorry about running off like this."

"Don't worry. I'll be right down to help." I made my own quick trip to the bathroom, then headed down the narrow stairs to find him. I didn't know a thing about sheep, but I was sure he could use an extra hand with rounding them up or something.

The stairs came out in his tiny living room: a secondhand couch, a chair, some exercise equipment, and not much else. Through the front windows, I had a view across the sheep-covered lawn to where a black Jaguar had stopped on its way out the gate. Chase stood with one hand on its roof, hunched over talking to the person riding shotgun. My grandfather. It looked like my uncle David was driving and someone was in the backseat. My dad.

My shoulders tensed. Last night, Dad hadn't mentioned going anywhere. He hadn't texted or left a voice-mail message, either. For that matter, I'd never seen all three of them go any-where together. What the heck was going on?

I found my cardigan on the coffee table next to our empty coffee mugs and Chase's blue yarn and knitting needles. Snag-ging it, I shoved my arms into the sleeves and launched myself out the front door.

Undoubtedly, my early morning presence at the cottage would confirm Uncle David's conviction that I had the morals of a sewer rat. Well, to hell with him. I was twenty, after all. Chase and I having sex shouldn't get anyone's panties in a bunch. But David would hassle my dad, who in turn would tell me to be more discreet and not to forget to use protection—and remind me that Chase was half-genie, as if that might call for some kind of magic contraceptive. That would make me blush and worry Dad might be right.

A knowing smile tugged at the corner of my grandfather's

mouth as I jogged between the sheep and up to the car. I put my hands on my hips and glared though the open front passenger window. "So, what's going on?" I asked.

"Apparently, they're going to Slovenia," Chase said, folding his arms across his chest.

I let my glare dart past Grandfather and to my dad in the backseat. "Slovenia? Don't you think you might have said something? What the heck's in Slovenia?"

Dad's eyes sparkled with excitement. "A bone flute, a twin to the Divje Babe. But more recently discovered and still in private hands at this moment. If our theory's correct, it can be used to open the veil between realms. Interesting, wouldn't you say?"

My pulse jumped at the possibilities and I nodded my agreement. My mother had been Malphic's prisoner in the djinn realm since before Chase had been kidnapped and enslaved. The family had tried to rescue her, but failed when Malphic used a warding spell to seal the veil before everyone could escape. If this flute could do what they thought, then we'd be able to attempt another rescue—like as soon as they got back.

I tilted my head, studying Dad intently. "Are you sure it'll work?"

"Fairly sure, but that's where we need yours and Selena's help," he said.

Grandfather patted my hand. "Talk to your aunt Kate, she'll tell you all about it."

"We need to get going," Uncle David grumbled.

The car rolled forward a few inches, but I held on to the window's edge a moment longer. Acquiring a flute in Slovenia had to be safer than fighting a vengeful genie and his shadow-henchmen, and we'd all survived that. Still I didn't believe for a second I was hearing the whole story. "Be careful," I said.

Dad gave me a quick air-kiss and a wave good-bye. "Don't

worry. This is going to be easy." His tone was light, but there was a catch in his voice.

I waved back, then hugged myself as the Jaguar glided through the open gateway and disappeared down the road beyond.

Dad wasn't that sure about the *easy* part. Not at all.